PENGUIN BOOKS

My Sweet Revenge

My Sweet Revenge

JANE FALLON

PENGUIN BOOKS

PENGUIN BOOKS

UK | USA | Canada | Ireland | Australia
India | New Zealand | South Africa

Penguin Books is part of the Penguin Random House group of companies
whose addresses can be found at global.penguinrandomhouse.com.

First published 2017
001

Text copyright © Jane Fallon, 2017

The moral right of the author has been asserted

Set in 12.5/14.75 pt Garamond MT Std
Typeset by Jouve (UK), Milton Keynes
Printed in Great Britain by Clays Ltd, St Ives plc

A CIP catalogue record for this book is available from the British Library

PAPERBACK ISBN: 978–1–405–91775–9
TRADE PAPERBACK ISBN: 978–1–405–91776–6

PART ONE

I

Paula

I want to make my husband fall back in love with me.

Let me explain. This isn't an exercise in fifties wifey-dom. I haven't been reading articles in old women's magazines. 'Twenty ways to keep your man'. That couldn't be further from the truth.

I want him to fall back in love with me so that when I tell him to fuck off out of my life he'll care. Or at least it'll register. He won't just think, 'Oh good.'

I want it to hurt.

Robert is sitting at the breakfast bar in the kitchen while I cook. Oblivious. Nose in his phone. Thumbs tapping away at the keyboard like a teenager. Probably texting *her*. He has no idea that I know. He looks like the same person. The person who, yesterday, was just my husband, the man I've been married to for eighteen years. Today he's someone who is cheating on his wife. I find myself staring at him, trying to look for tell-tale signs. How could I not have known? He looks up and smiles.

'What? What have I done?'

As he talks he tilts the screen of his mobile away from me slightly. He probably doesn't even realize he's doing it.

I try to mirror his smile. 'Nothing. I was just thinking.'

He picks up the bottle and refills my glass and then his. This has always been our ritual whenever he's home in the evenings. I potter around making dinner while he perches on a stool and fills me in on the goings-on at work. Although these days he's more likely to keep one eye on his phone and only give me half his attention. At least now I know why.

'Dangerous,' he says now. 'Too much thinking never did anyone any good.'

I force a laugh. 'Well, lucky I don't do it too often then. Actually, I was trying to decide whether to do rice or mash, so it really was life-altering stuff.'

'Surprise me. Want any help?'

I shake my head no. The last thing I can face doing is playing happy families. It's too soon.

He hops down from his stool, glass in one hand, phone in the other. 'Then I'm going to have a shower.'

'Don't be too long,' I say. 'I promised Georgia we'd eat early. She's meant to be meeting Eliza at half seven.'

'Ten minutes,' he says, and I have to stop myself asking why he needs his mobile if all he's doing is having a quick hose-down.

It was his phone that gave him away, by the way. That old cliché. I wasn't snooping. It never would have occurred to me to snoop. I've never even bothered to ask him for his password because he never uses it, he just wafts his finger over the button so it can read his print. So it's complete chance that I saw what I saw. This morning before he left for the studio – befuddled from the early start – he left it on the counter when he went off to get dressed. I always get up with him on studio days, even though he has to leave the

4

house at six and I am pretty sure I hadn't even realized there was a five fifteen in the morning until my alarm started announcing it one day. I like to keep him company while he eats breakfast. Kiss him goodbye when he leaves. Neither of us is a completely functioning human at that hour so I can only assume it slipped his mind that he really shouldn't be letting his phone out of his sight these days.

I didn't even notice it. But then it buzzed to say a message had arrived and I glanced down without thinking. The words 'Love you' happened to catch my eye and the name at the top. *Saskia*. Without thinking what I was doing, I snatched it up quickly, before the message faded away, never to be accessible to me again.

'Jesus! That was too close for comfort last night! WAY too risky! Hope Paula bought it!!! Didn't feel comfortable having to lie to her face! Love you xxx'

I stared at the screen in shock, pressed a few keys, hoping I could magically access the whole conversation but knowing it was hopeless. I heard Robert moving around in the bedroom, knew he would be back at any moment. I committed the message to memory and threw the phone back down on the counter as his footsteps thumped along the corridor, pretended to be preoccupied with something fascinating in the cutlery drawer.

He clocked his mobile lying on the counter. Did I imagine it or did the slightest flash of fear sweep across his face? I tried to look casual, I didn't want to give away the fact that I'd noticed it. He picked it up and shoved it in his pocket, not even looking at the screen.

A huge part of me wanted to throw accusations at him the second he walked through the door. Or punches. Actually, yes, punches would have been good. But thankfully, I stopped myself. I knew that I needed to mull over what I'd seen. I had to make sure that there was no innocent explanation before I went down a path I couldn't retreat from.

Now he saunters back into the kitchen, freshly showered, smelling of some kind of chemical fruit and wearing the old track pants and T-shirt that he likes to slob around in. I plaster a smile on my face.

'Will you give Georgia a shout? Five minutes.'

'Sure. Something smells amazing.'

I turn my fake smile up to ecstatic. Thank God for my drama-school training. Although we never actually did a class called 'How to convince your husband everything's fine when in actual fact you want to stab him with a fork'. Remind me. If I ever become a drama tutor, that'll be my first assignment.

'It's only chilli.'

Robert moseys on out again and I hear him shout to Georgia that dinner's ready. I know that above all else I mustn't give away that anything is wrong in front of our daughter so I try to steady my breathing, hypnotize myself into thinking that all is right with the world.

I fight the urge to cry. Unscrew the bottle of red wine and pour myself another small glass. When Georgia comes hurtling through the door, bag bulging with the books she needs for an evening of revision at her best friend's house, I'm sitting at the counter sipping it as if I don't have a care in the world.

'Want a glass?' I say, knowing what the answer will be. Georgia pulls a face that says I might as well have offered her some cat's pee.

'Yuk. Why can't you ever have white wine? Or vodka?'

'Because then you'd say yes when I offered you a drink.'

She laughs. 'That's OK. They're doing cheap Jäger-bombs at Vogue tonight. I can get legless later.'

'George . . .' I say, and she interrupts me before I can continue.

'I'm joking!'

'You'd better be.'

'I am . . . it's absinthe, actually.'

'Very funny.'

She leans over my back and plants a kiss on my head just as Robert comes back in, not a care in the world.

'Uh oh. What have you done?' he says. His old joke that any affection from our teenager must be an apology.

Georgia laughs and ruffles his hair as he sits down. I lean over and fill his glass.

We're the picture of a happy family.

2

I'm not a vengeful person by nature. Partly because I'm too lazy. Revenge takes effort. But I've never been the type who spends hours plotting how to get back at my co-worker because he doesn't contradict the boss when she praises him for something I've done. That makes it sound as if I have a high-powered career where rival colleagues are locked in a struggle for supremacy, clawing their way up the ladder to the top, shoving each other aside and trampling on the weak. Actually, I work in a bakery. Oh, the hilarity. The fat lady works in a cake shop. I can see it on people's faces when I tell them. No doubt dying to ask me if I get paid in produce or if my role is chief taste-tester. For the record, I do the selling, not the baking. Make coffees in our swanky machine, heat paninis and pasties, take the money.

But this time Robert has pushed me too far. I know he can be self-centred. He has a tendency to take himself and his job too seriously. And I know we've drifted apart a bit lately. It's not as if we haven't been getting along, more that he's stopped sharing his world with me. He used to come home in the evenings and we'd run through his lines for the next few days together, laughing at the ludicrous turns in the plot. Or he'd regale me with tales from the set over a glass of Merlot. He never asked me much about my own day – probably because nothing much newsworthy ever happens to me – but his stories about the other actors, the incompetent make-up artists and interfering producers always entertained me so much I never really minded. Because I always thought he still cared about me deep down. He just had a high-pressure job that left him a bit preoccupied.

I never in a million Sundays would have thought he was seeing someone on the side. Actually, that's not true. I've wondered, every now and again. Just over the past couple of years. Just the odd 'what if . . . ?' when he's told me he's going to be working late or he's been away filming on location. But I've always dismissed it. Told myself not to be paranoid.

And if I ever had allowed myself to think it might be true, I never in a million decades would have thought it would be Saskia.

Robert and I have been together for twenty years. We met at drama school, both of us with big dreams about the stellar careers that were undoubtedly in our futures, despite the statistics telling us otherwise. I think I once read that ninety-nine per cent of actors are unemployed at any one time. And that's not even taking into account the fact that only about five people share every single starring role on ITV. But that didn't stop everyone in our year at the North London School of Speech and Drama thinking they were destined to become the Next Big Thing.

Out of our classmates there's only Robert and four others who you ever hear about now. One because she went to Hollywood and was the new ingénue on the block for about five minutes. She lorded it over us all mercilessly, until the work started to dry up. Now she talks in a weird mid-Atlantic accent and pops up occasionally in the British press talking about her latest obsession with cupping or tantric meditation or the healing properties of cruciferous vegetables, even though she disappeared from our screens so long ago no really even remembers who she is. Two make very respectable livings in the theatre, and the fourth is doing fifteen years for fraud.

Financially, Robert is probably the biggest success story. He has been a regular in the prime-time Thursday-night rural-community drama *Farmer Giles* since it began five years ago. Sadly, he's not the eponymous Farmer Giles, who, with his wife and three children, is the heart of the piece, but second fiddle Hargreaves, Farmer Giles's nice-guy neighbour. Saskia, by the way, is Melody Hargreaves. Nice-guy neighbour's cantankerous but sexy spouse. Robert's on-screen wife. A woman he has professed to loathe for years.

What with repeat fees and the many overseas sales – the Americans, in particular, love the depiction of the countryside idyll that bears no resemblance to any place I've ever been – he earns a small fortune. He would give it all up to be one of our two former contemporaries who earn praise and respect for their work treading the boards, even if their bank balances are nowhere near as healthy. But he would never admit it.

We have – scrub that – we *had* a good life, the three of us. Me, Robert and seventeen-year-old Georgia.

Until now.

When we first left college, setting up home together in a cramped bedsit in Finsbury Park, we both went all out to try to get work, scouring the internet for open auditions and accepting every unpaid offer that came our way. Gradually, Robert started to get bits and pieces here and there. An agent took him on. Casting directors began to know his name. When I found myself pregnant with Georgia, it seemed that the obvious thing to do to – as Robert put it – was for him to work on his career first while I did all the childcare, and then, once he had got himself established, he could take a break and be the homemaker for a while, while I pursued my own dream. Even though it made me anxious that I was being left behind, it also made sense to me. And, if I'm being honest, I wanted to be the one taking care of our daughter. I just hadn't expected to have her so young.

Anyway, I'm sure you can all see where this is going. The years rolled on and Robert just never felt that the time was right for him to opt out.

Once Georgia hit Year 7 I nervously tried to dip my toe back in the water but with no track record, no agent, nothing on my CV except childcare and a bit of part-time clerical work when we needed the money, I couldn't even get through to anyone on the phone, let alone through their door. If I'd been prepared to go miles from home for an unpaid gig, performing a one-woman show to three people above a pub in the back of beyond then, maybe, I could have clawed my way into contention. But I was the wrong side of thirty with a soon-to-be-teenage daughter who needed her mother. And, besides, Robert always said it was important to him to know I was at home, keeping everything running smoothly. It meant he didn't have to worry about the mundane daily details of our life. It allowed him to shine.

Yes, you heard me correctly. He said that it allowed him to shine.

And somehow that was it. That was our life. Robert could take any job, work any outlandish schedule in any remote location, because he knew that everything was all taken care of at home.

Then he got the job on *Farmer Giles*, which meant for the ten and a half months of the year they filmed he would be flat out, dividing his time between the studio in west London and the exterior locations in Oxfordshire, and I threw away the glossy headshots I was still inundating casting directors with (which were already several years and many stones out of date), and took the job in the café. No qualifications necessary. He's become a minor TV star, or at least a recognizable face. I've become someone who works in a baked-goods store because the hours suit my desire to be home when Georgia gets back from school.

I imagine you have questions. I would. Like why would an intelligent, independent woman like me fall for an arrangement like that? The only answer I have is that I loved Robert and I honestly believed my chance would come. And I think he meant it when he first proposed it, too. I don't think he thought he was conning me. It was just later on, when he was enjoying his career, when he didn't want to give it up even for a few months, when he started worrying that to turn things down might mean he would never get offered anything again, that he changed his mind. And I suppose I could have insisted. Put my foot down and refused to wash another gym kit until he agreed to take a break. But the truth is that by then I had no confidence in the idea that I would be able to find work anyway. And the thought of watching Robert turn down some plum role just so he could stay at home and watch me failing to get a single audition was just too humiliating.

And because I never imagined he would throw it all back in my face.

The evening is agony. Trying to pretend to Robert that all is well while I work out what I am going to do. It doesn't help that Georgia leaves the second dinner is over, promising to be home by eleven at the latest. There's no ballast.

If Robert has any idea that I've found out his secret, he doesn't show it.

'Saskia turned up two hours late again today,' he says to me as we sit side by side in the living room. I'm scrolling through the Sky menu like there's no tomorrow, desperately hoping to find anything that might be a distraction and mean we don't have to spend the evening chatting.

I almost choke on my drink at the mention of her name.

'God,' I say. How would I usually react? I suddenly can't remember how to behave normally. 'Did she get a bollocking?'

Saskia's bad behaviour is one of his favourite topics. And, to be fair, I would be upset about it too if I were him. Although now I realize he probably isn't. It's just a smokescreen.

'Of course not,' he sighs. 'Because no one can face the tears and the threats to quit.'

Although Robert professes that he can't stand Saskia, a part of him lives in terror that she might decide to leave the show altogether. He is very much aware of the fact that while the show couldn't survive without Farmer Giles, it would most definitely live on if his neighbours moved away and were replaced.

'They'll probably sack her eventually,' I say, and I get a little jolt of satisfaction from the panicked look on his face. 'Oh, look, there's a new drama on BBC2 tonight. *Trouble in Paradise*. Didn't you go up for that?'

I know full well that he did. That he'd been gutted when he hadn't got it.

'Let's not watch that,' he groans. 'There must be something better on.' Robert hates watching programmes that he missed out on. Even worse if the actor who got the role he coveted gets any praise or, God forbid, an award nomination. He just assumes that he would have garnered the same attention too had he got the part. Never a doubt in his mind about whether his performance would have been as compelling.

'No, this looks good,' I say, pressing the button to watch. It takes all my strength to pretend to be absorbed in it for the next hour and a half. But it beats having to make conversation.

I slope off to bed as early as I can but I don't sleep at all, just go over and over it in my head. What does the text mean? What happened that made Saskia feel they were close to being caught? Caught doing what (yes, yes, I know). I think back. Last night I phoned Robert to ask if he knew what time he was likely to be home. The studio day finishes at seven but the cast are free to leave once their last scene is completed. A woman answered. Saskia, I now assume. I'd almost forgotten, it was such an insignificant event. Robert always has to leave his phone somewhere when he goes on set. No one wants to be the idiot who ruins a good take because some ironic eighties pop-song ringtone suddenly blasts out mid-scene. I've spoken to countless other people over the years who have answered on his behalf.

I didn't ask her name. Why would I have?

'Robert Westmore's phone,' she said when she answered.

I remember feeling like a bit of a saddo that I was calling my husband at work to ask what time he wanted his tea.

'Oh, hi. It's Paula, Robert's wife.'

I remember that she said, 'Hey!' in a very matey way.

'It's nothing important. I just wondered what time he was going to wrap tonight. Maybe you could get him to call me if he gets a moment?'

'No problem, Paula,' she said.

Twenty minutes later he called me back. Maybe a little flustered, but he often is if we speak when he's at work. He said that they might overrun a bit but he should be back by quarter past nine, latest. A mundane, routine call.

He got home at nine in the end. Nothing in the way he looked or acted gave away that he had been doing anything other than working. There was no lipstick on his collar, or anywhere else that I could see for that matter. He went straight upstairs for a shower, but then he often does. He was his normal, usual self. Which makes me think his normal, usual self is a man who is having an affair.

After he left this morning I turned on my computer. Googled Saskia Sherbourne. Of course, I already know what she looks like, but now I was confronted with hundreds of glamorous photos of her on red carpets and glitzy nights out. The thing that annoyed me most was how pleased with herself she looked. That 'oh yes, you think I'm attractive' smirk. It made me want to punch her.

Of course, she's slim, verging on half-starved. But she has that kind of round-faced, cleavagey look that – hopefully – doesn't age well. She'll be busty barmaid before she knows it. I checked myself for being bitchy. I've always tried not to judge people on their looks because I know from personal experience how hurtful that can be. Then I reminded myself she was quite possibly sleeping with my husband so I allowed myself to revel in the two pictures I found of her in a short skirt which showed off her surprisingly straight-up-and-down legs and bony knees.

According to her Wikipedia page, she's three years younger than me, which probably means we're the same age. Born Susan Mitchell. Ha! Not so glamorous now. Grew up in Exeter. Went to LAMDA (chip on its shoulder because it's not RADA). First job Nat West commercial.

I scanned down through the list of her credits, not really interested. Got to Personal Life. The Susan Mitchell/ Exeter/LAMDA information was repeated. Married at twenty-seven to Simon, divorced two years later. Then again in 2009 – which would make her either thirty-one or thirty-four at the time, depending on who you believe – to Joshua. They seemed to still be together; no mention of children, no mention of what it is that Joshua does.

There was a link to a profile piece in one of the Sunday magazines so, of course, I tortured myself by reading the whole thing. She's very grateful for the part in *Farmer Giles*, which came along just as she was wondering whether or not to call it a day. She would never take the role for granted. It's important for actors on TV shows to remember they're just a tiny cog in a huge machine. She reminds herself of this regularly to ensure she remains down to earth. If I didn't know it was all phoney, I'd probably have thought she was coming across quite well.

In the next paragraph she banged on about how lucky she was to work with Robert. How they've become good friends and so they instinctively work well together. I've read enough of these kind of interviews to know this could just be PR bullshit but that didn't stop it infuriating me. It was as if she was taunting me.

I found more interviews with her and then reread old ones with Robert that I must have read before with different eyes. Both of them are always at pains to tell the world how fabulously they get on, how they're so relaxed around each other they sometimes squabble about the most mundane things, like a real couple. I remember laughing with Robert when we scoured one of these spreads together. Teasing him about the way he managed to make it sound as if he and Saskia were such great friends when, of course, he hated her. I remember him telling me it was important that the viewing public bought into their relationship. That was the key to its success.

'I've never worked with anyone who cared so much', interview Robert had apparently said, and real-life Robert had read the quote out to me in a mock-serious tone and added 'about herself', which had me falling about, I seem to remember.

When actually it seems as if the joke's on me.

3

Usually, when Robert leaves for work, I go back to bed for an hour or so, but today I was on a mission.

I decided to hunt for clues to back up my suspicions. The text in itself wasn't enough to build a case on. But if he was up to something there would be other evidence. In a crime scene, I would spray our bedroom with luminol and see where the blood showed up. As it was, all I could do was poke through his personal belongings and hope something jumped out at me as incriminating.

I hated doing this, by the way. I'm not a natural snooper. I've always been that person who believes you shouldn't eavesdrop because you might hear something you don't like. So I didn't have a system. I just thought where I would hide my most precious secret things if I were him and started there.

Turned out he doesn't think the bottom of a suitcase he hasn't used in at least five years or the underneath of the drawer where he keeps random bits and pieces that I would never have any cause to go near – old receipts, two lighters from when he used to smoke, elastic bands, a Sony Walkman, a broken pedometer . . . it's like a museum of his life; we refer to it as the 'thing drawer' – are as good places as I would. In desperation, I called my friend and boss, Myra.

'Hypothetically, if you were going to hide something in

your home that you didn't want anyone else to find, where would you hide it?'

'Are you talking about Robert?'

'Hypothetically.'

'Think about where you'd never look. How about a box of old scripts? Has he got one of those?'

'I didn't say it was Robert. But yes, he has.'

'Try there. If you have no luck, call me back and I'll come up with another genius suggestion. Actually, call me if you do find anything because I want to know what's going on.'

I ignored that part and said goodbye. It took me a while to locate the piles of old scripts and call sheets that Robert has accumulated over the series. He's paranoid about throwing them away because it's drummed into all the cast and crew that they must never be leaked, as if the journalists of the world are lined up waiting with bated breath for the next implausible *Farmer Giles* storyline to break. Eventually, I came across them at the back of a big cupboard in a room we laughingly call the office but which is actually meant as a bedroom for a very tiny person.

There must have been twenty there. I remember that we had a purge a couple of years ago and got rid of all the ones that were for episodes that had already been aired. Robert has signed a few and given them to charities to auction off over the years. I shook them all out one by one and, even though the odd thing fell out (a parking ticket, a tissue), there was nothing that resembled a strange pair of ladies' knickers or a photo of him and Saskia in a compromising position. I piled them all back up and shoved the pile back into the depths of the cupboard.

I was thinking of phoning Myra again but I decided to rummage through the rest of the junk before I admitted defeat. I pulled out cartridges for a printer that we replaced about three years ago, an early laptop, its shell a garish orange, the empty case for Robert's old camera. As I picked the soft case up again to replace it I felt a hard lump at its centre. I opened it up and there was a wooden box I'd never seen before. About the size of a pack of cards but three times as deep. Ornate lacquered wood, a beautiful shade of amber. I picked it up and turned it over in my hand before daring to open it.

Inside was a small, intricately carved silver heart, one side flat. A paperweight, I assumed. With a card: *'Here's my heart, I told you you could have it. S xxx'*

I shoved it back in the box, the box back in the camera case, the camera case back in the cupboard. I piled things on top of it, tried to re-create the mess that was there before.

I warned you there was a reason you should never snoop.

For about an hour I paced around the flat. What was I going to do? How was I going to save my marriage? At last, it hit me. I wasn't. I didn't want to. I'd played a supporting role to Robert for too long and this is how he'd repaid me. I was done.

What I am not going to do is let him off lightly. I'm not going to allow him to ride off into the sunset with Saskia fucking Sherbourne and live happily ever after. I'm not going to look at smug spreads in *OK!* and *Hello!* as they set up home together. How cute! They played a married couple for five years and then they fell in love for real, their star power magnified exponentially by the number of photographs there are of them together. Fuck that.

So I came up with my plan. Like I said, we've drifted apart. He's stopped noticing me, stopped confiding in me. Started shagging his colleague. I sacrificed everything because I thought we were in it together, but it turns out he was just in it for himself. But if I just confront him with what I've discovered I'm scared he'll be relieved. He'll be able to move seamlessly into a new life. And I don't see why it should be that easy.

Most probably, he'd want to wait till Georgia goes to uni in September (medicine at Bristol, thanks for asking, she's a smart girl) before kissing our marriage goodbye. For selfish reasons, mainly. He wants her to think he's Dad of the Century. And, to be fair, I wouldn't dream of disrupting her A levels by dropping a bombshell of this kind on her now. So I have some time. I may as well make use of it.

I am going to turn myself into Robert's perfect wife. I'll make myself over physically – Robert has always been big on looks and I know the way I've changed bothers him. He used to be proud to have me on his arm; now if we go anywhere together he just looks a bit apologetic. He keeps his distance, as if he's hoping people might assume I'm his fat assistant, not his wife. I'm sure he doesn't think I've noticed, but I have.

Don't get me wrong, the way I've let myself go bothers me too, but for different reasons. It's a symptom of the fact I've given up. I feel lethargic, unfit, older than my forty-one years. So I'm going to do something about it. Slowly, so he doesn't notice. I'm banking on the fact that he's pretty much stopped looking at me. If I keep on wearing the shapeless baggy clothes that have become my uniform, then I don't think he'll be too curious about what's underneath. Then, when I'm transformed, I'll emerge, butterfly-like, and I'll take his breath away.

I don't think he's so shallow that my simply starting to look more like my old self will win him back. I'm going to go on a charm offensive too. Fake an interest in the day-to-day goings-on in his life, share my own work stories, read up on things that interest him, laugh at his jokes and offer up ones of my own, be there smiling with a G and T in my hand and a casserole in the oven whenever he comes home from work. I'll try to remember all the things that used to connect us before it all went wrong – what we used to do on days off, what we used to laugh at. I'll remind him who he fell in love with and, hopefully, he'll fall in love with me all over again. He'll dump Saskia and throw his all into his marriage.

And then I'll tell him it's all over.

It'll be my greatest acting role ever.

I want to put my plan in motion before I bottle out. Exactly what that means, though, I'm not quite sure. I have no idea how I'm going to force him to reconnect with me on a mental level but I can at least begin to work on myself. Try to relocate the woman he used to be physically attracted to. But it's so long since I've done any exercise that I have no idea what to do.

The world of fitness is a mystery to me. I know the basic principle is eat less, move more, but beyond that I'm clueless. I decide that walking to work is a good start. It's not that far – four bus stops – but I've never done it on foot since I've been there. And anything other than sitting around seems like progress. I eat my usual toast, butter and marmalade breakfast, knowing that's going to have to change but not feeling ready to think about it yet. I shower and dress, agonizing over footwear, as if I'm off to run a marathon. I settle on a pair of pink Converse I wear to do the weekly shop. The rest of my outfit is the same as I always wear to work – a baggy long top over stretchy black leggings. Very stretchy. My legs have the appearance of sausages threatening to escape their skins. Hair tied up in a high ponytail.

I almost throw in the towel before I've even started when Georgia shuffles into the kitchen at about quarter to eight. First thing in the morning she still looks heart-breakingly young in her pink flowery pyjama bottoms, grey T-shirt and no make-up. Can I really do this to her? I remind myself that Robert is the one who seems intent on breaking up our marriage. I would have stayed forever because that was the promise I made.

Georgia yawns, stretching her arms above her head.

'Did you have fun last night?' Eliza's mum dropped her back about five past eleven but I had already claimed a headache and sloped off to bed to think. Despite his early start, Robert had stayed up watching the news. He hates going to bed early.

With you, a voice in my head says, and I block it out.

'Mmm . . .'

I know there's no point even trying to talk to her before she's had a cup of tea and a bowl of something that looks healthy but almost certainly isn't.

'You in first thing today?' Georgia's school timetable has gone haywire now that her A levels are approaching.

She only has to turn up when she has a class scheduled. The rest of the time is deemed 'study time' and the students are expected to be cramming either in the library or at home. Clearly, whoever devised this system had never met a teenager.

She rolls her eyes at me. 'Why would I be up if I didn't?'

'Good point. I'm going in early. Make sure you lock up.'

I kiss the top of her head and leave before she can ask me why.

It's a beautiful morning. The sun is out and there's the promise of a warm spring day. I'm feeling positive. I've taken charge. Nine and a half minutes later, just before bus stop two, I feel as if I've been hit by a truck. My calves are burning and my feet, unused to being used for the purpose for which they were designed, are hurting in places I didn't know they had. Under my arms dark patches of sweat have formed. I'm a biped. How can simply walking be this hard? Have I really let myself go this much? I try to remember the last time I walked any further than the bus stop at the end of our road. Fail.

Behind me I can hear a bus rumbling along. Sod it. That's enough for day one. I have to trot the last few paces as it overtakes me, and when I heave myself on and sit down I can hear my breathing coming out in gasps. I try again to think when the last time I did any exercise was. Before I worked at the bakery, that's for sure. So at least five years. I'm hit with a wave of self-loathing.

No wonder Robert looked elsewhere.

I've only met Saskia once. Years ago, when the show first started and everyone was still being matey. Before all the petty resentments and jealousies that come with working in close proximity with the same group of people kicked in. Before the cast started counting each other's column inches and comparing storylines. I haven't met many of Robert's work family (as he calls them). Not since the early days anyway. But her face is as familiar to me as my own in the mirror.

I wonder what he's told her about me and then decide I don't really want to know. *My wife doesn't understand me. She's let herself go. We have nothing in common any more.* Tick all that apply. For the hundredth time I reread the text message in my mind. Is there any ambiguity? Could I be wrong? Could it just be a jokey text from a colleague? *'Hope Paula bought it!!! Love you xxx.'* No.

'Jesus, what happened to you?' Myra looks me up and down as I sneak past the queuing customers, heading for the back room, my T-shirt soaked in sweat. 'Is it raining out?'

'It's a long story,' I say.

I have a swift wash in the staff toilet, only remembering at the last minute that there are no paper towels to dry myself with, so I have to lean bits of my body at a time towards the hot-air dryer, which is not as easy as you might imagine, as the air comes out from underneath, and then cram myself into the same sweaty clothes I took off. My 'Myra's' overall (baby-pink retro chic with 'Myra's' embroidered in italics on the breast pocket) will have to act as a shield. Note to self: bring a change of clothes if you're ever going to attempt to walk to work again. Or maybe just walk home. It's downhill.

'God, don't stand downwind of any customers,' Myra says as I pass on my way to serve a couple at the front table. I take this to mean my clothes are a little rank.

When the café is quiet she corners me.

'So what was all that about hiding places? What's Robert done?'

'Nothing. I don't know.'

'Right,' she says sceptically. And then, thankfully, she leaves it. She knows I'll tell her in my own good time.

I finish every day at half two, after the lunchtime rush, a compromise I wrestled out of Myra by agreeing I would work straight through with no break, stuffing in a sandwich to keep me going whenever I get a second to nip out the back. Today I forgo my usual 'unsold leftovers from yesterday' pudding and plough my way through a banana instead. It's a start.

Once home (bus all the way, feet too sore, also weak from lack-of-chocolate-bar-induced deprivation), I plan what to make for dinner. Robert is a health nut. His body is his temple. He's an absolute sugar addict but he's involved in a constant tussle with himself over his weight for fear the glossy magazines might run a 'Look at the belly on him' story one of these days. Consequently, I usually steer clear of desserts and end up helping myself to biscuits halfway through the evening.

Today I spend what seems like hours baking two batches of brownies. One a sugar- and butter-laden heart attack on a plate, the other some kind of weird thing made from cannellini beans, coconut flour, sweetener and cacao powder ('NOT COCOA POWDER!!' the hyper

YouTuber I have already consulted for healthy dessert ideas before I left work screamed out at me from my laptop. Apparently, there's a difference, who knew?) Anyway, the health food shop I pass every day on my way to the bus stop (but have never been in) stocked it, along with the rest of the ingredients. Christ knows what it'll taste like, but it only has forty-five calories a slice. They look almost identical. Close enough that you would never notice the difference if you weren't looking for it. Later, I will tuck into one of the superfood varieties while claiming that the whopping three-hundred-calorie version I am serving Robert is the exact same thing. If I can do this every night he'll put on a pound every ten days or so and that will make me very happy. Petty? Me?

He's home at half seven. Showered and at the breakfast bar by twenty to eight.

'Where's George?' He pours himself a glass of red.

'Revising at Eliza's.'

And that's it. That's our conversation done. I rack my brains for something to talk about. These days, unless Georgia is here, we tend to eat in silence. I can remember when we used to trip over our words we had so much to say to each other.

'Good day?'

He grunts a yes through a mouthful of chicken.

'Saskia turn up on time?'

'She did.'

I can't think of anything else to say except 'Did you shag her today?' so I turn back to my food. Clearly, I need to work on finding some common ground.

4

What to do about Saskia? Apart from use her as a punch-bag and then mount her head on my living-room wall, that is. I need to make sure their relationship is well and truly dead before I tell Robert to pack his bags. I don't want him to have anywhere too cosy to run to. I've been racking my brains as to what is the best way to achieve this without giving myself away and the best plan I've come up with is this: appeal to her better nature (if she has one).

If Saskia grew to like me, then surely – unless she's a monster, which she may well be – guilt would start to kick in. It's one thing to have an affair with a married man if you buy into his lies that his wife is a harridan whose sole purpose in life is to make his existence a misery. It's another to meet her and discover she is sweet and unthreatening and she loves her husband and clearly believes that he loves her back.

OK, so it's not exactly foolproof, but it's all I've got. Plus, I get to satisfy my curiosity and get a close-up look at the woman my husband has picked over me. It's win-win. I just have to work out how to make it happen.

I need to move quickly because filming wraps up in two weeks for the month-long summer break, and after that I'll have no way of contriving to be in the same place as her at the same time.

As luck would have it, there is some kind of party coming up. I only know this because I was trying to find a time for us to visit Robert's mum and dad in Bath and, when I suggested a possible date, he told me he couldn't do it that weekend because it was the producer's birthday celebration on the Friday night. Robert always likes to show his face at any work-related social do. Now I know why.

In the early days he used to invite me along, but I always declined, thinking I would feel like a spare part and that, anyway, it might be nice for him to spend some time bonding with his co-workers. Yes. I know. After a while he stopped asking and, if I'm being honest, I felt a bit relieved. Making small talk with people I hardly know has never been my forte.

'Is it Josh's party this Friday?' I ask him when we're sitting side by side in front of the TV. We're watching *Countryfile*. Kill me. I mean, really, kill me. He loves it, though, and in my new capacity as compliant wife I've agreed to have it on for once. In fact, it was my suggestion. Ask me anything about growing corn. Go on. Ask me.

'Mmm-hmm,' he says, by which I think he means yes.

'I think I might come.'

The look that crosses his face is priceless. There's a moment when I think he might choke on the Cabernet Sauvignon he's just taken a swig of. He composes himself quickly.

'Really? What's brought this on?'

'I don't know. I just feel like I should make more of an effort.'

'It might . . . I mean, won't you feel a bit awkward? Not knowing anyone?'

'At first, probably. A bit. But . . . I mean . . .' Big, inno-cent eyes. 'Don't you want me there?'

Robert is looking anywhere but at me. Not such a good actor now. 'Of course, but . . .'

I wonder what's rushing through his head. Should he make a last-minute excuse not to go? Tiredness or illness? Will he phone Saskia and tell her she'll have to stay home? Is she even going in the first place? I have no way of knowing. Chances are, I will end up going to some god-awful do for nothing. But it's all I have.

'Is it at his house? Where does he live?'

'Out in west London somewhere. It's a long schlep.' He can't look at me.

'You were going anyway, though, right? That's why we couldn't go to your mum's.'

'I have to show my face. It's expected.'

Yeah, right, I think. There's an edict out that says all cast and crew must attend a random social occasion on the outskirts of London just because the producer says so.

'Well, then. Now you'll have company on the journey.'

'I wasn't planning on coming home first. It's the oppo-site direction.'

'I'll meet you at the studio. I can get a cab.'

There's nothing he can say. He's bang to rights.

'OK. I wasn't intending to stay long, though. Just so Josh knows I've made the effort.'

'Fine. I'm looking forward to it.'

I wonder if Saskia was expecting a lift. If she'll be left to make her own way now. Maybe she'll decide it's too much trouble.

*

On Friday afternoon I agonize over what to wear. For the third day in a row I have walked the first part of my journey to work, wearing some old trainers of Georgia's that she hasn't worn herself in years because the colour combination is so 2014. Next week I intend to do it both morning and afternoon. It's hardly training for a marathon, but it's something. Obviously, there is no change in my physical appearance as yet. Still a size eighteen. But that's fine. I don't want Saskia to think I'm a threat. I need her pity, not for her to dig her heels in and go into competition mode.

The look I want to go for is sweet and homely. That I care about what I look like but not too much. In the end I choose a black skirt that's rather flattering, if I say so myself, with a teal blouse that's pretty and feminine but with sack-like qualities. I take my time washing and blowing out my hair – one of my best attributes: long, thick, shiny and chestnut-brown – and making up my face. By five thirty I'm ready, even though my cab's not due to arrive till half six.

'How do I look?' I ask Georgia as she swoops into the kitchen and grabs a Diet Coke from the fridge. She looks me up and down.

'Fab.'

'I feel a bit nervous. I don't know why I said I'd go really.'

'Have fun, don't drink too much and don't do anything you'd be embarrassed for me to hear about,' she says, an exact rehash of the lecture I give her every time she goes out.

*

The cab drops me off outside the studio gates and, as agreed, I wait for Robert to pick me up. There was no suggestion of me coming in and having a look around. It's the end of the filming day and I spot a couple of faces I recognize from my TV screen on their way out. Presumably heading the same direction we are. David, Farmer Giles himself, spots me and waves, rolling down his window. I met him a couple of times during the shooting of the first series, when Robert and I went out to dinner with him and his wife. But we weren't a foursome that gelled. I'm flattered that he remembers me, though.

'Hello!' I walk towards the car.

David seems to be brandishing a ten-by-eight photo of himself. Flat cap on. In Farmer Giles mode.

'Who's it to?'

It takes me a moment to realize what's happening. He thinks that I'm a fan, waiting for a signed picture and maybe the chance to do a selfie with him. For a split second I almost go along with it to spare him the embarrassment of disabusing him, but then I decide that, as I'm bound to be seeing him again in an hour or so, that might be worse.

'No. I mean . . . it's Paula, David. Robert's wife.'

He looks confused for a second then, thankfully, lets out a big guffaw.

'Paula! I thought you looked familiar! What are you doing out here?'

'Waiting for Robert. Are you going to the party?'

'Sadly, yes. Home first, though, to pick up Grace. Why didn't you go on in?'

I almost say, 'Because Robert told me to wait out here,'

but I stop myself. I wonder briefly whether David knows about Robert and Saskia. Whether it's the gossip of the set. I push the thought from my mind. I can't think about that humiliation now.

'Oh . . . well . . . you know . . .'

Luckily, David isn't really interested in an answer and a couple of other cars have stacked up behind him, waiting to leave.

'Well, see you later. Are you sure you don't want that signed photo? You could raise a tenner on eBay!' He pulls away, chuckling to himself.

I make sure not to make eye contact with any of the other drivers in case the same thing happens again. Consequently, when Robert pulls up, I am examining a cracked piece of pavement.

'I just saw David. He thought I was an autograph hunter,' I say as I climb in, thinking it might make him laugh. I'm gratified that it does.

'Classic,' he says. 'He probably gives his parents signed pictures for Christmas.' David's self-importance is one of Robert's favourite topics. He's never recognized that he has similar tendencies himself these days.

'I should have just let him do it and then see if he remembered me at the party.'

'No! You should have told him it was my autograph you were waiting to get. That you didn't want his, thanks very much.'

'Ha! And then taken a picture of his expression!'

We keep going along these lines for a few minutes, making each other laugh, and it almost feels like old times. Then Robert says:

'I only want to show my face at this thing. I'm not feeling too good. Migraine, I think.'

Usually when Robert goes to a party thrown by one of the team, he arrives home in the small hours, waking me up with his over-exaggerated efforts not to wake me up.

'Oh. When did that start?'

'I felt it coming on this afternoon. I should have cried off, really.'

I'm not going to give him a get-out clause.

'Well, see how you feel when you get there.' What's he going to do? Drag me out kicking and screaming in front of everyone if he wants to leave before I've spotted my prey?

Robert is making a show of rubbing his temples and sighing. Acting lesson 1:01: if the character has a headache, rub your temples. I've been making sympathetic noises (remember, you are trying to be the perfect wife) and trying to keep the conversation light.

'So who's going to be there?' I ask as we sit in stationary traffic near Chiswick.

'No idea,' he says, which seems, to me, ridiculous.

'Well, who usually goes to these things?'

'Just the cast and crew, really. Whoever's around. I think he's having some kind of family do tomorrow.'

Rub, rub. Sigh, sigh.

'Do you want me to take over driving?'

'No,' he says in a martyred voice. 'I'm fine.'

Josh's house in Richmond is an old Virginia-creeper-clad beauty that's three times the size of our home. There are a couple of cars in the driveway already, and I'm relieved we're not the first. I want to be able to get lost in the crowd before Robert starts insisting it's time to leave.

'I should park out on the road, really. In case someone blocks us in.'

I don't argue. We pull up on the verge. It's a beautiful evening, still just about light. I take a deep breath of the sweetly scented air.

'We should move out to a quieter area.'

Robert grunts. 'I wouldn't want to do that commute every day.'

I don't point out that it takes way longer to get from our home in Chalk Farm to the studio in Acton than it did to get here from there just now. I imagine the last thing Robert wants to do at the moment is plan a future with me. Well, me too, I want to say. I don't want you either.

A man I assume is Josh greets us at the front door. Attractive. Mid-forties, I would guess. Very smiley. Jeans and a worn-out but expensive T-shirt. He's obviously rushed home and changed into his civvies. Cropped hair and a tan. One of those very easy in his own skin people. The opposite of me. He only joined the show a couple of years ago and I know that Robert doesn't think much of him. He's friendly enough, though. He offers us a drink. Robert refuses the Prosecco on the grounds that he's driving. Usually, by the way, when he goes to any kind of work do he books a cab there and back so that he can booze to his heart's content. Tonight he obviously wants to be on standby for a quick getaway. Plus, I wonder if he's thinking that, if he doesn't drink, then I'm less likely to. And if I don't get a bit of Dutch courage inside me I'm less likely to be asking questions.

'I'd love one,' I say, helping myself to a glass from the proffered tray. 'Thanks.'

'I was beginning to think he'd made you up,' Josh says, and his tone is so friendly it puts me at ease a bit.

'Paula's not usually one for parties,' Robert says, with a hint of accusation. I imagine he's terrified I'm going to start inviting myself along to every event from here on in.

'Well, it's good to meet you finally.'

'This is a beautiful place,' I say, looking around. Really what I'm doing is trying to spot Saskia.

'Thanks. We haven't been here that long. Still a work in progress.'

He and Robert start a conversation about something that happened on set today. It's quite a funny story about one of the older actors getting in a muddle with her lines and repeating the same one over and over again, regardless of what Robert, who was playing opposite her, said. It's the kind of thing Robert would have told me in the car once, doing the impression he's doing now for Josh's sake, making me laugh.

There are about twenty people already gathered in the spacious, dark-beamed living room. I make a quick scan of the women. Two I recognize as members of the cast. Neither of them Saskia. There is more activity in the adjoining room but I can't see clearly enough to make out who's there. As I'm planning my next move the front door opens and about twelve people all come in at once.

'I'm just going to nip to the loo,' I say as Robert gets swept up in a hail of hellos. He looks as if he wants to come with me but then someone collars him and I slip away. Josh points the way. Obviously, I've got no interest in going there really, so I head for the farthest corner and lurk around near a group of people, wondering what to do next.

And then I see her. Or, at least, I hear her first. That loud voice. Just a touch of her Exeter accent peeking through when she's not being vigilant.

'Honestly, it was a scream!' she's screeching. My head whips around and there she is, holding court to another woman who looks as if she wants to tell her to shut up but knows she'd never get away with it. Long, thick bob a rich, gleaming honey-blonde, self-satisfied smile on her suspiciously plump lips (I remember the headline in one of those gossipy magazines you read at the dentist's: 'Has Saskia the farmer's wife gone under the knife?' along with close-ups of various bits of her face that were looking a bit alien. It made no sense either. Robert's character Hargreaves isn't a farmer. He's an antiques dealer. But since when did accuracy get in the way of good copy?) Bright blue eyes the colour of the Mediterranean sky. Skinny as fuck.

I look around to check Robert is still occupied. I can only just see his head in the crowd so I figure I'm safe to make my move. I make my way over to the two women, taking in Saskia as I go. Without all her on-screen make-up, she looks younger but not quite as flawless. When I get close I hover. I can hardly march over and reintroduce myself. I try to look a bit lost and sorry for myself, hoping they'll take pity on me, but I imagine in reality all they think is, 'Why is this weird woman hovering next to us?'

They're talking about Saskia's frozen shoulder and how it doesn't seem to be getting better, no matter what. Saskia has a voice that I imagine a chihuahua might use if it could speak. Or a Pekingese. Yap, yap, yap. Or a fly. An annoying little gnat, nipping at your heels.

'And the worst thing is you lose your independence so

completely. You have to ask for help with everything. The other day I had to get Sarah to drive me home because it was hurting so much I couldn't change gear! I mean, it makes me think what it's going to be like when I get old and helpless, haha!'

She actually says the word 'haha!'

I manage to catch the other woman's eye and smile. Thank God for manners. She now feels obliged to smile back, and I'm sure she's going to think she has to include me in the conversation too. Unfortunately, she apparently missed the advanced etiquette class because she turns back to Saskia and freezes me out.

Their conversation moves on to exercise. Saskia is working hard to stay in shape despite her niggling injury. I discover that her passion is Bikram yoga. The one you basically do in a sauna.

'Sounds like torture to me,' the friend says when she manages to get a word in, and I warm to her a bit, despite her ignoring me.

'It's addictive,' Saskia says. 'I go every Saturday morning and it sets me up for the whole weekend. It's that feeling of purging everything from the week, starting afresh. It's really energizing . . .'

'I consider the weekend a rip-roaring success if I ever change out of my pyjamas,' the other woman interrupts, clearly desperate to be able to contribute to the conversation. 'Where do you go? I've got a friend swears by the one on Regent's Park Road.'

'Marylebone. West One Hot Yoga. It's more low key. Less crowded.'

'Well, it obviously suits you. Which reminds me, I must go

and stock up at the buffet before all the really fattening stuff gets snapped up. Do you want me to get you anything?'

'No, thanks. I ate earlier.' Liar. I bet she's one of those nibble on a celery stick and call it dinner kind of people.

'Back in a sec.'

The other woman moves off. I don't really have time for subtleties. Saskia is looking around for someone else to chat to. I can't just follow her to her next conversation and hope she decides to befriend me. A quick glance assures me no one is looking our way. The room has filled out and I can't even see across to where, I assume, Robert is still waiting for my return. Here goes nothing. I lob my half-glass of Prosecco at Saskia's scarlet-clad back. She squeaks and turns accusingly.

'Oh my goodness, I'm so sorry.' I reach for a tissue in my bag and start to pat her down. 'I tripped over the hearth.'

Face to face, Saskia is well put together but not drop-dead gorgeous. For some reason this gives me renewed courage.

'It's fine,' she says. 'Don't worry about it.'

'If you come to the bathroom I can wash it off. Otherwise, you're going to reek of alcohol.'

'Won't be the first time,' she says, and smiles. She has a lovely smile, damn her.

'Please let me help clean it off. I don't know anyone here and I don't want to be remembered as the woman who ruined someone's top.'

'It's nothing special,' she says, 'Nicole Farhi. And I've had it for years. At least three, I just fell for the shade. Don't you think there's something about red? It's such a happy colour . . .'

Has she finished talking? I take a chance. 'Even so . . .'

'OK, I suppose it won't hurt.'

I lead her in the direction of the bathroom. 'God, I really am so sorry. I'm Paula, by the way.'

If she registers the name she doesn't show it, although I'm sure Robert must have warned her I'd be here. 'Saskia. And stop apologizing. It was an accident. It could have happened to anyone. I once fell over the kerb and dropped an ice cream on a baby! Can you imagine!'

Once we're in the tasteful traditional bathroom – roll-top bath, floral tiles that are just the right side of kitsch, original, I would guess, porcelain sink – I start to pat down her back with toilet paper and then use my glass, which I still have in my hand for some reason, to dribble water down the stain. 'It's going to get wetter, I'm afraid. Then I can dry it off a bit more again.'

I work diligently for a moment, racking my brain for what to say. The whole point of this exercise is that Saskia will find out who I am and, maybe, be struck by a pang of guilt that I can build on somehow later. I'm rendered speechless by the ridiculousness of what I'm trying to do. Thankfully, Saskia feels the need to chat her way through the awkwardness.

'So why are you here if you don't know anyone? Just for the free food, haha? I can't imagine it's the scintillating company.'

Here's my in.

'Oh . . . because my husband works on the show. Robert Westmore.'

I try to avoid looking at her as I say his name, I don't want to give myself away. I can sense a change in the air, though. Almost imperceptible, but it's there.

'Oh! You're Robert's wife! Of course.' And I think I see the briefest flicker of her eyes up and down as she appraises the competition.

'I give her my brightest, most disingenuous smile. Open, friendly. Definitely not suspicious. I need to get her attention. Confide. Be vulnerable.

'We met once before actually . . . years ago . . .'

'Oh yes, at that dinner, wasn't it?'

It wasn't. It was at the wrap party for the first series, but I let it go.

'I don't know why I came, really. Usually, I say no. I'm not very good with big groups of people I don't know.' Careful. Don't cross over into pathetic. 'I mean, who is? I can't imagine that's on anyone's list of favourite situations.'

I've made her top way damper than I needed to in an effort to keep our conversation going. Now I'm flapping it back and forth as if that might dry it.

'Don't bother too much.' She peers over her shoulder at her back view in the mirror.

'A couple more minutes will make all the difference. I should pay for you to get it dry cleaned, really. Just to be sure.'

'Absolutely no need,' Saskia says, and I find myself thinking she seems nice enough. I would probably make much more of a fuss if someone drenched me in pungent liquid at a party. But then I remember she knows who I am, she knows she is sleeping with my husband. Not so nice after all.

I know that I can't keep this going forever. Saskia will start to get irritated with me if I don't let her go soon. I have one last flash of inspiration.

'Right,' I say. 'That's about as good as I can get it.' I want her to relax, just to give me one more opening.

'Thanks. It's so warm out there it'll dry in a second anyway.'

She turns to go.

'Oh, by the way,' I say. 'I couldn't help overhearing you talking about your shoulder. I know *the* best physio. A friend of mine had seen everyone for hers and she went to him and he cured her in a few weeks. She said she started seeing the difference right away.'

Saskia's eyes light up. How can she not bite? 'Do you have his number? Or even just his name . . . ?'

'I'll have to ask my friend. But I'll get it to you.'

I expect she thinks I'll give the details to Robert for him to pass on. No such luck.

'Thanks. That'd be great. I feel as if it needs a miracle worker at this point.'

'Well, from what I hear, that's what he is.'

Now I just have to research the best physiotherapist in London.

Saskia and I say a friendly goodbye and I fight my way through the crowds to where I left Robert. He's chatting to a man and a woman, but I can see he's also flicking nervous glances around, trying to locate me.

'Where have you been?' he says as I appear at his side. I could almost believe he's missed me.

'Long story. I spilt a drink on someone.'

'I think we should make a move soon,' he half-whispers into my ear.

'Fine,' I say. My work here is done.

5

Robert claims the need for a lie-in in the morning so I leave him to it. I strap on Georgia's trainers and walk around the block, buying two coffees on the home stretch as an alibi. Robert always used to sneak out and get me a latte if he got up first at the weekends. I can't remember when he stopped.

Back home I have a shower (nb: if walking four hundred metres makes you sweat, you should probably do something about it) and then potter about trying to decide what I can suggest we do with the rest of the day. Shopping? Too much like hard work. Robert is enough of a face now that he gets stopped for photos every few minutes by people who then want to engage him in their life stories. Art gallery? Ditto. We could drive out to a reclamation yard, or some kind of non-posh antiques place. We used to spend hours pottering around, picking up curios. At first fantasizing about what we would buy if we had any money to spare and, later, once Robert's career started to take off, purchasing the odd thing. A carved wooden box, a pair of vintage green glass bottles, an old variety poster. It was one of our favourite things to do.

'Fancy heading out to the Swan?' I say as I hand him his warmed-up latte when he surfaces.

'God, no. I intend to have a lazy day, doing nothing. The last thing I want to do is sit in the car for hours.'

So that's that then.

Later, I Google frozen shoulders. It seems London is awash with physios who claim to have the answer. There's just no way to work out who is telling the truth and who isn't. I send a quick text to Myra: *'Know anyone who's had a frozen shoulder who could rec a good physio?'* As a second thought, I add: *'Round here ideally?'* Myra knows everyone locally and all their business. She discusses it all loudly with them in front of the other customers. Their divorces, their wayward children, their haemorrhoids.

Three minutes later I get a reply: *'Are you OK? What did you do?'* So I have to fire off another message telling her I'm not asking for myself.

'Do you want to run lines later?' I ask when I take Robert in a chicken salad at lunchtime. He's propped up on the sofa in front of Sky Sports, watching the pre-match build-up. I've killed time clearing out cupboards in the kitchen. We are the embodiment of a 1960s gender-typical couple.

'I haven't had a chance to look at them yet.'

'OK, well, if you do . . .'

'Thanks, though.'

He turns his attention to his salad. This is hopeless.

'FA Cup today, isn't it?' I nod at the TV. Watching sport together used to be one of our 'things'. Any sport, it didn't matter what, so long as we could pick a side to back.

'First semi.'

I fetch my own salad – forgoing the new potatoes and big slice of bread I would usually have with it – and join him on the sofa. But not before I Google who's playing and check out a couple of forums to see what the contentious issues of the day are. I feel him tense up as if he thinks I've come to rain on his parade. So I keep quiet. Make the odd – I think insightful – comment once the match starts, and by ten minutes into the first half he's relaxed and we're discussing the team selection, as if either of us knows what we're talking about. At half-time he goes off and makes us both a cup of tea and brings in two biscuits on a plate, which I take as a friendly gesture. I take one and put it on the arm of the sofa beside me, although I have no intention of eating it (my body is also a temple, don'cha know). I know he won't eat the other one because he never does, but it's the thought that counts. When he's absorbed in the second half I stuff mine into the pocket of my cardigan. If he thought I was refusing a sweet treat he would definitely know something was up. It sits there, burning a sugary hole in my pocket, just demanding to be eaten, but I crush it between my fingers so I can't give in to temptation.

By the end of the match I'm feeling like we've had a pretty successful afternoon. And, actually, I'd forgotten just how much I used to enjoy mindlessly watching anything competitive.

'Second one tomorrow,' I say, clearing away the tea things.

'It's a date,' he says, and I think yes, I've made a breakthrough. And then his phone buzzes to tell him he has a message and I remember the reason I'm doing this. I wonder if it's Saskia. If she's texted him to tell him she spent fifteen minutes shut in a toilet with me last night. That'll scare the crap out of him. I can't help but watch his face as he looks at the message. Then he holds his phone up to me as if to show me what it says.

'*Mart*,' the name of the sender says, one of the first assistants. 'They've changed the schedule for Monday. Just as well we didn't do lines.'

'Right,' I say, remembering to smile. Everything's normal. You don't suspect a thing.

By Monday afternoon Myra has a name for me. I know that when I call Saskia to give her the info I need to seize the moment. There's no point just giving her the physio's details, saying goodbye and hoping that's enough. It's completely outside my personality to try to force my friendship on to someone but on this occasion that's exactly what I need to do. Hopefully, Saskia will be curious enough about her rival to take me up on my offer.

Thanks to the internet, I now know the main number for the production offices. My heart is pounding in my chest as I dial.

'Hello, *Farmer Giles*,' a woman's voice trills at me.

'Um . . .' I almost hang up. Tell myself to breathe. 'Could I speak to Saskia Sherbourne, please?'

There's a pause. Of course, it hadn't even occurred to me that they probably get all manner of crazies calling night and day to try to talk to the actors. I know that people send wreaths and condolence cards if a character dies. I curse myself for not having taken Saskia's mobile number.

'It's Paula Westmore, Robert's wife.' I wait for an intake of breath that tells me my name is infamous as the scorned wife, but there's nothing.

'Of course. Hi, Paula. Let me just see if she's in her dressing room.'

I hear the tone as it rings through. Then a click.

'Paula! Hey!'

I jump and almost drop my phone. 'Hi. I just . . . how was your weekend?'

'Great, thanks. Up to my eyes in lines to learn, you know how it is. Or you probably don't, lucky for you. Did you enjoy Friday? You didn't stay long.'

Bitch.

'Robert had a migraine. But, yes, it was fun. I want to apologize again for drenching you. I don't usually go around throwing drinks on people!'

'You should. It's very therapeutic. Anyway, the top came out fine. Good as new. No problem.'

'So . . .' I say. 'I have the name of the shoulder guy for you.'

'You're a lifesaver. It's got so bad I can hardly even undo my own bra at the moment.' She laughs. Well, she doesn't, she says, 'Haha.' I try to block out the image that her comment has created in my head and rattle off the details.

'I'm going to ring him now.'

'He's near where I work,' I say, which is, strictly speaking, true, although not that near. A five-minute bus ride rather than a walk. But she doesn't have to know that. 'Let me know when you're seeing him and we could meet up for a coffee or something. If you fancy it . . .'

I feel like an adolescent boy asking a girl out on a date for the first time. Why on earth would she say yes? What's in it for her? She hesitates for a moment. Probably trying to answer that question herself.

'OK . . . great. What's your number?'

There's no way of telling if she's just being polite. I leave it with her. There's nothing else I can do.

I'm late for work. Robert is away for a couple of nights shooting locations, as he is pretty much every other week. Episodes shoot over two weeks, ten days a pop, of which two are spent in Oxfordshire doing the exterior scenes. Depending on whether Robert's character is in any of those scenes, and how many, he can be away one or both of those nights.

I've always rather enjoyed those evenings when it's just me and Georgia, or even me on my own. Now I have mixed feelings. It's a relief to have time off from my new relentlessly upbeat and interested self (example: this morning over breakfast: Me (after some frantic Googling): 'Did you hear about that guy who's developing a head transplant?' Robert loves crazy science stories), but it's also agony to imagine what might be happening in the country hotel they all call home for the duration. Georgia was out last night, revising at Eliza's, so I tried to distract myself with the new series of *House of Cards* that had just popped up on Netflix, and ended up watching four episodes back to back, going to bed far too late and oversleeping.

I hear the bus rumbling along behind me as I head for the stop. I have no choice but to run for it as it overtakes me. I huff along in Georgia's trainers, flapping my arms at the people waiting in the hope one of them might hold it up for me. Of course, they just assume I'm the local lunatic and all make a point of looking away. I'm still trotting along as the last person climbs aboard and the door closes. Bugger.

I sit down heavily on one of the narrow, sheltered seats, trying to get my breath back. And then it hits me. I have just run further than I can ever remember running in my adult life. OK, so it was probably only a hundred metres, a hundred and fifty at the outside. And I am panting way more heavily than I have ever seen Paula Radcliffe pant after twenty-six miles. But I did it. A week of walking part of my journey has resulted in this gargantuan achievement.

Actually, it's not strictly true that I haven't run as an adult. A couple of years ago, shamed by a shopping trip to buy an outfit for a friend's wedding, I decided I needed to take myself in hand. I borrowed yet another pair of George's trainers and announced that I was going to go for a jog. Robert's reaction ('What? You??') didn't put me off. I left the house, walking at first. As I turned the corner into Prince of Wales Road I broke into some kind of shuffling trot. I was exhausted immediately. My lungs felt as if they were going to explode. I didn't own a sports bra (why would I?) so my boobs were flinging themselves up and down like they might detach from my chest altogether. But that wasn't what put me off. It was the shouts of 'Earthquake warning!' from a gang of lads and the peals of laughter afterwards. I saw a passer-by snigger as one of the boys mimicked my undulating gait. I turned

49

the first corner I came to and walked home, tail between my legs. Robert didn't ask me what had happened and I was grateful.

It occurs to me that this morning that no one gave me a second glance. In fact, they all did their best *not* to look at me, in case that would result in them having to engage in my plight. I wasn't a fat woman attempting to get fit, and therefore an object of ridicule. I was a fat woman running for a bus, something that is apparently much more socially acceptable.

It's a revelation.

6

Surprise surprise! Saskia texts me to tell me she has an appointment with Wonder Man. I remind her about the offer of a coffee after (if she wonders why I'm so persistent, she doesn't ask. She probably just thinks I don't have many friends, and she'd be right. I'm one of those classic 'lost touch with her female friends once she settled down' women. I hate to admit it, but it's true. Robert never had that much interest in my friends and I just sort of let the friendships slide in favour of new couply acquaintances – usually where the man was someone Robert had a connection with and I would have to engage in a slightly forced camaraderie with the wife. I have no doubt about who gets to keep them all in the event of a divorce. Not that I care. I'd take one Myra over ten of Robert's friends any day) and she accepts graciously.

I square it with Myra that I can take time out (hospital appointment that I somehow, conveniently, forgot to tell her about). I promise to work an extra hour or so at the end of the day. Saskia and I have agreed to meet in the Pain Quotidien in Highgate close to the clinic. I hop on a bus outside work and I'm there in less than ten minutes, casually sauntering along as if I've just nipped around the corner.

Saskia is already sitting outside when I arrive, nursing something in a large, handleless cup. She smiles when she sees me.

'Hey!'

Have I mentioned that I hate people who say 'Hey'?

'Hi. How was it?'

'Amazing. And he's taped it all up, look!' She rolls up the sleeve of her T-shirt to show me the blue kinetic tape. 'It's actually not agony for the first time in weeks. I owe you big time.'

Have I told you I hate people who say 'big time'?

I wave the waiter over and order a latte. We make a bit of small talk about our aches and pains and how shit it is to be getting older. I still don't really understand why she took me up on my offer but then she says:

'How long have you and Robert been married?' Just like that, out of nowhere. Ah! So what she wants is info. She wants to torture herself with all the details of her lover's home life that he won't share with her. I prepare to be interrogated. Remind myself: big eyes and no air of chippiness. Sweet, open and trusting.

'Eighteen years,' I say, smiling, as if that thought makes me happy. 'Nearly. It's our anniversary in a couple of months.' Might as well throw her a crumb for nothing.

'Amazing. Are you doing anything special?'

Remember, she needs to feel sorry for me, not like she's going to have to fight me to the death for her man. 'Oh, I don't know. Robert's so busy . . .'

'They do all blend into one after a while, don't they? Josh always says . . .'

I miss the rest of the sentence because all I'm thinking is, 'Who the fuck is Josh?' And then it all comes flooding back, Robert moaning because the broadcaster had hired Saskia's husband as the show's new producer. Bleating on about how she'd get all the best storylines now. I've met him. I've been to her house. Joshua, of the brief Wikipedia mention, is Saskia's husband, Josh.

'Josh's your husband?'

She nods. 'Didn't you know? Eight years.'

We're interrupted by a couple coming over to ask Saskia for a selfie. She manages to be both gracious and patronizing at the same time.

'You're even more beautiful in real life,' the woman gushes, and I have to stop myself from grimacing.

The couple move off, happy, and Saskia gives me a 'What can you do? Is it my fault I'm so popular' look.

'You don't have any kids, do you?' Now I'm starting to be as nosey as her, but I really do want to know if I'm not the only collateral damage. I'm pretty sure there are none, but for all I know Josh has three from a previous marriage and Wikipedia never thought to mention it.

'No. At least not yet. I'm in no rush. Not that I want to leave it till it's too late but, you know, the time has just never seemed quite right . . .'

I zone out, imagine swatting her away. When I tune back in she's still talking.

'. . . didn't have her first one till she was forty-three and it all went off without incident, but you just never know, do you? You just have the one girl, right?'

I snap back to attention. 'Georgia. She's off to uni this year. Well, hopefully . . . A levels, you know.' I could bore for England about George and everything that's so special and unique about her but I force myself to leave it there. I'll let Saskia play the role of over-talker.

'I bet you'll miss her. It must be terrible, after all those years of having to think about their every move and then, suddenly, you have no idea what they're up to. Not . . . I don't mean she'll be getting herself in trouble or anything like that. I just . . .'

I feel my eyes prick with tears. Swallow noisily. I'm trying not to think about Georgia moving away. Not with everything else that's going on. I grunt an assent and Saskia looks at me with – what looks like – genuine sympathy.

'Still, you know what they say. Life for a couple really starts again once the kids have gone. Maybe it'll be like a second honeymoon, haha!'

I don't even dignify that with a reply. Bitch.

And, by the way, I really can't stand people who actually say the words 'haha' instead of laughing. Especially when it's in response to something they've said themselves.

Here's what I think about Saskia. If I didn't know what I know about her, I would probably like her well enough. Not enough that I'd want to pursue a friendship, but enough that if I bumped into her at a party I wouldn't want to slit my wrists. She's a bit irritating but, on the surface, she seems to be a nice person. But I do know. And that makes all the difference.

I need to offer her more bait. 'I can never really get Robert to take a holiday,' I say sadly.

'Well, filming is a bit relentless. How about in the summer break, though? He must have time then.'

I shrug, look down at the table. 'I sometimes think it's that he doesn't want to. I don't know . . . I shouldn't . . .'

That's got her. 'No. Go on.'

'Well, that we're not enough for him, me and Georgia. Sorry, I don't know why I'm telling you this . . .'

She's loving it. Ears pricked up. Hanging on my every word. 'I'm sure that's not true. What makes you think it might be?'

'Oh, it's nothing. Really. I think these things just happen when you've been married a long time. We'll come out the other end of it, we always do.' I blink back imaginary tears. Or maybe they're real. I'm not sure at this point. The truth is that even though I'm done with Robert that doesn't mean I'm not mourning the end of my marriage.

'I haven't even asked you what you do,' she says, changing the subject as I down the last of my coffee.

'I work in a bakery,' I say. I wait for the customary downward eye-flick at my 'curves' and, to give her credit, she doesn't do it. 'Serving, obviously. Not . . .'

'Which one?'

'It's private. I mean, the place is privately owned. Not that I'm not going to tell you where I work. It's not part of a chain or anything. Over there . . .' I wave my hand in the general direction of work but don't add that it's a couple of miles away.

'God, how can you stand the temptation?' I imagine she's thinking that, clearly, I can't.

'I really need to get in shape as it is.' She runs her hands over her perfectly flat belly as she says this. Waits, as people like her always do, for me to contradict her. And, because I am being Mrs Sweet and Unthreatening, I force myself to do so.

'You look like you're in pretty good shape to me.'

She rolls her eyes. 'Looks can be deceiving. I'm one of those fat skinny people. I'm happy with the size I am but I have no definition.'

'That's better than being a fat fat person like me.' I nearly add 'haha' but I can't bring myself to.

'Oh, but you're not . . .' she starts to say, and then she stops because even she must know it would be ridiculous to finish that sentence.

Let me just put my size in context here because God knows what you're imagining. I'm big, don't get me wrong, but I'm not at the can't get out of bed without a crane stage. I am not yet familiar with extensions for airplane seatbelts, but they are starting to feel a bit snug. I have too much of everything – boobs, backside, thighs, upper arms – but it is all still identifiable, not yet one big, amorphous blob. I'm large enough that the first insult anyone reaches for when I piss them off – as I did yesterday when I accidentally barged in front of someone in the bus queue – is 'fat', though. Fat cow. Fat bitch. I'm a size 18/20. Fifteen stone and change when I last checked, although I don't do that too often. When people look at me they see fat first and everything else second.

By the time I have to leave to get back to work, me and Saskia are best buddies, even though it's taken all my self-control not to lean over the table and throttle her. And I'd say 'haha' while I did it too.

'We should do this again,' I say. Luckily, it looks as if Saskia is hooked on the idea of this private insight into her boyfriend.

'Definitely. I'll let you know when I book my next appointment.'

'Lovely.'

She actually leans over and hugs me as we say goodbye.

'Later,' she says as I walk off, and I pause for a moment, assuming there's the rest of a sentence to follow, which, of course, there isn't, so I'm kind of left in suspended animation until I realize, and off I go, waving a hand behind me.

If I didn't know what I know there would be no reason I wouldn't tell Robert that I've befriended one of his colleagues. It's a tricky one, though, because I'm assuming Saskia won't mention it, as it'd send him into a panic that he was about to be found out. I'm pretty sure he'd ask her not to meet up with me again. Then again, she must think that I'll innocently tell him. So, on balance, I decide that's the safest bet.

I wait till we're eating dinner, the three of us, and then drop it in as casually as I can. I do it with a smile on my face so he doesn't think I'm about to attack him.

'Oh, guess who I saw today? Saskia.'

There's a moment when I think he might choke on his risotto but then, actor that he is, he composes himself. 'Really, where?'

'We had coffee. It's a long story. Well, it isn't, but it's not that interesting.'

'I didn't even realize you knew each other.'

'We don't, really. She's the one I spilt the drink on at the party.'

'Right.' I can see that he's dying to ask more but he doesn't want to give himself away.

'She seems OK. Bit full of herself, obviously. Talks a lot. It's a bit hard to get a word in,' I add, to amuse myself.

Robert makes a laughing noise that doesn't really feel like a laugh. 'She does a bit.'

'Did you wash my white top?' Georgia says out of nowhere. And that's it, subject closed. I imagine he's thinking he can't bring it up again with me because I might start to wonder why.

7

I'm finding it frustrating that most of what I'm doing is waiting. Waiting for opportunities to try to reconnect with Robert, waiting to see if Saskia contacts me again, waiting for my pitiful efforts at weight loss to pay off. I need to make something happen.

Having a friendly chat about football every week or so is not going to rekindle the embers of our marriage. Especially now the season is all but over. I have to be more proactive or, before I know it, October will have come and Robert and Saskia will have run off into the autumn sunset without a care in the world. I've tried making a list of all the things Robert and I used to do together but, beyond hunting for antiques and watching sport, I can't really think of anything concrete. We just got on. End of story.

I suppose that I was different then. Not just in appearance. Less stressed. More confident. But then, so was he. Different, that is. More laid back. Less worried about how the world perceived him. Whenever I think back to the two of us in the early days, I always see us sitting outside a café, falling about laughing. We used to spend hours nursing a coffee, people-watching. Making up stories about the other customers or the strangers walking past. We used to try to imagine what they were saying, making up little dialogues, doing the voices. It sounds stupid now, but I can picture it like a snapshot of when I was happiest. I don't know when we stopped doing that.

I decide that the only thing I can take control of is myself. Since my near-miss-with-the-bus revelation I've come up with a strategy. Every afternoon now as I walk the first part of the journey home from work, I lag back, a couple of hundred metres from the first stop, until I hear the bus coming and then, as it rattles past me I start to run, arms flailing. I always miss it by a mile. And then, when I have got my breath back (a good five minutes), I huff loudly, as if I've decided to walk, and then I do the same again with stop number two. I only do it twice. That's enough to leave me sweating profusely, legs burning, face red for the rest of my journey on board.

The first few times I can't help glancing around to see who is sniggering. But, as before, no one is even looking at me, except with sympathy because I didn't make it to the stop on time.

I'm a mass of chafe marks, blisters, unidentifiable under-boob rashes. My knees feel as if someone has taken a sledgehammer to them. Some mornings my calves refuse straight out to allow me to do anything but hobble.

I know I need help but I'm not ready to ask for it yet. Not ready for the surprised looks and the stifled laughs behind my back. Even if I had the faintest idea who to ask.

So I add the first morning bus stop into my routine. Start packing a rucksack with a change of clothes and a towel. Keep my secret to myself.

Myra, though, witch that she is, knows something is up. She badgers me relentlessly. She is like a pig with a truffle when it comes to secrets. She knows they're there and she'd going to get to them if it kills her.

At first I think she thinks I'm having an early menopause. How else to explain the sweats and the need for a change of clothes every morning? Then, when I have made it clear that's not the case, she assumes I must have some terrible problems at home (which I do, but of course she doesn't know the half of it) and that I've moved into a grotty bedsit with no running water but am too ashamed to admit it. I'm running out of ways to put her straight when, one morning, she says:

'Have you lost weight?'

'I don't think so . . .' I splutter.

She stops what she's doing – which is cleaning the coffee machine – and the jangle of the armful of bangles she always wears, the soundtrack to my working day, cuts out abruptly. She looks me up and down critically, hands on hips. I have to stop myself from pointing out that her short crimson hair is sticking out from her head in five different directions, as it always does when she's been putting the effort in.

She squints at me. 'You have. Are you OK?'

This is what happens when you have paid no attention to the way you look for years; people assume weight loss equals illness, not that it might be a choice. Although I don't want to let anyone in on my secret, I also don't want her to start worrying about me and recommending holistic healers and cancer-killing juice diets.

'I'm fine,' I say. 'It's probably just worry about Georgia's exams or something.'

'Don't you think Paula looks like she's lost weight?'

Myra says at the top of her voice to one of the regulars, Mrs Cobham, who is just settling down with a pot of tea and a slice of a chocolate ganache cake. Mrs Cobham peers at me through her thick-rimmed glasses.

'I'm not sure. Maybe. Are you on a diet, dear?'

'No,' I say, and I make a big show of wiping down the counter, hoping that will signal that the conversation is over.

'Oh, I forgot you were as blind as a bat,' Myra says affectionately, and Mrs Cobham laughs indulgently. That's the thing with Myra: she can say the most awful things to people but she gets away with it because everyone loves her and it's obvious she doesn't really have a mean bone in her body.

'She's just messing with you, Mrs Cobham,' I say. 'Trying to wind me up'.

Worn down, I invite Myra over on an evening when I know neither Robert nor Georgia will be there.

'What's going on?' she says. Although we are good friends, I don't often invite her over to the flat. Robert isn't keen on unexpected guests. 'Oh shit! You're not going to tell me you've got another job, are you? Or that you want maternity leave? Are you pregnant?'

She peers down at my stomach.

'Of course not! I just want to talk to you about something, that's all.'

How can she resist?

She arrives on the dot of half seven, bearing a box of leftover cakes. I try to pretend they're not there. It's hard enough at work, but these are free and in my house.

We sit at the kitchen table and she opens the box, slides it towards me. I summon all my willpower.

'Not at the moment, thanks.'

'You *are* on a diet,' she crows. 'I knew it.' She makes it sound as if she's accusing me of a crime, which, in Myra's eyes, dieting is. One of the things I have always loved best about Myra Jones is that she is completely happy the way she is. She's bigger than me, older than me, she lives on her own and she couldn't give five fucks about any of those things. She's an inspiration.

'OK. Yes. I am.'

'Why? You're gorgeous.'

'It's a long story. It's . . . oh God, Myra, can I tell you something in absolute confidence?'

Her eyes nearly pop out of her head. She reaches for the bottle of red that's on the table between us and pours us both a glassful.

'Of course. Anything. I know I love a bit of gossip but I'd never repeat anything you didn't want me to.'

I know that's true. Myra is beyond loyal when it comes to her friends.

'It's Robert,' I say. 'He's seeing someone else.'

I wait for it to sink in. Her expression goes through shock to sympathy then fury and then back to sympathy again.

'That bastard. Are you sure?'

I fill her in on the story so far. Her mouth drops open when I tell her it's Saskia and only gets even wider when I reach the bit about meeting her for coffee, but I plough on through and she waits for me to finish.

'Jesus. And you're definitely going to kick him out, right?'

'Definitely. It's over.'

'Good. I've always thought he was a bit of a knob.'

I'm shocked. 'What?'

'He has that smug thing going on. Like he's waiting for everyone to recognize him.'

'To be fair, a lot of people do.'

'I know, but that's not the point. It's as if he thinks he's better than them. Like he's more important than they are because he's on TV.'

I know she's right. That's the thing with Myra. Her observations can be hurtful but there's always a huge grain of truth in them. I'm so used to Robert being Mr Popular, though, that it's hard to take in.

'I thought you got on with him OK.'

'He's your husband. I'm hardly going to tell you I think the man you love is a patronizing git. Shit, you're not going to change your mind, are you, and then this conversation will have been really awkward?'

'Loved,' I say. 'The man I loved. I don't think I do any more. I don't think I have for a while, actually.'

'So your plan is what? Get him to realize how much he loves you and then tell him it's all over?'

'Pretty much.' It sounds idiotic at best, I know.

'I love it,' she says. 'Serve him fucking right. You need to do a bit more than lose a few pounds and talk to him about football, though.'

'I know. I need help.'

She rubs her hands together, with a look on her face I've only ever seen when she's been scheming for ways to make her business more successful.

'The element of surprise is crucial. You need him to

64

look at you and think 'Wow!' Like he's noticed you for the first time. You're lucky you have that fat body thin face thing going on. It won't be obvious what's going on for a while. Well, apart from when you . . . do you still . . . ?'

Only Myra could ask this outright. 'Not so as you'd notice. And on the rare occasions we do it's when we've both had a few drinks so . . .'

'OK. Enough detail. Just wear baggy clothes. And you need to do more than just run after the bus. You need to join a gym.'

'Oh God, no.' The thought of all those perfect bodies pumping iron makes me want to cry.

'Or get a personal trainer. You need to do something to suck it all in so you're not just a big bag of flapping skin.'

'Why are you so keen on this all of a sudden? I thought you said I looked good as I am?'

'You do. You can put it all back on later but Robert's probably the type who wants a scrawny woman on his arm. I bet Saskia's stick thin in real life? Am I right?'

'Yes,' I say miserably.

'I knew it. So that's easy. You can do thin. Now all you have to do is to try and make him fall back in love with you the person again.'

'Sadly, not so easy.'

'One step at a time,' she says. 'Just keep doing what you're doing for now. It all helps.'

'I'm taking these with me,' she says, gathering up the boxes of cakes as she leaves, a bottle and a half of wine later. 'We don't want temptation right under your nose. Really, you shouldn't be drinking either.'

I raise my eyebrows in a way I hope conveys exactly what I think of that idea.

She laughs. 'No, you're right. That would be a step too far.' She gives me a big hug.

'Thanks, Myra,' I say into her shoulder. I feel much better for having unburdened myself.

'It'll all be OK,' she says. 'Or, actually, it won't, but at least he'll be miserable too.'

I'm cursing myself for not asking Saskia more about her own relationship. I was so thrown by her mention of Josh that it didn't occur to me to try to establish if they're the kind of couple who see her messing around with another man as acceptable (do those people really exist?), or whether Josh is in the same boat as me. Does he indulge her because she's an artist or some bollocks like that, or would he be devastated to find out the truth? I can't help thinking it would be useful to know.

It's out of the question for me to call her again but I do have one weapon in my arsenal. Saskia's love of hot yoga, specifically, Saturday-morning classes in Marylebone.

Of course, Marylebone is awash with Bikram classes. All those lithe, beautiful people slipping about in each other's sweat all day and night. I was paying attention when I was eavesdropping, though. I remember the name of the centre. West One Hot Yoga has three ninety-minute classes every Saturday morning. An early-bird special for superwomen at 7 a.m., and then nine and eleven. I imagine, in between, someone has to go in and mop up.

I have no intention of joining a class, obviously. Ambulances would have to be called. I don't even do cold yoga.

My plan, such as it is, is to be conveniently lurking outside when she emerges. Oh, the coincidence! Fancy seeing you here! It's worth a try.

There's no way I can convince Robert that I need to be in the West End at half past eight on a Saturday morning, when the first class would be heading out. I love my weekend lie-ins far too much. I can imagine that Saskia might easily be the type to leap out of bed at the crack of dawn on her day off to go and be pummelled into perfection, but even so. I decide to stake the next two out. If she's not there, she's not there. Even if she is, she might be in a hurry, or with a friend, or just have a life to get on with. But, at this point, it's all I've got.

There's a hairy moment when Georgia declares she wants to come shopping with me. I announced my intentions over dinner on Friday night. George, as usual, is on her way over to Eliza's. Robert is working his way through yet another fattening 'health' brownie. Tonight he declared my root vegetable mash 'fantastic' and asked what the mystery ingredient was. I just laughed and didn't tell him his portion had half a ton of butter added (missing from mine and Georgia's). I know it will take months for any of this to show around his flat middle, but it makes me happy. It's like I'm planting little bombs inside him and, one of these days, they're all going to go off together and the button will pop off his trousers just as a fan is asking for an autograph.

'You can't,' I say, all too abruptly. 'I'm hunting for your birthday present.'

Georgia's birthday isn't for another six weeks but, with the self-centred confidence of youth, she buys my story immediately.

'Oh my God! What? What is it?'

'I don't know yet. This is just a preliminary foray to give me ideas. A fact-finding mission.'

Robert groans. 'Are you expecting me to come?'

I laugh indulgently. 'No! Next time, when I've narrowed down the options.'

'You can take me out for brunch,' Georgia says and his face lights up. He loves it when she still wants to spend time with him. He's a great dad. In all ways except one.

On Saturday I get to West One Hot Yoga (which turns out to be West1 Hot Yoga! – I wonder if they paid someone to come up with that. I mean, really. Did they get extra for the exclamation point?) about fifteen minutes before the nine o'clock class is due to end. There's a café almost opposite (thank God for the wealthy would-be hipsters of Marylebone and their obsession with the flat white) so I pick the table with the best viewpoint, order myself a pot of tea and wait.

I try to come up with titbits I can offer up that will pique Saskia's interest but won't give her the impression that my marriage is dead and buried already. By the time the hordes of sweaty bodies start to exit at half past ten I've come up with a whole scenario that paints me as the loving wife, bemused and heartbroken by a sudden cooling-off on her husband's part. You'd have to have a heart of stone not to feel sorry for me.

I've also prepared some leading questions about her own marriage. I just have to find a way to work them into the conversation without giving myself away.

I daren't take my eyes off the exiting crowd for a

second. This is all for nothing if I miss her. I'm surprised to see there are a few men too. I'd imagined a room full of identikit pretty blonde skinny women. And, actually, they all do fit that description, for the most part. It's a bit like looking for a polar bear on an iceberg crammed with other polar bears. In a blizzard. I am rendered snow blind by honey highlights. I keep watching as the last few stragglers leave. Most seem to go home without showering (it doesn't bear thinking about) so I assume they all live nearby. They wear their sheen of sweat and damp skin-tight Lycra like a badge of pride. Look at what I've just endured! But wasn't it all worth it to get this body?

There's a small hiatus and, just as I think everyone has left, with no sign of Saskia, a couple of women emerge with (clean) damp hair and normal clothes on. Almost immediately, others start arriving, presumably for the eleven o'clock class. Of course, it hadn't even occurred to me that Saskia might spot me on her way in and then I would have no possible excuse to still be sitting in the same spot ninety-odd minutes later.

I do my best not to draw attention to myself. By which I mean I just sit there not quite knowing what to do. The waitress comes and asks if I'd like anything else and I flap her away, so intent am I on my task. At about ten to eleven I spot Saskia on the other side of the road. Hair neatly tied up at the top of her head. The obligatory skin-tight leggings and a colourful stretchy vest top. Gym bag over her right arm. She's talking into her mobile. Probably to my husband.

I keep my head down and my fingers crossed. If she notices me sitting there, she doesn't say anything, and I'm pretty confident she wouldn't want to pass up the opportunity for another close look at her rival. I allow myself to breathe out. Now I know she's definitely there, I have an hour and a half to kill. I'm loathe to give up my seat in case she leaves early (I've heard people are carried out faint and sick from these classes from time to time, something I'm sad not to have witnessed thus far) or I don't manage to secure another table later on. I can't just sit here drinking tea for all that time, though. I'll be a gibbering basketcase by the time she comes out. And the pastries look far too tempting. Besides, there are people hovering, glaring at me when they get the chance to let me know I should be giving up my table in the sun to them.

I pay my bill and wander down towards Selfridges. I might as well really do some scouting for gifts for Georgia while I'm here. It's her eighteenth so, of necessity, we have to make a big deal of it. We want to get her some things to help equip her for her new life away from home (don't think about it), but Robert and I also talked last night (companionable evening on the sofa watching people battering each other senseless on UFC. The things that can bring a couple together) about finding her something she can keep. Something to always remember. 'A framed decree nisi,' I almost quipped, but I reined myself in. Now I head to the jewellery section and stare boggle-eyed at the prices for a while.

When I get back to West1 Hot Yoga! all the tables at the café opposite are, predictably, taken. So I lurk in that fat Labrador waiting for a sandwich way beside the people who seem to be furthest along in their meal. Ideally, I will be sitting and looking at a menu at the point Saskia emerges. Then it would be easy to ask her to join me. Asking her if she wants to loiter by the side of the road for a while doesn't seem like such an attractive proposition.

The waitress who served me only an hour and a half ago shows no sign of recognizing me. This is how much I stand out from the crowd.

'Just one?' she says with a smile.

'At the moment. A friend's joining me.'

'We've got space inside.'

'I'd rather wait, if that's OK?'

The people at the table I'm coveting look up, disappointed. Clearly, they were hoping I'd take myself and my sad, hopeful eyes elsewhere.

'No problem. I'll bring you a menu to have a look while you wait.'

I check my phone. Three minutes till the class ends. My heart starts beating up a storm. And right on cue they start to trickle out. The sweaty glowers first – no sign of Saskia – and then, five minutes later, just as I am sitting down at the table – the clean, damp-haired showerers. Two, three, and then, there she is. Before I allow self-consciousness to overtake me I'm waving and calling her name.

She looks over. Sees me. Confusion. Then a smile.

She's looking good in cropped skinny jeans and Converse (I look hopefully for signs of cankles and, sadly, find none). She's wearing the same red T-shirt that I threw my drink over.

'Paula! What on earth are you doing here?'

Don't babble. You don't want her to think you're some kind of stalker maniac.

'Birthday shopping.' I roll my eyes. 'It's Georgia's

eighteenth in a few weeks and I'm trying to get ahead of myself.'

'Looks like you're hard at it, haha,' she says, indicating the fact that I'm holding a menu in my hand.

'Busted. Oh, do you want to join me? I'm just having a quick coffee before I go back into the fray.'

I'm relying on her thinking this is too good an opportunity to pass up. She can get a bit more info on the state of her lover's marriage and he can't be upset with her because, what could she do?

She hesitates for just a second. 'OK, lovely. Just a quick one.' She sits down next to me.

'What have you been up to?' I ask, feigning innocence. Hot yoga? What hot yoga?

'Bikram. I'm obsessed. Addicted to the sweating. Don't worry, I've had a shower, haha!'

'I've always wanted to try that! Do they do it round here?' BAFTA for the woman in powder blue.

'Over there.' She waves at the studio with its huge sign: 'West1 Hot Yoga!' 'You should come one day. I'm here every Saturday. I don't let myself miss it, whatever's going on.'

'Even with the shoulder?'

'Even with the shoulder. I just avoid putting any pressure on that arm for the time being. Oh, your guy really is working miracles, by the way.'

'You've been back?'

'Twice. I was going to call you, but it was all a bit last minute . . .'

Or Robert asked you not to, more like.

'Oh, that's OK. Work's been crazy so I probably

wouldn't have been able to . . . but it's getting better? I'm so glad.'

She fills me in on how she's getting on, and how much her range of movement has improved already and I pretend like I care.

'Is that the T-shirt?' I say when she's exhausted the topic.

'Oh yes! So, you can see there was no lasting damage.'

'Now I'm terrified I might accidentally spill my coffee on it. What if I have some kind of compulsion?'

'I'll take the chance. How have you been?'

'Yeah . . . good,' I say, with just the right amount of doubt. Don't tip over into self-pity or you'll just get on her nerves.

'That didn't sound very convincing.' That's got her attention. When the waitress comes she decides she's hungry and orders a salad for lunch. ('Niçoise, please, my darling. With the dressing on the side.') I follow suit. Dressing on the top. I'd only pour it all on anyway. I'm not ready for naked salad yet.

'So, what's up?' she says, once our order has been taken.

I give her a tight little smile. Poor, brave woman, trying so hard to keep it together. 'Oh, nothing much . . . I'm . . . we're just having a bit of a funny time. I think, with . . . I don't know . . . then there's Georgia . . .'

'It's a big thing for couples, suddenly looking at an empty nest. Not that I know anything about that, of course . . .'

I nod to let her know that she's already told me.

'It's understandable if you and Robert are finding it hard . . .'

73

She waits, hoping I'll elaborate. How much easier it would be for her if I told her our marriage was all but over. I won't give her that satisfaction, obviously.

'I sometimes . . . I shouldn't really talk about Robert when he's not here, especially as the two of you work together . . .'

'I would never say anything, don't worry about that. I know when to keep my mouth shut.'

I nearly laugh but instead turn it into a sigh, as if I'm thinking it over. 'I sometimes worry that once it's just us he'll start thinking, what's the point . . .' As I say this a genuine tear wells up in the corner of my eye. I'm acting but I'm not acting. Saskia reaches out and puts her beautifully manicured hand over mine, and it's all I can do not to shake it off.

'I'm sure that's not true. You have a history, that must count for something . . .'

I shrug. 'Maybe . . .'

Our salads have arrived and the waitress hovers awkwardly, not quite knowing what to do. Saskia moves her hand to make space. I dab at my eyes with my fingers.

'It's just . . . we've always been so close, and now he seems . . . distracted. Do you ever have that . . . you know, with Josh . . . that you feel as if he's not there sometimes?'

'Oh, Joshie's a darling,' she says. 'I'm lucky that way. I don't have to worry . . . sorry, that sounds awful, as if I'm saying you do. I don't mean it like that.'

'It's fine. You're lucky. I doubt there're many couples who can say they never have any periods where one or other of them is unsure.'

'We made a pact when we met,' she says, looking me

straight in the eye. She's a better actress than I thought. 'That we would always be honest with each other. If one of us did something that got on the other's nerves or made them unhappy we could say so without any recriminations. It works.'

'But what if one of you thought the other was cheating . . . ?'

She gives a little laugh. 'I'd cut his balls off, haha!'

So they clearly don't have an open relationship.

'How did he end up working on the show?'

'Nothing to do with me! Well, not really. He's freelance, you know, and he'd just come off another job for the BBC so he put himself in the frame. I'm not saying it didn't hurt that he was my husband – actually, that sounds awful, don't ever tell him I said that. He would have been in with a good shot anyway but the little word I put in with the execs might just have edged it for him.'

I can't imagine why the executive producers would have listened to an actress they must all consider a pain in the arse when it came to hiring a new face to run the show. Most likely what Robert said to me at the time was true: they thought it wouldn't hurt having someone on board who could try and keep her in line.

'How did you meet?'

She gazes off into the distance, a Tennessee Williams heroine having a bitter-sweet reminiscence.

'On *Under the Blue Sky*,' she says, referencing another god-awful series she was a regular on before *Farmer Giles*. This one was about an ex-pat couple settling into life in Spain. I think she played the cantankerous but sexy neighbour on that too.

'He was in the script department. I used to try to persuade him to write me all the juicy storylines, haha!'

I haha along with her, just to be nice.

'Have you and Robert been together since college, or have I imagined that?'

I nod, and rearrange my face into a more rueful expression again. 'Twenty years. It's hard to believe sometimes.'

'That's amazing. What an achievement.'

I bite my tongue. 'That's why it's so hard, you know, at the moment . . .'

'It's a big deal, isn't it? All that history,' she says, looking at me with what seems like genuine sympathy. That's it, the moment she bites down on the hook.

I lower my eyes. Lady Di at a press call. 'It's everything.'

By the time we say goodbye I know I've got her. A pang of guilt has got through. Now I just need to work on making it take hold.

'Don't . . . Maybe don't mention to Robert that we bumped into each other,' I say as she hugs me goodbye, having agreed that we will meet up again soon. 'Just because you work together and I would never want him to worry that I was talking to one of his co-stars about our personal life.'

The relief on her face is so palpable I almost laugh. I'm offering her a free pass. A front-row seat to the state of my marriage. 'Of course not. Hey, you should come to Bikram next week. We could have lunch again after.'

'I'd be in A & E. Maybe one day. Let's just do the lunch part.'

'Deal,' she says, hugging me again. 'I'll call you.'

*

I'm still trying to make a list of all the things that Robert and I used to love to do together so that we can have a few good bonding sessions that might remind him why he ever thought I was his soulmate. (Myra's advice: buy a mirror, hold it up and let him look at himself; that'll make him happy.) It's harder than you would think, pinning down exactly what shared interests you have with your spouse. Unless you still go ballroom dancing or dogging regularly, that is. And most of the activities that come to mind – dancing till four in the morning, taking ecstasy, going on anti-war demonstrations – are things neither of us have had any yearning to do, so far as I'm aware anyway, in the past eighteen-odd years. It's funny how everything I can think of that was a shared interest is from before Georgia came along. After that we became a family, doing family things, and the rest of it felt a bit immature, a bit trivial.

So far on my list I have: watching sport, browsing vintage markets, weekends away, walking. I added walking even though both Georgia and I gave that one up years ago. She because she thought it was a lame way to spend a Sunday, me because I was too busy comfort eating. It's one I think we could resurrect now, though.

The next sunny Sunday I start making a picnic before Robert has even surfaced. I've bought all his favourite things from the deli up the road – tiny red peppers stuffed with goat's cheese, taramasalata and pitta bread, mini quiches. I wrap them up, along with smoked salmon and cream cheese sandwiches (full fat for him, 'lightest' for me) and a half-bottle of Prosecco. I've planned out a route, just like we used to. Only about five or six kilometres (as opposed to the fifteen we used to happily tackle, but I thought Robert wouldn't be too happy if he had to carry me the last ten) across the Heath to the pergola in Golders Hill Park. We used to go and sit there for hours when Robert was between jobs and I was a stay-at-home mum, watching Georgia run up and down the steps, chuckling away to herself. I used to worry then about her being an only child. I still do. This whole thing would be much easier for her if she had a sibling to share it with. Somehow, it just never happened, even though we tried.

I hear him stirring in the bedroom. Brace myself. Rehearse my lines in my head. 'Don't just say them, live them,' I hear one of our old tutors say. I always thought he was a bit of a pretentious idiot but at the moment that feels like the exact advice I need.

The toilet flushes, then pad, pad, pad down the corridor and he's here.

I paste on a bright smile. 'Morning!'

'Huh,' Robert says. He's never been a morning person. He pushes his hair back from his face, a habit he's had ever since I've known him. The only difference being that he used to have thick dark brown hair and now I can see his scalp peeking through at the crown. I know how much he hates this. Loathes the fact that, whatever he does, he can't seem to stop the strands leaping from his head like rats from a sinking ship. He's considering a transplant. The make-up people on *Farmer Giles* do something miraculous with some kind of dark powder that means his impending baldness does not show up on camera, but it's only a matter of time. To compensate, he's grown a beard, like every other man in the country at the moment. He thinks it gives him hipsterish qualities. I think: young Santa.

Robert's otherwise handsome, chiselled face is a bit let down by his eyes. Not that there's anything wrong with them, but they're unremarkable. They don't have that piercing quality that marks out the leading men from the character actors. They're a muddy grey-blue. I've seen him in the mirror many times, practising his arresting stare when he thinks I'm not looking. He can't quite pull it off, though. In middle age he's in danger of looking ordinary. Shame.

I place a mug of coffee in front of him. He reaches for it, bleary-eyed, and slugs it back greedily.

'It's a gorgeous day.' I beam at him. 'So I've hatched a plan.'

He looks at me warily. 'Oh God.'

'No, you'll like it. We're going to park the car up the top of Hampstead and walk up to the pergola. We haven't done it for years. I've already made a picnic.'

I wait for him to object, wondering if I should have held off for him to wake up a bit more before I pounced.

'Since when did you want to go walking?'

'Since now. It'll be fun.'

'Last time I suggested going for a walk I think your exact words were 'Why would I want to do that?' He raises an eyebrow at me. A challenge, but a jokey one. I laugh.

'Yes, well, let's just say I've seen the error of my ways.'

He looks out of the window. 'It *is* a lovely day.'

I know he must be wanting to make some kind of

comment about the fact that I'll want to cop out halfway through. I try to distract him.

I wave the picnic bag at him. 'I have goat's-cheese-stuffed peppers.'

He gives me a slightly forced smile. 'Well, in that case . . .'

Bingo.

An hour later we're striding out past Whitestone Pond at the top of the hill. Robert always walks at a pace that suggests he's being followed by something big and scary but doesn't want to alert it to the fact he's trying to get away by actually breaking into a run. Consequently, I'm breathless already, which is affecting my sparkling attempts at conversation. (Among other things, I have researched the progress of the preparations for the Rio Olympics, what new shows are opening in theatres around the country and what's happening in *The Archers*, all topics that are close to his heart). I slow my pace, hoping he'll match it, but he just keeps moving. If we carry on like this, I'll have to sit down in a minute.

'Could we . . . um . . . I need to slow down a bit . . .'

He turns and then stops. 'Oh, sure. Sorry.'

So at least now we're ambling along next to each other. To an outsider it must look quite companionable. I decide to try out one of my topics.

'Oh! I was reading there's a new production of *Noises Off*,' I say, my breathing still coming out in deep rasps. 'It starts doing the regional rounds next month.'

'Right' he says. I can tell he's like a Jack Russell who thinks he might have seen a mouse; he's dying to be able to speed up and yomp off into the woods. Robert has always thought walking should be exercise, not just pleasure.

'We should go and see it. It's coming to Windsor, that's probably the closest.'

'Mmm-hmm.'

'Shall I look into tickets? We could stay the night down there somewhere . . .'

'Not if it's while we're still filming. You know I like to try and avoid too many commitments at the weekends.'

'Sure,' I say, deflated. *Noises Off* was one of my best weapons. It's a play Robert loves, coming to a town he adores. 'Well, maybe it'll still be going somewhere when you break.'

'Great.'

I try again. 'Oh! I was reading a thing about the Stone Roses! They're going back on tour, can you imagine? That might be a laugh.'

Robert pulls a face that basically says 'what the fuck are you talking about?' 'Sounds tragic to me.'

We walk on in silence for a few minutes and his phone starts to ring in his pocket. I wait for him to look to see who it is, but he just strides on, staring into the distance.

'Aren't you going to answer that?'

'No. It'll just be someone asking if I want to claim for an accident I never had.'

'It might be important. What if it's work?'

The ringing has stopped. He whips it out of his pocket and glances at the screen, holding it in a way that means I can't see it without making it obvious that he's doing so.

'Unknown,' he says. 'Told you. I'll put it on silent.'

*

We pass the muddy track that leads directly to the pergola and head for the main gates to Golders Hill Park. We don't discuss going this way, it's just the way we always used to go, and I feel a little jolt of sadness that our relationship still has muscle memory.

It's busy today because it's a weekend and the sun is out. Families chase each other around on the grass. Some are already having picnics, even though it's not yet twelve. There's a queue snaking out from the café but I want to stick to our old rituals as much as I can.

'Shall I get coffees?'

He looks at the line of people. 'Really?'

'Of course. You wait here, it won't take long.'

He leans against a wall outside as I join the back of the line and edge my way forward slowly. I watch as he takes his mobile out of his pocket and examines it. Dashes off a text and sends it. Let me guess. *'Don't call again! Am with Paula. Walking!!!!'* Something like that anyway. I imagine Saskia all fresh and shiny after yeaterday's Bikram session (and brunch with me after), smiling as she reads it. Flicking back her highlighted hair as unsuspecting Josh lovingly brings her a coffee.

When I look again Robert is posing for a selfie with an eager fan. The rule seems to be that once one person gets up the courage to waylay him and doesn't get punched in the face for their efforts, then everyone else within walking distance decides to have a go too. I know he'll be getting antsy. Cursing the fact that he's a sitting target and he can't get away because I won't know where he is.

I take a moment's comfort from his displeasure and then I do what any good, devoted wife would do. I send him a text telling him to head on up to the pergola and I'll find him there once I'm coffee'd up. Of course, he assumes it's Saskia texting him – I know he'll want to read her message as soon as humanly possible – and I watch as he holds up a hand to silence the fan at the front of the queue, who is almost certainly halfway through her life story by now, and dives a hand into his pocket, looking around guiltily to check I'm not about to surprise him any time soon. When he sees my name he looks over to the café and catches me watching him. I wave encouragingly.

He reads the text and smiles gratefully. I watch as he shakes off the rest of the autograph hunters, I assume by telling them that some emergency has arisen, and strides off.

Once I finally have my prize in my hands, I know exactly where I'll find him. We always used to camp out in the same spot, up some stairs and around a corner where there is just a single bench. Of course, if it was already taken when he got there, then I have no idea where he'll have gone to hide, but when I round the corner there he is. For once, his nose isn't buried in his phone. He's leaning back with his face turned towards the sun and his eyes closed. He's even made an effort to lay out the picnic in the middle of the seat. I stop myself from pointing out that the perishables would have been much happier staying in the cold bag for a bit longer. New Paula would never find fault.

'God, sorry,' I say as I approach. 'I had no idea it would take so long.'

'It's fine. It's nice sitting here, actually. Peaceful.'

I hand him his coffee and plonk myself down at the

other end. Tip my head back, close my eyes. He's right. It's nice.

Later, when I'm soaking in the bath, trying to calm my protesting muscles, I congratulate myself on a successful day. Not that I think sparks were flying between Robert and myself – far from it – but we passed a pleasant afternoon in each other's company. By the end of the walk back to the car I was wheezing like a pug with a smoking habit, but I did it. I didn't sit down on a bench and refuse to move until he went and fetched the car to pick me up. (I did consider it at one point but I managed to keep the thought to myself.)

When we got home I knew from the way he described to Georgia where we walked, how beautiful the woods were looking, the baby rabbits we saw, that he enjoyed himself. Round one to me.

8

How do you break it to someone that their wife is having an affair with your husband? It's hardly dinner-party conversation.

I may be playing with fire but I have decided I need something seismic to happen. Sitting around losing two pounds a week and waiting for either Saskia or Robert to feel remorse and break it off is not enough. I need to take control.

I wonder if either of them has considered what will happen to Josh once they come clean. He can hardly stay on the show. I can't imagine the humiliation. Are they expecting he'll just be a gentleman and step aside, losing his job in the process? I feel indignant on his behalf.

I can hardly just pick up the phone and tell him that his marriage appears to be over.

But I do know where he lives and when there's a good chance he might be home alone.

I just have to get up the courage to do it.

Meanwhile, I've decided to invite Robert's sister, Alice, over for dinner. I don't know how I can get across what a selfless gesture this is on my part. Let's just say that Robert adores his little sis. I, on the other hand, would rather be locked in a giant Bikram studio, doused in Saskia's sweat, and forced to perform yoga moves in forty-degree heat continuously for a week than spend time with her.

I know that sounds awful. She's my husband's flesh and blood, his only sibling. I would hate it if he felt about any of my family the way I feel about Alice. It's not as if I didn't try. When Robert and I first met I was excited to hear that Alice was only a couple of years younger. I imagined us as best friends, allies, confidantes. And then she came up for a visit.

I was intimidated by her right away. She oozed cool. Somehow, on her, faded jeans, ballet flats, a stripy T-shirt and an artfully placed scarf gave off Audrey Hepburn, and not onion-seller as it would have if I'd attempted it. She had long blonde hair that was just the right side of unbrushed, perfectly smudged kohl-rimmed eyes and a cigarette dangling from the corner of her mouth. And she didn't only ooze cool, she oozed confidence. Something I was already severely lacking in. My fantasies of her looking up to me in awe as I introduced her to the big city crashed and burned.

To say that Alice was spoilt would be like saying Hitler had a bit of a vindictive side. It was clear very quickly that whatever Alice wanted, Alice got. I'd organized tickets for us all to go to see something or other at the National – money I couldn't afford, but I wanted to make a good impression. Alice made it obvious right away that she wanted Robert to herself. An aspiring actress (his whole family were actors; I always imagined their house was like the capital city of luvvydom), she was desperate to see the play but when she found out the tickets were for three and not just the two of them she stamped her foot like Violet Elizabeth Bott and actually said the words 'I've come up to see you. I don't want to have to spend all evening with her' in front of me. I waited for Robert to tell her not to be so stupid but actually what he did was take me aside and say that maybe she had a point. So they went on their own. Didn't even try to sell my now spare ticket to pay me back.

To be fair, she was only eighteen that first time I met her. I assumed she would grow up and realize she wasn't the centre of the universe at some point, but it never really happened. She got into RADA the following year and so every time I went to their family home in the holidays I had to listen to the whole clan (Robert included) banging on about how it was the best drama school in the world and only the truly gifted stood a chance of getting in (the implication being that any old untalented nobody could train at the North London School of Speech and Drama). For some reason, Robert never took this personally, in the same way that I did. He was as convinced that his sister was the second coming as his parents clearly were. I should point out here that I adore Robert and Alice's parents. They just have a blind spot, that's all. And that blind spot's name is Alice.

Anyway, you get the picture. She was indulged and mollycoddled to the point of becoming insufferable.

Here's the thing about Alice, though. She's nearly forty. Thirty-eight. She has never had a professional acting job. OK, so neither have I. But she still calls herself an actress while I have long since accepted I work in a bakery. She still goes to workshops and open auditions and talks about herself as if she has a full diary of thespian commitments. Which she does, except none of them has ever paid her. She's one of the ninety-nine per cent for whom it just never worked out, however hard they tried. And she's never had any other kind of job. In so far as I know, she still lives off money her parents give her. AT THIRTY-EIGHT YEARS OLD! She lives in a flat they bought for her in Islington. They pay a monthly allowance into her bank account. And we all pretend it isn't happening. Between auditions she dabbles in various artistic pursuits, none of which ever comes to fruition.

And yet she has the audacity to still treat me as some kind of lower life form because I gave up the life of being an unemployed wannabee and actually got myself a paying job.

I tried for a long time to get along with her. Robert's own blind spot meant he would never hear any criticism and, besides, I didn't want to become that person who slags off their partner's family every chance they get. But I began to find her visits unbearable. It became harder and harder to listen to her pontificate about acting and the near-misses she had had (she was always down to the last two for any part she went for, according to her, and, of course, there would have been no way to prove this otherwise, as she well knew), and the directors who called her saying they were desperate to find the right role for her, when I knew it was all bullshit. Under other circumstances I might have felt sorry for her. But her attitude and the tendency of the whole Westmore family to treat her like some kind of undiscovered star made it impossible.

So I long ago stopped inviting her over. Whenever she surfaces I always suggest to Robert that the two of them meet up without me. (I try and make this sound as if I'm doing it for their sake.) And when I'm forced to see her – at Christmas or weddings and funerals – I bite my tongue as much as I can and just accept I'm going to be excluded from their conversations.

Alice has never married (too much of a self-centred fuck-up). And she's never had children because then, of course, she would have to assume some kind of responsibility and think of someone other than herself.

Georgia calls her 'Baby Jane', but only when Robert is out of earshot.

Anyway, in my effort to do things that will make Robert think what an all-round fantastic wife I am, I have emailed Alice and asked her if she fancies coming over for dinner on Saturday night. Even though I'm sure she's wishing I won't be there, the lure of spending time with her big brother, along with free food and booze, is clearly more than she can resist. I receive a curt '*Yes. Lovely*' a few minutes later.

'Auntie Alice is coming over at the weekend,' I say to Georgia, as she potters round getting ready for school.

'Oh God, really? When?'

'Saturday evening.'

Her face falls. I already know she has plans and I'm not about to mess with a seventeen-year-old's social calendar at this late notice.

'I know you're going out but it would be lovely if you could just be around long enough to say hello.'

She visibly relaxes. 'OK. But you have to defend me if she starts giving me the lecture.'

The lecture is the stuff of legend between Georgia and me. Alice had always assumed that Georgia would want to follow in the family footsteps and go to drama school. The news that she had applied to do medicine, that she

89

had zero interest in treading the boards, was met with something I can only describe as a gasp.

'All the Westmores go to drama school,' Alice said, as if she were quoting from the Bible.

'Not this one,' Georgia replied, laughing it off. Somehow she has always managed to take her aunt's insights with the pinch of salt they deserve.

'But . . .' Alice stuttered. I wondered for a second if she might ask for smelling salts for the shock. I wouldn't have put it past her. Instead, she looked at me accusingly.

'She must take after you.'

'I . . . I actually went to drama school myself, if you remember,' I said hesitantly.

'Oh yes, I always forget,' she said. 'It seems so unlikely somehow.' This, of course, from Alice, was the most damning thing she could think of to say.

'Ha!' Georgia snorted, and I marvelled again at the way my daughter could treat Alice's barbs as a joke. It made her untouchable. 'Honestly, Auntie Alice, I'm just not interested. I'm very happy with what I've chosen.'

Alice launched into a long (and boring) diatribe about the noble art of acting and how important it was to express your creativity and not be beholden to a job that would stifle you. I suppressed the urge to butt in to say that was all very well in Alice's case, she had parents who were still happy to support her, but George was actually going to have to make her own way in the world. I let her ramble on, Robert nodding every now and then at the wise nature of her words.

It's a speech that's been often repeated since and it's known, by Georgia and myself, as 'the lecture'.

'I will, I promise,' I say to her now. 'I just thought it'd be nice for Dad.'

When I break the news to Robert I actually feel bad for a moment that it means so much to him. Have I really got in the way of his relationship with his only sibling so much just because I don't like her? That feeling doesn't last long, though. She's a nightmare and he's . . . well, we all know what he is. Still, I know I've done the right thing. I've gone up a few places on the Perfect Wife scale.

'Will George be here?' he asks, on his way out the door.

'She's going out but she's going to stick around to say hello.'

'Just long enough to get the lecture,' he says, and chuckles. I'm taken aback. I had no idea he had picked up on Georgia's and my in-joke. It makes me warm to him a bit. A tiny bit.

'Exactly.'

On Saturday morning I leave home, ostensibly to head to Selfridges' Food Hall to stock up on delicious goodies for the evening ahead. Actually, I have already bought everything I need locally and it's all sitting in the bakery fridge, from where I can collect it later.

In reality what I'm doing is heading down to Richmond. Unless Saskia has woken up with a leg missing, she'll be heading in the other direction for her class at West1 Hot Yoga! I feel sick. I'm shaking. I'm wondering what on earth I think I'm doing.

I try to calm myself by thinking about the upcoming evening with Alice. This has always been my strategy with her. Try to think up calm and measured replies to any harsh comment she might throw my way to prevent myself from losing my temper. It's quite therapeutic. I try to think what the meanest, most tactless thing she has ever said to me is. In the end, I can't decide between two:

'You'd actually be quite pretty if you lost weight.' This was said a couple of years ago, when we were spending Christmas with Robert's family and I was tucking into a delicious home-made mince pie. It was the 'quite' that got me. Even in her twisted way of thinking she was giving me a compliment, she couldn't bring herself to be truly complimentary.

And 'I'm so pleased that Georgia seems to have inherited more than her fair share of Westmore genes. At least she won't have to worry about what she eats.' As if Alice's skinny frame was natural and not the result of serious self-deprivation, coupled with twenty Marlboros a day. As if Robert didn't spent hours on a treadmill trying to keep the paunch at bay.

When she actually says these things it's all I can do to stop myself from decking her. But when she isn't around I find the things she says endlessly amusing. It passes the time. Once I allow myself to look again, the train is nearly at Richmond. I walk for about ten minutes, to where the houses are bigger and set further back from the street. I remember the low stone wall with the hollyhocks behind it, honeysuckle spilling over the edge. A picture-postcard idyll in a tiny south-west London oasis.

I spot it from along the street and slow down. I have no way of knowing whether Saskia has actually gone to Bikram or not. I check the time – there's still about ten minutes until the class is due to start. I think about sending her a text but I wouldn't know what to say, short of asking her outright if she was there, which she might find a bit odd. I'm here now, though. I don't want to lose my nerve. I prepare a speech in my head explaining how I was in the area so I just stopped by on the off-chance, in case she's home. She'll think I'm a stalker but at least that's better than her knowing what I'm really up to.

Before I can bottle it I force myself towards their front door. There's a car on the drive but it could belong to either of them. Somehow I manage to ring the bell and not turn and run.

The wait is agony. Then I hear someone moving around. A man's cough.

Josh's face registers that he recognizes me but he's not quite sure from where.

'Hi.'

Then it dawns on him. 'Oh, it's Paula, isn't it? It took me a minute to work out who you were. What on earth are you doing here?'

He's so open and friendly – if a bit bemused – that I know he has no idea what I'm about to tell him.

'Um . . . Do you . . . is Saskia in?'

Now he looks really confused. Obviously, Saskia hasn't filled him in on our blossoming friendship.

'No. Was she expecting you?'

'No. Although we have had brunch a couple of times recently, so . . . Look, Josh, I know this is going to sound a bit odd but it's you I came to see. Can I speak to you?'

He looks cornered. I'm sure I'm spoiling his plans for a lovely quiet day off and I feel bad that he has no idea by how much. He thinks this is a mild inconvenience when, actually, I'm about to ruin his life. I almost back out.

'Sure. Er . . . do you want to come in? Is everything OK . . . Robert . . . ?'

Of course, he assumes I'm about to tell him that one of his biggest stars is sick or in rehab or something.

'Yes. It's not about work. Not really.'

I follow him into the front hall and through to the kitchen.

'Coffee?' he says, and I say yes, just because I always find it hard to refuse if someone offers me caffeine. I need to put him out of his misery quickly, though, I know.

'I'm just going to say this,' I start, and he pauses, filter in hand. Those are never good words to hear. He has nice hands. Capable hands, my mum would say. She loves a man with capable hands.

'I think . . . something's happened that . . . I think Robert and Saskia are having an affair.'

He actually laughs. 'What? Don't be ridiculous.'

'I'm sorry, Josh. It's true. I read a text.'

The colour has drained from his face. 'Show me.'

'I can't. I don't have Robert's password so I couldn't take a photo of it or anything, but I know it off by heart.'

He sits on a bar stool, coffee forgotten. I really could do with the caffeine, to be honest, but it feels rude to ask.

'So how come you saw it then?'

I explain the whole story. It sounds fairly implausible even to me, I have to say. His expression doesn't change.

'So, what did it say? Go on.'

I take a deep breath. I need to get this exactly right.

'Jesus. Exclamation mark. That was too close for comfort last night. Exclamation mark. WAY too risky! Hope Paula bought it. Exclamation mark, exclamation mark,

94

exclamation mark. Didn't feel comfortable having to lie to her face. Exclamation mark. Love you. Kiss, kiss, kiss.'

I sit back and look at him, unsure what to say next. He runs a hand over his cropped hair.

'And then I searched through his stuff and found a thing. A heart. Some kind of love token, I don't know. Anyway, there was a card . . .'

I repeat the words from the card, including the two kisses at the end, I don't want to leave anything out.

He's quiet for a second, then: 'Did you have any idea before?'

I shake my head. 'No. Well, I did sometimes wonder if he strayed occasionally . . .'

Because I have no proof to show him it occurs to me he might think this is some kind of elaborate wind-up. Or that I'm a fantasist with a grudge against his beautiful wife.

'How about you . . . ?'

He looks at me as if I'm crazy. 'God, no. Never. He's admitted it then, I take it?'

I pause for effect. I need him to take in what I'm saying. 'I haven't told him I know yet.'

'You only found out today?'

'No. A couple of weeks ago. Here's the thing, Josh . . .' I'm still standing up and I feel a bit lightheaded so I pull myself up on one of the other bar stools.

'I want to ask you not to confront her yet. Saskia. I know that sounds ridiculous. All you must want is to get on the phone to her now and ask her what the hell is going on. I was the same when I found out. But I'm worried that if they know we know, that'll just give them the excuse they need to make it official . . .'

'No,' he says, and it sounds like an animal in pain.

'I'm so sorry I had to be the one to tell you.'

'I'll fucking kill him,' he says, and I have to stop myself from reminding him that it takes two to tango.

'Get in the queue.'

He doesn't laugh like I hoped he would. Of course he doesn't, I've just shattered his world,

'Did you say you'd met up with her?' he says, as if it's only just sunk in.

'Yes, but . . .'

He cuts me off. 'How long's it been going on?'

I'm clueless. 'No idea. Nothing's really changed, that's what's so confusing about the whole thing.'

'Do you think . . . I mean, are we talking months? Years?'

'I don't know. Honestly. I've told you everything I do know.'

'And you're definitely right, aren't you? I mean, about what the text said and the fact it was from Sas?'

'Yes. Unless he has someone else in his phone under Saskia.'

He seizes on this as if I've offered him a lifebelt in a storm. Jumps up and starts pacing. 'That's it. Why would he ever risk being caught like that?'

I'm not lying, I've considered this too. But, on balance, I've decided I'm right. Maybe having some other woman listed under Saskia would protect whatever other woman it was if he got caught, but he would still be in a shitload of trouble. The point was, Robert never thought I would see anything incriminating. He had no reason to make a smokescreen.

Josh's doubt does give me a safety net, though. 'Maybe that's another reason to hold off from confronting her. Imagine if I was wrong and you accused her of something she hadn't done. Do you know her passcode?'

He nods. 'Of course.'

This slightly takes me by surprise. 'Really? I have no idea what Robert's is. He just uses that fingerprint thing.'

'Sas and I have always shared stuff like that. That's what makes this so . . .'

'You've never gone through her phone, though?'

He gives me a look like I'm accusing him of robbing a wheelchair-bound pensioner. 'Of course not!'

'Well, now might be the time to start. If you can look at any other texts between them, that might confirm it. Or disprove it, you never know.'

'Shit,' he says, plonking himself down again on one of the chairs by the gorgeous old wooden table in the centre of the kitchen. Now I feel a bit calmer that he's not going to blow the whole thing right away, I start to notice how stylish their home decor is. Like something out of a magazine, but lived in. Loved. 'I really don't want to become that person.'

I decide I need to wait before filling him in on the rest of my plan. He's not ready.

'Just please promise me you won't say anything till we've spoken again. We need to agree on what we're going to do and when we're going to do it. Otherwise, if you have it out with Saskia she'll go straight to Robert and tell him and it'll all be out of my hands. Please, Josh, the only thing that's keeping me sane is feeling as if I hold the cards at the moment.'

Even though I can tell he's devastated, he's a nice bloke. He feels bad for me. I know every fibre of him must be screaming to head to Marylebone and drag her out of her stupid hot-yoga class and demand the truth, but I don't think he will.

He asks me about the heart token and I describe it as best I can. The note. The 'S'.

'I'm sorry again that I had to be the one who told you. I just thought you deserved to know . . .'

'You did the right thing,' he says, and that's a relief, at least. 'It's as bad for you as it is for me and I know it can't have been easy.'

We exchange numbers before I leave. I put him into contacts as 'Gail'. I'm not stupid.

Robert is in a good mood. Ever since I told him I'd invited Alice over, he's been smiling at me. It's quite unnerving. He and Georgia have cleaned the flat. How he got her to agree to that on a Saturday morning I have no idea. Bribery, I imagine. Some kind of secret agreement to override a veto I had put on something.

I don't really care. Georgia is about as sensible as it's possible for a teenager to be about the importance of her exams. Robert has always been better than me in acknowledging that. I have a tendency to panic. To feel the need to remind her over and over again not to blow it. I can hear my mother doing the same to me and, even though I remember how it used to drive me crazy that she must have so little faith in me, I can't stop myself parroting the same.

Today I keep quiet. Partly because I'm so relieved I

don't have to clean up myself. I concentrate on the job in hand, unpacking the bag I've retrieved from the bakery on the way home (I almost couldn't get away from Myra, she was so desperate for the details), stashing the contents in the fridge. Smile, I tell myself. This is all pointless if you give away that something's up.

'What's Alice been up to lately? Anything I should know?' Robert speaks to his sister on the phone about once a week. I long since stopped asking for news.

He laughs a wry laugh. 'The usual. I think she had a new boyfriend for a while but that seems to be all over now.'

Alice has had a seemingly endless stream of rich, usually older, boyfriends. If you ask me, she's one of those people who thrives on conflict. She loves the highs and lows, the screaming rows and hysterical break-ups, followed by the gut-wrenching apologies and promises to change. I once asked her – when I was still pretending to try to form a bond with her for Robert's sake – why she was always attracted to relationships with added drama, and she raised an arched eyebrow at me, took a long drag on her cigarette and said:

'It makes me feel alive.'

It was all I could do not to laugh. But that's Alice for you. She's always starring in her own movie in her head. Usually French and incomprehensible and in black and white, I imagine.

'She'll probably have someone else on the go already,' Robert says now, an effort at friendly banter.

'Knowing her,' I agree.

'I wish she'd settle for someone,' he says. We've never

really talked about this, not for years anyway, because I would always express a similar sentiment, and Robert would get all defensive and say something twattish like that Alice was a free spirit or a butterfly. So I'm surprised to hear him say this now. Even more surprised, given that settling for me seems to be the last thing on his mind these days.

'I know. Not that she'd thank us for saying so.'

'No,' he says. 'Best not offer any advice on that front.'

Alice arrives in a flurry of silk scarves and Chanel No. 5. She has an electronic cigarette dangling daintily between the fingers of her right hand and a bottle of something fizzy clutched in her left.

She flings herself at her brother, air-kissing him noisily on each cheek, then does the same to Georgia and, slightly less enthusiastically, me. I hear her actually say the words 'Mwah! Mwah!' as she hovers near my ear. She's looking good in a Breton top and faded, rolled-up jeans. Ballet flats on her feet. Basically, the identical clothes she was wearing when I first met her nearly twenty years ago. Her long blonde hair is side parted and carefully tousled. Her green eyes are kohl-rimmed. She's still a beauty, there's no doubt about it.

'You've lost weight.' She holds me at arms' length, trapping me there while Robert and Georgia turn to look. I actually blush guiltily. Trust body-obsessed Alice — stick-thin even to this day — to notice.

'Oh, I don't think so. Maybe a little. We went for a walk . . .' I add, as if so out of shape was I that one walk on the Heath could make a visible difference. Although that's probably not too far off the truth.

She grabs at my waist and I squirm. As usual, I'm in an oversized top and leggings. She hangs on to – what looks to me – quite a handful, while I stand there feeling like livestock being appraised at market.

'You have. Definitely.'

'Actually, Mum, you do look like you've lost a bit.' Georgia gives me a big smile. I know how much my getting fit would mean to her.

I'm actually quite flattered that Alice noticed, although then I remember that she has always been obsessed with how big I've become. She's a size fascist. To her, a woman letting herself pile on the pounds is on a par with her neglecting her children. Whenever she's having some kind of grubby liaison with a married man she'll always say in a knowing way that the wife has 'let herself go', thus implying it was the wife's own fault that her husband ran off with a skinny narcissist who spends all her waking hours worrying about how she looks. And always with half a glance to me.

Thankfully, Robert has lost interest in the state of my body already. 'What can I get you, Alice? Is that fizz cold?'

She hands over the champagne. 'Not really, but it'll do.'

'We have cold,' I butt in, a big smile plastered on my face. Champagne was on my list of Alice favourites and my supplies bag contained a bottle.

'We do?' Robert looks at me quizzically. We never do.

'I got some in,' I say. 'Special occasion.'

He rewards me with a smile, pleased that I'm indulging his sister's expensive tastes. 'Excellent. And I'll put this in for later, shall I?'

'You're looking gorgeous, as always, Alice,' I say, eyes wide, no hint of sarcasm.

She attempts modesty: 'Oh no, I just threw on any old thing.' I nearly laugh. I'm a much better actress than she is.

We settle down at the kitchen table, doors to the tiny balcony open, as it's a beautiful evening. Alice begins her one-woman monologue 'Tales of Me' – which basically means she talks about herself and her fabulous life non-stop for the next half-hour. There are stories of man friends who have whisked her off to the south of France and unrequited suitors who are half dead with desire for her.

As she holds court I find myself tuning out and just watching her. Despite my suspicions of Botox (paid for by God knows who), her skin is starting to look a little papery. Fine lines are creeping vine-like around her eyes. It suddenly strikes me as rather tragic. To be someone for whom looks have always been the most important thing. To define yourself as a ravishing beauty all your life, only to watch it begin to fade before anything else has started to have any meaning. At least I stopped relying on what I looked like years ago. I can't imagine how tiring it must be.

The thing that really knocked me sideways about Alice when I first met her wasn't her complete lack of interest in me, it was her confidence. She always knew that everyone in the room had noticed her. I remember her once bemoaning to me the fact that girls didn't like her because they were intimidated by her beauty. She's always been a master of the humble-brag. Poor me, poor me – by the way, have you noticed I'm gorgeous? She had absolute faith in the fact that if people didn't want to be her friend they were just jealous.

I, on the other hand, thought that her indifference to

me must mean that I was dull. Provincial and unworldly up against her glittering urban sophistication. It took me years to work out she was just scared I would come to be more important in Robert's life than she was.

I get up and potter about, getting the food ready. The olives are already on the table and, as she speaks, Alice nibbles on one with her tiny, perfect teeth. The starter is a goat's cheese salad, already made, apart from lightly grilling the cheese. Cheese that I know Alice will take one bite of, declare delicious and then leave. At the moment, I'd love to be able to do the same, but it looks so yummy that I'm giving myself a night off my diet. This evening is enough of a trauma as it is.

'So,' I say, in an effort to be friendly, 'what's happening with you? Didn't Robert tell me you were doing some kind of new show or something?'

He did, several weeks ago, before the new me was born. I know that because when he came off the phone and told me Alice had decided to write and perform a piece about her own fascinating life I said something like 'Jesus Christ, who's going to go and see that?'

Her face lights up, another opportunity to intone about herself.

'Yes! I'm only at the early stages, you know. I just thought I have so many extraordinary stories to tell that I should get them all down on paper. I'm looking for a director at the moment.'

'Amazing,' I say. It isn't. I've heard a version of this many times, plays Alice is on the verge of producing and starring in. None of them ever gets off the ground. 'Where are you thinking of putting it on?'

She twirls her champagne around in her glass. 'Oh, well, ideally somewhere like the Donmar . . .'

Georgia snorts and then recovers herself. The Donmar Warehouse has a capacity of about two hundred and fifty. There aren't two hundred and fifty people in the world who would want to go and see Alice wank on about herself if her play ran from now for the rest of her life.

'Right. Wow! Doesn't . . . I mean, that must get booked up a long way in advance . . .'

'Well, of course,' she says. 'And a part of me wonders if it wouldn't be better in a more intimate setting anyway. More, you know, conversational. Like the King's Head. Or the Etcetera.'

The venues she's naming are getting smaller and smaller, but she's still dreaming. One night in a broom-cupboard-sized theatre, capacity one, would be about right. She could take whatever man she was seeing at the time. Oh, and Robert would probably want to go. She could do an extended run of two performances. Of course I say none of this.

I can see that Robert is looking at me, no doubt waiting for me to scoff, so I keep my expression open and friendly.

'You'll have to tell the story about the bloke who cast you in that film that didn't exist. That was a great one.' This, I know, is one of Alice's favourite stories about herself. I don't believe a word of it. It has to do with a very attractive, successful man (all the men who pursue Alice are attractive and successful, apparently) setting up a fake audition just to meet her. I remember I pissed her off the first time she told me because my reaction was that he was obviously some kind of dangerous sex pest and she should report him to the police. Now I listen to her tell the whole thing again and laugh and ooh in all the right places.

I pull out the grill pan and slide the cheese on to the plates. Georgia takes this as her cue to escape. There's a flurry of hugs and perfume.

'I haven't even had the chance to talk to you properly,' Alice says sulkily.

'I'll see you again soon. I'm late,' Georgia lies, and she flees before the lecture can even begin.

Sadly, that means I get to hear it myself.

'Such a shame,' Alice starts as soon as the front door closes. 'But I suppose we have to let her make her own mistakes.'

Usually, this is where I would pounce. I can't abide the way she thinks she knows best about everyone. Worse that she thinks everyone wants to end up like her. Today I bite my tongue.

'Exactly. You can't force anyone to do anything they don't want to do. However much you may want to.'

'Sadly true.' She sips on her champagne. Then turns her attention to her brother. 'So, Robbie . . .'

She's the only person who ever calls him Robbie. He is so not a Robbie. I called him Rob once, early on in our relationship, and he made it very clear that he was a Robert.

'. . . how's the great Farmer Giles?'

They chat away happily and I leave them to it, concentrating on eating my way around the cheese, just like Alice. Great, she can be my new role model.

Robert smiles expansively. 'Isn't this nice? We should do it more often.'

*

By the time she leaves in a taxi I'm exhausted with the sheer effort of pretending like I care all evening but Robert is in such a good mood that it must have been worth it. He reaches for the red wine and pours us both a glass.

'I'm going to get ready for bed,' I say, yawning. 'I'll be back to drink this. Leave the clearing up till tomorrow.'

'I'll just load the dishwasher.'

I leave him to it. Head for the bedroom to change. Halfway through, I do something I never do and go and stand in front of the full-length mirror in just my underwear. I know that Alice is right. My clothes are feeling looser and I'm sure I must have lost a few pounds. If I was expecting to be pleasantly surprised, I'm in for a letdown. Rolls of fat still spill out in every direction. My arms flap when I move them and my legs knock in at the knees from the sheer effort of carting the rest of me around every day. Even though I'm starting to feel stronger, there's no evidence of anything resembling muscle anywhere.

Smaller I may be, but I can't see it. Of course, I have avoided seeing my naked reflection for so long that I never witnessed myself at my biggest. But it was bigger than this, obviously. Bigger than huge.

I shove myself miserably into my pyjamas (a different oversized T-shirt and leggings, funnily enough) and head back to the kitchen. Robert is back at the table, glass in hand.

'I think I'm going to go to bed, actually. I'm knackered.'

'Oh,' he says, and he looks disappointed. He's never been one to sit up drinking alone. I know I can't afford to lose the brownie points I've accumulated this evening so I force myself to give in.

'OK, well, I'll just drink that one, seeing as you've poured it.'

I sit down opposite him.

'Thanks for this evening,' he says. 'I know she can be difficult sometimes but it means a lot to me to have her round.'

Another gold star slots into place. I'm fishing around for some small talk – there's only so far I can go with the 'wasn't it lovely to have Alice round?' conversation. I'm terrified he's going to want to start inviting her every weekend. Luckily, I'm saved by Georgia barging in, clearly a couple of vodkas down.

'Is it safe?' she hisses in a conspiratorial whisper.

'Are you drunk, madam?' Robert laughs.

'Only a little bit. Is there any of that champagne left?'

'No!' Robert and I say in unison.

'Spoilsports.'

'Now I really am going to bed.' I down the last of my red wine. 'You too, I'd suggest.'

She rolls her eyes at me but ambles off in the direction of her room, waving a hand as she goes.

'Do you think we're terrible parents because our seventeen-year-old has come home tipsy?'

'What, and we never did at that age?' he says with a smile.

God, I think, we were only a couple of years older than Georgia when we met. How depressing. 'That was different.'

He raises an eyebrow. 'In what way?'

'I have no idea.'

Things are going so well that I start to wonder if he'll

want to have sex with me. Robert always initiates it. I gave up on that one years ago because I started to get scared he might take one look at my roly-poly tummy and reject me. And it doesn't happen very often. Rarely, in fact. Especially lately, for – it now occurs to me – obvious reasons. But when it does it's usually on a night like this one. A few drinks, a bit of conversation about the old days, both of us making an effort. Oh God, I hope not. Not when I know it won't be me he really wants to be with.

I bend down and kiss the top of his head. 'Night.'

By the time he gets into bed I'm doing a good impression of someone who's fast asleep.

9

When my phone dings to tell me I have a message and I see the name Gail I'm confused for a moment. I have no idea who it is. Then it hits me and I look around guiltily as if I'm about to get caught out.

It's short and to the point.

'Can you talk?'

Robert is sleeping off the champagne and red wine. I send a message back, *'Try me in 5'*, pull on Georgia's trainers and head down to the street, still in my PJs but with a hoody over the top. Phone clutched in my hand, willing it to ring. I daren't try him because I don't know if he's somewhere where it would be safe to answer. It strikes me that this must be what having an affair is like. The simultaneous jolts of fear and excitement.

I'm half crazed with anticipation, just turning the corner on to the main road, when my ringtone – that generic tune that I've never got around to changing that means whenever half the population's phones ring I reach for my bag – kicks in. I check the name and answer before it has the chance to play through again.

'Hi.'

'Paula. It's Josh,' he says, as if I might not have worked that one out by now.

'Yes. Hi. Where are you?'

'Out on a run. You?'

'Walking. So?'

I hear an intake of breath. 'I think you might be right.'

'Shit. Tell me.'

'I only got the chance to look late last night when she went to have a bath. There's only one other message between them . . .'

'Really?' I'm finding it hard to imagine how one text can be so devastating as to constitute irrefutable proof. 'And . . . ?'

'It's a reply to the one you saw. It just says, *All fine. Don't text, she might see.*'

I wait to hear if there's more, but that's it. A part of me wants to scoff and tell Josh this proves nothing, but I know that, actually, it does.

'Shit.'

'This is . . . I don't know if I can handle it.' Josh's voice cracks. I feel desperately sorry for him. Unlike me, he still believed his marriage was perfect, until yesterday.

Here goes. 'Here's what I think. I want Robert to get what's coming to him. I know you probably don't feel the same. You probably want to try and save your marriage. But, whichever way you look at it, we need to try and break them up. Trying to force them to separate will make them resent us and probably push them together.'

I cross the road to the park and keep walking. The air is heavy with the scent of lavender. Dogs, delirious with freedom after a night being cooped up, run around, frenzied. I explain my whole plan, such as it is, to him. He listens without interrupting.

'I'm not suggesting you should do the same thing or that you would be out for revenge too, I just want to ask you to help me break them up. And not to let them know we know until they do.'

That's it, my pitch. Who could blame him if he refused to have anything to do with it?

'I don't know, Paula. I don't know if I can act normally around her. Around either of them. I have to work with them, for Christ's sake.'

'I'm not saying it's going to be easy. But at least that way when they do break it off you'll know it's because they wanted to, not just because you told her she had to.'

The silence goes on so long I wonder if we've been cut off. I take my phone from my ear and look at it. Three bars.

'Josh?'

'I'm here,' he says. 'I'm thinking.'

'After it's over you'll hold all the cards. You can decide to confront her or not.'

'I know, I know,' he says impatiently. 'Sorry, I didn't mean to snap at you. It's a lot, you know.'

'You can opt out any time. Just make sure you tell me.'

There's another pause, and then he says, 'OK. I'll try, that's all I can say.'

'Thank you.'

'So what's your plan for splitting them up?'

'Not much beyond trying to make them feel guilty, really.'

We agree to meet up in a couple of days. It's a start.

I'm too full of nervous energy to go straight home. I pound up to the top of the hill, wanting the discomfort of physical exertion to overwhelm any other feelings I might have. I think about Saskia waking up, full of the joys of Sunday, and whether she'll notice that her husband's view of her has changed forever. He'll smile at her indulgently but it won't quite reach his eyes. It gives me a little thrill to think about it. By the time I reach the top I'm pouring with sweat and puffing like a steam train. I turn around to head back down and I'm seized by the urge to run. So I do. With all the grace of Lee Evans stumbling around the stage, I career down to the bottom, arms flailing. It's exhilarating. And it's downhill all the way, obviously, which helps.

The next time I see Josh is two days later. He's called and asked if I want to meet for a coffee. I'm surprised, to say the least, but I'm not about to pass up the chance to find out what's going on. We meet in a café in Holland Park. All chi-chi green tea and macha powder.

'Aren't you supposed to be at work?' I ask as I sit down. He's already there, drinking something that looks suspiciously like a flat white but might be a latte. I defy anyone to tell the difference. It's the middle of the filming day and, I assume, producers are a necessity.

'They won't miss me for a few hours.' He shrugs. 'Robert and Sas are doing a run of scenes in their kitchen, so at least I know they're occupied.'

'How's it been?'

His eyes are red-rimmed, as if he's not been sleeping, with added bouts of crying. I panic that he's given himself away.

'Bad,' he says. 'Don't worry, she still doesn't know I know,' he adds, as if he can read my mind.

'No disrespect, but she must be blind if she can't see something's wrong. You look like shit.'

'Thanks.' He laughs. 'I've told her I've got terrible hayfever. There's lots of sniffing and rubbing my eyes going on.'

'Have you noticed anything different about her . . . now you know?'

He hesitates for a moment while the waitress hovers and I order myself a peppermint tea. I was so nervous about meeting up with him that I downed three coffees in quick succession this morning and then had to go for a walk to calm myself down.

'No, but then I've always known she was a good actress.'

I manage to hold my scoff.

'She even talked about Robert. Complained that he kept stepping on her lines in some scene or other.'

'Classic. Robert's always moaning about her too. That's obviously their smokescreen.'

He takes a sip of his giant coffee. 'I think they genuinely used not to get on. Unless you think this has been going on since series one?'

It doesn't bear thinking about. That Robert might have been deceiving me for five years. I shake my head. 'No. It's like the plot of a bad play. Two people loathe each other so much there's obviously some kind of underlying sexual tension.'

Josh laughs, and his face is transformed, the hard edges gone 'We actually did a story like that last year, do you remember? I thought it was a stinking cliché at the time. I wanted to cut it but I'd only just arrived and I didn't want all the writers to walk out.'

'Oh yes! Saskia's character and the vet! You see, truth mirrors fiction.'

His expression changes again. 'Do you think the writers knew about Sas and Robert and they thought it'd be funny to base a story on them?'

I shrug. 'Stranger things have happened. You can't start worrying about whether or not people know. Not now.'

He stirs his spoon around in his half-drunk coffee. Looks up at me with a slight smile on his face. 'It's the story conference next week.'

Farmer Giles is like a cross between a soap and a regular drama in that it never really stops filming. They make twenty-three episodes a year with a two-week break at Christmas and a month off in the summer. People can't get enough of its cosy rural shenanigans. It's ridiculously old-fashioned and melodramatic and it goes through storylines like Taylor Swift goes through boyfriends.

Every year, just before the summer break, the producers and writers have a big story conference where everyone pitches ideas and they try to make sure they have enough material for the coming series. This is also the point where the decision is made to write characters out or introduce new blood. I think for a moment that he might be hinting he could write Robert out. Much as I want revenge, I don't think my daughter's father losing his job would be a good idea.

Josh must be able to read my expression because he says, 'I don't mean ... we could have some fun with storylines, though . . .'

Once the cast members are secure that their contracts

have been renewed for another series, their attentions turn to their story arcs. Because, post story conference, straight characters have been known to become gay, or vice versa, lovers have turned out to be siblings. One actor who had been playing a sweet and gentle husband and father for three years discovered overnight that he had apparently been a serial killer all that time. Let's just say there's not much point in a cast member trying to give their character depth because they don't really know them at all. No one does.

It's always amazing how personally some of them take it. Robert used to laugh at the annual protestations of 'my character would never do that' as being precious. But that's probably because Hargreaves has remained fairly consistent since the beginning.

'Ha! Oh my God, can we give them something awful?' I suddenly feel the most positive I have in weeks. Even though this is a pointless exercise in terms of breaking Robert and Saskia up, it will make me happy. And I'll get the chance to play sympathetic wife. 'What would be Saskia's worst nightmare?'

He doesn't even have to hesitate. 'Losing her looks.'

'So you could have her disfigured somehow. An accident.'

'No, that would be too dramatic. She'd love it, because she'd think she'd end up winning a BAFTA. Better if we just have it as an ongoing theme that she's let herself go.'

'Put on weight! You could make her really fat.'

Even though everyone is sworn to secrecy after the story conference until the scripts emerge weeks later, there are always leaks. Robert always comes home with some titbit he's picked up, face glowing with schadenfreude. Because Josh and Saskia are married, though, he can obviously fill her in with whatever he feels like. And anyway, in this case, the actress would need to be let into the secret, whoever she was, so she can start stocking up on pies.

Josh laughs. 'She'd have to spend the whole summer break putting on the pounds. Oh God, that might be genius.'

'Do it, please.'

'She'll kill me.'

'It'll be worth it. It'll help too. Robert is such a looks fascist.'

'I'd have to convince the writers too, obviously. Somehow, I don't think that'll be too hard. I'm not sure she's their favourite person.'

I've heard stories of Saskia storming on to the set announcing that the latest script is shit and whoever has written it couldn't get a job writing manuals on how to use a fridge-freezer. Mind you, I've only heard this from Robert, so who knows how much truth there is in it?

'And I'll need to come up with a story to go with it. You can't just say "someone gets fat". There needs to be a reason.'

'Details,' I say. 'You can do it. What else?'

'OK,' he says, and I can see he's warming to the theme. 'Something for Robert.'

'He couldn't stand to be a hate figure. He loves the adulation he gets. All those old ladies thinking he's a sweetheart.'

Josh smiles. 'What would be the worst thing we could make him? I know! A paedophile!'

'Jesus. That might be going too far. I don't think Georgia . . .'

'You're right. Wrong show anyway. We'd lose half our viewers. What else? Violent drunk? Wife beater?'

'Haven't you already done both of those with other characters?'

'God knows. Probably. Fraudster? I've got it. You say the old ladies love him? Well, let's make Hargreaves a con-man, conning the local elderly out of their savings.'

'Perfect. Turns out he's been ripping them off for their precious family heirlooms for years. He needs to be really mean.'

'Vile,' he agrees. 'And I'll try and back-seed it into the first couple of episodes.'

The first two or three episodes of the next season are already written to some extent or other because of the fast turnaround, he tells me. Post story conference there is always a scrabble to rewrite sections to accommodate the new story arcs. This way Robert will get to hear the news soon. There's no point planting these landmines and then not detonating them till after it's all over.

We get on to other things we might do to make their working lives a misery. Hargreaves will have a fling with Marilyn, the younger (and soon to be prettier, once Saskia's Melody has 'let herself go') local barmaid. Pneumatic and raven-haired. Obviously, Robert will love this, the idea that Hargreaves is still perceived as virile enough to appeal to a woman half his age, but it'll be a huge blow to Saskia's pride. She likes to think of herself as the show's siren. In turn, we decide, she'll make a pass at a handsome stablehand and he'll laugh in her face.

Robert's Hargreaves will go into business with the brash alpha male Smyth. Not a problem in itself, except that Robert loathes Jez, the actor playing Smyth, with a passion. (Mind you, he 'loathed' Saskia, in so far as I was concerned, until a couple of weeks ago so, who knows, maybe him and Jez are an item too.) He can't stand to be in the same room as him and, from what Josh tells me, is actually scared of him because Jez is a bit of a violent psycho. Robert is not good at being scared. It's definitely not his happy place.

'I'll need to work on these ideas to make sure I can get the writers to agree. We all vote on each story so I need to get them on side,' he says again, and I find myself hoping he's not an ineffectual wet lettuce who they'll all gang up on and walk all over if they don't like his ideas. He doesn't seem as if he would be, but you never know. I remember Robert moaning about him being unimpressive but then Robert had his own agenda.

'Of course,' I say, 'even if only one of them gets through, it's something.'

I look at my phone. We've been here an hour and it's flown by. Who knew revenge could be such fun? I think Josh is feeling the same. I can't imagine living with Saskia is a barrel of laughs. It's hard to picture the two of them cracking up over something stupid.

'I should probably get back,' he says now, waving at the waitress for the bill. He brushes away my offer of a fiver.

'You're OK, though?' I say, feeling a bit guilty.

His face falls and I wish I hadn't asked. Maybe the past hour making each other laugh and poking fun at the people who are betraying us was worth far more than talking about how upset we are. 'It's shit, what can I say. I'll be glad when we break for the summer.'

'It can't be easy having to watch them together.'

'Why do you think I asked you to meet me now? It was either that or watch them having a make-up snog in their kitchen fifteen times in a row.'

My stomach turns over. I've always felt OK with Robert having to do love scenes with his on-screen partner. I mean, it's not as if he's in *Fifty Shades of Grey*. In *Farmer Giles*, even sitting in bed next to someone of the opposite sex fully clothed and with the covers pulled up to your chin is seen as a bit risqué. But kissing, hugging, all that stuff, I didn't care. Why would I? Acting is a job like any other. But the idea of them doing it now, thinking they're getting one over on everybody by hiding in plain sight, makes me feel sick.

'No more kissing scenes,' I say, before I can stop myself.

'Agreed.'

10

'I'm only going for a few weeks!'

Georgia looks mortified. She's on her way to Ibiza with a bunch of friends, exams over. We are both taking her to Luton to wave her off. She's been away with her mates several times before so it's no big deal, but this time it feels symbolic. She's left school. She's on her way out of the door for good. I get the impression Robert is thinking a version of the same thing because he sniffs back a tear as we wait to wave her through Departures.

'Three weeks,' I say. 'I've never not seen you for three weeks in a row since the day you were born.'

She looks around, notices that Eliza's mum and dad are looking a bit sniffly too and relaxes just enough to accept our hugs. Robert and I end up circling her with our arms at the same time, which makes it feel as if we're embracing each other with George squashed in the middle. I fight the urge to pull away and push him off at the same time.

After she's left, Robert and I stand there, waiting, as if unsure what to do next. And then a pair of old ladies, smartly dressed for their trip in that way that old people dress up for travelling, like they do for dinner, spot him and start beetling towards us, no doubt to ask for a picture.

'Shall we go?' I say, not letting on that I've seen them.

'Sure,' he says, but they're too quick for me, calling out his name in loud voices that cause every other person in the place to turn around to look too. All of a sudden it's like being in a zombie film, although the protagonist isn't in danger of being eaten, rather of being photographed to death.

'Shit,' I mutter under my breath before I can stop myself. I know that's half the morning gone right there.

'I'd better just . . . sorry . . .' He turns to the crowd with a beaming smile, ever the professional.

As I watch him get engulfed, elbowed out of the way by more than one old dear, I check my phone for messages. I've been doing this all week, like it was my full-time job, waiting to hear from Josh. So far only one short missive. In return to my question *'How's it going?'* on Thursday I received a not very enlightening *'All good'* back. The story conference, I know, was on Wednesday and Thursday. I wonder if he bottled out of pitching any of our ideas and whether that's a sign that he might bottle out in a bigger way altogether.

I'm about to dash off another text when one appears as if by magic.

'Are you free to chat?'

Of course, Saskia will be at Bikram, toning up her lovely body. I'm tempted to risk it. Robert is still surrounded by the undead and by the look of it will be for some time. I decide it's worth the chance. If anyone will understand if I have to end the call suddenly, it's Josh.

'If I hang up, don't call me back,' I say before he even has a chance to say hello.

'Of course,' he says, as if that's the most natural thing in the world. 'I'll be quick anyway. I just wanted to tell you it couldn't have gone better. All our ideas went through.'

'Ha! That's amazing. Well done.'

'The script editors are just plotting them through, but it's safe to say Saskia will be having to eat for three or four from now on.'

'Have you told her yet?'

'No. She's going to kill me. Obviously, I'm never going to admit it was my idea. I'll tell her I argued against it but I was outnumbered. She'll just think I'm ineffectual.'

I glance over at the throng around Robert, see him look my way as if to say, 'Can you come and save me?', turn back to the phone.

'Well done, you.'

'I thought you'd want to know. And we're going to plant the first seed of Robert's villainous conman career into ep one. That means I'm justified in telling him about it during the break.'

I look at my husband, surrounded by his adoring demographic, not one of them under seventy.

'Perfect.' I suddenly realize that Robert is on his way towards me, beaming apologetically at his fans and gesturing at me as if to say I need him to get moving for some reason. The second he's out of the clutches of the last of them, his expression changes to one of accusatory irritation.

'Got to go,' I say, and end the call with Josh without waiting for him to say goodbye.

'Why the hell didn't you rescue me?' Robert says, furious. That's always my role, by the way. I have to play bad cop and drag him away while he protests that he'd much rather stay and talk to the 'great unwashed', as he refers to them in private.

'Sorry. Myra called.'

He rolls his eyes. 'I thought I was never going to get away.'

'It's so sweet how much they adore you, though, isn't it? At least you're lucky you're playing such a sympathetic character.' I try not to smirk as I say this.

Because Robert professes to dislike Saskia so much, I am allowed to slag her off whenever I get the chance without it coming across like I'm a bitch. It's a hobby. Robert always likes to watch the show. He claims it helps him develop his character but I know he really just enjoys seeing his own face and marvelling at the way he acts everyone else off the screen. (He actually said this to me once. He likes to draw attention to the nuances of his performance and make sure I'm aware of how special it is.) We missed it on Thursday night because we took Georgia out for a meal to celebrate the end of her exams, so on Saturday evening we settle down to watch, glasses of wine in hand.

'God, what's happened to Saskia?' I say when there's a close-up at one point. 'Her face looks really weird. Do you think she's had a dodgy facelift?'

To set the record straight, Saskia looks ten times better than most of us on a good day, but I know how to push my husband's buttons.

Of course, he has to agree with me. 'Ha! Probably.'

'She probably feels threatened by Marilyn,' I say, mentioning the character who, unbeknown to Robert, his own character will soon be having an affair with. 'It must be hard to have based a career on what you look like and

123

then watch it start to fade. I mean, it's not as if her acting skills are going to get her far.'

It's true that Saskia is not a great actress. She gets away with it – just – but only because she's always cast so close to type.

I'll be honest, I don't really feel comfortable making comments like these. I'm not a natural bitch and women get a hard enough time as it is about the way they look without me joining in. But when he only grunts his assent I feel cheated. I wanted to force him into saying something mean about her too.

'That girl playing Marilyn's gorgeous, isn't she?' Maybe I can help move his focus on to the other woman. 'And she's good too. Believable.'

'She went to RADA,' he says, as if that explains everything.

'That was a good episode for you,' I say as the credits roll. I'll be honest, *Farmer Giles* bores me to tears. It's so twee but then with these sensationalist storylines every now and again to keep the viewers hooked. Everything is a little bit too heightened, from the rivalries to the hairdos.

He yawns and stretches. 'That's one thing I'll say about Josh. He's made the writers buck their ideas up a bit. The scripts are definitely better.'

'Why don't you like him? It seems like he's doing an OK job.'

'He's a nice enough bloke. Well, you've met him. I'm just not sure he's a strong enough pair of hands, that's all.'

'Did you tell me he was married to Saskia? Or have I imagined that?'

Robert grimaces. 'He is.'

'Is that why he got the job?'

'God knows. Actually, that's not fair. I think he's got the experience. On paper, at least.'

'Has Saskia got any better since he arrived?'

'Not so you'd notice.'

To give Robert his due, he doesn't even flinch when I mention her. There's no moment when he looks as if he's trying to work out what the right thing to say is or to stop himself from giving himself away.

'It can't be much fun being married to someone and then having to try and discipline them at work.'

'It can't be much fun being married to her at all.' He laughs heartily at his own comment and I force myself to join in.

11

It's my first session with the personal trainer Myra has found for me. I tried to protest, but she wasn't having it. Despite her feeling as if I'm letting the side down by attempting to get fit, she's determined to help me achieve my aim of getting back at Robert. I've told him I am working an extra hour in the afternoon. And even though I'm dreading it, I'm glad to have an excuse not to go home. The idea of him hanging around the house for the next four weeks is filling me with dread.

Myra waves me off like it's my first day at school.

'Don't come back all super-skinny, will you?'

'Very funny. I'll be lucky if I come back at all.'

I'm expecting the gym to be full of buff young people, oiling their muscles and twirling giant weights around their heads like batons. As it happens, the place is quiet. While I wait nervously in reception for the girl behind the desk to finish her phone call, I look around. One woman – older than me, I would guess, but in fantastic shape – is being shown how to do something that looks tortuous in one corner of the room, but she's laughing while she's doing it so that's a good sign. Maybe she's getting the endorphins they always talk about, or maybe she's just a masochist. Other than her and her trainer, the gym is empty.

There's a row of machines that even I recognize – two cross-trainers, two bikes, three treadmills – and then a bunch of black metal objects with the appearance of torture-chamber implements. I almost turn and walk straight out again.

Just as I'm thinking seriously about it, the receptionist hangs up and turns to me with a smile.

'Paula?'

I nod nervously. 'That's me.'

'Don't look so scared. You'll be fine. I'll tell Chas you're here.'

When I booked the appointment, Myra standing over me while I made the call to make sure I didn't back out, I was disappointed that only male trainers were available in the slot that I wanted. For some reason, having a woman would feel far less humiliating. I've been having nightmares ever since about some young lad laughing with his colleagues about the fat bird he's having to try and knock into shape.

Chas, when he appears, turns out to be older than I'd expected – I would put him in his mid-thirties – and a thoroughly nice bloke. Just as well, because the first thing he does is tell me he has to weigh me and test my body fat. I tell him it's fine, I don't need to know how much I weigh, and he just laughs and says there's no getting out of it so we may as well just get it over with.

In a small side room he chats to me as he grabs bits of the flab round my waist and on the back of my arms with what looks like a pair of tongs.

'So what's your usual fitness routine?'

I actually laugh. 'Walking to the fridge?'

I hate it when I do this. When I make jokes about my own size. My way of saying, 'Yes, I know I'm fat too.'

He's kind enough to smile. 'Seriously, though . . .'

'Um. Nothing really. Walking, I suppose. I ran down a hill the other day.'

'How often do you walk? And how far?' Now he's doing some kind of calculation on paper, based on whatever the tongs told him.

'Every day, pretty much. Only for about fifteen, twenty minutes.'

I wait for him to scoff. Instead, his expression doesn't change from one of friendly positivity. 'Well, that's something. You can't underestimate the value of walking.'

'It's only been for the last few weeks . . .'

'OK, slip your shoes and socks off and step on the scales. Any idea how much you weigh?'

I shake my head, no. I'm lying. A few weeks ago, the day I started my new regime, I forced myself on to confront the truth. Fifteen stone four ounces.

He peers down at the electronic scales. '93.89 kilograms.'

I try to do the calculation in my head. Fail. 'I don't know what that is.'

'That's . . . that's fourteen stone eleven.' He writes it down on my notes.

I can't believe it.

'Wow. I've lost half a stone. Just in a few weeks.'

Chas smiles. 'I thought you said you didn't know what you weighed.'

'I was telling the truth. Because I thought I weighed fifteen stone four and it turns out I'm only fourteen eleven.'

'That's walking for you.' At this rate, Chas is going to talk himself out of a job and I'm just going to spend my days hoofing it around north London. 'And is that your main goal? Weight loss?'

'Yes. And tightening it all up, you know. I don't want it all to be flapping about.'

'The weights will do that. How's your diet?'

I talk him through the improvements I've made and he seems to be impressed. Chas himself is like a poster boy for healthy eating. Even his hair, which is thick and slightly bouffant, screams that his diet is perfectly balanced. His teeth are the white of a man who has never even tried red wine. He reminds me of David Hasselhof but without the lying on the floor demanding a burger bit. He looks up from his calculations.

'So your fat percentage is forty-four. We'll measure it regularly to see if it's going down.'

Forty-four per cent. I am forty-four per cent fat. Forty-four per cent of me looks like the gloop you find in the U-bend of a blocked-up sink.

'Jesus.'

'We'll get it down, no worries.'

I wish I had Chas's faith in me. A large part of me is hoping he'll say that's it for today and the hard work will start next time but, of course, that's not how it works. I have never felt so out of my comfort zone. We don't even use weights ('I'll ease you in gently') but after a slow but steep walk on the running machine, a sequence of squats and lunges and stepping up on to a low box, and a few arm movements with stretchy bands, I'm sweating like I'm in a sauna and wheezing like a bulldog.

'I can't . . .' I say about a thousand times and, to give him credit, he lets me have a breather every now and then. I get the impression this is the last time that'll happen.

The last five minutes is bliss as he stretches out my

aching muscles while I lie on my back on the floor, feeling like I've been hit by a truck.

'When are you in again?' he says as I peel myself up off the mat, revealing a sweaty impression of myself. I imagine alien scientists examining it in aeons to come, like the Turin Shroud. Concluding that humans were large, shapeless mammals made up of forty-four per cent fat.

I want to say 'never', but I bought a block of twenty sessions to force myself to attend (and because of the hefty discount). 'Thursday,' I pant.

He beams at me with his big, straight teeth. 'Great. And well done. You've started, and you've made a commitment, that's the main thing.'

I want to punch him but I don't have the strength.

Knowing that Robert will probably be home when I get there, I have a quick shower and change back into my work clothes. Walking is out of the question. Perspiration is still dripping from every bit of me when I get on the bus.

'She went ballistic.' Josh is smiling at me across the table. We're back in the same café, coffees on the table. Officially, I'm putting in a few extra hours at Myra's, and Josh is in his office, prepping for the next run of filming after the break.

'OK, tell me everything. What did you say?'

'I tried to make it sound positive. Like she had this great story coming up . . .'

'What is the story, by the way? I imagine "woman gets fat and lets herself go" doesn't cut it.'

'She's been compulsive eating ever since she found out she couldn't have children.'

'Jesus. Who'd be an actress?'

'I know. It's soap at its worst. But, to be honest, our viewers will probably love it. It's a tragedy.'

'So when you come back after the break it's already happening?'

'Exactly. But she's trying to keep it a secret from Hargreaves, because she's scared he'll leave her if he finds out they can't have kids.'

'She's eating her feelings!'

He laughs. 'Right.'

'OK, so you sat her down and told her this.'

'I told her she had this great story coming up and that she was going to get so much attention, and she got all excited, obviously. Then I told her what it was and she asked me if she was going to have prosthetics to wear. Of course, that's out of the question because of the cost and the time it would take to put them on every day . . .'

'And?'

'And then it dawned on her. She asked me if I was asking her to put on weight and I said that was why I was telling her about the story now, so she could start right away. Oh, I forgot! I'd bought her a big cake. All cream and chocolate. And I went and got it then.'

'Ha!'

'She practically threw it in my face. Out and out refused to do it. So then I said, "Look at Charlize Theron. She made herself look terrible when she played that serial killer and she won loads of awards".'

'Oh God, she really might end up winning a BAFTA.' Even though I shouldn't care about this, even though it would happen long after everything was over, because the

BAFTAs aren't till April or May, I still hate the fact that it might end up being the best thing that's ever happened to Saskia.

'Oh no she won't.'

'How can you be so sure?'

'Because I'll forget to enter her. It's up to the producers on each show who gets thrown into the mix. If she's not in the race, she can't win.'

'Won't she find out?'

'How? So long as we don't tell anyone.'

I can tell he's proud of this twist in the plan from the way he sits back and looks at me.

'Oh my God, you've turned out to be an evil genius.'

'I'm trying my best.'

'So Charlize Theron clinched it then?'

'Not immediately. There was lots of her trying to nego- tiate how much weight she would be expected to gain. How quickly she would be allowed to lose it again. Lots of tears and "what if you don't still find me attractive when I'm fat?"-type comments. Which was rich, to say the least. The truth is, I wouldn't care if she was twenty stone if she was still the same person I thought she was until a couple of weeks ago.'

'Well, you say that now . . .'

He cuts me off, more animated than I've ever seen him so far. 'It's the truth. I love my wife. I'm not that fucking facile that it's all based on how she looks.'

'She's lucky,' I say wistfully.

'She obviously doesn't think so.'

There's an awkward silence where I don't know what to say and I think he feels a bit embarrassed about his outburst. Eventually, I say, 'No, well, who knows what they're thinking?'

'I can't concentrate at work, wondering what she's up to. At least when we're filming I have an idea.'

'Robert was out all afternoon yesterday. Said he'd arranged a golf lesson.'

Josh puts his face in his hands. 'Sas told me she went to the spa. Said there was no point trying to call her because she'd either be having a massage or too blissed out afterwards to have a conversation. Shit.'

'There's no point torturing ourselves trying to work out the details. We know what they're doing, we don't need to know the hows and wheres.'

He puts his coffee mug down and looks at me. 'You really think they're planning a future together?'

'I have no idea.'

There are tears brimming at the corners of his eyes again. He flicks them away and I can see him trying to keep his mouth under control, to stop himself going into full-blown crying mode. I look away, to give him a chance to recover his composure. I wonder if the waitress thinks we're a couple going through a bad time.

'I've been going over the schedule for when we're back,' he says, trying to smile. It's actually heartbreaking to watch. 'I'm trying to have them in on different days whenever we can. Make it harder for them to see each other. Obviously, half their scenes are together though so . . .'

'Good one. Any obstacles we can put in their way. Maybe I should book us a holiday or something. Get him away for a week or so. Not, to be honest, that I want to spend any more time alone with him than I have to at this point.'

'Will he go for it, do you think?' He looks hopeful and I know it would make him feel so much better if he wasn't having to wonder what his wife was up to every minute when he was supposed to be working.

It's years since Robert and I went on a proper summer break because, wherever we go, he gets paranoid that people are sneakily taking photos of him in his trunks. Which they are most of the time.

'Sod it. I'll just book it. Tell him it's a surprise. If I make it somewhere he's always wanted to go, then I'll look like Wife of the Year even if he's pissed off with me.'

In the end, all the good places are booked up because it's holiday season and most people have the sense to plan ahead. I settle for asking Myra for two weeks off and announcing to Robert that I've done it so we can spend time together while he's not working. To say he looks horrified when I tell him would be a disservice to the word 'horrified'. I know as soon as I say it that he and Saskia had planned to spend their days together. I don't even have to stick to him like glue to make sure that doesn't happen now. The potential is enough.

We're sitting on our little balcony overlooking the gardens below. After a week of rained-off Wimbledon the sun has suddenly come out and half of London seems to be outside making the most of it. Robert is idly picking dead leaves off the geraniums in the pot beside him.

'I thought we could have a staycation,' I say, pretending not to have noticed the look on his face. 'I didn't like the thought of you having to entertain yourself all day with me at work and George away. I thought you'd be bored stiff.'

He can't really argue with this. Robert would (usually) be the first person to admit he hates being on his own for too long. He needs an audience.

'I've got things arranged, though. Plans,' he says petulantly.

I shrug, as if that's not important. 'Like what?'

'I told Alice I'd spend a day doing galleries with her. And golf. I thought I'd get some more lessons in.'

'You can still do all that,' I say brightly. 'I could join you and Alice. Or, I know, even better, I could leave you to the cultural stuff and then meet you both somewhere for lunch. Where are you going, do you know?'

'We haven't sorted out the details yet.'

'And you've always been on at me to learn golf. I could come for a lesson with you.'

He scoffs. 'You hate golf.'

I do. I hate it. It's up there with darts and motor racing for me. Sports that really should not be called sports. 'Only because I've never tried it. It'll be fun. Anyway, Myra's already got someone in to cover for me, so you're stuck with me now.'

'Fine,' he says, with complete disregard for how curt he sounds.

'I thought you'd be pleased,' I say, turning on the tears. Just enough to make him feel bad, not so much he wants to run a mile. I do a good job of looking like I'm trying to hold them back too. Look away, as if I'm trying to hide them from him.

He softens, because he's not a monster. I don't think for a moment he wants me to be unhappy, whatever he's doing.

'I am, love. I just wish you'd have talked to me about it first. Maybe the following week would have been better . . .'

'I wanted to surprise you. I didn't think.'

He leans over and kisses me on the top of the head. 'I appreciate it, thank you.'

'And if you have plans, that's fine,' I say, knowing that I've pissed on his bonfire so thoroughly that he won't feel invincible enough to sneak off for extended periods of time any more. And I can make sure he doesn't anyway, by springing the odd surprise on him here and there. 'I'm happy pottering around on my own, you know that.'

When I text Josh to tell him what I've done, I get a smiley face back in return.

12

I'm back outside West1 Hot Yoga!, this time by arrangement. I sent Saskia a friendly text a couple of days ago – '*Fancy brunch on Saturday?*' – and she almost bit my hand off to accept.

She's positively glowing, although whether from the Bikram or the extended session I'm pretty sure she had with my husband when Josh and I were both at work on Thursday I don't know. It was pretty surreal knowing it was going on (when I'd told him I'd be home from work a bit late – because of Chas and his metallic torture implements, although I didn't fess up to that, obviously – he said he wouldn't be there anyway because he'd arranged a game of golf with the pro at the club he's a member of in Highgate) but not being able to do anything about it. I'd tried to channel my anger into my exercise, like I'd read people apparently did, but all that happened was that I told Chas he was an arsehole when he asked me to hold a bigger weight the third time I did a set of step-ups on to the box.

Anyway, whatever is going on with Saskia, she looks well. She gives me a hug and tells me how lovely it is to see me.

'You look really good,' she says disingenuously.

'You too.' She's wearing a pair of white rolled-up jeans and a tight raspberry-coloured top that shows off her mighty cleavage to anyone who's interested. Some kind of fancy flip-flops. Her legs and arms are tanned a honey stain that's too perfect to be natural. She's still looking as toned as ever so I imagine Josh is losing the battle to have her eat herself fat. I tug my T-shirt down over my stomach and hate myself for doing it at the same time.

'How are you enjoying the break? I thought you might have gone away.'

'Well, of course Josh doesn't get the time off, does he? And it's no fun on your own. And all my girlfriends are working, so poor old me is stuck at home on her lonesome.'

I seize on that, putting down the menu I've just picked up. 'Oh yes! Wasn't it the story conference last week? Robert's always on eggshells, wondering what awful fate they're going to impose on him.'

'Tell me about it.'

I fake a laugh. 'Surely you don't have to worry. Josh wouldn't dare.'

She gives me a pious look. 'I've always told him he mustn't treat me any differently to the rest of the cast.'

Yeah, right. 'So have you got any spoilers? Or is he sworn to secrecy?'

There's a pause where she thinks about whether or not she can tell me her bad news. On balance, she likes me, and she knows that, being married to one of the other actors, I know the rules, so I think she will. I wait patiently.

'Usually, but . . . oh God, Paula, you mustn't tell anyone, not even Robert . . .'

'Of course not. I haven't even told him we're friends, remember.'

So she takes me through the whole thing. How challenging it's going to be and how Josh said she would probably win awards. I feign surprise when she gets to the bit about having to pile on weight.

'Wow. That's dedication! Good for you.'

'I know this sounds shallow, but I don't know if I can.'

'Trust me, it's easy.'

'Haha. You know what I mean. What if I can't lose it again and then I'm . . .' She peters out, probably realizing she's about to insult me.

'You will. Think of it as a challenge. Josh's right, you'll be drowning in BAFTA nominations.'

'Do you think?' she says, looking hopeful for the first time, and I think, God, they're so alike, her and Robert. They just want praise and attention. They're like that needy girl at school who knew she was prettier than everyone else but needed to hear it said. Repeatedly.

'Definitely. And hey, I can help you. I'm an expert.'

'You really should stop putting yourself down all the time,' she says, which is a nice thing to say, I have to admit.

The waitress appears to take our order. Saskia goes for her usual salad Niçoise with the dressing on the side.

'Oh no you don't,' I say. 'Pick something more lardy.'

She makes a show of protesting and then she selects a baked potato with cheese and butter. The sweaty ladies of West1 Hot Yoga! would have a stroke.

'Extra cheese,' I say on her behalf. 'And extra butter. Extra everything.'

I order the salad Niçoise for myself, force myself to ask for the dressing on the side.

'How about you?' she says as we wait for our food. 'Are

you and Robert jetting off somewhere?' There's not a hint, not the tiniest giveaway, that she knows anything. I assume Robert's told her about our 'staycation' by now. How I sprung it on him and ruined his summer. I decide to mess with her head a bit. When I told Josh we were meeting up – having filled him in on the history – his advice was not to keep playing the sympathy card.

'She'll see a weakness and she'll pounce. Sas doesn't really do female solidarity. Or empathy, for that matter. Where you might start to feel sorry for the other woman, she'll just see an opportunity.'

I interrupted him. 'I wouldn't be doing it in the first place.'

'Well, yes, there is that. All I'm saying is that I don't think trying to get her to feel sorry for you will work.'

I wanted to say, 'She sounds lovely, I can see why you want to save your marriage,' but of course I didn't.

'No, we left it too late,' I tell her now. 'Although Robert's persuaded me to have a couple of weeks off work so we can at least spend some time together.'

This isn't the story in so far as she is concerned. In the – true – version that she will have been presented with, Robert was as horrified as I imagine she was by my decision. I watch for a reaction and, because she's not that good an actress, she can't help but give away that this is news to her. She covers it up quickly, though.

'How lovely. You're getting on better then?'

'You know, actually, we are. Just the last couple of weeks he's been, well . . . let's just say, really attentive.'

I raise an eyebrow in a way that I hope conveys that Robert's and my sex life has swung back into action. It works (God, I'm good). Saskia looks a little as if she might be sick. She gives me what I can only describe as a grimace. A rictus grin that has nothing behind the eyes.

'Wow. That's great. I'm so pleased for you.'

'Me too! I don't know what's happened but we've been a bit like randy teenagers for the past week or so.' I almost laugh as I say this. It's so far from the truth. Her expression is priceless. Eyes wide, mouth open. 'I mean, sorry to be so graphic but . . . you know . . . I know I can trust you.'

Actually, I am taking a bit of a risk that this gem will make her forget our agreement to keep our friendship a secret and she'll storm straight over to confront him. Deep down, I know she won't, though. She would never want to risk him finding out she's been sneaking around, discussing him with his wife behind his back. It would make her look far too insecure.

'Of course you can. No wonder you're looking so well.' She attempts a laugh. Settles instead on a dry 'haha'. I wonder if I do look different. Better. In the couple of weeks since I saw her last I've done more exercise than in the previous ten years combined.

'So what are you planning to do with your two weeks off? Now that Robert's "persuaded" you?' She can't help herself, she has to know the details. 'What treats has he got in store?'

'I'm not sure yet. He's being very mysterious.'

'Gosh. How exciting.'

'I think he just feels guilty for being a bit distracted lately. I feel bad now about ever mentioning that to you. I was over-reacting, I think.'

She's squeezing a corner of her napkin in her fist.

I don't think she even realizes she's doing it. I savour the moment.

'Let's hope so. I'm sure you're right.'

We sit there in silence for a moment. I'm buzzing from my tiny victory. Saskia has a face like fury, as if she blames poor old me for the fact that my husband is apparently showing signs of caring.

'He said something at work on Friday about you taking Georgia to the airport last weekend . . .'

I knew it! Robert had tried to protest that George was only going away for a few weeks so it didn't need two of us waving her off and making a show of ourselves. And I knew, I just knew, that he was hoping he could sneak off and meet Saskia then. Josh would think she was at Bikram. I would be hanging around, otherwise engaged in Luton. It would have been the perfect crime. So I made a big thing about George having said she wanted us both there. How she was being all sentimental because it was her last summer before she left home. A little while later he'd sneaked out 'for a run', no doubt mobile in hand. One point to me.

There's no need for me to tell Saskia all that, though.

'Well, I did. He cried off because he would have had to get up too early, bless him. I left him sleeping in like a teenager.'

Honestly, if someone knew how to develop an invisible camera that you operated with just the blink of an eye, I would stump up the money for it right now, just to capture her expression.

'Oh. From the way he was talking about it, I thought it was a matter of life or death.' She's trying to pass it off as a joke but I know her brain must be screaming out that he lied to her. That they had the perfect opportunity to meet up but, for some reason, he chose to make up an excuse.

'Typical Robert,' I say, and roll my eyes in a way I hope conveys affection.

I feel I've done enough for one day. Now, she's the paranoid, insecure one. I don't want to risk losing her altogether, although I imagine curiosity is going to make her desperate to meet up again.

'How was yoga?'

'Fine.' I wait for more. For the usual yapping nonsense. But she's concentrating on her newly arrived baked potato – the size of a small submarine – like it's a script she has to learn for tomorrow.

I leave my dressing firmly on the side and tackle my salad.

Because I'm going to have to cancel two weeks of sessions with Chas, I've scheduled extra for this week, knowing that Robert will be off most days, trying to understand why his carefree, confident lover has suddenly become clingy and suspicious. Don't get me wrong, I still hate Chas and all he stands for with a passion (that's not fair, he's perfectly nice, I would just rather never have to see him again) but I am on a mission. As Saskia expands, so I'll contract.

I've picked the middle two weeks of Robert's break to take as holiday. It felt the most disruptive. This way, hopefully, Saskia will be in a mood with him for the next few days, following my bombshell, but unable to tell him why. Then she'll spend a fortnight wondering what he and I are

143

up to, unable to call him when she wants, at the mercy of him contacting her. And then it'll only be a week till filming recommences, during which time, almost inevitably, relations will be strained, because I will have laid it on thick about what a great time we had. Hardly the long summer idyll they were hoping for.

I arrive home from work every day, bruised and battered, bits of me I didn't even know I had screaming in protest. Despite Chas's efforts to stretch me senseless at the end of each workout, I ache like I've never ached before. I've been sick once (after he made me push a heavy wooden box up and back along the gym floor), cried twice (when he asked me to push the heavy wooden box for a second and third time), and sworn more times than even I think is acceptable. Through it all, Chas has smiled his big, cheerful smile with his big, white, straight teeth and barked words of encouragement. I tell him I want to punch him so he suggests we add boxing into our routine from now on. I'm too worn out to argue.

There is no denying that bits of me are getting smaller, though. Random bits, like the couple of inches just above my knees and the wobbly stuff that hangs over the side of my bra. Chas tells me everyone is different but he's reassuring about the fact that the rest of my body will catch up soon. I won't end up essentially a fat person but with unfeasibly small upper knees and bras that are too baggy. All my clothes already feel looser to one degree or another, and there is something that I think resembles muscle tone appearing under my surface. Deep under the surface, but still. On the third day I walk all the way home after my hour with Chas and I actually enjoy it. I decide that I must have been brain-snatched by aliens. This can't be me.

Robert is absent every afternoon except one when I get home so I lie in a hot bath and soothe my war wounds. I try not to think about where he is and what he's doing. Josh and I compare notes about timings and excuses given and we're both pretty certain they have spent most days together, although where, we have no idea. I scour our bedroom for signs, just in case Robert has the nerve to bring her here, but I don't find any stray blonde hairs or catch a waft of her cloying flowery perfume anywhere. When I tell Josh this he admits he's been doing the same. Although what he actually says is that he scoured their bed with a magnifying glass for unfamiliar pubes, which makes both of us slightly hysterical when we think about the absurdity of it.

In the evenings Robert and I sit in – what must seem to him – companionable silence with a bottle of wine and the TV. I never quiz him about what he's been doing with his day, I don't mention that his breath smells of wine when he tells me he's spent the afternoon walking in Hyde Park, or that there's a faint smear of pink lipstick near his left ear when he's describing the frustrating time he had in John Lewis, trying to find us a new chest of drawers. I don't even tell him I don't want a new chest of drawers, nor have I ever said I do. I smile and I laugh and I make jokes and laugh at his. Who wouldn't want to be married to me?

On the Friday evening, when Robert finally gets back from a 'game of golf', he seems frazzled. Agitated. Hardly the demeanour of a man who has spent all day wandering around the countryside in pursuit of a ball he keeps los-ing. For someone who tans easily, there isn't a speck of colour on his face on this beautiful, sunny summer day. I have to stop myself from asking if he wore a veil, or if Highgate has its own microclimate which meant he was under cloudy skies while I bathed in sunlight. I went a shade darker just walking home, despite the factor thirty, that's all I'm saying.

Of course, what I actually do is ask about his game (conveniently played against someone I have never met, someone he got to know at the golf club and seems to have no intention of ever seeing outside). His heart's not in it, though. Something's happened.

When I get a moment I send Josh a text, asking if he's safe to talk. The reply I get back says, '*No. Half an hour?*' I can't risk it. Robert has gone for a shower but then we're in for the duration.

'*Can't*', I reply. '*Tomorrow?*'

We agree to chat once Saskia has safely left for Bikram. I'm half tempted to try to arrange to meet up with her, but I've already told Robert my Saturday-morning massage session has been cancelled. I'm eaten up with curiosity, though, so I send Josh another message:

'*She seem OK?*'

I'm still waiting for a response when Robert strolls back in and heads for the cupboard to get the wine glasses. Later, when I get the chance to look, there it is:

'*No, actually*'.

Saskia was red-eyed, he tells me when we speak in the morning. I'm walking around the park in circles, having told Robert I was going on an emergency mission to get milk because we'd run out. This involved me having to pour what semi-skimmed we did have down the kitchen sink when he wasn't looking. I knew he wouldn't argue, though. Neither of us can contemplate facing the day without coffee.

'Do you think they've broken up?' I ask, breathless. 'It seems too easy.'

There's a pause and then he speaks. 'I checked her phone when she was asleep. Nothing, obviously.'

'Christ, it's so frustrating not knowing what's going on.'

'I wonder how they communicate,' he says.

'Telepathy,' I say, and he laughs. 'That's how intense their relationship is.'

'I feel as if I have no idea who she is any more.' He sighs. I sit down on a bench, my face in the sun, wait for him to speak.

'Maybe I should cut my losses . . .'

'Just wait. We have no idea what's going to happen.' I watch as a little girl in a red hoody flaps along after a pigeon.

'Do you think I'm an idiot for wanting to stay with her?'

'It's not about what I think.' I stand up and keep walking. Might as well get some exercise in as we talk.

'But do you? Be honest.'

Well, he did ask. 'OK. Yes, I do. She seems like an absolute cow. You could do better.'

He laughs and I'm relieved. 'No, really, tell me what you think.'

By the time I'm in spitting distance of the flat, I realize I've forgotten the milk. I turn around and head back towards the main road again.

13

With Myra's help, I've planned a tireless schedule for Robert's and my staycation. Art galleries, matinees, walks in the park. I'm exhausted just thinking about it and, to be honest, I'd love to just flop around for a couple of weeks doing nothing, but that's hardly the idea. I attempt to arrange one event for each day in the hope that will stop him being able to nip off for a 'game of golf'. And I keep my plans vague so that he daren't plan ahead. I've even organized a couple of nights at Robert's mum and dad's because I know he always feels as if he doesn't see them enough. It suits me too. I love Robert's mum and dad. How they ever produced Robert and Alice is beyond me.

Lloyd and Christine are both actors, of course, although neither of them works much these days. Both had some modicum of success in the seventies. In fact, they met on the set of a sitcom about a school – a twenty-four- and a twenty-three-year-old playing kids of sixteen – that ran for about four years. After that, they both struggled, and, happily for Robert and Alice, set up an antiques business on the side that actually did rather well. Robert likes to say in interviews that this is one of the reasons he feels so comfortable playing Hargreaves, as if picking up a vase and turning it over was a skill that needed to be crafted over many long years. Neither of them threw the towel in, though, and, occasionally they will pop up briefly in random dramas. In fact, Lloyd just did a couple of days on *Game of Thrones* and came home saying he'd never seen so many nipples gathered in one place in his entire life.

They are ridiculously proud of Robert in that way that only parents can be. And, best of all, they love me, seemingly unconditionally, too. Georgia, their only grandchild, can walk on water, as far as they are concerned.

They live right in the heart of Bath, in a house they bought in 1975 for a steal and which is now probably worth five trillion. It's the house Robert and Alice grew up in and every time I go there I have to fight off pangs of envy for the childhood they must have had. Not that mine was bad. Not at all. It was just a bit dull. A bit colourless. Two-up, two-down suburbia with a miniature willow in the front garden and church on Sundays. I always imagine that Robert and Alice grew up in a frenzy of art and sophistication. While I was playing Kerplunk with Cathy from next door, they were at the theatre or being allowed a sip from a champagne cocktail at a fabulous party in the garden. I wonder whatever happened to Cathy. She was exceptionally gifted at Kerplunk. She's probably a surgeon now, with those hands.

Robert's family home is one of those honey-coloured, four-storey, terraced beauties that Bath is famous for. Set back slightly from the street with black railings surrounding the below-ground courtyard at the front. Unexpectedly large garden at the rear. Wooden floors and original shutters restored to their former glory. There is always much discussion about parking and how hard it is to find a space nearby this close to town, but I can't imagine I would ever find anything to complain about if I lived here. Well, apart from my husband's infidelity, that is.

Because of the parking issue we've come down on the train and, when we show up in a taxi after the short ride from the station, Christine is looking hopefully out of one of the front windows, waiting to spot us. She's presumably been there all morning, as I don't think I told her which train we were catching.

'Bless her,' I say as I wave, and her face lights up.

Robert smiles indulgently. I'll give him this. He genuinely does love his mum and dad.

The reason I've organized this visit now isn't just because I know Robert will enjoy it, or that it's easier for me to be relaxed around him when Lloyd and Christine are there, because I would never want them to pick up on any bad atmosphere. It's because I want to guilt-trip him. Overindulgent and prone to blindness in so far as their children's faults are concerned they might be, but I know that the one thing they would find it hard to forgive their son would be him cheating on me. Lloyd and Christine have stuck together through thick and thin and they're proud of that fact. All the temptations were there, they always say about their life in the spotlight, but they steadfastly avoided them. They knew what would really matter when the dust settled.

'Darlings!' Christine says, throwing open the front door. She's not one for an understated entrance. She hugs us both in a flurry of scarves and musky perfume that smells as if it was bottled in the seventies. Christine is still a beauty but she's starting to take on the look of a startled bushbaby just woken from a nap because of the tiny bits of surgery – which she will never admit to – she's been having here and there. Her eyes are now round in a way they never were when she was younger, all droop eliminated with the nip of a scalpel. She over-plucked her eyebrows when she was young (as was the fashion) and they never really grew back so she now has unnatural dark brown lines permanently arching above her eyes a good half a centimetre above where any hairs used to be. This time, I notice her cheeks are smooth and appley. Plumped up like two fat chicken breasts. I'd love to be able to tell her she should stop, that she's just gorgeous as she is, but that would mean admitting I'd noticed and it's an unspoken law that none of us does that.

'Come in, come in. Lloyd is at the shop but he'll be home soon. He's dying to see you.'

We dump our bags in the hallway and follow her down to the huge basement kitchen. Doors open on to the garden at the back and the courtyard at the front. Lloyd and Christine's house is so big that Robert and I have our own bedroom permanently (as does Alice), even though we only visit a handful of times each year. But we all know the first order of the day on any visit is a pot of tea (pre-watershed) or a gin and tonic (after six).

I actually feel myself relax as I soak up the warmth that Christine gives off, as if she were a mobile radiator turned up to maximum. If I were a cat, I know whose lap I'd sit on.

'How are you, sweetheart?' She holds me at arm's length. 'You look as lovely as ever.'

'You too,' I say, because she does. Whatever she did to her face wouldn't make me think any differently.

When Lloyd gets home (I'm half crushed by the bear hug) we FaceTime Georgia while she's lying on a lounger on the beach. Lloyd and Christine can't quite get the hang of what's going on and keep saying things like 'When did she film this?' (Lloyd) and, at one point, when I explain that this is actually happening in real time, waving and shouting, 'Coo-ee!' over and over again (Christine). I'm almost crying with laughter by the time we hang up, having established that she's having a great time and she doesn't miss us at all. I look over at Robert and see he's the same way.

Over dinner (cooked by Christine and Lloyd together in a sort of reverse *I Love Lucy* double act) I can't believe my luck when Lloyd mentions how sad it is that some old family friends' son is getting divorced, having discovered his wife has been seeing another man for years. It's exactly the in I need.

'That's just awful. How can someone be so cruel to the person they're supposed to love?'

I know I'm preaching to the converted here in so far as Lloyd and Christine are concerned. I just have to light the touchpaper and off they go.

'It's ghastly,' Christine says. 'I mean, he had no idea, can you imagine?'

'People aren't prepared to work at anything nowadays.' Lloyd picks up the baton. 'One sniff of boredom and they're off with someone else.'

'Everything's instant gratification these days.' Christine and Lloyd use phrases like 'these days' a lot. Rarely in a positive way. Now she leans forward on her elbows, warming to her theme. 'In our time, you made your bed and you lay in it. Didn't you, Lloyd?'

'You did. Mind you, we were lucky.' He reaches over and puts a hand over hers and I have to bite back a tear. They're so sweet.

Robert is keeping schtum. Maybe he's worried that if he says anything he'll give himself away. Christine's not having it, though.

'I think you know him, actually, Robert. Mark Tyler. Wasn't he in your class at school?'

'Oh, um, yes, I think so. I wasn't really friends with him, though.' He's looking a bit shifty, clearly wishing we would all change the subject.

'Isn't it awful, though? He's such a lovely boy,' Christine persists. 'Can you imagine? They've been married for twenty years. Two children.'

'Mmm . . .' he says. 'Nasty.'

'We've met her several times, haven't we, Lloyd?'

Lloyd nods his agreement. 'I'd give her a piece of my mind if I saw her now.'

'Well,' Robert says loudly, changing tack. 'I could do with another glass of wine. Anyone else?'

For two days, Robert's mum and dad spoil us and indulge us. They're so thrilled to have the pair of us to look after that, even though my instinct screams out at me to help out with the cooking and cleaning, as I would in anyone else's home, I hold back and let them get on with it. It's not hard to see how someone like Alice would take advantage.

When talk turns to her as we sit at the big table in the back garden with our post-dinner brandies, the smell of the honeysuckle almost overpowering, I keep my opinions to myself. Far be it from me to be the one to tell them she has about as much chance of getting her one-woman show off the ground as of being cast as the next James

Bond. Not just because no one would be interested, but because she would never actually put in the hard work to make it happen in the first place.

'I wonder where she'll do the first run . . .' Christine says, and then they're off, reminiscing about theatres they worked in in the sixties and what they were called then or what they've now become. Robert and I just let them ramble on. I imagine this is how they spend their evenings when it's just the two of them, happily meandering along down memory lane, holding hands.

'We saw her the other week, didn't we, Robert?' I say when they eventually slow to a stop.

'Mmm . . .' Robert says. He's quiet this evening and I wonder if he's trying to decide whether it's safe to sneak off and call Saskia from a phone box. He wouldn't dare ring her now, though, not in the evening, when Josh might be about. Despite their no-texting rule, he's clearly nervous that she might, because every now and again he looks at his phone, tilting it up from where it lays face down on the table beside him, in a way that means only he can see what's on the screen. At one point he nips inside, taking it with him. He thinks I don't notice, or, if I do, I wouldn't understand the significance.

'I know. How lovely. It's so wonderful that the three of you get along so well,' Christine says, and I bite my tongue and smile.

I check my own mobile when Robert is in the bathroom as we get ready for bed. There's a text from 'Gail' that just says, '*This*', along with a screen grab of what seems to be Saskia's Wikipedia page.

I'm a bit confused about what I'm meant to be looking at at first but then I notice the part where it states that her age now reads 'Sherbourne claims to be thirty-eight but, in reality, she's forty-three.'

I snort.

I listen to make sure Robert's not on his way back. Josh is probably asleep by now but I send him a reply anyway.

'Did you do this??'

His reply comes almost immediately. *'Me? As if I would.'* He follows it up with a smiley face. I actually laugh out loud just as Robert comes in from the bathroom.

'Stupid cat video,' I say, as if in explanation. I'm banking on him not asking to watch it. Robert isn't big on animals.

He rolls his eyes, but not in a mean way. 'Thousands of years of progress have led to this. Videos of cats banging into glass doors.'

I laugh along.

'Let's have a look then,' he says, and I know this is him trying to make an effort to be nice. I, on the other hand, am caught out. I press a random button on my phone to clear away the incriminating messages.

'Oh, I don't know where it was now. I just saw it on Twitter.'

'Oh, well,' he says, climbing into bed beside me. 'There'll be a thousand more tomorrow.'

'Have you had a nice evening?' I say as he turns off the light on his side of the bed.

'Lovely,' he says. 'I should come down more often.'

He might not think I pick up on it. He's probably not even aware he just did it. But there it is, that subtle shift from 'we' to 'I'. It tells me all I need to know about what's going on in his head.

By the second week I'm going stir-crazy and desperate to go back to work. Even to have a session with Chas, which just goes to show how bad it's got. I crave my own company in a way I've never experienced before. I'm exhausted with being nice, positive, supportive Paula, but I have to say, I'm doing a great job of it. Robert has definitely enjoyed it, despite himself. He's had all his favourite things (well, apart from one particular yappy blonde) handed to him on a plate like little Lord Fauntleroy – why wouldn't he have had a good time? We've seen plays, gone around the Courtauld and the Royal Academy, walked on the Heath. I have held my own in conversations about *Top Gear* and spent hours on the internet in the mornings looking for funny stories to drop into the breakfast-table conversation. I even booked us both a golf lesson (at the same time, but with different people, obviously. I didn't think an hour of someone going 'So you hold the club like this. No. Like this' would make him very happy), and even though I wanted to hurl myself off a bridge before the lesson was even halfway over, afterwards I raved to him about how much fun it had been and how I've been wrong all these years. He was chuffed, I could tell. Not that he wants me to join him on the green, of course, especially because half his games are actually not really games at all, but he appreciated the sentiment nonetheless.

As fortnights go where you spend all your time with someone you don't really want to be with, it's gone about as well as it could have gone.

14

Saskia has gained nine pounds, Josh tells me gleefully when we next speak. I'm on my way to work, practically skipping my way down the road with happiness to have left Robert still in bed. If the last two weeks have shown me anything, it's that I'm not afraid to be on my own. In fact, I'm looking forward to it.

'In three weeks? That's pretty good going.'

'It's showing too. She's devastated.'

'Does she look awful?' I know as soon as I say it that this is a step too far for Josh. He's too nice.

'No. God, no, that's not what I'm saying. She still looks great. It's just that she can't see it like that. It's making her lose her confidence.'

'Story of my life. Well, I'm pretty sure she and Robert will be meeting up today, so let's hope he notices.'

He tells me that he's going to call Robert in for a meeting this week to discuss his new story arc. It's only a week to go till filming recommences and the whole treadmill gets going again for another year. Two actors have been culled (one unpopular with the viewers, Josh tells me, and the other too dull to keep finding stories for) and they've already been told that they'll be written out in the next run of episodes. I feel a bit sorry for them, losing their jobs out of nowhere. It will probably be months, or even years, before either of them gets another paid acting gig.

'And when do you get to take time off?'

He laughs. 'God knows.'

Chas has decided it's time to weigh me again, like a prize cow at a meat market. He's already poked me with the forceps, although he has yet to complete his calculation. Humiliating as it is, I'm so glad to be back.

When he tells me the news, I think I've misheard.

'Thirteen five.' He looks down at his notes from last time. 'That's great. Nearly a stone and a half down.'

'Are you sure that doesn't say fourteen five?' I peer down, trying to see. Chas has changed the readout to stones and pounds at my insistence.

'Well done,' he says, beaming. 'And your fat percentage is . . .' He scribbles on his bit of paper. It's like waiting for them to announce the winner of *The X Factor*. The suspense is unbearable. '. . . thirty-eight.'

'Wow. And that's good?'

'It's great. Thirty-nine per cent counts as obese, so now you're down to the overweight category.'

That burst my bubble. 'So I'm not obese any more by one per cent?'

He picks up on my change of mood. 'That's right. And that's an achievement.'

'But if I eat a couple of bags of crisps and sit on the sofa for a day I'll probably be back in obese again.'

'All the more reason not to do those things.'

When we get back to the gym he pushes me harder than ever before because, as he keeps reminding me, he hasn't seen me for two weeks. I don't care. Even though I feel sick, I do everything he asks. I don't even complain.

Something's happened.

Something big.

To say it was unexpected is a bit of an understatement. It wasn't on my top hundred list of things that might happen, if I'm being honest. Probably not my top million.

It's been a lot of years since I kissed someone in a park in broad daylight. And it's been a lot of years since I kissed someone who wasn't Robert. For those two things to happen at the same moment must be about the same odds as Donald Trump becoming president. Oh, wait.

It didn't last long. It was only a moment before I came to my senses and pushed him away. But I'd be lying if I said I didn't enjoy it while it was happening. Mostly because of the novelty value, I think. Not because of who was doing the kissing. At least, that's what I'm trying to tell myself.

Later, I try to piece together the whole picture. It's a bit hazy because the final outcome sort of blurred what had been there before. We were leaning on a railing in a quiet part of Hyde Park, admiring the pond beyond, having agreed to meet at the entrance closest to the Mandarin Oriental. I was telling Josh about my having sacrificed everything I hold dear in order to pretend I was interested in golf.

'He doesn't deserve you,' Josh said, and I'd laughed and said that we both deserved better, actually, he and I.

'No,' he said with – I realize in retrospect – a kind of intensity. 'I mean it, though.'

Next thing I knew, it was happening. He didn't just grab me either. There was a moment of staring into each other's eyes, which I went along with, I hold my hands up. And then his mouth was on mine and I was so shocked I let it happen.

I came to my senses pretty quickly. This wasn't going to help anything. Nice though the sensation might be, flattered though I undoubtedly was, it wasn't right.

I moved away as gently as I could in the circumstances.

'No,' I said, a little breathlessly. 'We shouldn't.'

'I really like you, Paula,' he said, and I have to admit it, my stomach did a little flip because it was so long since anyone had spoken to me like that. But, really? Did he?

'It's not right. We'd be as bad as them.'

'Hardly.' He brushed my hair away from my face and I felt myself blush. I tried to hold my nerve.

'Josh, you're trying to save your marriage. How's kissing me going to help?'

He looked off into the distance. Exhaled. 'I don't think I am any more. I don't think it's saveable. I've stopped caring what she's doing. I'd say that meant it was over.'

This was news to me. I still felt uncomfortable, though.

'Even if that's true, it's too soon. We'd just be each other's rebound person.'

He smiled. It's a crying shame him and Saskia never had kids, because they would have had killer smiles. 'Would that be so bad?'

'It'd be messy. We need to keep focused on what's important. Get them split up . . . wait, why do you care if they split up or not now?'

'Because you do. And because I don't want her to have

a happy ending either. Your desire for vengeance has rubbed off on me.' He raised his eyebrows and waggled them so I knew he was joking.

'OK, well, let's just work on that and then see what happens.'

'Are you sure I can't kiss you again?' He ran his fingers down the side of my face so gently I felt it in completely other parts of my body. What was going on? Having never thought of Josh in this way, my body seemed to have decided that perhaps I should have.

It took all of my willpower but I managed to say, yes, I was sure. Actually, no, I didn't say that at all. What I in fact said was, 'OK. Just once, though. So I can remember what it feels like.'

So he did, and I allowed myself to sink into it and enjoy the sensation. For the briefest moment I forgot about everything: Robert, Saskia, the fact that a gang of teenagers were hooting at us with derision as they passed.

'You're gorgeous, you do know that,' he said as I broke off again, and I, with all the social graces of a thirteen-year-old, snorted, and said, 'Stop it.'

'I'm fine to wait,' he said. 'Or not, if you don't . . . I love that you wouldn't want to do anything behind their backs.'

As he said that he pulled me towards him and kissed my forehead. I was so confused, such a mix of being flattered, excited, turned on and horrified, that I hardly knew where to put myself, so I just turned and moved away.

After that there was an awkwardness that had never been there before. We walked on – both clearly thinking it was better to keep moving – but our conversation felt forced. I started to worry that I might have lost him as an ally. I'd hurt his pride at a point when it was damaged anyway. When we emerged at Bayswater Road he announced he ought to be getting back to work. Filming started again on Monday and the place was in chaos.

'Don't worry,' he said as we said goodbye, a respectable couple of feet between us. 'It won't always be this awkward. I just have to go and lick my wounds a bit.'

'It was nice,' I said. 'It wasn't that it wasn't nice.'

'God forbid that would be the official review.' He laughed and I felt myself relax a little. 'When was nice ever irresistible?'

So here's what the problem is. Try as I might, I can't dismiss what happened. I have no doubt that Josh just wanted to get back at Saskia, or to feel as if he'd taken control of the situation or something. Maybe in the moment he really did think he fancied me, I don't know. And now his pride's a little hurt but he'll get over it.

The problem is actually with me. I keep replaying the moment in my head. I've never even considered that I might find Josh attractive – obviously, he's good-looking, but I've never really been a sucker for good-looking; not without other stuff to back it up – but suddenly it's clear to me that I do. Am I really that sad that, as soon as someone shows the slightest bit of interest in me, I talk myself into having a massive crush on them? Yes! I hear you all shout. Clearly.

I can at least console myself that I did the right thing. Not just because I want to be able to occupy the moral high ground where Robert is concerned, and it's hard to do that if you're at it with someone yourself. 'You did it first' doesn't really cut it. It's more that I don't want to open myself up to any more heartache. I don't want to fall for someone only to have them turn around and say it was all a big mistake and they're moving on.

Not that I think I'm about to fall in love with Josh. But you know what I mean.

So now I feel too awkward to text him. Just in case he thinks I like him. Did I mention to you that I'm thirteen years old? I might as well be, for all the emotional maturity I'm displaying. Interestingly, my realization that there might be other men out there who I like the look of who would be interested in me seems to make it much easier to get along with Robert. It's as if it takes the edge off my hating him. Makes me care less.

On Friday I got a message from Saskia asking if I wanted to meet up at our usual time on Saturday. '*Or are you and Robert still on your staycation?*' she asked accusingly. She was obviously desperate to hear the worst. I decided to let her sweat and sent her a short text. '*Can't do Sat. R wants us 2 spend last 2 days together! Next week?*'

I tried to picture her face when she read it. Imagined the agonies she was going through, thinking we'd had such a great time that Robert couldn't bear to be apart from me even for a second.

'*I might be coming up to the physio on Mon or Tues,*' she sent back. '*Coffee near there?*'

I decided not to point out to her that it was odd she didn't yet know when her appointment was, given they're apparently like gold dust. And that it was hard to believe she would be able to get one timed exactly to fit around my availability. She knew she was lying and so did I; we didn't need to acknowledge it. Monday is a Chas day so I agreed to meet her in the usual café in Highgate on Tuesday, at about quarter to three.

I decide it's time to step things up a gear and so, on Saturday morning (still on my 'course of massages'. You'd really think I'd be relaxed enough by now), Myra meets me in Oxford Street and we do something I haven't done in at least seven years. We buy nice clothes. Actually, strictly speaking, that's not true. I've bought the occasional pretty outfit but I've always gone for the big and shapeless variety. I have pitched a small but decorative marquee over myself and called it dressing up. Today my new thirteen-stone-something self is looking for clothes that fit. That flatter. Chas would be proud of me.

'Fucking hell,' Myra says when I try the first ensemble on in H & M. 'You've got a waist. Where the hell did that come from?'

'Chas,' I say, and she gives me a lascivious grin. Myra loves Chas. He came into the café one day (coincidentally, I hadn't told him I worked there) and she practically drooled when I introduced them. She likes that rippling-muscle look. Ever since then she's done that really annoying thing of raising her eyebrows at me whenever I mention his name, as if we're in a conspiracy of fancying him. She won't believe me when I tell her I don't so I just let her get on with it.

'And your bingo wings aren't flapping like they used to.'

'Gosh, Myra, you do know how to flatter a girl.'

'What? I'm just saying. Like mine do. Look.'

She lifts up an arm and wafts it back and forth. I do the same. We're creating such a breeze that the girl closest to me actually moves away.

'Mine still do, see.'

'Yes, but only when you make them. Mine do it all the time of their own accord.'

'This is why you made me get Chas, remember. It was your idea.'

'Traitor,' she says affectionately.

To be honest, I'm as astonished as she is when I look at myself in the mirror. It's not so much that my body has changed more than I think I'd noticed, it's that I feel comfortable with it. I don't want to smother myself in an outsized T-shirt any more.

I buy a cute gingham summer dress with a fitted top and no sleeves (no sleeves!) and an A-line skirt, some cut-off cargo pants and a couple of tops that actually fit me. In Topshop I add a short-sleeved cardigan and a floaty thing that's fitted around the bust.

And, for the first time in living memory, some dedicated sportswear. OK, so they're just another version of leggings, but they're sporty leggings. Not 'I've given up, take me outside and put me out of my misery' leggings. And they 'wick away sweat', whatever that means. So it's win-win.

Back home, I hide it all in Georgia's wardrobe. I'm not quite ready yet.

On Sunday I tell Robert I'm off to have my hair cut and he opts to hit the golf course. Several hours later I emerge with a half-head of highlights and a spray tan. I smell like a dog that's been wallowing in a weedy pond and, at the moment, I look as if I've been dipped in mahogany wood stain, but the girl – who has seen bits of me while I stood there in a paper thong, throwing shapes and trying to ignore the humiliation, that no one else has seen in years – tells me it will all look much more natural when I can wash it off later.

'Did you fall in a vat of gravy?' Robert says when he arrives home. I'm in my usual shapeless outfit and with my new shiny, bouncy hair tied back, but there's no disguising the fact that I'm a different colour from when I went out this morning.

'Oh, I decided to have a spray tan. Myra swears by them.'

He's not so interested that he questions me further, and that suits me just fine.

On Tuesday morning I blow-dry my hair and put on the gingham dress. I have to wear it with trainers because I'm still determined to walk everywhere but, actually, the combination looks quite cute, even if I say so myself.

Robert is just getting up as I'm about to leave the house. I swear he does a double take when he sees me.

'You look nice,' he says, possibly the greatest compliment he's paid me in years.

'Thanks,' I say casually. I want him to notice but I don't want him to think there's something afoot. 'Sorry if the sheets look like there's been a dirty protest in there. I thought I'd showered it all off.'

'I can change them.'

He doesn't say any more but I'm aware of him looking at me as I move around the kitchen.

All day long the regulars ooh and aah over me. I feel like a show pony having my fetlocks appraised. Or an avocado awaiting approval of its ripeness on the fruit and veg counter in Tesco. For some reason, it's deemed acceptable for our customers to touch my hair and grab at (albeit smaller these days) handfuls of flab on my upper arms while exclaiming about my transformation. It's flattering, but it's also crossing all sorts of boundaries I wouldn't usually allow people to cross.

Saskia is already there when I get there on Tuesday. I've walked all the way, and not even broken a sweat. I almost don't recognize her. Nine pounds is only nine pounds but, unfortunately for Saskia, eight of it seems to have gone on to her face.

'Hi! You look well,' I say as I accept the hug she gives me.

'Don't.' She grimaces. 'You, on the other hand, really do.'

She looks me up and down. I wonder if my transformation looks as radical to other people as hers does to me. From the way she can't take her eyes off me, I'm pretty sure that it does.

'What did you do to yourself? You look incredible.'

'Oh, you know. I've been trying to be good for once . . .'

'Well, it's obviously working. I feel wretched.'

Earlier, Josh texted me to tell me that the rest of the cast and crew's reaction to Saskia's ballooning up in size had been a joy to watch. She'd managed eleven pounds, by the way, he said. Not bad going in four weeks. She had already come crying to him that she felt they were all staring at her and talking about her behind her back. Which they probably were. It's called schadenfreude. Or karma, even. She's spent all these years treating them all like dirt and now they're revelling in her obvious misery.

'*I can't wait till the first ep. airs*,' he texted. '*I can see the headlines now!*'

Unfortunately, the first episode of the new series won't be broadcast for weeks, but it gave me a warm glow thinking about the reaction she'll get. One nasty comment on Twitter about the way she looks will probably send her over the edge. People slag off her acting all the time on there and she barely reacts, but I imagine one mention of her double chin would start a meltdown.

The truth is that she still looks gorgeous. And even Robert, with his obsession with appearances, is going to think so. But we've landed a big blow to her self-confidence. She's not going to be the same person.

'Think of the awards,' I say now, and laugh to show I'm joking.

'Yes, and think of the fright I'll look going up to collect them, haha! I've had a miserable couple of weeks, actually,' she says, and I can see that there are rings around her eyes like she hasn't been sleeping.

'Just because of the eating?' I say disingenuously. It's hard not to smile as I say it. I make my eyes wide. I'm worried.

'Oh, that and a few other things. I won't bore you.'

'No, go on. I'm always banging on to you about my problems . . .'

'No, it's nothing really. I just spent too much time on my own, I think. You know how that can drive you crazy . . .'

I don't actually.

'. . . Much more importantly, tell me how your – what did you call it? – staycation went.'

Here we go. My face lights up at the memory. 'It was fantastic. Better than going away even . . .'

I drone on about the things we did and the places we visited, as if that's what she really wants to hear about. It isn't. You know that look a dog has when you're holding a ball and they're waiting for you to throw it. That.

As soon as I pause for breath she's straight in there.

'How did you and Robert get along, though? That's the million-dollar question.'

Throw it. Throw the fucking ball.

I wish you could see her expression. Honestly, you'd laugh, and it's all I can do to stop myself in the moment.

I choose a face that I think says bliss.

'Great. Really great. Honestly, Saskia, he's like a different person. We just . . . I don't know, we just got on like we used to.'

Her face, by contrast, reads 'on the verge of throwing up'.

'Why do you think that is?'

I've thought about this, knowing she might ask. 'I don't know. I did wonder if it had got something to do with George being about to leave home and him thinking we needed to reconnect somehow, but I think, actually, it's deeper than that. Something's happened to make him fall back in love with me . . . I know that sounds stupid . . .'

Saskia looks around as if trying to locate the sick bucket.

'Gosh. No. It sounds like a fairy tale. Has he said anything?'

'Only . . . I can't actually say them because I'll feel stupid . . . but, yes, nice things. Lovely things.'

She puts a heap of sugar into her tea, something I've never seen her do before, and stirs it vigorously. The cup rattles she's so violent. People at other tables look around.

One woman double-takes as she realizes who exactly it is making such a racket. She reaches for her phone. I recognize the gleeful anticipation from the way people look at Robert just before they attack. In a second, she's out of her seat and on her way over. All passive-aggressive nervous hesitation.

'It is you!' she says, far too loudly. 'I wasn't sure. Oh my God, I'm such a fan. I know you must hate this, when you're just trying to have coffee with your friend, but if my daughter —'

Saskia cuts her off. 'Can't you see I'm trying to have a private conversation?'

She practically shouts it, and everyone in the place turns around. I have never, in all the times I've met her, seen Saskia be anything other than gracious with her fans. She once said to me that a bit of loss of privacy was the price she had to be prepared to pay, because if it wasn't for the fans she would be out of a job. I smile at the waiting woman nervously but she's not the slightest bit interested in me.

'Wow. No need to be so rude,' she says.

I decide to step in and save Saskia from herself. This time. Only because I'm worried that if she gets into a row someone might video it and put it on YouTube, and I wouldn't want Robert to see us together. And besides, she'll owe me.

'Saskia just had some very bad news,' I say in my softest voice. I put my hand over Saskia's to show solidarity. 'Sorry. It's literally just happened, so . . .'

The woman's face drops. 'Oh my God, that's awful. I'm the one who should be sorry, barging in . . .'

'You weren't to know.'

I imagine she's wondering if it would be OK to still ask for the selfie she came for. It wouldn't surprise me. Luckily, at that moment, a tear rolls down Saskia's cheek. It must be real because I've heard from Robert before that they have to fake her tears with glycerine if she's ever called upon to cry on the show. Robert himself has a whole repertoire of angry/regretful/heartbroken weeping he can call up in a moment if required. He's very proud of this.

'I'll leave you alone,' the woman says, backing away now. 'I hope everything will be OK.'

I give her a little shake of my head as if to say, 'Too late for that,' just to make sure she really does leave.

'Are you OK?' I say to Saskia once the coast is clear.

She nods her head, wipes the tear away. Gives me a watery smile.

'I'm good, aren't I? I knew that'd scare her away,' she says unconvincingly.

'How's Josh?' I ask out of nowhere.

She waves a hand dismissively. 'Oh, you know.'

I'm surprised. Usually, she's at such pains to tell me how deliriously happy her marriage is.

'Is everything OK?'

'Yes! Gosh, yes, it's fine,' she says, as if she's just remembered that that's the picture she's supposed to present to me, of all people. 'It's just hard, you know, that we can never get time off together, that's all.'

I want to ask what his mood is like. If she's noticed a change in him. If kissing me has left its mark. Obviously, I don't.

'For fuck's sake'.

Robert has returned from his meeting with Josh. Of course, I've already had Josh on the phone so I know it didn't go well. Or, actually, it did, depending on who you're rooting for.

It was the first time we'd spoken since our encounter in the park. When he'd texted me to ask if I was free to talk I'd almost said no because I was so worried it might be awkward. Thankfully, the grown-up me had won out because, in fact, Josh was completely Josh-like. Open, friendly, no hint of an edge. It cleared the air without us having to sit down and clear the air.

I filled him in on my latest meeting with Saskia. 'She's rattled,' I said, and he laughed.

Robert slams his keys on the table. 'They might as well make me a fucking kiddy fiddler.'

'Hardly,' I say. 'Then you really wouldn't be able to go out in public.'

We're standing in the hallway. Robert had barely got through the door before he blurted out his news. Now he stomps off into the kitchen, and I follow. Of course, I hadn't thought through that I'd have to deal with his bad mood.

'Hargreaves would never rip anyone off, let alone the elderly.'

'When did the writers ever worry about what was real?' I switch on the kettle and reach for the coffee jar.

'He did that fundraiser, do you remember, when old Mr Watkins was going to lose his home. And he paid Mary Simmons over the odds for all her old tat because he felt sorry for her after her husband died. I've built that whole bloody character on knowing that he had a heart of gold.'

I almost laugh. I know that Robert takes his acting seriously, but really. To say Hargreaves is two-dimensional would be pushing it. Although, to be fair, if he is, up to this point, one of those dimensions has probably been 'heart of gold', the other being 'a man'.

He's slumped on one of the kitchen chairs. I go over and put my hand on his shoulder in sympathy.

'Is it that bad? It might be a good story. You're always saying there's nothing to get your teeth into.'

'You know what my fan base is. Old ladies love me. And now I'm going to be a villain. They'll be baying for my blood. There'll be a petition to have Hargreaves sent to prison and me written out before you know it.'

'Don't be silly.'

'I should complain to the big bosses. That Josh Carpenter hasn't got a clue. He's destroying the show.'

'Is this his decision then?'

'Him and the writers. Honestly, they couldn't organize a piss-up in a brewery.'

I sit down next to him, the voice of reason.

'It might be better not to rock the boat. Just see how it pans out for a while.'

'This is the end of my character, that's the bottom line. One way or another, I'll get axed next year.'

'Well, if you do, you do. Go out with a bang, that's what I say.'

He thumps his fist on the table. 'And what then?'

'You've always known it wasn't forever. There's no such thing as job security in acting.'

He worries at his beard like it's got fleas.

'They're destroying the show. They've given Saskia some bloody storyline where she has to walk around looking like a beached whale because she can't have kids or something. I mean, what kind of story is that? They had her fattening herself up in the break. Obviously, I'm not supposed to say anything so . . .'

'What?' I say lightly. 'I shouldn't go calling up *OK!* magazine?'

'You know what I mean.'

'God, I bet she hates that. I get the impression she's one of those people who are obsessed with how they look. How much weight can you put on in a month? Maybe I won't even recognize her when I see her again.'

He makes a grunting noise that could mean anything.

'Imagine the conversation between her and Josh when he had to persuade her into that.' I laugh. 'He must be a brave man.'

'He's a fucking idiot,' Robert spits, and I remember I'm supposed to be being supportive.

'He certainly sounds like he is. Don't worry too much, they'll probably end up sacking him.'

Later, I text Josh. '*That went well then.*'

He favours me with a swift reply. '*Classic. I wish you could have been there.*'

'*Me too,*' I send back, and, for the briefest moment, I find myself wishing I could be sharing this triumph with Josh face to face. An image of his intense brown eyes jumps into my head. I have no idea where that came from.

15

Saskia and I are sitting in the sun. Or, at least, we're sitting in the heat. The sun is making only an occasional appearance. The weather has turned heavy and oppressive. People walk around sweating, as if they've just got out of the shower. There's the tiniest of breezes from the river, though, and we're making the most of it.

She called me while I was at work this morning. She had a day off, she told me (Robert was filming solidly all day. A sequence of scenes in Farmer Giles' barn, all of the animals conveniently out in the pasture, thus saving the production money. They would dub the odd moo and baaa on later) and she was bored. Did I fancy meeting up?

So I've trekked all the way down to Richmond to meet her at one of the cafés near the bridge. That's the thing about Saskia. She has some kind of Jedi power that means you end up agreeing to spend hours schlepping halfway across London to somewhere that's two minutes from her home, even though she's the one who suddenly wants to meet up out of nowhere. She manages to make everything about her.

There's something on her mind, I can tell. We've ordered drinks – Diet Coke for me, sugary version for her – and we're waiting for them to arrive, sitting silently, looking out at the ducks and the boats. Saskia not talking is unusual enough in itself. But there's something shifty about her. Something I can't put my finger on.

'So, how's things?' I say, stuck for anything more interesting.

'Oh . . . you know . . . fine. Still eating for England blah blah.'

'Josh OK?'

'Yep.'

She turns back to look at the river. The suspense is killing me. I'm about to try and engage her in conversation again when she looks right at me, a worried expression on her face.

'Paula, can I? . . . I have to tell you something.'

I feel my heart start pounding. Is she going to tell me she's sleeping with my husband?

'OK . . .'

'It's about Robert. He's . . . oh God, please forgive me for telling you . . .'

Just get on with it, I want to scream. I know anyway.

'What? Go on.'

'He's . . . he's having an affair.'

I wait for her to say 'with me', but she doesn't. She just sits there and looks at me, all concern.

'I don't understand.'

'I'm so sorry to be the one to break it to you, but I've come to really like you and I just couldn't live with myself knowing and not telling you . . .'

Alarms bells are going off in my head. My brain is whirring, trying to take in what she's saying.

'Who with?'

This is it. This is where she'll confess it's her. She's just building herself up for it.

She breathes in slowly.

'Samantha.'

I look at her, clueless.

'Samantha,' she repeats. 'The girl who plays Marilyn.'

16

I'm stunned into silence, my mouth hanging open. Could I have got this so wrong?

'Samantha?'

Saskia nods. 'It's been . . . I've known for a while.'

I think about the way she always questions me about how things are with Robert. Could that be because she was trying to gauge if I knew? To work out if she should say something or not?

'How did you find out?'

She's looking anywhere but at me. 'I walked in on them once.'

I actually hear myself gasp.

'I'd gone to her dressing room to borrow something, I can't remember what. The lock is broken on hers so it's always unlocked – ever since that actor who played Ryan, do you remember him? Anyway, he used to be in there and he locked himself in once and wouldn't come out. They had to break the door down. 'Roid rage it was, apparently. He didn't get those muscles from just anywhere . . .'

I wait, willing her to get back to the point. She must pick up on my impatience because she shuts up about Ryan and his steroid habit.

'Anyway, there they were on the sofa. It must have been

early days, I think, because they were taking such a risk. I suppose most people would knock but it didn't even occur to me.'

'Were they actually . . .'

'Pretty much. Anyway, I backed straight out again and they didn't see me. But a few weeks later he was being really annoying at a party – you know how pompous he can get? So I told him what I'd seen, just to burst his bubble. He denied it at first but he'd had a few drinks and eventually he admitted it was true. I think he regretted it immediately because he begged me not to repeat what he'd said to anyone else. And, of course, I didn't. And then you and I became friends . . .'

'You knew when I first met you?'

She nods. 'I did. I'm sorry. I wanted to say something to you – I was cheated on in my first marriage and I know how awful it is to find out you've been completely deluded – but I didn't think it was any of my business. And, besides, I'd promised Robert. But then you started saying how well things were going and how he seemed to be a changed man and it started to niggle away at me. Because it's still going on.'

That doesn't explain the text message, though. I try to recall exactly what it said.

As if she can read my mind, Saskia says, 'I even covered for him once. When you phoned. Do you remember? He'd left his phone in the green room and when I saw your name I answered because I was afraid if anyone else spoke to you they would go looking for him in his dressing room. I knew they were in there together.'

It all comes back to me. *Jesus! That was too close for comfort last night! WAY too risky! Hope Paula bought it!!! Didn't feel comfortable having to lie to her face! Love you xxx'*

It's possible. The 'Love you' is a bit over the top, but Saskia is the kind of person who blurts out endearments to waitresses she's known for five seconds. They don't mean anything to her.

It doesn't make sense to me why Robert would confide in her though. He's always telling me they don't get on. So much so that I thought it was a smokescreen.

'Why would he tell you? It doesn't make any sense.'

She shrugs. 'I think — and forgive me if this sounds crass — I think he wanted to make a point that he was attractive to a woman like her. I mean, you've seen Samantha — younger, you know. Beautiful. I think he was showing off. He really was quite drunk.'

'Shit,' I say, and Saskia, thinking I'm upset because I've just found out my husband is seeing someone else, puts her hand over mine.

'You deserve much better,' she says.

I can't tell her that what I'm really upset about is that I just kissed her husband.

Her husband, who wouldn't even have considered kissing me if I hadn't just persuaded him that his wife was having an affair.

I can hardly look at her. I make an excuse about having to get home. I need to process what's going on.

'The only thing I'd ask,' she says as we say goodbye, 'is that you don't let him find out it came from me. He could make my life a misery at work.'

'Of course not,' I say. 'I'm not just going to storm straight home and accuse him. Not until I can work out a way I could plausibly have found out. I'd never drop you in it.'

'I really am sorry, Paula,' she says, for the hundredth time. 'I agonized about whether it was the right thing to do or not.'

'It was. Stop worrying. It's much better that I know.'

She hugs me and I hug her back, feeling like the worst person in the world.

All the way home, I toss it around in my head. Was I so convinced that I was right about Robert and Saskia that I twisted the evidence to fit the prosecution's thesis? I try to look at it rationally.

— If she wasn't trying to probe into the status of our marriage, why did she meet up with me in the first place and then keep on meeting up with me?

Maybe she genuinely liked me? Maybe it's hard for her to make new friends because of who she is, so she seized on the opportunity when it came along?

— If they weren't having an affair, why would Robert reply to her message telling her they shouldn't text?

Because he was afraid she would say something about Samantha and I would see it? Because he was worried about her accidentally giving stuff away? Because he can't stand her and it was an easy way to get her off his back?

— If they weren't meeting up, why were they out at the same times? Why did their moods seem to mirror each other's?

Coincidence. That's all I can think of. That and the fact that I was so keen to see the signs you would probably have read anything into anything so long as it supported your theory.

When I look at it like this, there's nothing concrete. Nothing that would convict her. Nothing that would justify me running to her husband and announcing that she was cheating on him. Nothing that would justify me allowing him to think his marriage was over.

And, of course, it's all too obvious to me now that there's more than one woman in Robert's life whose name begins with an S.

Shit. By the time I reach home I've convinced myself I'm the most loathsome human ever. When I see Robert I almost start offering up apologies for ever doubting him, until I remember he's just as guilty as he ever was. It's only Saskia I should apologise to.

Saskia and Josh.

I can't even think about what I'm going to say to Josh yet. He's going to hate me, and rightly so. Not only have I sown a huge seed of doubt about his marriage, I've also encouraged him to do things that could jeopardize his career. I think about how funny I thought we were coming up with Saskia's weight-gain storyline and I feel sick. What seemed like karma now strikes me as nasty, petty and bitchy, all qualities I despise. Terrifying though the thought is, I have to put this right as soon as I can.

Robert is droning on about work but I'm only half listening. I'm wondering whether it's too late for Saskia's character to suddenly conceive. The weight gain could be explained by her being pregnant. They could stuff padding of ever-increasing proportions up her dress and the real Saskia could lose the pounds that I know are making her so unhappy. I can suggest it to Josh once he's got over what I have to tell him. If he ever does.

Something Robert is saying jolts me back to reality.

'What did you just say? Sorry, I was miles away.'

'I was saying we got the next batch of scripts. And now they've got Hargreaves having a fling with Marilyn! I mean, I'm not saying it couldn't happen, but he's always been devoted to Melody. It's as if they have no idea who he is any more.'

Oh crap, I'd forgotten about that. Our plan to put Saskia's nose out of joint. I don't imagine for a second that Robert is really upset about this storyline. I imagine it's all his Christmases come at once.

'Isn't she, like, twenty-two?' I can't help myself. Even though I'm preoccupied with the mess I've created, I can't let him get away with that.

'Sorry?'

'What's her name? The actress who plays Marilyn. Isn't she really young?'

'Samantha? About that, I don't know. Why?'

'Because you said it could happen. Her and Hargreaves. And it just seems really unlikely to me, that's all. It's not as if he's meant to be stinking rich or anything. I mean, he's in his forties and she's twenty-two . . .'

'He's forty-one,' he interjects and, for the first time this afternoon, I almost laugh.

'Whatever. He's way too old for her. It's tacky.'

'It's not that it's tacky. Plenty of young women find older men attractive. It's just that Hargreaves wouldn't do it.'

'Trust me, it's tacky. He'll look like a dirty old perv.'

'Well, that's not making me feel any better, thanks.'

'I'm just agreeing with you. It's a terrible idea. If the old ladies don't hate you for becoming a conman, they're going to hate you for chasing after a woman young enough to be your daughter.'

'Him, not me.'

'Of course, that's what I meant. But we all know they won't see it that way.'

'For Christ's sake, Paula. I'm worried about this enough already. You're not helping.'

I can tell that, deep down, even though he's worried about the reaction this story will get from the public, he's a bit proud of this one. The world will see that Robert Westmore aka Hargreaves is still attractive enough that a gorgeous young woman finds him irresistible. And sadly, that does seem to have come true in real life. Although I'm sure that the fact that this is probably Samantha's first job and Robert has been a well-known face for a few years must have helped. He's a big fish in a medium-sized, banal, mainstream pond and I imagine she found that impressive.

'Why don't you talk to Josh if it's really bothering you?' I say, knowing what the response will be.

Robert huffs.

'What's the point?'

I shrug. 'At least you'd know you tried, I suppose.'

Later in the evening, to try to take my mind off Josh, I Google Samantha. I know that I have to do the grown-up thing and tell him the whole truth as soon as I'm able.

I keep thinking about him and Saskia at home and her not understanding why he's changed towards her. Why their happy, near-perfect marriage seems to have suddenly taken a turn for the worse. I've managed to convince myself this isn't something I can do over the phone and I've sent him a text saying we need to meet up urgently. I got a reply within minutes:

'*Of course. When? X*'

I try not to think what he thinks I want. A repeat performance. That I've changed my mind and I'm happy to dive headfirst into a relationship with him and to hell with keeping the moral high ground?

We make a plan to see each other tomorrow. I have to push it. He claims a busy schedule (which I don't doubt for a second) and I reply offering to meet him anywhere (apart from the studio, obviously) any time (sorry, Myra). I get a couple of concerned messages back – '*Everything OK??*', that kind of thing. I try to reassure him as best I can without getting into specifics. Because everything is most definitely not OK.

To try to distract myself, I decide to go for a run. An actual, legitimate run, not a run disguised as a chase after a bus. When I announce my intentions to Robert, dressed in my new, form-fitting, sweat-wicking sportswear, I notice his eyes flicking up and down. I'd forgotten he's never seen me like this. I wait for the sarcastic 'What? You?'

'Have you lost even more weight?' he says and, actually, there's no hint of sarcasm.

There's no point me denying it. 'I think so. I've been trying.'

'You definitely have. Are you working out?'

For some reason, I find this embarrassing to admit to. 'Kind of.'

'Blimey. What? Running?'

'Walking, mostly. Weights. I joined a gym . . .'

'Ha! What's brought this on?'

I can feel myself going red.

'I just thought I should get fit, that's all.'

He jumps up. 'I'll come with you. I haven't been for a run for ages.'

I know that this is good, him wanting us to do something together – they say that the couple who work out together stay together, which is obviously not what I want, but I want him to want it, if you know what I mean – but it's the last thing I need. I need a bit of space to clear my head. I need time to work out how I'm going to explain myself to Josh. 'I don't really run. More just walk and then trot the odd bit. You'll be frustrated.'

'I can always leave you to it and meet you back here. I'll get changed.'

I can hardly refuse. I tell myself to make the most of it, to use it as a bonding exercise. The fact that Robert isn't seeing who I thought he was seeing doesn't change anything. I still need to focus on convincing him it's me he loves. And this is progress, there's no denying it. Huge progress.

'OK. Don't be pissed off with me if I conk out, though.'

For the first time ever, I start running when I leave the front door and I don't stop until I reach home again. Partly because I want to get it over with, but mostly because it feels good. My body feels strong. It's impossible to dwell on negative thoughts when you're doing something so physical. Despite Robert puffing along beside me, I'm able to forget everything that's going on and just concentrate on putting one foot in front of the other.

After a while I notice that Robert is struggling to keep up. I slow my pace to let him catch me up.

'What have you done with my wife?' he says, as he stops and tries to catch his breath.

I laugh, despite everything. 'Come on. No stopping.'

Now I'm fresh out of the shower and sitting in the bedroom with my laptop. The exercise-induced euphoria has worn off and I've come crashing back to earth with a thud.

'Samantha Smith' brings up a whole slew of results, but I head straight for Wikipedia. It's a short entry, she hasn't been in the public eye for very long. Samantha, it turns out, is an ancient twenty-three, born in Kent. No mention of any significant other, either now or in her past. *Farmer Giles* is her first professional job.

I look at a few photos just to pass the time. One of them is a cast picture from last year. Robert and Samantha are side by side. Her all fresh-faced and eager-looking, the new sexpot on the block. Him avuncular, genial in character. It's impossible to imagine the two of them getting it on either on the show or in real life. Saskia is on the other side of Samantha, dressed in one of Melody's trademark riding outfits. I'm hit with a pang of guilt so strong it takes my breath away. I shut the laptop down. I need to find a way to put things right.

17

'What a fucking mess.'

I've had to fill Myra in on the Samantha-not-Saskia story because I overheard her telling one customer that she had it on good authority that Saskia Sherbourne was a bit of a slut and not a very nice one at that.

'For fuck's sake,' she says when I tell her. 'I've worn myself out trying to make sure everyone knows what a bitch she is.'

'Well, she isn't. You'll have to go around saying nice things now.'

'Not in my nature,' Myra says. 'And you're definitely sure about this Samantha? I'm not going to waste my precious time slagging her off to anyone who'll listen, only to find out she's actually Mother Teresa's more saintly sister.'

'Saskia walked in on them.'

Myra pulls a face like a toddler who's been conned into eating Brussels sprouts. 'Grim. It makes it seem like it wasn't so bad when we thought it was Saskia. At least she was age-appropriate.'

Thank God I never confided in Myra or anyone else about my feelings for Josh. I don't think I could stand being labelled a potential home-wrecker on top of everything else.

'Hold on. Didn't you snog her husband?'

Shit, I forgot. I did tell her, after a couple of glasses of wine one night, and then swore her to secrecy.

'Shhh! I did, but only because I thought it was all over between him and Saskia. I feel awful about it.'

Myra shrugs. 'It was only a kiss. It was, wasn't it?'

'Of course! But that's bad enough. Imagine how she'd feel . . .'

'So that's it for you and him? All over.'

'Definitely all over. Not that anything had even really started. He's going to hate me now, anyway.'

I've been trying not to think about Josh. I would hate me if I was him. All I can do is hope that him and Saskia come out the other end OK and that, eventually, he'll realize that nothing I ever did was malicious.

'It was too soon, anyway. You need to sort yourself out before you go getting in a relationship with anyone.'

'Exactly,' I say, and I mean it. 'I need to remember what I'm supposed to be doing here.'

'I mean, you were so convinced it was her.'

'Don't rub it in. I know.'

'Oh shit.' She suddenly walks over to a customer, a semi-regular whose name I don't know.

'Do you mind if I have a look at that?'

She practically snatches a newspaper out of his hand before he can say no. I catch a glimpse of the front page. A very unflattering picture of Saskia, looking miserable and stuffing in what looks like a cake at the catering truck, covers most of it. I'm distracted for a moment by the fact that Josh is beside her, paper cup in his hand. The head-line screams out: 'SUPERSIZED SADSKIA.'

'Give me that.'

Myra hands it over. It promises more pictures on page seven, so I flip the pages over.

Inside there's another grainy photo, this time shot from low down to accentuate the changed contours of her jaw. And another showing a tiny excuse for a stomach curving under her T-shirt. Underneath, they debate whether or not she might be pregnant, or whether she just ate a big lunch.

Bizarrely, over the years, I've popped up in the tabloids occasionally too. It's unavoidable when your husband is a TV star. In the early days of *Farmer Giles*, on Robert's arm at some do or other, more recently reluctantly hovering in the background of a paparazzi shot, midway through tugging my T-shirt down. Of course, they never comment on me except to say 'his wife of many years' or 'his long-term partner'. Anything that implies I wouldn't have been the kind of woman he'd have gone for if he'd been famous when he met me. I hate it.

On this occasion, someone on the production with either a grudge or the need for a bit of fast cash has obviously tipped off the papers. I wonder if Saskia has seen it. I'm sure whoever did it has made sure she has. It must be killing her.

I hand the paper back. 'Thanks.'

'That's nasty,' Myra says when I rejoin her by the till. 'Poor cow. Although "Sadskia" is quite inspired. I always thought I should get a job writing headlines for the tabloids.'

I feel wretched. A couple of days ago, I would have celebrated. Revelled in imagining her upset. 'This is all my fault.'

'Don't beat yourself up, there's no point.'

*

We're in a greasy spoon in Acton. Close to the studio but not so close that one of the cast or crew might walk past when they're on their lunch break. He leans in to hug me, burying his face in my hair, when I arrive late, having got lost on my way from the tube, and I feel myself stiffen. There's an anxious, nervous energy about him that I assume is because he's worried about what I have to say to him that's so urgent, but then he produces the tabloid from his bag and puts it on the table with a flourish.

'Did you see this?'

Another tiny alarm bell starts to ring in my head.

'Yes. It's . . . um . . . a bit harsh.'

'She's devastated,' he says, and not in a way that makes it sound like that's a bad thing.

Of course. How could I not have realized? After the Wikipedia alteration, it should have been obvious. 'Did you . . . ?'

He nods. 'Anonymously, of course.' He sits back and looks at me expectantly, waiting for praise.

'Shit, Josh.'

'What? This is perfect. Her confidence is shattered. Plus, Robert is going to look at her in a whole other way after this.'

I try to get the words to come out of my mouth. My carefully prepared speech has gone out of my head. Josh puts a hand over mine.

'I always used to think getting revenge was pathetic, that it made you as bad as the person you were punishing. I don't think I'd realized how cathartic it was. How it could make you feel like you were the one in control.'

It's true, he's looking happier than I've ever seen him. I swap our hands over. Squeeze his in mine.

'I have to tell you something. It's not good.'

He looks so concerned for me that I have to look away or I'll lose my resolve.

'What's going on?'

'There's no way of saying this that won't sound awful. I've fucked up. Really fucked up . . .'

'Paula . . . ?'

I shake my head. 'Just let me say it. And I want you to know I'm so, so sorry. It was obviously just a huge mistake. It . . . I'm just going to come out with it. Don't hate me.'

I'm still clinging on to his hand and massaging it like a stress ball. I feel sick. Breathe deeply to try to calm my stomach.

'It's not Saskia that Robert's having an affair with. It's Samantha.'

For a moment he looks sympathetic. Then the realization of what my words mean for him starts to filter in. He tugs his hand away.

'You are kidding, right?'

I feel tears prick up in my eyes and blink them away. 'No. Not kidding. I jumped to the wrong conclusion. I'm so sorry, Josh.'

'You convinced me my wife was being unfaithful because you "jumped to the wrong conclusion"? What the fuck?'

He puts his elbows on the table, runs his hands over his stubbly head.

'I'm so sorry,' I say again. It's all I've got. 'It was a huge mistake. I put two and two together and got five.'

I tell him what Saskia had told me about Samantha. How she was just trying to be a good friend.

'Oh my God!' he says, and it comes out like a howl. Luckily, the café is half empty. Josh picks up the newspaper and thrusts it at me. 'This. This is all my fault.'

'They would have commented on it anyway at some point. Don't blame yourself.'

'I'm not,' he says, in a vicious tone I've never heard from him before. 'I blame you.'

'I didn't ask you to leak a story to the papers.' I know as soon as I say it that it's the wrong thing to say.

'No, you just asked me to help you ruin her and Robert's lives. You asked me to help you with your stupid plan to make yourself feel better.'

I know it's all my fault but I feel as if I have to defend myself. 'Well, maybe that's a good thing because, otherwise, you would have gone straight to Saskia and confronted her.'

'Yes, and then she would have convinced me that you were talking a crock of shit and I would have felt like a stupid jealous husband for a while but it would all have blown over. I wouldn't have jeopardized my job and my – what turns out to be happy – marriage. I wouldn't have made my wife feel belittled and unconfident and worthless.'

'I don't know what to say. I'm sorry. I feel like a complete fucking bitch, if that helps.'

He stands up, snatches the newspaper from the table. 'It doesn't.'

18

Of course, I don't hear from Josh and I don't try to contact him. I find myself thinking about him and Saskia all the time, though, and I'm relieved when I get a text from her asking if I'm OK. It takes me a moment to remember that she thinks I'm still dealing with the shock news of Robert's affair.

'I'm fine thx. How are you, more to the point?'

I don't get a reply back for a while, presumably because she's needed on set. Then:

'You've seen the papers then.'

'Absolutely shitty' I send back. *'Don't let it get to you.'*

'Too late.'

She asks if I want to do our Saturday usual and I accept gratefully. I'm desperate to hear what, if anything, has changed since I dropped my bombshell on Josh. A part of me wonders whether he's told her everything, to explain why he's been being cold towards her, but I don't think he'd ever want her to know about the revenge he had planned. I don't think she'd find that very easy to forgive.

To try to keep my mind occupied till then, I go running every day. I still can't go far but I increase it by a little every time. Back home, I'm all bags of ice and hot compresses and ibuprofen for my aching joints. Chas, impressed by my sudden commitment (I list my achievements to him every session, like a child trying to impress their parents with what they've done at school), decides to get the calipers out again and declares me to be down another six pounds and two fat percentages. I beam with pride like the teacher's pet.

Saskia just wants to talk about me when she emerges with her post-Bikram glow. I'm sitting in our usual spot and the waitress, with whom I am now on first-name terms (Monika, Polish student teacher, lives in Wembley, traumatized by the prospect of Brexit, English twice as good as mine), has already brought me a giant skinny latte without me even having to ask. As Saskia sits down another appears, along with two menus. I'm not sure either of us is going to be in the mood to eat.

'I've been thinking about you constantly since I last saw you. I assumed you hadn't said anything to Robert because he seems to be his usual self at work. How are you coping? Are you feeling wretched? I'm sure you must be . . .'

Saskia always does this, asks a question and then doesn't give you space to answer it. I've started to find it quite endearing. Restful. I don't have to think about how to formulate an answer, I can just let her carry on till she runs out of steam. It doesn't feel as if it's going to happen any time soon.

'. . . I still can't decide if I did the right thing or not telling you. But I couldn't look at one of my closest friends and know I knew something bad about them that they didn't know . . .'

I'm touched by the fact she's called me one of her closest friends. It had never really occurred to me that she might view me that way, I was so sure she had a hidden agenda. Now it occurs to me that I've never really heard her talk about any girlfriends. I get the feeling that, for all her success, Saskia is lonely.

I put her out of her misery. 'You did. You definitely did.'

'So have you decided what you're going to do?'

I shrug. 'Nothing at the moment.'

She looks at me as if I've lost my mind. 'You're just going to let him get away with it?'

Even though I've grown to like Saskia, I'm not about to tell her my plan to punish Robert.

'No. But I'm not going to just steam straight in and accuse him. He'd just deny it, and then where would we be?'

'I'd kick him out, if it was me. Actually, I'd cut his balls off first, then I'd kick him out.'

'It's not that easy . . . there's Georgia . . .'

'Who's a grown woman . . .' she interrupts me.

'Nearly,' I say. 'She's home this week and I want her to be able to enjoy it. It's probably the last summer ever when she won't have any responsibilities. I don't want her having to deal with this.'

'I have no idea how you have so much self-restraint,' Saskia says. I can't tell her that I wouldn't if I hadn't already decided it was over with Robert. If I cared.

'There's no rush. It makes more sense for me to think before I act, anyway. What's that saying? "Revenge is a dish best served cold."'

'Just don't let him get away with it. You deserve so much better.'

She wouldn't think so if she knew what I've been doing. How I've been scheming. I bury the urge to confess.

'Thank you. I really do appreciate your advice, by the way.'

Saskia takes a sip of her latte. 'Do you remember how exciting everything was at Georgia's age?'

'Just about. I don't think it was as stressful then as it is now, though. Can you imagine having all your mistakes up there on social media for the whole world to see?'

'Haha! All your friends posting photos that would hang around forever. I mean, I had braces, glasses, acne, you name it. At least newspapers are tomorrow's chip paper, I suppose. Do they still wrap chips in newspaper? It seems so unhygienic.'

I laugh fondly. Trust Saskia to bring it back to looks. She can't help herself.

'Newspapers are all online now, though, aren't they?' she says. 'Those Sadskia pictures will be doing the rounds for the rest of my life.'

We sit there in contemplative silence for a moment. Then I can't help myself.

'What's Samantha like?' I know I shouldn't care but the words are out before I have a chance to remind myself of that.

'Don't even waste your energy thinking about her.'

'I mean, beautiful, obviously . . .'

Saskia huffs. 'She has youth on her side, that's all. She'll look as rough as anything when she gets to our age, you'll see.'

I suddenly remember Saskia's Wikipedia page. I wonder if Josh has changed it back, if Saskia ever even saw it.

'I doubt he's thinking he'll still be with her when she's our age. Or if he is, he'll be so old by then he'll think forty is positively youthful. What's she like as a person, though?'

It's not that I'm planning on getting involved with Samantha – I've learned enough from my lesson with Saskia to keep my distance – but I have to poke the scab. And, anyway, any intel might be useful. Maybe Robert's fallen for her because of her love of knitting and I can take a crash course.

Saskia ponders. I can tell there's no love lost between them but it wouldn't be like her to be out-and-out bitchy, although, to be fair, the line about Samantha's looks not lasting the test of time was a bit near the mark.

'She's ambitious,' she says. 'And she has that thing where she thinks she's invincible. We were all like it at that age, I suppose.'

'I certainly was,' I say.

I'm about to launch into a rant about the pressure on today's young people to succeed when Monika, thankfully, saves me from myself to ask if we've decided what we want to eat.

'Tuna Niçoise, dressing on the side,' Saskia says, and I wonder if she's forgotten she's meant to be calorie-loading.

'Aren't you meant to have a side of fries with that?' I say as soon as Monika leaves.

Saskia gives me one of her big smiles. 'Josh says I can stop. He said they're pulling back on the story a bit because they were worried Melody was going to get a bit dull if she just moped about the place. Now . . .' She looks around to see if anyone is eavesdropping, as they so often are whenever I go anywhere with either her or Robert. '. . . Obviously, it's top secret. Don't even say anything to Robert, because I don't know if they've told him yet.'

'Of course not.' I'm curious to hear what Josh has managed to pull off.

'Well, Melody is still fed up because she can't give Hargreaves the kids he so desperately wants blah blah, and everyone thinks the weight gain is because she's depressed but . . .' She takes a big, dramatic pause and I hear a drum roll in my head. '. . . then it turns out she's pregnant. The doctors have got it all wrong. So I can just wear one of those prosthetic tummies. I don't have to get any bigger!'

'Wow. Didn't they tell her categorically at the end of the last series that she didn't have all the right equipment to conceive?'

Saskia flaps her hand dismissively. 'Details.'

'Well, I'm pleased for you. That'll show the papers.'

'Exactly.' she laughs. 'Haha! I know I'm shallow, but you try having your double chin up there on show for everyone to laugh at.'

'Story of my life,' I say, smiling.

'Stop that. You're looking amazing. You always did.'

'Thank you. That's a nice thing to say.'

She leans forward on her elbows. 'So, tell me more about how you're going to stick it to Robert.'

Saskia and Josh, it seems, have come out unscathed. I don't know this for certain, obviously, but from what I can tell it looks this way. I'm glad. That's an understatement. I'm delighted, relieved and a little bit sad at the same time. I find myself thinking about the moment Josh kissed me and, although my overwhelming feeling is of guilt, I still get a jolt of pleasure when I allow myself to indulge in the fantasy unchecked. And then a feeling of regret that it can never go any further. Not even that, but we can't even be friends any more.

But Saskia, I tell myself, is what matters. I almost ruined her life. Deliberately. It doesn't bear thinking about. Even though she has no idea, I need to do everything I can to make it up to her, to make sure she's happy.

I need to be a good friend.

PART TWO

19

Saskia

Strike a match. Light the touchpaper. Sit back.

Although, to be honest, I'm a bit disappointed she's not going to storm in and confront him straightaway. That's what I was expecting to happen. What I was hoping for. Who knew she would be so calculated? I didn't think she had it in her.

That's the thing about Paula. She has hidden depths. When I first met her I thought she was a bit passive, a bit wet. She struck me as the kind of woman who would doggedly wait it out while her husband screwed around and then be there like a doormat when he decided to come home again.

Except, of course, Robbie wasn't meant to be going home again. He was meant to be moving in with me once the coast was clear. And by 'coast', I mean Georgia, and by 'clear', I mean she'd left home and gone off to college or wherever she's going. You know what I mean. I never was any good at metaphors. Or is that a simile? Anyway, you get my drift. Once Georgia had safely left the nest, unscathed by parental drama, Robert was planning to leave Paula, I was planning to leave Josh and we were going to set up home together.

That was the plan anyway.

Until, that is, he told me it was over a couple of weeks ago. Just like that. Out of nowhere. It was just before their stupid 'staycation', as Paula insisted on calling it. The day before, in fact. We were at my house. Robbie always got a thrill out of being in Josh's bed. He hates Josh. I, despite everything, do not. Joshie is a thoroughly decent man. He's kind, he's sweet, he loves me. He's good-looking, there's no doubt about that. He's successful in his own way. He's just not very . . . exciting. He's safe. And, at one point in my life, I thought that safe was what I wanted. Now I know better.

Anyway, Robbie and I were lying in bed in the middle of the day. I'll admit I was a bit unsettled. All that talk from Paula about how attentive Robbie was suddenly being. All the hints about how he couldn't keep his hands off her. It made me feel sick to my stomach but I couldn't stop pressing her for details. I had to know the worst.

That's what led to me making friends with her in the first place, if truth be told. I really had no interest in meeting up with some strange woman who I'd only ever spoken to because she spilt her champagne down me, except that I realized as soon as she suggested it that it was a golden opportunity to get an insight into Robbie's life. He's always been very closed about revealing personal things.

Back to the point – we're lying in bed. Post-coital, just so you can picture it. Notice he got one last hurrah in before dumping me by the way, haha! I was asking him about something, I can't even remember exactly what. But I know it had to do with him and Paula – something stupid and humiliating that I should have kept to myself, like when did he last sleep with her and who initiated it – when he suddenly sat up. He looked straight at me and I knew something wasn't right.

'Sas, we can't keep doing this.'

I genuinely didn't know what he meant at first. Meeting at my house? Doggy-style? Eating Ferrero Rocher? (I forgot to mention we were eating Ferrero Rocher at the time. He was trying to help me with my weight gain, even though I knew he hated the whole idea of it.) I think I said something along the lines of 'What do you mean?'

'This. Us.'

It hit me then. You'd have to have the skin of a rhino to miss what he was trying to say. I felt a rush of adrenalin, but I knew I had to keep my cool. Robbie hates hysteria in any form.

'What's brought this on?'

'I can't deal with the fact you don't trust me.'

I'll come clean. Since Paula had told me about his new-found affection, I'd had a bit of a wobble. And even though I obviously couldn't tell him what my suspicions were based on, I had started to badger him about his wife and why he hadn't left her yet and, most of all, why he had agreed to spend time exclusively with her for two weeks at a point when we were both off work and could have seen each other every day. I'd even started to look at flats for us to rent together when the time came. Just until we could sort out our divorces and buy something.

'It's not that I don't trust you. Of course it's not. I just had a moment, that's all.' I couldn't say what I wanted to, which was that I had it from the horse's mouth that he and Paula were shagging each other senseless again.

The thing with seeing someone who has a wife – or a

husband, I suppose – is that you have to accept that they're having sex with their partner sometimes. That's a given and anyone who tells you they're not is lying. But there's 'I'm doing this because I have to' sex and there's 'I'm doing this because I fancy the arse off them' sex. And Robbie had always been very clear that what he was doing was the former.

Side note: Josh and I still make love in a very pleasant but utterly routine fashion about once a week. Probably not bad going when you've been married for eight years but I wouldn't really miss it if it stopped tomorrow.

'You've been going on and on about it. It's as if, after all we've been through, you still think I'm choosing her over you.'

I couldn't help myself. 'Well, you are spending this ridiculous two weeks with her.' I was dying to add, 'She told me it was all your idea, she told me you were desperate for the two of you to spend some alone time together,' but of course I couldn't so I had to plump for looking like a paranoid bunny-boiler.

'For fuck's sake. This is what I mean. I've told you and told you there's no way of getting out of it. It's only two fucking weeks.'

'It's not just that,' I said, but then I couldn't elaborate on what else it was so I didn't say any more.

'What then? What are you accusing me of exactly?'

He was getting angry, I could tell. I could feel tears welling up and I tried to blink them away because I knew they weren't going to help.

'Nothing. I'm not accusing you of anything. Forget it.'

'You can't just keep making little comments and then

saying, 'Forget I said anything,' he said, and I knew he had a point. I'll be the first to admit I had been doing that a bit lately.

'OK then,' I said, trying to sound as rational as I could. 'I've been worried you were going to choose her over me. I'm being stupid, I know. I won't mention it again, I promise. Just give me another chance.'

Christ, no one likes a beggar.

'I think we need a break,' he said, getting out of bed and reaching for his clothes. 'I'm not saying permanently, but let's slow things down a bit.'

And then I don't know what came over me. I saw red. I've always been a bit of a green-eyed monster. With blue eyes, haha. Before I could stop myself I said, 'There's someone else, isn't there?'

He yanked his T-shirt over his head then, almost ripping the sleeve.

'I'm not even going to dignify that with an answer. I'm leaving now, OK, let's just take these next two weeks to think about things. Don't call me, OK? Really, Sas, I mean it. Don't call.'

A noisy sob escaped before I could stop it. Robbie and I almost never call each other anyway. It was a decision we made early on. No calling, no texting. We see each other almost every day at work so our rationale was that phoning must only be for emergencies. He was furious with me when I broke the rules by sending him a text that time after I answered his phone and it was Paula on the other end.

I panicked and wanted to stop it ringing in case one of the runners heard it, I thought they'd come in and grab it for him to be helpful. I was naked on his sofa at the time so it would have been a bit of a giveaway. He was in the shower. Stupidly risky, I know. We just got carried away. Usually, we're much more discreet. We both learned a big lesson from that one, I can tell you.

I was lying when I told him I didn't check who was calling, though. Of course I did. I knew exactly who was going to be on the other end when I said hello. I just wanted to hear what she sounded like, that's all. There was no way in a million years I was going to give anything away, I'm far too good an actress for that.

When I sent the follow-up text I'd had a big glass of wine and I was filled with adrenalin thinking about what might have happened. I suppose I just wanted to relive the moment with him. A bit of excitement. I knew as soon as I pressed send that I shouldn't have, and his curt reply confirmed that. So, no more texting. We got away with it that one time and we both agreed we shouldn't do it again.

'Promise me,' he's saying now. 'I don't want to have to spend the whole time guarding my phone in case you do something stupid.'

'I won't. Jesus Christ.'

'We'll talk in two weeks, OK? I'll call you from the golf club when I know Josh will be at work.'

'Please just say it's not over,' I said. I know, I know. Pitiful.

He leaned down and kissed me on the forehead. I angled my face up so our mouths met, and I knew from the way he allowed it to happen that there was still hope.

'Two weeks. Then we'll talk.'

20

Those two weeks were agony. Not only could I not talk to Robbie, I couldn't even meet up with Paula to quiz her about what was going on. I did try texting her a couple of times. Generic things that wouldn't make him suspect anything and go into a panic if he caught sight of them, even though he'd wonder why I was texting her at all – *'Having a good time?'* and *'How's it going?'* She replied *'Blissful'* to the first and *'Wonderful'* to the second, which just fuelled my paranoia without actually telling me anything.

So I just had to wait it out. Hope that Robbie would miss me. So maybe him and Paula were getting on better, but it wasn't enough. It couldn't compare to what we had, he and I.

I'll be honest, the weight gain I'd been prescribed wasn't a stretch at this point. I can see why they call it comfort eating. Josh kept on telling me how well I was doing. I could see him being a feeder in another life. He seemed to really get a kick out of watching me stuff myself and, whenever I'd get on the scales and report back on another kilo gained, he would beam like a proud parent watching their slightly stupid child get a certificate for 'best attendance' or 'plays well with others'. I'm not going to deny he was getting on my nerves.

And I did try calling Robbie, even though he'd asked

me not to – from my hairdresser's mobile, from a pay phone (have you got any idea how hard it is to find a pay phone these days, especially one that's still connected and not being used as a coffee shop or some kind of free community library?), even once from my gym, under the pretext that I'd lost my own phone and it was an emergency. He didn't answer any of them. He must have decided not to pick up any unknown calls just in case they turned out to be me.

Anyway, to cut a long story short, I didn't wait for him to call me once it was over, I phoned him the first day I could, when I knew Paula would be back at work. I managed to persuade him to meet me – he wouldn't come to the house, so I knew then that the outcome wasn't going to be good. We met in Richmond Park, in a part I'd come to think of as ours, where it's always quiet and you can sit there for hours and barely see another living soul. It was drizzling so we had the place to ourselves. As soon as he arrived he told me that he'd been thinking about almost nothing else for the past two weeks and that he was sure what he was doing was for the best. We'd run our course. No building up to it. No hesitation.

I begged, pleaded, cried. It wasn't pretty, I'll tell you that much. And, like I said before, Robbie hates crying. So that didn't help. He hates drama of any sort, which is ironic, if you think about it. I felt helpless, I didn't know what to do. The only thing I could think was that he'd decided to try and make it work with Paula. Why, I have no idea. He's barely had a good word to say about her since I met him.

Actually, that's not fair. He doesn't badmouth her. But

he's never exactly talked about her as if she's the love of his life either, even before we got together. 'Indifferent' is the word I'd use.

Like me with Josh. It's not as if you hate them. Or even dislike them. You just wish you weren't married to them because there are other people you'd rather be with.

At one point I – and I'm not proud of this – even said 'Is it because I've put on weight?' Robbie's always loved my body. I've always known that, in his praise of its lithe, slim contours was a buried criticism of the way Paula had let herself go.

'Don't be so ridiculous,' he said. 'Even I'm not that shallow.'

But something had clearly changed. It wasn't Paula, he told me. Even though they were getting on better, this wasn't about them. Their marriage was still dead in the water. It was about him.

Nothing I said would persuade him. It was over. He asked me to respect his decision, not to make things hard at work. At home. I had to agree – what else could I do? Of course, he had no idea that I was friends with his wife. That I would hear the whole story of the past fortnight from another perspective. That I'd find out he was lying to me.

And that's when I decided I couldn't let it happen. I couldn't let him just slide back into his marriage as if I didn't exist. As if nothing had happened.

And then, when I saw Paula all smug and glowy because she'd won, even though she hadn't even had any idea she was taking part, it hit me. If I couldn't have him, then neither could she.

Her face when I told her about him and Samantha – inspired, don't you think? Given the storyline he has coming up, where he's going to have to spend hours on set with her every day. What wife wouldn't be threatened?

She totally bought it. She trusts me. We're 'friends'.

And even though she's taking her time I know that it's all over for him and her now. I can make sure of that. She'll tell him to pack his bags and go eventually. Once Georgia leaves home. God, what is it with those two and their precious daughter? You'd think she would barely be able to feed and dress herself, they wrap her up in so much cotton wool. It's all I've heard for the past two years – that's how long Robbie and I have been seeing each other. Two years – how nothing must upset little Georgia until she's safely off at uni and making a new life for herself, blah, blah, blah. As if being a hundred miles away is going to protect her from being devastated once it happens.

And, when she does, where will he go? I know Robbie. He's not one to leave one home without having another all set up to go to. He's one of those people who could never live alone. And, in the meantime, I'll break it to Josh that it's over (I am a little worried that he might end up sacking me or something, but I'm hoping that if he thinks it's all about me having some kind of mid-life crisis and not about me wanting to move on to someone else, he won't be that vindictive. He's not the type anyway. As I said, he's a thoroughly nice man. Yawn. Haha) and I'll set myself up in a cosy little flat somewhere nice (note to self: Robbie loves Maida Vale) and wait.

It's the perfect plan.

21

Paula

I just ran five kilometres. I'm not even kidding. Without stopping once, except to cross the road here and there. OK, so I might have altered my route a couple of times so there were more roads to cross. And I may have stopped at every crossing even when there was no traffic, looking left and right to be sure, while I got my breath back, but I did it. It's a milestone. I text Chas and tell him. He's obviously not with a client because I get a typically Chas-ian reply straightaway.

'Awesome!'

Myra, on the other hand, sends, *'Freak'* followed by *'Traitor'*, followed by *'LOL.'*

Knowing that Robert's relationship is with Samantha, not Saskia, leaves me both better and worse informed. I know, for example, that they can't have been seeing each other for more than two years because that's how long she's been on the show. But I know nothing about her home life or whether she's cheating on anyone herself. I can't force my way into her life like I did with Saskia, partly because I wouldn't know how but also because I don't have it in me to do it again. I haven't got the energy.

I've been trying to remember whether or not she was at

Josh's party, but she wasn't on my radar at the time so, if she was, I've forgotten. As far as I can remember, I've never met her. Unlike with Saskia, Robert has never slagged her off. He's never really spoken about her at all. I've always got the impression that the younger actors on the show are a bit cliquey, all hanging out together in the evenings, as if they can multiply their star power by running in a pack.

Of course, I've Googled her some more and read a couple of short interviews, although, as one of the lesser characters, she doesn't command the same column inches Saskia does. Things I've learned include: she went to stage school in London from the age of thirteen, she's a Daddy's girl (is that the same as having a Daddy complex? I don't know), she has a small dog who seems to have lost the use of his legs, because in every picture I see he's sitting in a handbag, she likes cheese and onion crisps. Fascinating stuff.

I found her Twitter page. Photos of the dog. Photos of Samantha and the dog. Selfies with fishy, pouty lips and more than a hint of cleavage. She seems to call people 'babes' a lot. All my worst prejudices flooded out and I decided I had to stop looking. Me turning into a bitch wasn't helping anyone, least of all me.

I decide I need to approach things from a different angle. What does he get from her that he can't get from me? Yes, yes, I know. Apart from that. Do I need to gen up on One Direction or *Geordie Shore*? What do they talk about? What do they do when they're not in bed? They must have something else in common.

'Do you think she's got a designer vagina?' Myra says

helpfully when I ask her advice. 'Apparently, that's a thing now.'

I don't even dignify that with an answer.

Georgia is home for a few days, brown as a Dundee cake and full of stories that make my hair stand on end. It's always easier for Robert and me to bond when our daughter is around but I think that it helps that I no longer care what he's doing when he's not with me. I've finally told him about Chas and, instead of being dismissive or baulking at the expense, he told me he thought it was great and that it was obviously working because he'd never seen me look so fit and healthy.

For one scary moment I thought he was going to suggest joining me on my sessions, but in the end all he did was suggest we go running together more often, which we've started doing. It's fine. It makes me push myself harder. And while we're puffing along there's no pressure to be talking or trying to show him how devastatingly witty I am. It's all I can do to breathe.

Oh, thirteen stone dead, by the way. Just in case you were wondering. Robert, on the other hand, has gained a couple of pounds. I wonder why that is.

22

Saskia tells me the Robert/Samantha thing is causing a bit of a bad atmosphere on set. Which, of course, means that everyone knows about it. I try to brush away the feelings of humiliation.

'So they're not even trying to hide it now then?'

'Oh no, they are,' she says. We're sitting in the café on the ground floor of Fortnum and Mason, rain battering the windows outside. She pours herself more tea, toys with the sugar, decides against it. 'But that just means there's this weird tension. They've been shooting their first kiss scenes this week, did you know that?'

I shake my head.

'Anyway, one of the make-up girls told me it was awkward. A bit intense. Usually, people joke around when they're shooting that kind of stuff. Not that she was saying she thought there was anything going on, it was just an observation. I don't want you to start worrying that everyone knows.'

'I'm not.'

'I mean, I don't know why, because they must have been seeing each other for a while, so it's not as if they couldn't control themselves or anything . . .'

'How long ago was it you found out?' I realize I've never asked her this.

She thinks for a moment. 'About six months ago.

Obviously, I don't know when it started but I'd say it can't have been long before that or they wouldn't have been taking such a risk.'

So not as long as I thought then. I think back to six months ago. Was there any big change in Robert's behaviour? Nothing that I can remember. We had well and truly drifted apart by then.

'Maybe it was just the fact that they had to do it in front of other people. They were probably over-compensating or something,' she says. 'I don't think everyone's gossiping about them now or anything . . .'

I wish I still had Josh to talk to. Someone who knew exactly what was going on, who would just give me the real lowdown, knowing he didn't have to try and spare my feelings.

'How's Josh?' I say, partly to change the subject and partly to scratch the itch. I still get flashes of us kissing in the park – the second time, the time I just decided to go for it so I could lodge the memory in my head – and it makes me all warm and fuzzy for a moment, till reality comes crashing in.

'He's good,' she says. 'Relieved that he no longer has to force-feed me, I think, haha!'

'It must be difficult for him. Knowing things that are going on behind the scenes of the show and not always being able to talk to you about them.' This is my penance, trying to make sure Saskia thinks the best of Josh. Trying to make sure they're OK.

'He has to do his job, I understand that.' She shrugs.

Guilt about what I've done to Saskia is still eating me up. I can't ever tell her. Not so much the Josh thing, which was, after all, just a kiss, even though, for me, it's loaded with far more – and I think for him it was too. But for making him feel differently about her, even if only for a while.

I want to give her something to cement our friendship. I want to make her feel I value her. And, to be honest, there's an element of self-interest too. If I can't share my thoughts with Josh, I can at least share them with her, get her take on things. She knows all the parties concerned. Maybe she can help me come up with ways to put a bomb under Robert and Samantha's relationship. I do worry a bit that she'll think I'm vindictive and nasty, that it'll change her opinion of me, but actually I think she might be impressed. She's been so confused about why I'm not confronting Robert, throwing him out and making a new life for myself. On balance, I decide it's worth it.

Obviously, there will be glaring omissions in my confession. I can never tell her that this whole thing started because it was her I thought Robert was seeing.

'Can I tell you something?' I say as our lunch arrives (seabass fillets for me, fish cakes for her).

'Of course,' she says, intrigued. 'Anything, you know that.'

23

Saskia

So little Paula has a plan. I told you she had hidden depths. It's not good, though. Not for me.

I was hoping that my telling her some story about him and Samantha would either a) make her throw him out or b) make her so paranoid and suspicious he'd leave of his own accord. Because we all know how much he likes those traits, right.

What I never imagined is that she would go all out to win him back first.

But let's see how long his rekindled passion lasts when she keeps asking him where he's going and what time he'll be back. Because even if she sticks to her resolve not to confront him, she's not going to be able to keep up the pretence that they're love's young dream 24/7. Imagine his righteous indignation if he thinks she's accusing him of something when, for the first time in years, he's not up to anything! I'd love to be a fly on that wall.

The good news – for me – is that it's all over for Robert and Paula in so far as she is concerned. The endgame is that she dumps him.

The bad news is that, by then, she's hoping he'll be hopelessly in love with her again. And, if he is, where does that leave me?

She wants me to help her break up him and Samantha, which is genius, given I put them together for her in the first place. I can certainly help her with that, haha!

Between Robbie and me, things are very strained. Obviously, we're making sure no one picks up on an atmosphere – although most of the crew think we can't stand each other anyway, so a bit of animosity wouldn't give anything away – but I'm struggling. I can't accept it's over just like that. Just because I doubted him.

Paula is giving me no insight at all. Thankfully, she's stopped banging on about all the fantastic sex they're having. I assume because she's cut him off now I've told her my Samantha story. I like to picture him confused, thinking it was all suddenly going well at home and then being shoved out in the cold again. Wondering if he did the right thing giving me the boot after all.

I'm not going to lie, getting older is hard. I'm only thirty-eight (OK, forty-three when no one's listening, although I've practically forgotten that myself), but that's positively ancient in TV terms for a woman. Not that there aren't roles, there are. It's better than it used to be anyway. But mostly those roles are frumpy mum, dull auntie, boring teacher. Nothing juicy. And, God forbid, nothing where you're meant to be the eye candy. I miss it. I miss being the centre of attention.

Call me shallow ('You're shallow, Saskia!'), but there you go. I appreciate I'm not the world's best actress. I know I've always got parts based on the way I look. It never bothered me. I wasn't trying to be Judi Dench, I wasn't trying to win Oscars. I was trying to enjoy a bit of fame and fortune. Is that a crime?

I knew I was taking a risk getting together with Robbie with Josh working on the show. Sometimes I wonder if one wasn't a direct reaction to the other. I suggested Joshie for the job, he got it, and then I immediately felt boxed in. As if I didn't have anything any more that was just mine. And a part of me has always wondered if Robbie saw it as some kind of competition. He didn't take to Josh, he made that quite clear. So maybe he thought seducing me was a way of getting back at him. At first, anyway. I like to think he really did fall for me after that. That him suggesting we set up home together (because it was his suggestion, just to be clear; I didn't ask him to leave his wife) meant he wanted to spend the rest of his life with me.

I gambled on the fact that when it all went tits up I would be more indispensable to the show than Josh would. I'm one of the central characters, I won 'Best Supporting Actress in a Long-running Drama' at the TV Voters' Choice Awards after the second series. How could a backroom boy even compete? I never thought that my own position would be threatened.

Now I wonder whether I haven't had a lucky escape. On the hierarchy of who's who in *Farmer Giles*, Hargreaves currently comes a definite second after the farmer himself. I'm probably fourth in importance, after Giles's wife. And Marilyn is creeping up, hot on my tail. This story with Robbie will give her a massive boost. I've started to wonder if I could be vulnerable if Robbie suddenly decided he didn't want me around any more. If it was a case of 'either she goes or I go'. There would only be Josh standing between me and unemployment.

So I need to tread a bit carefully. I can't even imagine what Robbie would do if he found out it was me who started the Samantha rumour; who has poisoned his wife's head just when they were getting on so well. Lucky for me, Paula has always been adamant that we don't mention our friendship to him. If we keep it to ourselves, then no one'll be any the wiser. And then, one of these days, she'll hit him with an accusation out of nowhere. Who will he think is paranoid then? I'll look like Miss Super-rational 2016.

He'll need somewhere to run to and I need to make sure that somewhere is me.

24

Paula

I don't know whether something has happened to make the production run more smoothly, or whether Robert's character isn't being used as much as he used to be, but the days of filming running over seem to be gone, at least for now. Or, what I should say is he isn't coming home late at the moment. I never really believed it was filming that made him stay back two hours several times a week. Maybe it's because Georgia's home – not that she's really home even when she's home, if you know what I mean – and he wants to spend as much time with her as he can. Either way, he's around a lot more in the evenings.

Georgia is planning her birthday. She wants a party but she doesn't want it at the flat. (Thank God; I had been worrying about how to square it with the neighbours for weeks. Let alone the pressure there would have been to invite them.) We've left it a bit late so, right now, I'm desperately phoning around trying to book a venue that says 'cool' but doesn't cost the earth. Robert is in the shower.

I've tried three clubs (hopeless), two pubs (no large-enough space) and four restaurants (too short notice). I'm scrolling through half-heartedly on my laptop when I hear a phone ringing. I know it's not mine because it's sitting right in front of me, dark and silent. So it can only be

Robert's, because Georgia is out, and anyway, her ring tone is always a song – last count 'Hotline Bling'.

I track down the noise to a jacket slung across one of the kitchen chairs. It was raining when he left for the studio this morning so he slung it on over his T-shirt. It's so rare that he leaves his phone unguarded that I can't help myself. I'm in the pocket like a Jack Russell down a rat hole. I check the caller ID: Sam S.

Samantha.

Really? She's calling him when she must have a good idea he's at home? I'm so angry about the out-and-out rudeness of it, the fact that she doesn't give a shit about whether he's with his wife and daughter, that before I know what I'm doing I've answered.

'Robert's phone,' I say, in a tone I could only describe as hostile. I take a long breath to try to calm myself down. Never show the enemy your cards.

'Oh, is that Paula?' I recognize her voice from having seen her on the show. She sounds stupidly young and perky.

'It is. He's in the shower, I'm afraid. Can I give him a message?' I know I sound like an officious secretary but it's the best I can do at the moment.

'It's Sam Smith,' she says, and then she laughs. 'Not *that* Sam Smith. Samantha. From work.'

There's no hint in her voice that she's committed the ultimate faux pas.

'I was just going to talk to him about this stupid scene we're filming tomorrow. I can't get my head around it.'

'Right,' I say. 'I'll ask him to call you.' I just want to get off the phone before I say something I'll regret, but Samantha's still chatting.

'It's this ridiculous storyline we've got going on. Has he told you about it? Hargreaves and Marilyn?'

She may as well add the word 'eew'. This doesn't sound like a woman who secretly has the hots for him.

'I mean, the age gap is ridiculous. It's like she's going out with her dad. Not . . . I don't mean Robert's old or anything . . . or that he's not attractive . . . oh God, sorry, that all came out wrong. It's just . . . there's never been any hint of it before and it feels a bit unlikely, you know. We both think so.'

I'm more than a bit confused. 'That's *Farmer Giles* for you.'

'Tell me about it. Anyway, sorry, Paula, I don't want to disturb you . . .'

I can hear Robert heading this way.

'It's fine, hold on, he's coming.'

'Nice to talk to you, by the way,' she's saying as I hold the phone out to him. I want to be able to gauge every detail of his reaction. There's a tiny flicker when he clocks that the phone I'm holding is his.

'It's Samantha.'

Anything? If I'm being absolutely truthful, if I was in court and told I had to name one emotion that he couldn't one hundred per cent keep in check at the moment I said that name, I would have to say relief.

'Oh. Thanks,' he says, as he takes the mobile. I wait for him to leave the room, for any hint of tension in his voice, but instead he settles down on a bar stool next to me.

'Hi, Sam,' he says in a matey voice. 'No, no, it's fine . . .'

He laughs at something she says. 'I haven't even looked at it yet. Hold on.'

He rummages about in the sides he's brought home from work. Finds the offending scene, scans it.

'Jesus. I see what you mean . . .'

I tune out then, hijacked by my thoughts. If I'd walked in on this conversation without him realizing I was there, there would have been no doubt in my mind that he was just talking to a friend or colleague. Is he really this good? Is she?

'She's a nice kid,' he says when their conversation is over. 'Bloody awful actress, though.' He laughs and I laugh with him. But does that answer my question? Would Samantha be incapable of convincing me there was no hidden agenda in her call to Robert? Or is it just that she doesn't care? That she's the kind of person who wouldn't be fazed by their lover's wife answering the phone because she couldn't give a shit about her or their marriage?

When I can get away I call Saskia.

'Hey!'

'Hi. Have you got a moment?'

'It's Amanda,' I hear her say to whoever she's with. I assume it's Josh. I picture them there, sharing a glass of wine. Maybe sitting in their beautiful garden, now the weather's cleared up again. I'm touched that she's still honouring my request to keep our friendship a secret. Christ knows what Josh would think was going on if he knew I was phoning her now.

There's a pause and then she says, 'Hi, sorry, I've come upstairs to the bedroom. Everything OK?'

'The weirdest thing just happened.'

I relate the whole story. How open and friendly Samantha sounded. How their conversation seemed completely natural.

'You couldn't have been mistaken, could you? I mean, obviously, you saw him with someone, but could it have been someone else? Someone who looks like her maybe?'

'Sorry, Paula, it was definitely her.'

Maybe I'm just gullible. 'She sounded so genuine.'

'She'd probably been practising. I mean . . . if she was going to risk calling him at home . . .'

Now I feel like an idiot. I imagine Robert and Samantha laughing about how they got one over on me. 'Oh well, it doesn't make any difference anyway, I suppose. The fact is that he's seeing someone, not who it is.'

'Atta girl.'

'I can't wait for this all to be over. I can't wait to start a new life all on my own.'

'Then kick him out now,' she says.

'You know I can't. Or he's won.'

'Then we need to get on with trying to split them up,' Saskia says, and I feel so grateful that I have an ally. 'The sooner that happens, the sooner you'll be free of him for good.'

By the time I finish speaking to her I feel much better. Because Saskia saw it with her own eyes, there's no doubt that it's Samantha Robert is seeing. Regardless of how pleasant she seemed on the phone just now, I know it's all make-believe. I'd be lying if I said I wasn't shocked by how easily Robert slipped into having a friendly worky chat with her. It makes me think his conscience hasn't been pricked at all despite how well we've been getting on. It makes me think I've got a much harder battle on my hands than I thought.

25

Robert is due to be away for two nights, filming scenes in Oxfordshire. When he's not around I flick through the schedule for the week. The first day, he's only in a couple of scenes, one with David, one with Samantha. The rest of the time is taken up with two-handers between David and Saskia. That means the four of them will stay up there the night before to be ready for the crack of dawn on filming day.

Day two is more David/Robert and then stuff between other cast members, who I have no interest in. So Robert and David will stay for a second night, along with a few additions, and Saskia and Samantha will make their way home after the first day's filming is completed. At a rough guess, Robert will be home late Tuesday afternoon

I text Saskia and ask her if she'd like to come over to the flat on Monday evening, once she gets back to London. I wait for her to suggest I go to hers – Josh, I assume, will be away till the following day – or somewhere near hers, but to my surprise she agrees to trek across town to meet me, for once. Georgia has gone off again – working in the parking field of some festival or other with Eliza, doing a twelve-hour shift in exchange for a pittance and a pair of free tickets to the next two days – so I know we'll have the place to ourselves.

Chas puts me through my paces after work.

'Look at those guns,' he shouts when I push a pair of weights above my head. I look in the mirror that covers one whole wall of the gym – the one I usually avoid looking at – and I can see the tiniest hint of muscle under all the soft squishy stuff.

'Pea-shooters maybe,' I say, laughing at his enthusiasm. 'Or water pistols, at a push.'

'You can get some very big water pistols. Be proud of those things,' he says when I heave the dumb-bells up again. 'You've earned them.'

'Did you just buy a dictionary of clichés? Or *How to Give Positive Affirmation in Ten Easy Lessons*?'

'I'm naturally upbeat,' he says. 'It's a big part of my charm.'

Saskia arrives, bearing a bottle of wine. She looks tired. Even though she has been allowed to ease off the weight gain, it's still a shock to see her rounder contours. She's replaced her usual skin-tight clothes for a more flowy T-shirt and pale pink pedal pushers. She looks great.

'Hey!'

We hug and she follows me inside, looking around. I'm glad I made the effort to tidy up before she got here.

'This is lovely,' she says, peering into the lived-in living room as we pass it on the way to the kitchen.

'It's small,' I say, and I chastise myself for making apologies. I love our flat. It's shabby but it suits us perfectly. Or, at least, I've always thought so. I've never understood the need to move somewhere flashier just because you can. I'm already worrying about whether Robert will let me stay here once we separate, because I can't imagine living anywhere else. 'We've been here for years and we just never got around to scaling up. Even though Robert thinks we should have years ago.'

'Don't ever scale up,' she says, laughing. 'It just means more maintenance, more things to go wrong. I spend half my life waiting in for people to come and fix things.'

'OK, good, I'll bear that in mind when I win the lottery.'

As if she can read my mind, she says, 'Are you going to stay here when . . . you know?'

'I hope so. He knows how much I love it. It's been Georgia's home her whole life. And I doubt Samantha's going to want to move in here anyway. Where does she live now?'

I put two large glasses down in front of Saskia and she fusses about opening the wine.

'Oh. I'm not sure. For some reason, I think she still lives with her mum.'

I take one of the now full glasses and down a large swig. 'Jesus. And don't tell me, her mum's my age.'

'Hardly. Not that I've met her.'

We sit by the open patio doors, looking down on to the tiny communal garden below.

'So, how's things? She was there last night, right? At the hotel.'

'She was. Oh, so guess what? I found something out.' She pauses for a reaction.

'What? Tell me.'

'We were stuck in Make-up at the same time so I ear-wigged on her conversation. Those make-up artists are like therapists, honestly. Or priests. People seem to feel they can tell them all their darkest secrets. I think it's because you're sat there for hours and you've got to talk about something . . .'

I have to stop myself from telling her to get to the point. I know by now that Saskia moves at her own pace when it comes to telling stories.

'. . . anyway, she was talking about her boyfriend – by whom I assume she means Robert. I certainly haven't ever heard her mention anyone else – and she was saying she's desperate for a baby . . .'

She sits back and looks at me triumphantly. I'm hit with a wave of nausea. It hadn't even occurred to me that Robert might want more children. Of course he will. He's still young. But now? Already? Before he's even walked out the door?

'Shit,' is all I can come up with.

'Sorry. Oh God, has that upset you? It has, hasn't it? I just thought it might be a good weapon somehow. I mean, there's no way Robert is going to want another baby, I would have thought. Not at this stage. And she was saying that he – her boyfriend – wasn't keen. It sounded as if she was thinking about just going ahead and letting it happen . . .'

'Jesus, really?'

'Anyway, I just thought it might be useful intel. It would frighten the life out of him, I imagine.'

She's right. Robert would hate the idea of Samantha getting pregnant behind his back. I have no idea how I can use it to my advantage, though.

'I thought I could drop it into the conversation some-how,' Saskia is saying. 'Just that I overheard Samantha saying she's plotting to "accidentally" get knocked up. That's got to sow a seed of doubt, surely.'

'That's brilliant. I don't want to ask you to get any more involved, though . . .'

She shrugs. 'What do I care? It'll actually be quite entertaining to see the look on his face. After everything he's done to you . . .'

I top up our glasses. I can hear the theme tune from *Coronation Street* blasting out from one of the other flats.

'Why do the two of you dislike each other so much?'

I've always thought I understood Robert's irritation with Saskia – her lateness and her diva-ish behaviour – but who knows now if any of that is true? Josh certainly never spoke about her in that way.

She gives me a wry smile. 'Oh, I don't know that we do. We just don't get on particularly. There's a difference. Well, unless he's told you something else. Maybe he hates me, haha!'

'No, no, I didn't mean it like that. I was just curious, that's all.'

She thinks for a moment. 'Two big egos fighting for attention. Something like that anyway.'

'Makes sense.'

'I think Robbie and I both like to be the centre of attention. Although, to be fair, most actors do, in my experience.'

'You sound like Alice. His sister. She's the only one who ever calls him Robbie.'

'Did I call him Robbie? I didn't even notice. That's because I have a friend called Robbie who would think I'd gone insane if I called him Robert. I don't think I've ever called your Robert it before . . .'

She picks up her glass, takes a sip. We sit there in silence for a moment. Well, silence and the sound of Steve McDonald's voice cutting through the air. I feel as if we've talked about me and my problems enough.

'How are you, anyway?'

'Good. I mean, I'm fine. I hate it when people say "I'm good." It doesn't really make any sense and it sounds so American, don't you think? And then I go and start saying it myself, haha!'

And they're off. I let her ramble on for a bit. I'm staggered by the idea that Samantha might deliberately get pregnant without even discussing it with Robert. That she would be prepared to trap him in that way. It actually makes me feel sorry for him, although it would definitely be one way for him to learn the perils of dating someone young enough to still think playing games with people's lives is acceptable. When I realize Saskia has ground to a halt, I have no idea what she was saying.

'Sorry, what did you just say?'

'I was just talking about Josh. He wants us to go to Barcelona for the weekend for our anniversary. It's where we went on our first holiday together.'

She rolls her eyes at me.

'What's up with Barcelona? Barcelona's lovely.'

'That's not the point. I don't know why he wants to go away at all. I mean, it's nine years, it's not as if it's anything special.'

I think how much I would have loved it once if Robert had been the type of person to want to whisk me away for a romantic weekend. It's as if she reads my mind because she says:

'I know that sounds horribly ungrateful. I'm just knackered, that's all. I'd rather go out for a nice meal but he's making a big fuss about wanting to spoil me.'

Of course he is. It's his way of saying sorry. Not that Saskia knows he has anything to be sorry for.

I think of his kind eyes. His habit of running his hand over his head. The way he looked at me before he kissed me.

'I'd let him do it,' I say, reaching for the wine bottle. 'If it means that much to him.'

26

Saskia

I probably shouldn't have said anything to Paula, but the truth is, Josh is being annoyingly lovey-dovey at the moment. Not like *that*, but asking me if I'm OK every five minutes and bringing me cups of coffee in bed when I'm trying to have a lie-in. I know, I know. Most spouses would kill to be married to someone who was still attentive after eight – nearly nine – years, but I could do without it. It's getting on my nerves.

That's the thing when you know someone just flat-out adores you. It makes you want to test it. To kick out and see how they react. What would be their breaking point? Well, I imagine finding out about me and Robbie would have been Josh's. A small dalliance, a one-off with someone he didn't know, he would probably get over in time. A full-blown two-year love affair with someone he can't stand, I very much doubt.

So, that was weird, being in Robbie's – dear God, I called him Robbie in front of Paula! You idiot, Saskia! – home with him having no idea I was there. It was the first time – he never felt comfortable taking me there because of his daughter, blah blah. We were both taking a risk with our partners but Georgia was a risk he wouldn't even consider. So I jumped at the chance when Paula invited me. I couldn't wait to get a look at it. Even though all I really wanted to do was enjoy having the house to myself for once.

It's smaller than I imagined. Hardly where you'd expect a big-shot TV star to live. Big old block. Their flat is on the fifth floor (thankfully, there's a lift, haha!), overlooking a sort of small communal garden out the back. Probably six rooms in total, including the bathroom. Sunny aspect. Original-looking parquet floors.

But that's enough of the estate-agent spiel. I always find it fascinating (and sometimes a bit off-putting) how everyone's home smells different. It's as if each household creates their own fragrance unique to them. On first impression, Robbie and Paula's place smelled of laundry, girly bath products, a residue of some kind of garlicky something she must have eaten the night before, and the tiniest hint of underlying damp. All in all, not too bad.

I can't even describe how weird it was seeing Robbie's things in this context. Odd bits and pieces that were so familiar to me, in amongst evidence of the whole other life he has that doesn't include me. I managed to have a good look around on the two occasions I visited the loo, which was conveniently situated next door to their bedroom. There was a pile of clean washing on the bed (hence the laundry smell) and I recognized items I know so well in its jumble. Largish, dark wood-framed bed against the wall, white bed linen with a cheerful poppy-motif duvet cover. Wardrobes built in along one side. It was obvious which side of the bed was his. Just the copy of the latest John le Carré alone was enough to give it away. I couldn't help myself, I pulled open the top door of his bedside table and had a quick look. The usual mess of bits and pieces – cold medicine, ear plugs, coins. For some reason, it made me a bit sad. It was so mundane. That's the thing Robbie and I never got to share, the mundane. The everyday detritus that makes up a life.

On my second visit I had a trawl through the bathroom cabinet, but there was nothing illuminating beyond a box of Just For Men. Ha! And there was me thinking he was all natural!

It was hard to picture him there, I'm not going to lie. It made him seem smaller, somehow. I remember when I was a teenager and going out with a boy I had had a crush on for months. It was all going really well. All my friends were envious. I thought he was about the coolest creature I had ever encountered, until he invited me home for the first time. One glimpse of his room with the faded flowery wallpaper that his parents obviously wouldn't allow him to change under his posters, the mess of dirty socks and underwear, his potions to ward against acne on the little desk, and I could never look at him the same way again. Never mind that my own bedroom still had Five Star on the wall and my fluffy cartoon-character slippers nestled on the floor next to my old dolls' house. He diminished before my eyes. Thankfully, the same didn't happen with Robbie. Rather, I had an overwhelming feeling that I wanted to rescue him from it all.

And the baby thing was inspired. I mean, come on. Now I can just report back that I 'accidentally' let slip my piece of gossip to Robbie. That the look on his face gave away a million secrets. That, suddenly, she's red-eyed and tearful and the two of them don't seem to be speaking to one another any more.

And then Paula will feel as if she can kick him to the kerb when he's down and has nowhere to run to.

Except, of course, that I need to make sure he feels he can run to me.

I just hope she never decides to give Samantha a piece of her mind because that would leave everybody very confused indeed. Samantha most of all.

Robbie has started filming a new storyline involving Hargreaves going into business with wide-boy thug Smyth, the village ne'er-do-well. Every TV idyll has one. I know he's not happy about it. It's part and parcel of the bigger revelation that Hargreaves has been a conman all along, preying on his elderly friends, selling them bits of old tat in exchange for their life savings or paying them a pittance for what he knows is a priceless antique.

Personally, I think it's inspired, in that classic soap way. (I can hear Robbie's voice in my head now: '*Farmer Giles* is not a soap, Saskia. It's a long-running series. It only runs for half the year, that's the big difference.' Most of us know it's a soap in all but name, though.) Take the person you would least expect to do something and have them do it. It'll have them hooked even if it'll also have them throwing their pension books at him in the street.

I did ask Josh if the storyline was anything to do with him. He's never been Robbie's biggest fan and he doesn't even know the half of it. If I had his job I would be wanting to wreak havoc on any of the actors who had pissed me off, I can tell you that. He went a bit po-faced, though, and said he would never let his personal feelings get in the way of work.

The more immediate issue is that Jez, the actor playing Smyth, is a psycho. He only joined the show last year – an ex-cage fighter turning his hand to acting for the first time – and he's managed to terrorize pretty much every-one ever since. Luckily for most of us, our characters have no reason to cross paths, except for the occasional scene in the pub where there's safety in numbers.

Robbie is terrified of him. Actually terrified. He would never admit it but I've seen him do that overly enthusias-tic matey thing whenever he's with Jez which means, 'I'm just like you. Please don't hit me.' He was outraged when they cast him, saying it was a stunt and it was bringing the credibility of the show down (really, though, I don't know how he kept a straight face). Someone clearly told Jez because he made it clear he couldn't stand Robbie from the start. And he's a big bloke. Not to mention unhinged.

Anyway, now they are having to spend whole days shooting two-handed scenes in a set that looks like a back alley where someone might be murdered and not discov-ered for days (where this is meant to be in our sleepy fictional village is unclear. Everyone stopped caring about the geography years ago), some of which involve Jez pin-ning Robbie up against the wall and shouting in his face. One of the make-up girls – never Robbie's greatest fan, since he shouted at her for chatting during rehearsals once – tells me it's a joy to watch. Robbie's fear is palpable. Between takes, Jez apparently paces the set, barking at anyone who comes near him, trying to stay 'in the moment', while Robbie cowers behind the director.

On a day when I'm in early, waiting to shoot a scene at the hairdresser's – one of those annoying, slightly comedic filler scenes that you know will almost certainly be cut from the finished product – I decide to wander over to the studio to see how it's going. Maybe Robbie will see me as a friendly face, the safest port in a storm.

They're rehearsing a new scene when I get there. Arguing about the price of something or who owes who what. At one point Jez shoves him with all his force and Robbie stumbles back. He looks to the director for help.

'Can we . . .' he says nervously. 'Could we just save it for the take?'

The rule, as everyone worth their salt knows, is that with anything uncomfortable you pull back on the rehearsals, blocking out what you intend to do but not actually doing it. Same with kissing. Although Robbie used to conveniently forget that when we first got together and, suddenly, Hargreaves and Melody were snogging like randy teenagers whenever the script called for them to have a quick kiss.

'Just block it through, Jez,' the director calls. I think she's terrified of him too. Most of the directors are. 'Half pace.'

'Sure,' Jez says, and then adds, 'Sorry, mate,' to Robbie, although said in a way that means anything but.

'From the top,' the first assistant shouts. 'Quiet, everyone. Rehearsing.'

They run through the scene again. Same point, same shove. It's almost comical. No, not almost, it actually is.

Robbie stops again. 'For goodness' sake . . .'

He catches sight of me then and the look he gives me is one I'll treasure. He can't hide the fact he's pleased to see me. He rolls his eyes inclusively.

'Let's just go straight for a take,' the director calls. She can clearly see the situation is getting out of hand.

'First positions,' the first assistant shouts. 'Quiet!'

Everyone stands like statues, as they always do when a scene is being filmed. Jez's acting is laughably bad. He stumbles on a line and ends up saying something that makes no sense at all.

'OK,' the director says as the scene judders to a halt, clearly giving up. 'I think we've got that. Let's move on.'

The first assistant barks out the details for the next scene, also involving Robbie and Jez. There's a short hiatus while they discuss some technical stuff and I'm gratified, out of the corner of my eye, to see Robbie sidling over to me.

'Did you see that?' he says before I can even say good morning. 'He's out of fucking control.'

'It's a joke,' I say. 'It's not as if he can even act.'

'I'm thinking about taking it up with Josh. Apart from anything else, it's turning the show into a farce.'

'It's not that you're scared of him,' I say, taking the risk that he'll see the funny side.

He rewards me with a smile and my stomach flips. 'Terrified. But Josh doesn't need to know that. I'll convince him it's about integrity.'

'I can speak to him too if you like.' Even though I'm enjoying Robbie's discomfort, I know I could win myself serious brownie points by helping him out here.

'Would you?' he says, in a voice full of gratitude.

'Of course.'

He's called over to start rehearsing the scene then. Just before he moves off he puts his hand on my arm and says, 'How are you? Are you OK?'

'Surviving,' I say. 'Just about.'

It's a breakthrough.

27

Paula

Twelve stone twelve and still thirty-six per cent fat. My descent has slowed right down now that my body expects exercise as part of its everyday routine. I don't even care. I feel – and look – better than I have in years.

I'm filling Myra in on the baby news. I can't get it out of my head. It's hands down one of the worst things I think a woman could do to a man. Let alone to the new life they'd be bringing into the world.

'Christ.' She bangs a mug of coffee down in front of me. I'm sitting at one of the tables after my latest session with Chas because I can't face going home yet. Robert has the day off and I'm at a loss as to what the two of us would do to pass the time. Even though I'm, strictly speaking, a customer at the moment, I still jump up to help every now and then if someone is waiting to be served.

'Make sure you sort your divorce out before it happens, just in case he suddenly decides to start taking his parental responsibility seriously.'

'Shh!' I say, looking around to see if any of the customers are listening in. 'He already does take his parental responsibility seriously.'

'So there you go. You don't want him trying to say you

have to sell the flat and live in a hovel because he has a new mouth to feed.'

'I don't think . . . that's not the point anyway. If he wants to have a whole other family, then that's his problem. The point is, she's doing it behind his back.'

'Well, not all of it,' Myra smirks.

'You know what I mean. What kind of girl does that?'

'A nasty, manipulative one. I couldn't wish her on a nicer person.'

I pick up a napkin and wipe the table where my cup has left a mark. 'They do deserve each other, I suppose.'

'So Saskia's going to drop her in it?'

I nod. 'I didn't ask her to, she volunteered.'

'I'm starting to like Saskia.' She flops down in the seat opposite me and then jumps up again when someone comes through the door. 'It's a clever move.'

'It might just work,' I call after her retreating back.

For the next few days I watch Robert for a sign that anything has changed. I'm extra nice to him, so that at the moment the scales fall from his eyes as far as Samantha is concerned he'll see me and think, 'That's who I should be spending the rest of my life with.' Or something like that anyway.

On the Sunday night, when we're chatting about Georgia's impending A-level results I hit him with the genius 'Can you believe it's been eighteen years?' line.

'Next week,' he says, helping himself to a home-made truffle (his, half a pound of butter and enough sugar to satisfy a room full of slow lorises; mine, coconut oil and sweetener. Appearance – identical. I clock his tummy sagging a little over the top of his Ralph Lauren PJs and wonder how his heart is standing up to the assault).

'I'll miss it, won't you? I don't just mean I'll miss her. I can't even think about that. I'll miss the whole mother-hood thing.'

'You'll still be her mum,' he says, patting my leg as if I were a horse. We're slouched on the sofa, side by side. Close but not too close.

'I know. And I wouldn't want to do it all again from the beginning, truthfully. Not now. Not the baby and toddler years.'

'Christ, no! Can you imagine? I don't think we slept for three years, did we?'

I reward him with a laugh. 'Something like that. And imagine trying to deal with an adolescent thirteen years from now.'

He shudders. 'Are you trying to give me nightmares?'

I decide that I've pushed the point enough. Clearly, Robert isn't on board with the idea of new fatherhood. I just have to wait for Saskia to work her magic.

'Tell the truth, are you sad she's decided not to have a party?'

In the end, George got too frustrated with the lack of a decent venue and decided that, rather than spend the next week or so stressing that her party would be rubbish, she wouldn't have one at all. She's chosen, instead, to go for a posh dinner, followed by a club with her eight closest mates. Bankrolled by us, obviously, but we're only too happy to do it. Mostly because it means we don't have to go, and we can just take her out for a meal ourselves another night.

'"Sad" doesn't even come close,' he says. '"Relieved", "thankful" and "grateful" would be more like it.'

'Me too. Is that terrible?'

He takes a swig of his licorice tea. We're both having a night off the wine in an effort to fool our livers into thinking we might be going teetotal so they should buck up their ideas. I'm on the lemon and ginger.

'Dreadful,' he says. 'We're awful parents.'

And he leans over then and puts an arm around me, pulling me a bit closer and kissing my head, just below the hairline. It's hardly foreplay but it's an unprompted gesture of affection, and that's progress in my book.

I'm on eggshells waiting for Saskia to tell me what's going on. Eventually, on Tuesday afternoon, she calls me.

'Oh my God,' she says before I can say anything. I'm just home from work and about to get in the shower. 'You should have been there.'

'You told him! Tell me everything!'

She leaves a dramatic pause. I try to be patient.

'OK. I'll have to give you the quick version because I'm going to get called any minute now. So, we were chatting between scenes. They were doing a re-light so we had to hang around for a while. I had to wait till it was just me and him, obviously, because I didn't want anyone else running to Samantha and saying anything. Anyway, eventually, we were on our own so I just came straight out with it. Like I was concerned for his welfare . . .'

'What, out of nowhere?' I have to admit I'm in awe of Saskia's front.

'Sort of, but I kind of led up to it by saying something

else about Samantha, something nice, about the fact that she'd done well in a scene or some such nonsense, I can't remember, and then I said, "Oh, but there's something I have to tell you. I might have got the wrong end of the stick or something, in fact I'm sure I have . . . but if it were me I'd want to be told . . ."'

'And . . .'

'Of course, he couldn't resist the bait. So I told him what I'd "heard". His face, Paula! Obviously, he was trying not to give away too much, because there were people around, even though they weren't in earshot, but it was all there to read if you knew what you were looking for.'

'Brilliant. And what did he say?'

'He asked me a few things, like was that really exactly what she said, and did I think she was actually trying to make it happen or was it just a flippant thing? He was making little quips like it was all a big joke but I could tell he just wanted details. And then we got called back, so that was that. I could tell he was rattled, though. His concentration was way off after that.'

'Genius,' I say. 'I owe you one. I can't wait for him to come home today now, see if I can spot anything.'

'I saw them in a huddle at lunch and she didn't look very happy. I hope he doesn't drop me in it with the make-up girl, but hey, what can you do. I'm on a mission, haha!'

'Thanks, Saskia, that was above and beyond, really.'

'Well, let's hope it works.'

'Even if it doesn't make him see sense right away, it's a nail in their coffin, surely.'

'If it isn't, then I don't know what we have to do.'

I promise to update her on Robert's state of mind later. Then I pace around, wondering what to do with myself, until I remember that I need to look as appealing as I possibly can when he gets home fresh from – hopefully – a fight. So I have a shower, wash my hair and blow it out. I moisturize everything in sight, put on a new pair of jeans that have been waiting for just such an occasion (size fourteen, I'm not even joking. I could have wept when I tried them on and they fitted) and the floaty-top thing I bought on my first shopping expedition. Then I touch up the polish on my toenails (this involves having to take the jeans off again because I can't bend down in them. There's fitting and then there's fitting, if you know what I mean) and put on just the right amount of make-up so I look good but not like I've got made up for him.

All of this takes me over an hour, and then I start pacing again. I never know what time to expect Robert home on filming days. Sometimes he's only in the first scene, so he can be finished for the day by nine thirty. Earlier, even. They shoot fast on *Farmer Giles*. Today, I seem to remember, he's in most of the scenes, so I probably won't see him till half past seven, or even later, if he decides to stay behind and argue with Samantha. It's still only five so I could have several hours of sitting around in my finery, waiting.

I pass the time by baking more treats. Puffy cupcakes, one batch with sugary cream frosting on top, one with frosting made with sweetener. It's a bit grainy but it still tastes delicious. I decorate mine with a P in protein-enriched sugar-free sprinkles (yes! There is such a thing! Who knew? And who would have thought I would care till now?) and Robert's with an R in the all-calories and no-redeeming-qualities-whatsoever version. Then I mix them up on a plate and set them to one side under a cloche.

By the time I've cleaned up there's still no sign of him so I decide to give Georgia a ring to pass the time. She's due home from another festival jaunt in a few days, and she'll be here for a couple of weeks, which will encompass both her birthday and the arrival of her A-level results, so that could be an emotional rollercoaster. If that roller-coaster only had one giant up and then another, even more giant up, that is.

She's in a field, she tells me, when she answers. She's always in a field these days so that doesn't really give much away. She's in the middle of a thirteen-hour shift, show-ing people where to park their cars so that any of them have a hope in hell of ever finding them again.

'Honestly, Mum, I've never argued so much in my life. No one wants to park where I tell them to.'

'What do you care?' I say. 'You won't be there when they leave. Let them all block each other in.'

She laughs. 'Is that one of your life lessons? Don't care about doing a good job if you won't be around to see the consequences?'

'Just this once. They'll all be off their heads anyway, probably. They won't even see cars, just giant frogs or something.'

I can practically feel her rolling her eyes. 'This isn't Woodstock.'

'Just for the record, I wasn't even born when Wood-stock happened. And it was in America. But I take your point that festivals aren't the same as they were when I was your age.'

'What I meant was, this is a book festival. There are seven tents serving tea and cakes. And a glass of white wine costs thirteen pounds. No one's getting off their heads.'

'So, when are you heading home?'

'Day after tomorrow. Hold on . . .'

I hear her barking out directions to someone in a tone of voice I've never heard before. It's as if there's a whole different, more grown-up, version of my daughter out there in the world. Which, I suppose, there is. I should be proud. It means I've done my job. Then she's back.

'Sorry. Just had to stop some idiot blocking an exit.'

'Maybe you should consider a career as a prison officer. Or a football referee?'

'I'm going to ignore that. I should go, really, we're not meant to be on our phones . . .'

'Of course. Love you!'

I hear a click as the front door opens. 'Oh, hang on, George. Dad's just walked in. Let him say a quick hello . . .'

I head out to the hall, holding the phone out to Robert. 'It's George.'

His face lights up, as it always does when there's an opportunity to talk to our daughter, so it's hard to tell what kind of mood he's really in. He looks the same. Not as if he's spent half the afternoon arguing with the love of his life.

'Hi! Let me guess. You're in a field . . . ?'

I leave them chatting happily and go and open a bottle of wine. When he comes in he has a big smile on his face.

'Sounds like she's having a great time.'

Nothing about him says he's had a tough few hours. I pour him a glass of red.

'She's loving it. You have a good day?'

'Great, actually, yeah,' he says, and he looks as if he means it.

'Why so good? Anything special?'

'No,' he says. 'Just one of those days, you know.'

Someone give that man a BAFTA.

28

Saskia

Hallelujah!

I knew he still wanted me! I knew he wouldn't be able to stay away forever.

I was relaxing in my dressing room a few days after my little set visit. It was my first day back in since my brief chat with Robert so I hadn't been able to capitalize on the inroads I'd made. We were running a bit behind and I knew they wouldn't get to my scene till after lunch now. This is something people never realize about actors in film and TV. Half of your life is spent just waiting around. Even when things are running smoothly, you have hours to kill every day. Dead time.

People handle it differently. Some take up hobbies, so it's no surprise to walk in on someone and find them knitting or embroidering some ghastly object. Some try and engage whoever else is around in games of poker or canasta. Some even take to drink (mentioning no names, Jez, haha!). It can be deathly boring. You're not even allowed to go off premises for a walk, in case they suddenly decide to re-jig the schedule. I try to make myself do yoga or meditation. Something that adds value to my life. Of course, when Robert and I were still an item, it was a different story if we found ourselves at a loose end at the same time.

So I was lying on the sofa, eye mask over my eyes

(cucumber to reduce puffiness) when there was a tentative tap at my door. I assumed it was one of the runners come to ask me what I wanted from Catering so I just called out, 'Come in!' and didn't move.

Then I heard his voice. 'Very fetching.'

My heart almost burst out of my chest. I whipped the eye mask off and there he was. Robert. Standing in front of the closed door, looking right at me.

'Can we talk?'

I sat up, running my hands through my hair to flatten it. Luckily, I was wearing a short, silky robe over just my underwear. I didn't have to worry whether he'd like what he saw. 'Of course. Sit down.'

He cleared a pile of clothes and God knows what else off the only other chair.

I opened my mouth to speak again and then forced myself to close it. I had to wait for him to say what he'd come to say. It felt like an hour before he spoke.

'I just want to clear the air,' he said. 'I don't want us to be enemies.'

'We're not,' I said. 'We never could be.'

'Thank God for that. I've hated us not really talking for the last few weeks.'

I resisted the urge to say, 'It was all your decision. I never wanted to separate in the first place.' I've learned my lesson. Don't be accusatory, don't be needy; above all else, don't ask him how things are with Paula.

'Me too.'

'Have you been OK?' he said, and he gave me what I knew was his sympathy look – head slightly tilted to one side, eyes slightly screwed up.

It did actually make me a little teary, I'm not going to lie. I felt as if something had shifted, as if there was a chance we might be able to start again where we left off. I didn't want to blow it.

'Mmmm hmmm,' is all I could manage.

'I wasn't . . .' he started. 'I didn't ever want it to end. You have to understand, I just felt as if you didn't trust me. Like I couldn't do anything right.'

You can imagine how frustrating it was. I could never explain to him why I suddenly became jealous. Not because I'd been that type of person all along, and I just hid it well. But because I had proof. I had the words of his wife, telling me how fantastic things were, how he couldn't keep his hands off her suddenly, how he wanted to spend two weeks of his precious holiday holed up with her in some kind of John and Yoko love-in.

Of course, I said none of this. Now that I've poisoned Paula's mind well and truly against him, I think the love-ins are over. Whether he wants them to be or not.

Don't get me wrong, I know how pathetic I'm being. It reminds me of a phrase my ex-husband used to say (not Josh, he's not my ex yet, haha! Simon, who I married way too young and who then drank his way through all our savings. I left one night when he was on a bender, with just whatever I could carry, and I never looked back. I might be being pitiful at the moment but I'm strong underneath. I work hard to achieve what I want). Anyway, sloppy seconds, I've always hated that saying. The image it conjours up! Yuk. But there I was anyway, scrabbling around for Paula's sloppy seconds, content to be second best. Because the thing was, I knew if he gave me a chance I could win him back round. I could make him forget her all over again. But, like I said, I didn't say any of that.

'I know, and I'm sorry. That's not me. You've known me long enough to believe I'm not jealous or paranoid or any of those things. I just had a wobble, that's all.'

He worried away at the cuff of his shirt. He was dressed in Hargreaves' favourite outfit, a cross between Lovejoy and the Davids Dickenson and Essex. I could just imagine the first costume meeting. What do antiques dealers wear on TV? Dapper but eccentric with a hint of whimsy. That'll do. No point in trying to be original.

He sighed. 'I don't want Paula. I haven't wanted Paula for years. You never had anything to worry about.'

Stay calm. 'I realize that now.'

There was a long silence. Neither of us spoke and I started to worry that some idiot runner might come and knock on my door after all, with the list of what was available for lunch. If the atmosphere broke it would take a gargantuan effort to rekindle it. I tried to send out vibes. 'Keep Away!'

I looked across at him and he was staring at me intently. I held his look, and before I really knew what was happening he was right in front of me, kneeling on the floor, and then his mouth was seeking out mine.

We locked the door after that. Someone did knock eventually, but we stayed really quiet until they went away. And then we started giggling like a pair of schoolkids and I knew it was all going to be OK.

29

Paula

Saskia looks happy. I find her on a bench in Regent's Park, where we agreed to meet, because, thankfully, she has a meeting in town. She's positively glowing, as if it were she that was pregnant and not her character, Melody. I wonder for a second if that might be it. Maybe Josh's way of showing that he's fully committed, that he regrets the way he almost threw his marriage away on a misunderstanding, has been to knock her up. Not that I think either of them has any great desire to have a child. And she is, of course, forty-three, whatever she says, which is pushing it a bit to have a first baby, but stranger things have happened.

'You look amazing!' I say as we hug hello. 'Whatever you're doing at the moment, it's working.'

'Don't even get me started on you,' she says. 'I barely even recognize the woman I first met a couple of months ago.'

'OK, let's just agree we're both fabulous.' I still feel awkward accepting compliments about the way I look. I just don't have that gracious gene.

We buy coffees (well, I buy a coffee and Saskia gets a green tea because she has a 'no coffee after lunch' rule) and then we walk up towards the rose garden, even though the roses are past their best. We catch up with all the mundane stuff but, actually, I find it hard to concentrate because I'm dying to hear the lowdown on Robert and Samantha. When she leaves a rare two-second pause in a story she's telling me about having her parents over for lunch, I pounce.

'So you have to tell me what's going on with Robert . . .'

'What? Oh . . . sorry. There's me babbling on about God knows what. OK, so, I've been keeping a close eye on the pair of them since I gave him the good news, and I would definitely say relations were frosty.'

I take a sip of my coffee. Burn my tongue. 'Ouch. He seems like his normal self at home, though. Not as if he's upset about something.'

'That's what he seems like at work too, actually. I wonder if he thinks he's had a lucky escape.'

'Do you really think they've split up?'

'God knows,' she says, swatting away an over-excited wasp. 'But they definitely aren't acting like love's young dream any more. We did a big scene in the pub yesterday and he didn't even look at her. Whereas she didn't take her eyes off him for a second. Plus, her eyes are all red and puffy. One of the make-up girls told me she'd been crying too. It took them hours to unpuff her eyes, apparently. Is that a word, "unpuff"? If it isn't, it should be.'

'And he hasn't said anything to you?'

'We haven't really seen each other since. Oh, I did pass him in the corridor on my way out yesterday, and I asked him how he was and he just rolled his eyes. There were people around, though, so we couldn't really talk. But I'm sure he'll tell me what's going on because, who else can he talk to? Even if he doesn't like me much, I'm all he's got.'

It's huge, but it's not enough yet. I need to make sure that relationship is well and truly dead.

'What else can I do to make sure they don't just pick up where they left off after a few days?'

Saskia thinks for a moment. I watch while a large dog takes a small woman for a walk, straining at the end of its leash like a rabid ox pulling a plough.

She turns to me with a triumphant look on her face. 'I think you just have to keep on doing what you're doing. I, on the other hand . . .'

'What do you mean?'

'Think about it. Robert knows I know about him and Samantha. So I can tell him anything. I could make something else up that she's supposedly said or done that would really piss him off . . .'

'It needs to be something that couldn't be proven,' I say. I can't deny I'm getting a buzz of excitement, thinking about it. 'If he's feeling like he doesn't quite trust her because of the baby thing, then even the tiniest hint of something might push him over the edge.'

'Oh my God, I've got it!' She bangs her tea down on the bench and it slops over the rim of the cup. 'I'll tell him I've seen her flirting with Jez. Or worse. Kissing him. He's so terrified of Jez he would never confront him in a million years. He'll check with her. She'll deny it. He won't believe her. I just have to find a way to make sure he doesn't tell her it came from me. That should be easy enough, given that I'm the keeper of his biggest secret . . .'

'God, Saskia, do you think we should? Is it too much, involving someone who's completely innocent?'

'Jez'll never find out.'

'No, he will, because Samantha would probably tell him. She might go and beg him to explain to Robert that it's not true. That's what I'd do, wouldn't you?'

'You're right. I have to think this through. I'll come up with something.'

'You know how much I appreciate this, don't you?'

'You can pay me back by agreeing to come to a Bikram class one weekend, haha!'

I reach for my default response: no thanks, followed by some kind of disparaging remark about my weight and general lack of fitness. It dies on my tongue, though. Before I know it, I'm agreeing to go.

'Really?' she says, raising one eyebrow, something I've always wished I could do myself. I used to practise for hours in front of a mirror when I was a teenager because I thought it would give me an air of sophisticated mystery. I never managed it, though, even when I stuck Sellotape over the one I wanted to stay down. 'I was convinced you'd put up more of a fight than that.'

'I'm a changed woman.'

'This Saturday?'

Now I've said yes, I'm rapidly losing my bottle. What if I'm one of those passing-out people? It's all very well doing a bit of yoga (I say, as if I have any idea. I attempted a DVD once, because I thought it looked like the easy, pain-free alternative to real exercise, and I had to give up after ten minutes because I pulled something in my thigh. That's my sole first-hand experience), but it strikes me as another thing entirely doing it while being slow-roasted.

'I'm not sure. It's Georgia's birthday this weekend . . .'

'Chicken. Well, if you decide you're brave enough, let

me know ahead of time, because I'll have to book you in. And I'll have a word with Adrienne, the teacher, so she knows there's a beginner in the room. Otherwise, she'll just steam ahead, and you'll end up with no idea what's going on.'

I tell myself it's time to be brave. 'OK, sod it, I'll do it. Not this Saturday, though. Next.'

Saskia claps her hands together like a small, over-excited child. 'Excellent. Good girl.'

I can't wait to tell Myra. This one might just push her over the edge.

30

Saskia

It's too funny. No, it really is. Paula is going to attempt a Bikram class! I mean, I know she's lost a shedload of weight, but she's still a big lady. Still what – if she were me – I would consider too big. I suppose you have to admire her, though, she's done well.

I thought my suggestion of a fake Samantha and Jez romance was inspired, but she's right, of course, if any of this were real, Robert would confront Samantha and she would go straight to Jez. I have to keep reminding myself that, even though Robert and Samantha aren't having a thing (they'd better not be!), Paula absolutely has to believe they are so anything I come up with has to be watertight. No plot holes. Really, I should get one of the writers to come up with something for me. Although, on second thoughts, they never seem to worry if their story-lines hold up under scrutiny.

There does need to be something, though, that will help convince Paula that Robert has dumped Samantha for good (or the other way round, of course, but I think this way is more believable, given how I've portrayed their relationship for her). The time is coming when she'll feel she has to kick him out before he dumps her to set up home with – she thinks – Samantha. Georgia must be leaving home in the next few weeks. When do universities start? End of September? So, six weeks maybe. Six weeks for me to convince her it's well and truly over with them, never to be revived. Six weeks for me to make sure he walks straight out of their flat and into the one I will have lined up for us.

Oh, that reminds me. I've booked a day to go and look at a few places. I know it's a bit premature. Robbie and I have only just made the first tentative steps back towards each other (well, not steps so much, we were lying down most of the time, haha!). So I'm not telling him about it because he'll feel like I'm railroading him. But I need to make sure I have the perfect bolt-hole ready. And six weeks is tight. By the time I've seen somewhere perfect and jumped through all the hoops you need to jump through to secure it (that's assuming it's already empty. In fact, I need to tell the estate agent that's non-negotiable. I don't have time to wait for previous tenants to get their act together and move out), found a decorator, had any work that needs doing done, bought all the little bits and pieces that make a house a home . . . well, let's just agree it's tight.

So I'm going to view four flats. All in Marylebone. Why, I don't know, except that I like it around there and it feels sufficiently far away from both Josh in Richmond and Paula in Chalk Farm. You don't get much for your money so my budget has gone through the roof but I fig- ure, once Robert has moved in, we'll share the rent and it'll only be a matter of time until we find a perfect dream home to buy. I'm leaving Josh with the house. Much as it breaks my heart, because I've sweated blood making it exactly how I want it. That is, I hired someone else to sweat blood, but it still cost a fortune, and it's not even finished. But my earning power is greater than his. And given that he'll be out of work soon, it feels only fair. Not to mention that this whole thing is going to be devastating for him. He has absolutely no idea. So it's the least I can do. Likewise, Robbie has always said he wouldn't insist on Paula selling the flat or anything like that.

Three two-beds, one three-bed, although that one is really out of my price range. All with an underground parking space because I know Robbie would stress about trying to find a spot on the road every time he went out. They're like gold dust in an area like that. I'll just have to put up with it myself until we work out where we're going to settle long-term. All with some kind of balcony or roof terrace. All, I have to say, a lot nicer than the place he's in now.

And as soon as it's ready to move into I'll break the bad news to Josh. I don't even want to think about that yet. I know I'm a horrible person, I know what I'm doing is cold and calculated but I really have never wanted to hurt him. None of this is about him. It's about me. And Robbie.

And the future we're going to have together.

31

Paula

Georgia is eighteen. It feels as if there should be bunting and a parade, it's such a big day for me and Robert, but, as the youngest in her year, George has done nothing but celebrate eighteenth birthdays for months now. She has eighteenth-birthday ennui. Still, she lets us make a big fuss with Bucks Fizz at breakfast (Georgia: 'Is there actually any alcohol in this, because it just tastes like orange juice?') and puts up with us reminiscing about the day she was born – how she nearly arrived on the number 24 bus, because we didn't have a car and we couldn't afford a taxi – without ever once saying she's heard this story a thousand times.

She loves her presents – both the sensible, practical stuff and the Tiffany necklace that has her birth date inscribed on the back of the heart. I've booked the three of us a table for lunch at the Oxo Tower, somewhere she has always wanted to go, and the weather perks up from humid and dull to humid and sunny just in time for us to take our table outside. Robert and I are on our best behaviour – him thinking he's getting away with it, me comforted by the fact he definitely isn't going to – and I silently congratulate myself on the fact that Georgia is seemingly unaware of any underlying tension.

I'm struck with a sudden thought. Is that going to make it worse for her, though? We've protected her to such an extent that she has no idea anything is wrong between us. When we break it to her that we're going to go our separate ways, is it going to be ten times harder for her because she hasn't had a chance to prepare herself? She might start thinking her whole happy childhood has been a lie and start questioning everything. But on the other hand, we could have messed up her future by adding worries about her parents' happiness on to her A-level stress. Not to mention the fact that Robert and I have never even discussed the fact that anything might be wrong in our marriage with each other. He's just done what he's done and I've found out about it. There was nothing concrete we could have said to her anyway. The bottom line is that there's no right or wrong way to tell a child her – supposedly happy – parents are splitting up. All we can do when it comes to it is try to handle it as best we can.

'Are you OK, Mum?' she says now, as we wait for our main courses. 'You look miles away.'

'I was just thinking about that time we went to Devon,' I say, reaching for a happy family memory, 'and you made friends with that statue of a cherub in the hotel garden. You didn't want to leave its side.'

'I was three!'

Robert laughs. 'You told us it was called Tinky.'

'You were obsessed with *Teletubbies*.'

'That's about the first thing I remember,' Georgia says. 'That holiday.'

'What about the time we went to Scotland?' Robert says, and we allow ourselves to be swept away by a sea of collective memories of her childhood. Whatever is happening to us, nothing can change those.

'Want to watch this week's show?' Robert says, once George and Eliza have fallen into their taxi to go to her birthday dinner, dressed up to the nines for the club night that will follow. I mean, you have to admire his front. He's still enough of a narcissist that his idea of a fun way to spend an evening is to watch himself (and his mistress, let's not forget) on the telly.

'Sure,' I say, ever the compliant wife. Besides, it'll be interesting to see the chemistry between him and Samantha, given their characters are heading towards an affair. (I remember with shame that the idea for that storyline came about because Josh and I – or was it just me? – thought Saskia would hate watching herself portrayed as the older woman usurped by a younger, more glamorous model. I wonder whether Josh ever put in motion the storyline that had Saskia's character throw herself at a younger man only to be rejected, before he put the brakes on everything. I'm not proud of myself, just so you know.)

We settle down at opposite ends of the sofa as the familiar theme music starts. Pastoral scenes of rolling hills and winding country lanes. Farmer Giles and his cows, Mrs Giles walking their border collie across a field, Hargreaves standing proudly outside his little antiques shop, Melody riding a horse. The idea that someone got paid good money to come up with this hackneyed pile of crap is mind-blowing and more than a bit depressing. Neither Samantha's nor Jez's character is sufficiently important to make the credits yet, although their upcoming storylines might soon catapult them to the top.

'Saskia really is stunning,' I say when she first appears. I feel as if I want to say something nice about her. To make amends to her. And, let's face it, he would never believe me if I complimented her acting.

He grunts, non-committal.

'It's hard to believe Hargreaves would cheat on her with anyone, let alone Marilyn.'

'I told you,' he says, pressing pause, because he hates to miss a second of the action. 'I tried to argue that with Josh, but he wouldn't have it.'

As usual, I doze off by the time the plot of the week kicks in (something to do with a tractor going missing and being spotted at a local auction among stuff put up for sale by Jez), but I do manage to see the first scene with a hint of what's to come between Hargreaves and Marilyn. I try to decide if her real-life attraction to him is translating on to the screen and, actually, she does manage to make her flirtation fairly convincing.

'She's quite good, isn't she?' Robert says, and I can't bring myself to answer.

Josh has just walked into the café.

Let me just say that again. Josh. Has. Just. Walked. Into. The. Café.

It's hard to emphasize enough how momentous this is. Josh, who hasn't spoken to me since he found out I had falsely accused his wife of having an affair, who lives on the other side of London and so couldn't just have stopped by at random, who is supposed to be in the middle of a filming day in Acton, is standing in the doorway, looking around, as if he's trying to spot someone. Me.

I'm about to finish for the day. I have one of my regular sessions with Chas in twenty minutes and Chas does not tolerate lateness. I've been looking forward to it, actually, as I often do these days. I'm already wearing my sweat-wicking finery under my 'Myra's' uniform. The top is an aqua-coloured fitted thing from Lululemon that just skims my waist. There are a few lumps and bumps on display still, but I feel confident in it. Strong. I like the idea that it says, 'I work out,' although it could equally say, 'I bought some clothes at Lululemon and put them on for work because they're comfortable.'

I'm in the middle of telling Myra all about the rest of George's birthday weekend (it mostly involves her moaning and saying she felt sick while I made her toast and mopped her brow, I won't bore you) when I see him out of the corner of my eye. Something about him, some sub-conscious familiarity, makes me turn around to see who's come in. I screech to a halt halfway through a sentence.

Josh half raises an arm at me. I catch Myra looking from me to him and back again. I compose myself and walk over towards him.

'What on earth are you doing here?'

He waits for me to get close enough so he doesn't have to shout. 'I need to talk to you. It's important. Is now OK?'

To say I am confused really doesn't do my state of mind justice.

'Um . . . sure . . . I mean, I was just leaving to meet my trainer . . .'

'Oh God, sorry,' Josh says, and everything about his body language tells me he hasn't come to shout at me again for potentially ruining his marriage. 'I didn't even think you might be going somewhere else. I just remember you saying you finished at half two. I'll come back. Or I can call you. It's fine.'

I've never been good with cliffhangers. I always want to know what's going to happen. 'No, it's fine. Let me just ring him. My phone's out the back.'

I'm loathe to leave him with Myra because she's defin-itely picked up that there's something going on here, but I have no choice. I can't just leave Chas hanging. Out in the back room I chicken out of phoning his mobile and call the gym instead. I don't feel up to feign-ing illness (putting on that sleepy, drugged voice, like I used to when I had a job I hated, temping in an insurance office, and I often phoned in 'sick') so I claim a family emergency and Justine the receptionist promises to let him know right away. I know they'll still charge me for the session, because it's so late in the day, but there's nothing I can do about that now. I promise myself I'll go for a run later.

Back in the café, Josh is sitting at a table being given the third degree, along with a slice of carrot cake, by Myra. I imagine she will have tortured it out of him that he's Josh, the producer on Robert's show, which means she'll have worked out that he's Saskia's husband and that I had a bit of a thing for him. That we had a bit of a thing for each other, to be fair. I actually feel myself blush when I walk back over to join him.

'Shall we go for a walk? You can bring your cake with you.' No way am I hearing whatever it is he has to say with an audience.

Myra, thankfully, gets the hint and springs into action. 'Oh yes, I'll wrap it for you.'

I can tell he wants to say no, he'll leave it, but he's too polite. Or too scared. Myra is very protective of her cakes and he might have picked up on her Rottweiler-like tendencies.

As we leave, him clutching his bag of cake like a five-year-old leaving a birthday party, she raises her eyebrows at me, and I shrug.

'See you tomorrow.'

I follow Josh out of the café and up the hill. He seems to know where he's going and he's not saying anything yet so I decide it's pointless to badger him and, besides, I'm using all my breath trying to keep up. He rounds a corner away from the main road and stops at a bench by a little triangle of green.

'This OK?' he says.

'Sure.'

We sit side by side, a foot and a half between us.

'Sorry if I made you miss your appointment.'

'That's . . . Josh, tell me what's going on . . .'

He inhales slowly and I have to stop myself from shouting at him to get on with it. A fat black and white cat wanders past, giving me an accusing look. I imagine this is usually his bench.

Finally, he speaks. 'I think it's Saskia after all. Who Robert's been seeing. I think it's been her all along and this Samantha thing is just a distraction.'

'What? Why . . .'

He rubs his hand up over his forehead and back across his stubbly hair. He's got an unshaven thing going on today. Despite what's going on, I find myself thinking that I like it.

'OK,' he says. 'I'm not proud of this.'

'Don't even get me started on things I've done I've not been proud of lately.'

'She's been acting strangely. I don't know . . . I don't think I ever would have picked up on it if it wasn't for everything that went on before . . . nothing I could really put my finger on, but I would notice that, if Robert wasn't around, she wasn't around, that kind of thing.'

I'm starting to feel a bit queasy. I notice that Josh still has his carrot cake clutched in his hand. It's almost funny.

'And I've been watching him and Samantha ever since you told me about them. And there's just no way. Unless the two of them are the best actors in the world, which . . . no disrespect . . .'

273

I pull a face that I hope means: don't feel you can't slag him off on my account.

'There's literally no chemistry between them at all. Not even in their love scenes. And she's a really nice woman. I just don't think she would . . . And then I started thinking about why you knew about them in the first place and, of course, it was Saskia. Saskia told you, right?'

I nod. I can see why that might look a bit incriminating. Shit. 'Yes. That's the only piece of evidence we have, Saskia's word.'

Could she have been lying to me? I've felt so guilty ever since then that I've allowed myself to become close to her. I consider her my friend.

'So then I started to think, why would she do that? And there was only one explanation I could think of.'

I stare at the ground, racking my brain for why else Saskia would make something like that up.

'I don't think we can assume she's lying just because Robert and Samantha might be covering their tracks well.'

'There's more,' he says. I knew there would be. Josh is too rational to come halfway across London to tell me this on a whim. 'This is the bit I'm not proud of. I went through their dressing rooms. I'd get sacked, honestly, if anyone knew, but I waited till everyone had gone home one night – I'm quite often the last to leave; there's a spare set of keys locked away in the main office safe that are only meant to be used in emergencies. It's strictly forbidden to go in there without permission, unless it's life or death. Not to mention how unethical . . .'

'Don't you have security guards on at night?' I remember

Robert once saying to me in the very early days that he'd had to accompany some burly man to the wall where all the cast photos were posted to prove to him that he wasn't a burglar or a nutter when he went back to collect something after everyone else had left. I hadn't even questioned why he might have been there so late at the time.

Josh nods. 'Yes. Two. But they know me, obviously. And I knew I could have made up some plausible story about what I was doing there if they spotted me. I am the producer, after all. And so long as no one started claiming anything had been stolen, they would probably never give it another thought. As it turns out, I didn't see either of them.'

'So . . . ?'

'So I looked in Saskia's first. In the bin, there was a note. Ripped into a few pieces but hardly difficult to put together again. Here.'

He produces a crumpled mess of paper from his pocket and hands it to me. There are five small pieces and I assemble them easily.

'Five o'clock? Mine? Wait for me if I'm not done.'

There's no name, no initial. The writing most definitely looks familiar. I get that feeling that hits you when you go backwards on a swing too fast. Not because of Robert. Him betraying me is old news. Because of Saskia.

'Shit. It's still not proof, though. Maybe they were going to go over lines for today.'

'They "loathe each other", remember. It seems unlikely. And, anyway, once I'd been through all Sas's stuff, I went and had a look in Robert's.'

I know I'm not going to like what's coming. 'Go on . . .'

He rewards me with a smile. 'What would be the biggest cliché you could think of? Imagine this was an episode of *Farmer Giles*.'

That's easy. 'A pair of her knickers.'

'Bingo!'

No way. 'You cannot be serious? You found a pair of Saskia's knickers in Robert's dressing room?'

He nods. 'It's almost too good, isn't it?'

'But . . . I mean . . . not that I'm doubting you, but there are only so many brands . . . couldn't they be Samantha's?'

'What size would you say Saskia is?'

'I don't know. Something stupid like an eight.'

'Exactly. And . . . at a rough guess . . . how about Samantha?'

I think about Saskia's skinny form and Samantha's curves. That girl has hips.

'OK, point taken. But someone else then? One of the crew? A cleaner?'

'She has the exact same ones. In the exact same size. She's been playing you. Both of us.'

I try to take it in. The cat is now rubbing his head against my legs, but I'm not in the mood. 'That bitch. And I'm meant to be doing her stupid hot yoga with her next weekend.'

Josh looks at me, confused. Of course, he has no idea Saskia and I are in touch. Why would she have told him? I always assumed it was out of respect for me not wanting Robert to know, but I now realize she had an agenda of her own too.

'We're friends now, if you can believe that. I felt bad for what I'd done to her. I'd got to like her.'

'You're still meeting up?'

I nod. 'Sorry. It's nothing sinister. Just a coffee now and then. Like I said, I thought we were friends.'

Josh sighs, and his silence says it all.

'Oh,' he says, after a few seconds where I take this in. 'I forgot the *pièce de résistance*.'

'How could anything beat the knickers? I mean, really, though . . .'

He rewards me with a sad smile. 'Sas is looking at flats to rent.'

'For the two of them?'

He nods. 'I assume so. There was a pile of particulars in her room. All in Marylebone.'

'Near West1 Hot Yoga! She loves that place. She can roll in there every morning and sweat to her heart's content.'

'I guess it's neutral territory. Anyway, one of them had a big tick on it, so I photocopied it.'

He digs around in his work bag. Pulls out an estate agent's sheet with a picture of a very fancy-looking living room, complete with floor-to-ceiling windows overlooking a large balcony. Is this it? Robert and Saskia's love nest to be?

'It's nice,' I say, handing it back.

'It's expensive.'

I exhale. 'God, wouldn't it be great if you could just sack them both? See how long they last living in a bedsit.'

'Don't . . .'

'Just indulge me for a minute. It would be funny.'

'It would.'

'So they're really going to do it.'

'Looks like it.'

277

'Why don't I at least phone up and enquire about it? Find out if it's gone.'

'It can't hurt, I suppose,' he says, handing the details back to me.

'God, I'm sorry, Josh. This is a million times worse for you than for me. Obviously.'

I'm struggling to make eye contact with him. I don't know whether I'm more worried he might think I was trying to make a pass at him or whether I actually would be. So I lean down and stroke the cat, who is now curled up by my feet.

'I don't know,' he says. 'Things haven't been the same since . . . you know . . .'

Really? Since you kissed me?

'I don't mean me and you . . .' he carries on quickly, clearly concerned I might think he did. Which I did. For a second. Sue me. 'Me and Sas. I started to look at her differently when I thought she was cheating on me, and then, even though I felt incredibly guilty for getting it so wrong . . .'

'Or not, as it turns out . . .'

'Or not. I tried – I really did – to throw myself back into it, but it was as if I'd allowed myself to see all her faults and then I couldn't *unsee* them. How self-centred she is. How she thinks she's above everyone else. How badly she treats people sometimes. I started almost wishing she *had* cheated on me so I had an excuse to leave.'

'Why not just leave anyway?' I wonder if he's like Robert after all. Unable to leave one relationship without having another to fall into.

'Because I'd promised her commitment. I stood up and

said all those things like '"Till death us do part" and "For better or worse". You can't marry someone and then just decide to opt out because you don't like them quite as much as you thought you did.'

'Sounds like a good enough reason to me.'

'That's why you stayed with Robert all these years?'

'That was different. We had George.'

'I just didn't want to be that person, that's all.'

'Which is admirable. I'm not saying it isn't.'

'I guess part of me was hoping I might snap out of it. Like it was just a hangover from having convinced myself it was over.'

'This is all so fucked up,' I say. The understatement of the century.

'Anyway,' he says, 'I thought you should know.'

We sit there in silence for what seems like a decade but is probably thirty seconds. My cat friend has wandered off, bored with the lack of attention, so I just stare off into space, wondering what to say next. Eventually, something hits me.

A light bulb flashes in my head. 'She called him Robbie! She covered it up pretty well but I should have realized something was up then. No one calls him Robbie except Alice. So it's not like she's even ever overheard someone else calling him that and it just slipped out. That must be her pet name for him.'

He rolls his eyes. 'She calls me Joshie.'

'Lucky you. So what are you going to do now?'

He smiles a sharky smile. 'Help you,' he says. 'Break them up. Kick them out. I'm done with being the nice guy.'

'Are you going to throw her out of the house?' I'm

surprised. Josh was always adamant that this was something he would never do.

'Only figuratively. When I say I'm done with being the nice guy, I mean I'm planning on being marginally less nice now than I was before. But that doesn't have the same ring to it.'

'Always speak in soundbites,' I say, laughing. 'Then you can qualify them afterwards.'

'That's always been my motto.'

I'm glad. Although I'm pleased that he's going to stand up for himself more, it would have been a shame if this whole mess turned him into some kind of bitter, vengeful saddo. I'm only too happy to fulfil that role.

When I get back to the café – in my haste to get out of there to find out what Josh had come to say to me, I left the keys to the flat in the back room – Myra is all over me before the door is even closed behind me.

'OK. Explain yourself,' she says, stacking a pile of clean plates. The bakery is quiet. It's too hot and humid for tea and cake. 'What was he doing here, and why haven't you set me up on a date with him?'

I flop down at a table. Gratefully accept the ice-cold can of Diet Pepsi she puts in front of me.

'He's found out it's Saskia Robert's seeing after all.'

Myra plonks herself down opposite me, ignoring the young woman with the toddler in a buggy who has just come in.

'You are kidding me.'

'Hardly.'

'But . . .' For once, she is lost for words.

'Customer,' I say, waving at the toddler, who smiles and flaps a hand back at me. The mother looks at me gratefully. I remember what it was like when George was that age and taking her anywhere induced looks of horror from all the people whose day she might potentially ruin with her out-of-control noise levels. Why anyone ever thought glaring at a small child was going to help keep them calm and quiet I don't know, but you'd be surprised how often it happens.

Myra doesn't engage in any of her usual small talk as she makes the mother a tea and hands the little one a box of juice. She can't wait to get back and hear what I have to say. I fill her in on the whole sorry situation and she sits there, wide-eyed.

'Well, I can see why you liked him,' she says, as if that has anything to do with anything.

'What? I don't! I mean . . . I did . . . it's so irrelevant at this point . . .'

'You can always pass his number on to me.'

I ignore her. 'Can you believe she's been playing me this whole time?'

'Telling you he's shagging someone else is pretty shitty, I must admit.'

'She made up that whole thing about Samantha secretly trying to get pregnant! I could have made such a fucking idiot of myself. I could have confronted her . . .'

'She knew you wouldn't, though, didn't she?'

'She still took a risk. I mean, God, how desperate.'

I glug back the last of my Diet Pepsi. I may have broken the record for fast fizzy-drink downing. 'So, what now?'

'Now you truly do have the upper hand,' Myra says. 'Now you know everything and she knows nothing.'

'I don't know if I've got the energy.'

'Of course you have. Deny them their happy ending. It'll make you feel better, I promise.'

I give her a hug before I leave.

'Oh,' she calls as I'm about to go out the door. 'Can I put that "Sadskia" picture up on the wall now that we don't like her again?'

33

Before he left, Josh promised to stay in touch. I think we've both learned from the last time that random nastiness doesn't suit us. There will be no more petty revenges with hurtful storylines or leaked photos to the papers. We have a goal: to split up Robert and Saskia once and for all, and that's it.

It makes sense for me to keep up the pretence of my friendship with her. I don't want to alert her to the fact that anything is wrong. And, besides, there's still the possibility I might glean some interesting bit of information that she accidentally lets slip. So, I am intending to keep my Bikram appointment – Saskia has already texted me to tell me she has reserved me a place – although I am now no longer prepared to make an arse of myself in the name of friendship. I download a video of the moves and I practise them every morning and afternoon. OK, so I'm not going to suddenly become lithe and supple in less than a week, but I can at least make sure I don't look like a total idiot.

I also squeeze in a spray tan after my Chas session on Wednesday. If I'm going to have to stand next to Saskia dressed in Lycra, I want to make sure I look as good as I can. I don't want to be there just to boost her already massive ego.

Chas gets the calipers out. Pronounces me thirty-five

per cent fat, and the scales tell me I've lost another three pounds. To celebrate, I brave Sweaty Betty to find myself the perfect yoga outfit (by which I mean the one that I'll look best in, not the most practical), and I'm beside myself when I come away with everything in a medium. Cropped leggings and a fitted sleeveless top that shows off the muscles Chas and I have been working on. When I show the clothes to Georgia she makes me model them for her. I can see by the look on her face how proud she is of me.

'You look fucking brilliant, Mum.'

'Language, young lady,' I say but her obvious pride in me gives me a huge boost. I've told her – and Robert – that I'm trying out yoga for the first time on Saturday morning, but not that it's Bikram or that Saskia will be there, obviously. And as a dedicated yoga bunny herself, Georgia's been giving me tips.

She's off to another festival for the weekend herself – as usual, half-work, half-play – but, even though none of us is mentioning it, we all know that tomorrow is THE BIG DAY. The day all A-level students both dread and look forward to in equal measure. Tomorrow is the day she'll find out if she's got the three As that she needs to take up her place at Bristol. I have never doubted for a second she'll ace it. She couldn't have worked any harder and still retained her sanity.

Still, on Thursday, I'm grateful that I'm working, because it would be hard to concentrate on anything else while I wait for her call. I know she and Eliza are heading into school at about eleven and I have to stop myself from looking at my watch every thirty seconds from ten o'clock onwards. Myra tries to distract me by making me serve everyone who comes in. It doesn't matter. I might be smiling and making small talk but, inside my head, all that's going on is me willing my mobile to ring. At five past eleven, when I accidentally give someone a slice of cheesecake instead of triple-chocolate gateau, Myra steers me towards the back room.

'Try her,' she says. 'Put yourself out of your misery.'

The first two times it rings until it goes through to voicemail. They're celebrating, I tell myself. They're all screeching and screaming in that way only teenage girls can. I try again and I'm relieved to hear the repetitive ringing stop halfway through.

'Mum?'

I was right about the celebrating. I can hardly hear her for the high-pitched hysteria.

'Hi, sweetie. I couldn't wait . . .' I close my eyes. Wait for her to say 'Three As' or even 'Three A stars'. I'm jolted back down to earth by what sounds like a wail.

'I didn't get them!'

'You . . . ? What do you mean?'

'I got a B and two Cs.'

In my day, that would have been fine. Cause for celebration. I know that things are very different now. Everyone and their mother gets As. Georgia was slated to sail through easily with the top grades. I don't understand what's gone wrong.

'What? Sweetie, are you sure you've read the right thing?'

'I know I'm obviously thick, Mum, but I'm not that thick.'

'You're a million miles from thick. Do you want me to come and get you? We'll figure out what to do.'

'No, it's OK. We're going to go to Tinseltown.'

'We need to ring the uni as soon as we can, don't we? See if they'll still take you?'

'They're not going to take me now. I'm miles off. Not unless everyone in the world messed up too.'

'We should still call them.'

'Jesus, Mum,' she snaps. 'Just let me have a few hours for it to sink in.'

I know I'm right, that if she has any hope of somehow overcoming this obstacle we do need to get on to it right away. Hundreds of other parents around the country will be scrabbling around at this moment doing exactly that. Ensuring their child doesn't miss out on the future they hoped for. But I also know I need to give her a bit of space. What harm is a couple of hours drowning her sorrow in milkshakes with her friends going to do?

'Of course. I might make some preliminary enquiries. Then we can get on to them later. Don't worry. Everything'll be OK.'

I don't want to sound as if I'm checking up on her but I can't help adding, 'Is Eliza with you?'

'Yes,' she sniffs. 'She got two Bs and a C.'

Eliza is supposed to be going to Leeds to study chemistry. Clearly, that's not about to happen now. I want to say, 'There must be a mistake. You must be looking at the wrong list.' I'm so confused about how this has happened. They've been studying together pretty much every evening. Or, at least, that's what Georgia told me. Shit.

'Don't be late, OK. We need to sit down and talk, you, me and Dad.'

Of course I call Robert immediately. There's no reply and I can't help imagining him and Saskia sitting there looking at my name on the screen, laughing about how hilarious it would be if she answered instead of him. Even though I know that, in reality, he's probably in the middle of filming a scene, I'm overcome with anger at him. I need to talk to him and I need to talk to him now.

I bite the bullet and call the production office, tell the very friendly boy who answers that I need to speak to my husband as soon as is humanly possible. He tells me he can see Robert on the monitor in the office, sitting in Farmer Giles' kitchen, but that he thinks they'll probably break for lunch once this scene is completed.

'I can get a message to him then.'

'No one's died,' I say. 'But it's still an emergency.'

Myra is hovering when I finally emerge from the back room.

'Shit,' I say when I see her. 'Fuck.'

I fill her in. Thankfully, she doesn't try telling me that everything will be all right in the end or list the people who went on to be rich and successful but who failed to gain any qualifications at school.

'So,' she says, sitting me down and pouring me a coffee. 'You ring them and beg, is that it?'

'Basically. But she's so way off and it's such a sought-after course.'

'So then what? You try other unis? Other subjects?'

'I suppose so. I don't really know how it works because I never bothered to find out.'

'Well, it wasn't exactly on the cards.'

'Do you think she's been lying to me all this time? That she and Eliza weren't really studying? I mean, it's a bit of a coincidence, them both getting such low grades.'

Myra shrugs. 'Why don't you speak to Eliza's mum?'

'I hardly know her,' I say. 'But yes, I will. Where the fuck is Robert?'

An elderly lady nursing a tea and an eclair whips her head around to see what the drama is.

'Sorry,' Myra calls over to her. 'Family emergency.' She drops to a whisper. 'Nosy old bat.'

'I need to tell George she can't go off to that festival tomorrow,' I suddenly remember. 'She needs to stay and sort this out.'

'You can tell her tonight. Let her have a couple of hours blowing off steam.'

Robert finally gets me when I'm on my way home, stomping down the hill, barging past anyone who gets in my way.

'Where the hell have you been?' is the first thing that comes out of my mouth.

'I only just got your message,' he says. 'They left a note in my dressing room but I didn't go back there.'

No, too busy fucking Saskia in hers, I think.

'What's happened? Is George OK?'

'She's missed her grades. By miles. B and two Cs.'

'Jesus, Paula, I thought she'd had an accident or something.'

'I told them to tell you no one had died.'

'Poor baby. Is she OK?'

'Yes. I think so. She's with her friends. Do you think she's been lying to us all this time about how much she was studying? Do you think she and Eliza have been going out every night?'

Robert sighs. 'Probably. They're teenagers . . .'

'What, and that makes it all OK?'

'No. Of course not. I just mean it doesn't make her bad. All teenagers lie . . .'

I can't help interrupting. 'I wonder where she gets that from . . .'

If he registers what I've said, he pretends he doesn't. 'The important thing now is that we help her sort this out. Not that we give her a hard time for it. If she has been sneaking around, then I'd say she's learned her lesson. It's her future she's in danger of messing up.'

He's right. I know he is.

'What time's she getting home?'

'I don't really know. She probably doesn't want to face us.'

'I'll speak to Josh. See if I can get released early. They might be able to move stuff around.'

'It's OK. She might not be back for hours. Thanks, though.'

By the time Georgia arrives home – looking a bit teary-eyed and a lot sheepish – my anger has burnt out. Robert was right. It's her future that's at stake here. Whatever she's been up to, this is way worse for her than for us.

'Come here,' I say when she lets herself in, and I pull her into a hug. She sobs into my shoulder.

'I'm really sorry, Mum.'

'It's OK. You can tell me what's been going on later. Let's make a plan first.'

'There's no way anyone'll take me for Medicine now,' she says, and she looks so heartbreakingly sad it almost kills me.

'No', I say. 'Probably not. So you have two choices.

Retakes and try again next year, or try and get into another course somewhere that's not so demanding.'

'I don't want to do anything else.'

Even though I feel so bad for her, I still have to stop the words, 'You should have thought of that before' coming out of my mouth.

'What happened, do you think?' I'm not going to accuse her. For all I know, she and Eliza really did spend hours studying and they're just not as academic as everyone believed. And I want her to tell me the truth. I don't want to force it out of her. She needs to learn that being honest pays off. At least, with me it does.

'I don't know . . . they must have told us to revise the wrong stuff or something.'

'Right. God, so everyone's grades were down in those three subjects?'

I wait. I can see in her face that she's struggling with what's the right thing to do. Weighing it up against what might get her in the most trouble. I have to force myself not to bail her out.

'No . . . Mum, I think I messed up . . .'

A weight lifts off me. We can deal with her low grades. The thing I couldn't have dealt with would have been knowing she didn't trust me enough to be truthful with me.

'What happened? It's OK.'

'I didn't revise. Well, I did, but nowhere near as much as you think I did.'

'So all those evenings round at Eliza's? What were you doing? Watching TV? Going out? I'm not cross, I just want to understand . . .'

'We were working.'

George and Eliza both have an occasional evening and weekend job at a diner in Camden. And by 'occasional' I do mean occasional. One night a week.

'At the diner?'

She nods. 'We thought we should try and get as much money together as we could before we left home. It seems stupid now.'

Well, at least they weren't out getting drunk or taking drugs, I suppose.

'How often?'

'Four or five nights a week. Whenever you thought I was there.'

'And Eliza's mum was OK with this?'

She looks down at the table. 'She thought we were here.'

A thought occurs to me. 'Who was bringing you home in the evenings then?'

'I got the bus.'

'Jesus Christ, Georgia. If something had happened to you, I would have had no idea where you were.'

'I'm sorry. I'm really sorry.'

I reach across the table and take her hand. 'It's OK. Thank you for telling me the truth. Now we just have to work out what to do next.'

'Don't tell Dad,' she says. She's such a Daddy's girl that the worst thing she can imagine is him being disappointed in her.

'I already have. He's taken it better than you think.'

I persuade her that we should call Bristol just in case, even though I know it's hopeless. And it is. They're very nice, and they tell her they'll put her on a list, but obviously there are other people who only just failed to get the requisite grades who they are much more likely to make an exception for. They don't even suggest an alternative course that might take her, that's how much they don't really want her at this point.

'So clearing or retakes?'

Neither of us can get up much enthusiasm for going through clearing. Georgia makes it clear that she wouldn't really want to go to any uni that would take her on to do Medicine with such poor marks.

'I mean, imagine what the course must be like if they're so desperate they'd take me,' she says, and I'm pleased to see she laughs.

'Do you want to try for anything else? What else are you interested in?'

She barely even gives it a thought. She's wanted to be a doctor since she was eight years old.

'I'm going to have to retake. Oh God, the humiliation.'

'Don't be stupid, loads of people have to. What's Eliza thinking?' Much as I have always liked Eliza, I'm not sure the idea of the two of them going through retakes together is the best one I've ever heard, given what's happened. I don't know who influenced who, but I definitely wouldn't want the whole thing to just repeat itself again.

Georgia shrugs. 'She doesn't know yet.'

It's only once I'm cooking dinner and Georgia and Robert are sitting talking it over at the kitchen table, that it occurs to me that she now won't be leaving home in a few weeks. Obviously, a huge part of me is thrilled. No empty nest for another year. No feeling as if that whole, major chapter of my life has closed. But I know this also throws everything up in the air for me and Robert. Will he still leave to set up home with Saskia in October, as I believe he plans to? Can I bring myself to throw him out with her still living at home?

And it hits me that, just as I expect her to behave like an adult and take responsibility for her own future, so I have to treat her like one by not cosseting her from the fact that her parents' marriage isn't perfect. I owe it to her to present her with the facts – once I'm ready to admit to Robert that I know them – and let her react however she reacts. I'll try and make it as painless for her as possible, obviously – I'm never going to ask her to take sides or dictate who she lives with – but I'll be as honest with her as I can be. It's only fair.

34

Saskia

Annoyingly, Paula looks quite cute in her yoga outfit. And confident. When I first met her she seemed to spend most of her time apologetically pulling her oversized T-shirt down over her stomach, but not any more. I wonder whether Robbie has noticed the changes. Probably not. If you see someone every day, you stop looking at them. They become wallpaper. White noise.

I have to make sure that never happens to us.

I've found us a flat, by the way! 'An apartment', the brochure called it, because I think the agent was trying to sound all New Yorky. And it does remind me of New York. All clean lines, big windows and dark wooden floors. It's on the seventh floor, so the views of Regent's Park are fantastic.

It's empty, both of people and furniture, which is perfect. I've ordered the basics – by basics, I mean the things you need to live (sofa, bed), not that I've purchased them at knock-down prices at DFS or Furniture Village. I've spent hours in Heals agonizing over whether a couch with a chaise works better than a corner arrangement (it does). My Amex card has taken a bashing. Luckily, Joshie and I have always kept an element of our finances separate. That is, we share everything, but every month we divide an equal amount of our income into our own accounts so we don't have to have a discussion every time one of us wants to buy a pair of shoes. That's what kills a lot of marriages, in my opinion. The endless petty squabbling over whether it's fair that she wants to spend two hundred pounds on a jacket when he just bought one for fifty. Of course, Josh and my marriage is about to fall apart anyway, despite our clever accounting. Oh, well, maybe it wouldn't have lasted as long as it did without our illusion of financial freedom. Who knows?

Anyway, the point is that he doesn't need to see my American Express statements because the money comes out of my own account.

The rest of the furniture I thought it would be fun for me and Robbie to choose together. I know he loves antiques, and so do I. We can take our time. Choose the perfect piece for each corner. It'll be a labour of love.

Meanwhile, I have asked the owner of the 'apartment' if I can paint a couple of walls to give the place more character. I've spent hours in Farrow and Ball, trying to discern the difference between String and Cord and then more hours painting tiny squares from tester pots on different sections of wall and trying to work out how the colour will look in different lights. I'm doing the work myself, would you believe? I wanted to put something of me into the place. Something I could point to and say, 'I did that'. I've enjoyed it, for the most part. Dressed in old jeans and a big shirt, scarf wrapped around my hair in a very Norma Desmond kind of way. Radio on.

I've had to take a year's lease. Cancellable (is that a word?) at three months' notice but you don't get your (ginormous) deposit back. It seems funny sitting (on the floor!) in this big, beautiful space that's going to be our home but which Robbie still knows nothing about. I'm planning on bringing him here in a week or so – once my 'basics' have arrived and I've found a handyman to put the TV on the wall and connect it up. I'm going to make up the bed with crisp white linen (who knew thread counts could go so high and cost so much!), stash a bottle of champagne in the fridge and surprise him.

I can't wait.

I usually like to put my mat at the front of the class. Fewer distractions, plus Adrienne can see what I'm doing more easily, and make those little adjustments that make all the difference. But I'm going to have to give up my spot and move to the back today, downwind of all those Lycra-clad behinds, because it's Paula's first class and she'll need to be able to watch what other people are doing and follow them. The front is a place for those of us who can move seamlessly through the postures. It's almost a performance.

I love the buzz I get as soon as I step into the heat of the room. The instant feeling of relaxation, like walking into a sauna or one of the hothouses at Kew. The sheen of sweat that covers you almost instantly. ('Perspiration,' I hear my mum say in my head. 'Ladies don't sweat.') I like to get there a few minutes early and just lie on my mat and get myself into the right frame of mind. Try to forget all the stresses and strains of the week. I see a lot of the same faces each class but there are usually a couple of newbies craning their necks to get a good look at me. I can always tell. The subtle double-take when they spot who I am. The furtive glances that follow. I try to block it out. Once someone went back out to the changing rooms and got their phone – strictly forbidden, of course – and tried to take a sneaky photo. Adrienne threw them out. Banned them from returning. I pretended to be shocked at the severity of her punishment but, afterwards, I thanked her profusely.

I'm not really in the mood for having to play the role of teaching assistant. I'm trying to remember why I thought it would be a good idea to insist Paula came along in the first place. I think I thought it would be funny. She'd make a fool of herself and I could feel superior. It's sad, isn't it, that life's all about these petty victories? I could feel fabulous in my skin-tight gear (even despite the few extra 'pregnancy' pounds I've been forced to gain) while she would, no doubt, be feeling self-conscious and uncomfortable. It's a power thing, I'm fully aware of that, thanks very much. Survival of the fittest. Literally, haha!

And at our usual brunch afterwards I can lay it on thick about Robbie and Samantha (Robert. Must remember to call him Robert. Christ, that was a close call the other day.) I can drive another nail into their coffin.

So I'm being extra attentive. Smiling at her encouragingly when I get the opportunity. Whispering little helpful hints when I can. She looks as if she's enjoying it, despite it being hard work, so I suppose that's gold stars in the bag for me. I'm waiting for her to have to sit down, like most first-timers, but she battles on through. She's fitter than I ever would have imagined and, you have to hand it to her, she's determined. By the end of the ninety minutes

I can see she's hooked. It hadn't even occurred to me that she might decide to take it up properly and I'm a bit put out at the thought of it. This is my thing, my space. I don't want to have to share it. Also, it could become a little awkward, come October, haha! I wonder how subtly I can say, 'You'll have to find a different club, or at least sign up for a different class,' and I decide I can't. Damn.

35

Paula

Saskia is in full-on Robert and Samantha mode. Robert and Samantha this. Robert and Samantha that. She tells me that she has another scheme to help split them up, still involving telling Robert that she has seen Samantha with Jez, but this time adding in the detail that she's not sure if she saw what she saw, but offering to try to prise the truth out of Samantha if Robert will just hold off accusing her for the moment. Sound familiar?

'Brilliant,' I say, with all the enthusiasm I can muster. I'm finding it hard to concentrate. I have a list of local schools going round and round in my head and, while she talks I mentally run through the pros and cons of the sixth form in each one. George is adamant she doesn't want to return, tail between her legs, to the one she's just left.

'Then I can eke it out, just giving him a few little tidbits here and there, but not enough for him to confront her, and so we won't have to worry about her going straight off to Jez to get him to confirm the whole thing's a pack of lies. It'll just make him feel rattled. Do you think he'll go for it?'

In reality, not in a million years. Robert would go straight to Samantha and have it out with her, regardless of what Saskia had asked him. As I now know this whole thing is a pack of lies, though, why not?

'Definitely,' I say. 'Just emphasize that he doesn't want to make himself look like an idiot by accusing her falsely. Robert hates to look like an idiot. And that women value trust over everything, so if he shows Samantha that he doesn't trust her without reason it'll affect their relationship. Some bollocks like that.'

'I should be taking notes,' she says, and then, of course, she adds, 'haha,' for good measure. It's odd how I'd become used to it, even started to find it endearing, but now it sets my teeth on edge all over again.

We're sitting in our usual café – too drizzly for outside, even though it's still hot. Saskia is freshly showered, smelling of Molton Brown, and damp-haired. I, on the other hand, look like I've had a fight with a garden hose and the hose won. The idea of stripping naked in front of my husband's lover with her über-judgemental body image issues was too much for me so I am taking my sweat home to wash it off there. I know I smell, and not in a good way.

I loved hot yoga, by the way. Loved the slow pace, the instructor's soft voice murmuring the transitions as if she'd said this same thing a thousand times – which she almost certainly has – and it had lost all meaning, the feeling that my body had become like a piece of elastic, the rivers of water running down my back after only a few minutes. I can see why it's addictive. I was rubbish, obviously (Adrienne: 'Yoga is not a competition. There is no such thing as being good or bad at it. It's a personal journey'), but it didn't seem to matter. Two people gave up partway through and lay down on their mats like they really were just there for the sauna element, and no one batted an eyelid. I'm proud that I stuck it out, though. I'm proud that I'm strong enough.

Saskia nibbles on a bread roll, perfect little veneered teeth like a row of shiny tiles. I've never understood that veneers thing. People with healthy but slightly wonky teeth replacing them with something that looks like your great-granny's falsies that she only got very reluctantly because her real ones rotted and fell out of their own accord.

She looks exactly the same as she did the last time I saw her, except that I now know she's way more of a bitch than I ever imagined. The vain, vacuous husband-stealer I thought she was then seems like a saint in comparison to the piece of pure evil I think she is now.

I now know that the flat is already hers. I called the agents, claiming to be her assistant (what was the worst that could happen? They have no idea what I'm talking about, have never had any dealings with Saskia and tell me I must be mistaken? Saskia has, in fact, rented a different flat and they think I'm incompetent? What do I care?), and asked if they could remind me of the end date of the lease. I gave them the address confidently, dropped Saskia's name, and the woman I spoke to sounded all smiles.

'Well,' she said. 'It was twelve calendar months from August the fifteenth, so that would be August fifteenth next year.'

I thanked her and got off the call as quickly as I could. It had been over a week since Saskia took possession. I didn't really know what to do with this knowledge except to phone Josh and let him know.

'Check in the cupboards and see if her favourite dinner service has gone missing.'

I was glad to hear him laugh. 'She's welcome to it. It's hideous. Maybe I should start making a pile of all the stuff I'd rather see the back of.'

I told him all about Georgia and how, now that she was no longer leaving home, everything had changed.

'It makes no difference now if I kick him out in October or next week. And I suppose Robert must feel the same. He could announce he's going at any moment. Especially now they have the flat to go to. If we're going to do anything to try and derail their future, we have to move fast.'

'Do you still have the appetite for it?' he said, and I had to think for a moment to work out what he meant.

'I don't know. It seems a bit petty, doesn't it? Maybe we should just let them get on with it?'

'No chance,' he says. 'I don't want to do anything cruel, I just don't want it all to be so easy.'

'That's how I felt at the start. Still do, I suppose. I don't know now. It doesn't seem that important any more in the scheme of things.'

'Georgia will be OK,' he says, getting right to the heart of what's really bothering me. 'It'll be one of those things where, in a year's time, you're saying, 'Well, thank God she failed the first time . . .''

I can't help but laugh. It's such a sweet attempt to make me feel better. 'Let's hope so.'

We agreed to meet up on Sunday night, when both Robert and Saskia would have travelled up to Oxford, ready for filming on Monday. Ordinarily, Josh would be there too, but he told me it's not unusual to leave filming in the hands of one of the script editors if he has things to do in London. I find myself looking forward to it. Not because I think anything is going to happen between us. That was a blip, a knee-jerk reaction to the fact that he was feeling rejected. But it won't hurt to spend the evening in the company of an attractive man.

'It's nice around here, isn't it?' I say to Saskia as we eat our salads. She has her dressing on the side again, of course. I, assured by Chas that a bit of olive oil and balsamic is actually going to do me more good than harm, have slathered mine over the top. Chas is big on eating right, not (necessarily) eating less. Saskia's starvation method of weight control fills him with horror. And who am I to argue because, so far, I've lost more than two and a half stone. And – more importantly – a whopping ten per cent fat. At this point, if Chas told me to put olive oil and balsamic on my breakfast in the morning I would probably do it. Except that he never would because Chas, above all, does not believe in fads.

'Yes,' she says, looking around. 'I love it.'

We're about three minutes away from the 'love nest', as Josh and I have started to refer to it. Of course she loves it.

'I could live around here.'

'Me too!' Her overly smooth face lights up (although she's never admitted as much, it's obvious that forehead is full of Botox). No doubt she's laughing on the inside about the fact that she thinks she's got one over on me. 'There's so much life but it still feels like a community!'

I sometimes think that, if there were a limited supply

of exclamation marks in the world, Saskia would have used them all up by now. I'm getting a bit bored. I'm not learning anything new about her and Robert, and I'm finding her company really tiresome. It's hard not to tell her what I know, just to see her smug façade crumble. I can't wait for all this to be over.

36

'I've had a great idea.'

Josh is in my kitchen. That's not a sentence I thought I would ever say. Robert left a couple of hours ago, kissing me on the cheek and telling me he'll miss me, as he always does. It stopped having any meaning years ago. Georgia, having secured a place at a local sixth-form college for retakes (school was considered too humiliating, and who can blame her?), travelled down to Wiltshire to the festival yesterday in the end. I didn't tell her she shouldn't. She's an adult and, besides, there was nothing else for her to do here. Once the new term starts I'm pretty confident she'll knuckle down. So it made sense for Josh to meet me at the flat, but it still feels weird. As if we're doing something illicit. Which we are. But not like that.

I hand him a glass of wine, sit down opposite at the kitchen table.

'Go on.'

He's looking good. Happier. Healthier. More relaxed. He's in a T-shirt and jeans. Tanned. He arrived with a soft, dark grey hoody over the top because the temperature has suddenly dropped. I have to admit I find it hard to resist a man in a hoody. Not a chav, sitting in a park with it pulled up over his head and a can of beer in his hand, obviously. But a soft hooded top (I would guess Josh's is cashmere) on a fit-looking man – especially one with a bit of a tan – does something unmentionable to me. It's a thing, OK?

But then, I'm looking good too. I'm in my retro gingham summer dress. Bare legs. Bare, *toned* legs, I should point out. Bare, toned, tanned legs. No shoes and cute teal polish on my nails. Hair piled up on top of my head and held with a big clip. Not that it matters how I look. That is not what this is about.

'The plan to make him fall back in love with you obviously isn't working.'

I laugh. 'Thanks.'

'That came out wrong. But you know what I mean.'

'You're right, it isn't. We are getting on better than we have in years, though.'

'So we haven't got time for that to play itself out.'

I nod. 'A couple of weeks at the most, I reckon. If that.'

'We have two choices. We either just let it play its course, let them dictate when it happens and go off to their happily ever after . . .'

'. . . thinking they've got one over on us . . .' This is the one thing that sticks in my head every time I think I should just stand back and let it happen. The idea that they'll think they played us. That they'll feel sorry for us. And, no doubt, laugh about how clueless we are at the same time. I can't stand being laughed at.

'Exactly. Or we have to force the issue now. Do something that blows the whole thing up and then see what the fallout is.'

'Like . . . ?'

He sits back, smiles at me, runs his hand back across his head.

'We tell them we're having an affair.'

It takes a moment for what he's saying to sink in, it's so left field. I can't think what to say, so I say nothing, wait for him to explain.

'We play it totally straight. Sit them down and confess, as if we feel terrible but we're powerless to ignore our love, or some shit like that. We make it sound like it's been going on for ages.'

I'm confused. 'Won't they just say, "Great, that leaves us free to do what we want"?'

'Maybe. But it'll take the wind out of their sails. It'll stop them feeling like they got one over on us. And, you never know, sometimes people start to want something they thought they had no interest in just because someone else wants it . . .'

I mull it over for a second. 'But won't it look as if we're the bad guys? To other people, I mean. Robert and Saskia could claim they only got together because they found out about us.'

Josh scratches his chin. Thinks. 'No, because we'll come clean as soon as we've told them. Either they'll pretend to be devastated – how could we do that to them when they love us so much? And then we tell them we know and they look like a pair of massive hypocrites – or they admit to what they've been doing and expect us not to care because we're doing the same and we say, "Actually, we're lying. We just wanted to force you to tell us the truth." It's win-win. For us, anyway. We get what we want and they no longer feel like they played us and won.'

I pick up my glass. Clink his. 'It might be genius.'

'It's all we've got at this point anyway.'

We talk it over some more and decide that sitting them down and 'confessing' is the best way forward. If we arrange for them to catch us out there's too much potential for everything to go wrong. I see a whole Ray Cooney farce play out in my mind. Me and Josh running around in our underwear while Robert and Saskia chase us.

After a second glass of wine Josh raises an eyebrow at me. 'Of course, we might have to practise.'

'What do you mean?' I know what he means. At least I think I do. Hope I do.

'We need them to believe us, so we need to be really convincing. Like we can't keep our hands off each other.'

OK, I think. I almost say it.

Josh laughs. 'I'm joking. Your face!'

Of course he is! Of course he's joking. I channel Saskia. 'Haha!'

'Although, you know . . .'

'Shut up, Josh.'

To be fair, that clears the air between us a bit. As if we were both wondering whether something might happen and that was stopping us from relaxing in each other's company. I feel the atmosphere shift.

'When did we get together?' I ask. We need to get our facts straight if we're going to pull this off.

'After you came to our party? Or is that too recent?'

'I quite like the idea of them thinking we were already an item then, because that's the only time they've seen us in the same place. It'll make them relive that whole evening to see if there were any clues.'

He leans over and picks a dead leaf off one of my geraniums. 'Nice.'

'That's the night I threw a drink at her.'

'Ha! Yes. Is it plausible we could have hooked up before that, do you think?'

'It's a bit of a stretch, given that, as far as they know, we'd never even met. So long as we don't make it sound like a coincidence, though, we should be OK.'

'So I'll say I approached you somewhere – Selfridges Food Hall – and said, "Aren't you Robert Westmore's wife?" because I recognized you from paparazzi photos with Robert or something?'

'We could probably get away with that. The whole thing's going to be so shocking for them anyway I don't think they'll be analysing the details.'

'And we got talking, and then the next thing you know . . . how long ago do you think?'

'Six months? No, that's too neat. Seven months. So January – I love that it'll be when I was at my biggest. Nothing will confuse Saskia more than thinking you made a play for big old me when you had her at home. Or Robert, for that matter.'

'Oh, please. You were still as hot as anything. I remember thinking that at the party.'

I blush from my scalp to my heels.

'And anyway,' he continues quickly. 'Who says I made a play for you? Maybe you threw yourself at me and I was powerless to resist?'

'Because I was so big. I had you in an arm lock.'

'OK, you have to stop with the fat comments,' Josh says, leaning forward and filling our glasses again. I like that he's so at home in my kitchen. I suddenly remember I haven't eaten anything and wonder if he has. I get up and open the doors to the balcony. I need some air.

'So, that's how we met,' I say, to get us back on track. 'And the reason we didn't tell them we met is because we started our affair straight away. One minute you're saying "Are you Robert Westmore's wife?", next we're . . . where? In a hotel? I think they'd remember if we both didn't come home one night.'

He thinks for a moment. 'We didn't just jump right into bed but there was an obvious attraction. Overwhelming. So we arranged to meet up again one afternoon.'

'OK, good. Are we intending to leave Saskia and Robert for each other?'

'Definitely. That's why we're breaking the news.'

'I don't want to tell him he can keep the flat. It might put ideas into his head. Not that he'd want it.'

'I love this place,' Josh says, looking around. 'So much character.'

'Not flash enough,' I say, and he rolls his eyes. 'He's been trying to persuade me to sell up and buy something more impressive for years.'

'We can say we haven't worked out the details.'

'Do I call you Joshie?'

He narrows his eyes at me. 'Definitely not.'

'Joshykins? Squidgy? Fluffums?'

He picks up a handy takeaway menu and throws it at me. 'Are those the kinds of things you call Robert?'

'I call Robert Robert. It suits him. By the way,' I say, picking the menu up from the floor. 'I should eat something. Not this shit, though.'

'Let's go out,' he says, standing up.

'What if someone I know sees us?'

'Even better. We're having an affair, remember.'

We wander down the hill and over the railway bridge on to Regent's Park Road. Luckily, there's a rare free table in Lemonia so we don't have to do that embarrassing thing of wandering around getting turned away from everywhere. I order a big bottle of water before I do anything else because I'm feeling lightheaded from the wine and the big plan. Before the waiter has even put down the plate of olives I've grabbed three and stuffed them in.

'Sorry,' I say, smiling at him. 'Starving.'

By the way Josh attacks the plate of tiny radishes and carrot sticks that arrives next I assume he's feeling the effects too. That calms me down. We're both a bit worse for wear. I'm not the only one in danger of making a fool of myself. I browse the menu, trying to make a healthy choice. Plump for swordfish kebabs with a side of spinach. Josh orders the mixed fish special with a portion of fries.

'Wine?'

Say no. Stick to water. 'Go on then.'

Josh, like me, prefers red, even though we're going to be eating fish, and that, according to Robert, is a cardinal sin. We order a bottle of Merlot. ('That's only two big glasses each, we might as well.') Sod it.

An hour later, we're staggering back up Chalk Farm Road because Josh is insisting on walking me home. We've barely stopped chatting since we sat down – partly the fault of the wine, obviously, but also because he's just so easy to talk to. He's so non-judgemental, so enthusiastic about things. Robert's default setting is cynical disdain, which can be amusing but eventually becomes wearing. You end up too scared to express an opinion about anything. Sometimes I just want to talk about how much I like something without worrying about whether or not it's the *right* thing to like.

Josh, I now know, grew up in Brighton with his mum and dad and two older sisters. He moved up to London at eighteen to study English at uni (he's very sympathetic about Georgia. Totally thinks she's doing the right thing, holding out for better results and trying to follow her passion) and ended up getting a job as a runner in the offices of a TV production company, a very lowly, underpaid but privileged foot on a much sought-after ladder.

It was easy to tell him all about my frustrated plans to act, how I watched the train leave without me while I stayed at home being a mum and making sure Robert felt supported enough to go off and build his own career. He laughs when I tell him about Robert's 'we'll work on my career first and then, once I'm established enough to take a bit of time out, we'll work on yours' promise.

'When did that ever work?'

'I know, I know.'

'Still, you probably ended up saner than you would have. Not having to compete for every little job you get. Not constantly worrying about whether you're too old or whether you're pretty enough. Actresses have it really hard. It's still all about what they look like, whatever anybody says. No wonder Sas is so obsessed with being skinny and not getting wrinkles, because everyone else is.'

'Hence Sadskia.'

'I shouldn't have done that. However badly she's behaved, that was below the belt.'

'It was a direct reaction to a shocking piece of news. Don't beat yourself up.'

'I know. Nothing I can do about it now, anyway. But still,' he said, swirling a chip around his plate.

'I wish I could have tried it once, the acting thing,' I found myself saying, something I haven't even admitted to myself for years. I don't know where that came from. 'I don't think I would have wanted it to be my whole life, but just so I could say I gave it a go. Anyway . . .'

I told him all about Alice. Made him laugh with stories about her pitiful attempts to have us all believe she had a glittering career.

By the time there was a pause in the conversation the wine had run out and we – very sensibly, for which I am so, so grateful – decided against ordering another bottle.

Back home, he follows me up the stairs to the fifth floor. I'm equal parts hoping and dreading that something's going to happen. I know we shouldn't. I know we especially shouldn't in my flat while my still-husband and daughter are away. But I want to so much it's all I can do to stop myself from shoving him into the flat and locking the door behind him.

I let myself in, wait for him to follow me.

'Do you want a coffee or anything?'

He hangs back on the doorstep. 'Better not.'

My bubble bursts. He's not interested. Of course he's not, why would he be? So, we kissed a couple of times before, but he didn't really know what he was doing then, he was so cut up about Saskia. So we get on, but that doesn't mean he thinks of me as anything other than a friend.

'No. Well, thanks for coming over and walking me home . . .'

'I'll call you tomorrow when neither of them is around . . .' Josh is heading off to Oxford first thing.

'. . . just to check we still think this is a good idea when we're sober. Thanks for a lovely evening.'

'Thanks. It was fun.'

I wait for him to turn away before I shut the door, just to be polite. He hovers for a second.

'I have a request,' he says, still standing there. He's doing the slightly sheepish smile thing he does where only one corner of his mouth turns up. It makes me feel a bit weak at the knees.

'Right . . .'

He exhales noisily. I wonder what's coming next.

'Can I kiss you goodnight? I know we both think it's important to keep the moral high ground but I figure we've done it before and, if we don't do it again, I'm actually going to go crazy . . .'

I experience relief, then joy, then lust, all in a millisecond. A huge grin breaks out on my face and there's nothing I can do about it. No playing it cool for me, fabulous actress that I am.

'Definitely.'

'Just a quick kiss, here on the doorstep, and then you have to kick me out. Even if I beg. Which, I'm telling you now, I probably will.'

'It's a deal.'

He leans forward, and his lips touch mine. Bits of me

light up like a pinball machine. It's all I can do not to pull him inside and shut the door.

After a few ecstatic seconds I pull away.

'OK. We have to stop now.'

He smiles his crooked smile. The one that makes me feel funny. 'Already?'

'Already.'

'Spoilsport. I'll talk to you tomorrow'.

I watch as he heads down the stairs, slightly wobbly on his feet, one hand raised in a goodbye gesture.

'I had a lovely evening,' he calls up from at least two floors below.

I laugh. 'Me too.'

I wait to hear the click of the street door and then I go inside to my lonely bed, wondering why I have to be so fucking principled.

37

'I'd take any old course just to get to uni. Why wait another year before you start having fun? And you might still be able to go to Bristol. They have a *great* drama course. Although that would probably be hard to get on to this late in the day. You could go and do English or something and transfer . . .'

Guess who's round?

I forgot that, in my effort to be wife of the year, I had told Alice to make sure she set aside a weekend night to come and have a farewell dinner with Georgia. I didn't want to make it the last weekend George would be home because I wanted her all to myself then, and Georgia had plans for the two before, so we settled on this one. And then, when it turned out Georgia wasn't leaving home after all, I forgot to cancel.

Robert is, of course, delighted. Listening indulgently to his sister's bullshit with a smile on his face. I wait for him to step in and defend George's choices but he just sits there, nodding.

'It's fine, Auntie Alice,' Georgia says, just as I'm about to steam in. 'It's worth waiting another year to do what I really want to do.'

We're sitting at the kitchen table. Alice in her faded ripped jeans, ballet flats and a flowy peasant blouse, with tousled hair and smudged mascara, is vaping away like a good 'un. Two bottles are open on the table – red for me and Robert, white for Alice and Georgia. Tesco's finest.

We've already lived through Alice's thoughts on my weight loss. Her: 'You look amazing! If you keep going like this you'll be thin in no time'. Me: 'Actually, I'm feeling happy as I am. I don't really want to lose much more. Just tone up.' Her (giving me the kind of pitying look you give the malnourished, runty schoolboy who tells you he wants to be a rugby quarterback): 'Of course. Good for you.'

Now she moves on to another old favourite, berating Robert for not putting a word in for her with the *Farmer Giles* casting director. I tune out, think about Josh and the plan we're about to put in place.

We have to think of a way to get the four of us – me and Robert, Josh and Saskia – in the same place so that Josh and I can make our big announcement. We agonized over whether telling them together was the way to go, or whether we should each break it to our own partner in private. On balance, we thought it would be good for us to present a united front, for them to see us together, so obviously a couple. It seems more definite, more shocking. And shock value is what we're going for.

So we've decided that Josh will throw another party. I'll invite myself to come along. Somewhere during the evening (we're a bit hazy on this part) we will take them into Josh's study and break our news.

We're pretty confident that we have a bit of time on our side. Josh had a sneaky look at Saskia's latest Amex statement and discovered that she has ordered some very expensive items from Heals, so I dug out my best 'Saskia Sherbourne's assistant' voice again, and rang up, asking to check on the delivery date. I was told that the sofa and coffee table were being delivered in just over a week's time, but the bed not for another two and a half. There is no way, Josh and I surmised, that Robert and Saskia are going to move into the nest without a bed. Of course, if they were that desperate to get away from the two of us, they could go to a hotel but, we figure, they've stuck it out this long, what's a couple more weeks?

So Josh is going to organize the do for two weekends' time. That way Saskia won't be wondering why the sudden urge for a gathering. And, as luck would have it, it's her birthday in a couple of weeks, so that will give him the excuse he needs.

'Her forty-fourth?' I say when he tells me. We're chatting on the phone. We haven't seen each other in the flesh since our night out, but the memory of the kiss is still front and centre of my mind.

'God, no!' he says, in mock-horror. 'Forty-second. Or third. Or maybe even first. I lose track.'

'It's so sad that she thinks a couple of years makes all the difference.'

'I don't think she does. But she's stuck with it now, she's kept the pretence up for so long.'

Josh and I are making a big effort to be generous when we talk about our partners. We're trying very hard to be the nice guys.

Alice has a new boyfriend she wants to introduce to us. Oh joy. Over the years I've managed to avoid having to meet most of them because they come and go so fast and, usually, if duty called, I would just send Robert to oblige. I remember one who was supposed to be some kind of millionnaire businessman but disappeared to the loo as soon as the bill arrived, and one who clearly was wealthy but couldn't seem to give us an explanation why. I think that one ended up in prison, actually.

Alice is hardwired to be incapable of not driving every man she dates to the brink of insanity. Her self-obsession, her paranoia, her inflated sense of her own importance. Her refusal to eat anything that might accidentally have a couple of calories in it. So the fact that this one has, apparently, lasted three months is big news. Not that I have any interest in meeting him. None.

Of course, I can't say this, so I find myself agreeing to a dinner on Thursday night. Alice tells us he – Ivan – will be able to get us a reservation at City Social even though it's such short notice, because he's very well connected. She waits for us to be impressed. I can't quite muster it but Robert indulges her and oohs and aahs.

I ask her what he does and she tells me he's a film producer. She rattles off a list of films he's had an involvement in, some of which I've heard of, but, as most films have a gazillion producers and half of those have just contributed sums of money that they hope to recoup with interest, it's not necessarily a job in itself.

She's very over-excited about how it's going. 'I really think this could be it,' she says dreamily. Mentally, I give it another month.

Later I text Josh. 'Can't we pull the plan forward? I've got to meet Alice's new boyfriend on Thursday and I need a way out of it.'

He rewards me with a smiley face that I'd find irritating coming from anyone else, but – like Alice with her new boyfriend, I realize – I am in the phase of being blind to his faults. Maybe he just feels that a silent expression of laughter counteracts all the 'haha!'s he's been subjected to over the years.

38

Saskia

Well, that didn't go as well as I'd hoped.

Robbie is pacing about the apartment – looking spectacular, with its freshly painted accents, and cleaned to within an inch of its life by *moi* – like a tom cat who's been locked in all day, watching out the window as his rivals run riot around his territory.

In the end, I couldn't wait for the furniture to arrive. I was so excited. I arranged to meet him in a café around the corner. He was grumpy, to say the least, about coming into town, and I should have realized then that maybe this wasn't the right time. He'd had an early start – I was off today and I spent my time adding a few little touches. Fragrance sticks and vases of flowers on the windowsills. I went to John Lewis and picked out fabric for new blinds and curtains. Bought wine glasses and a couple of bottles of bubbly and stashed them in the fridge – so he was tired and a bit crabby from the off. I should have suggested we go to the pub up the road and have a couple of glasses of wine. That might have loosened him up. But he knew there was something up and he just kept asking me what it was, so we didn't even order a coffee, I just led him straight to the apartment block and asked him what he thought.

He guessed as soon as we got there. Unsurprisingly, as the concierge on the desk downstairs (nine to six, Monday to Friday; they don't call them porters around these parts) greeted me with a 'Hello again, Miss Sherbourne' as we walked into the lobby.

'Oh no,' I heard Robbie mutter under his breath. 'What have you done?'

I gave him an encouraging little smile as the lift doors closed. Of course, with his fresh eyes on the place, I noticed every little scuff and paint smear. The faux flowers on a little table outside 7B suddenly seemed a bit sad rather than charming.

'Close your eyes,' I said as we got to the door. I was still determined he was going to love it, even though he hadn't said a word to me since that first comment.

'Saskia . . .'

'Close them!'

He did as he was told and I let us in – although I got the key stuck at first so it took longer than I'd hoped. I grabbed his hands and pulled him inside behind me. Turned him to face the room. The sun was still shining, although low in the sky, and the place looked stunning.

'OK. Open them.'

I waited for a reaction. He looked around. Blinked.

'You haven't taken it yet, have you?'

'Of course I have. Just for a year. It'll give us time to decide where we really want to be.'

'Where I want to be certainly isn't in the West End.'

'Marylebone isn't the West End. Not really. And you've got the park right there.' I flapped my hand in the direction of the window. 'Don't you think it's lovely?'

'It is. It's a lovely flat. But I thought we were going to do this together. Find an area that worked for both of us. Chiswick, or Hampstead . . .'

'Isn't the café Paula works in in Hampstead?'

'Not Hampstead then. But somewhere like that. Dulwich. Maida Vale.'

'It's fabulous around here.' I knew I sounded petulant but I couldn't help myself. I'd put so much thought into this place. I loved it. Love it.

'It's noisy, and there's no parking . . .'

'There's a parking space in the basement just for us.'

'Only one?'

'It's only for twelve months. I mean, the first one's practically up already.'

'Couldn't you tell them you've had some kind of family emergency? That you need your money back?'

'It doesn't work like that. And besides, all the furniture's arriving next week.'

'Oh, for God's sake, Saskia. We're supposed to be in this together. That means making decisions together. Choosing furniture together.'

I stomped across the floor towards the kitchen area. Opened the fridge and extracted the champagne. He started pacing the floor, up and down, which is where we are now.

'I didn't think you'd want to waste time hunting for the perfect coffee table.'

'Well, I would. Because it would be *our* perfect coffee table. Both of ours.'

I have to say, that takes the wind out of my sails. It's such a sweet thing to say.

'Oh God, I'm sorry. I've messed up, haven't I?'

I start trying to get the wire off the top of the champagne bottle, but it only winds itself on more tightly. A tear plops out of my eye, rolls down my cheek and on to the counter before I can wipe it away. This isn't how this evening was meant to go.

Robert is by my side in an instant. 'Don't cry.'

He pulls me towards him and I sob on to his shoulder. 'I overreacted,' he says. 'It was a bit of a surprise, that's all, and you know how I am with surprises.'

It's true. He hates surprises. Why didn't I think of that before?

'I've spent hours painting it . . .' I say – rather pitifully, I admit, because I've invested so much time and effort into trying to make it perfect. But also because I can sense he's softening and I could end up having my cake and eating it too, if I play my cards right.

'It's a beautiful flat,' he says into my hair. 'And you're right, it'll be perfect for us for a few months while we get on our feet. Clever you.'

I have no doubt that I've won the biggest battle. Once he's been through the emotional turmoil of telling Paula and moved all his stuff in, he's hardly going to want to move out again right away. And if he does, I can put up a fight. Dig my heels in.

'Thank you,' I say, handing him the champagne bottle. There are two chairs already on the balcony – thankfully, John Lewis delivered them yesterday – and I'm planning that we take our glasses out there and watch the sun go down before we each head home to our spouses. If the bed was here we'd make love to seal the deal, but we're

324

both a bit old for the floor. What with my back and his knees, we'd need a paramedic on standby, haha!

He pours out two glasses and I take one and clink it against his. 'Here's to our future.'

He clinks back. 'Together.'

'Two more weeks,' I say as we leave. We've been making plans. As soon as the rest of the furniture is here, that's it. He's a bit hesitant because, of course, bloody Georgia messed up her A levels and now she's staying at home for another year – why she couldn't just retake after a couple of months and then go off travelling or something I don't know, but he tells me her grades were so far removed from what she needs that they've decided she needed another full academic year to catch up – but I leaned on him. Made it sound a bit now or never – without going full-on bunny-boiler, obviously. I told him I was leaving Josh in two weeks' time, whatever, and then I'd be young(ish), free and single, living it up in my swanky flat in Marylebone. Chiltern Firehouse every night, hanging out with God knows who. I didn't actually say it was over for us if he didn't leave Paula at the same time, but the threat was there. In the end, he agreed that it would be ridiculous for us to wait another year. Georgia is eighteen. She can stand on her own two feet. And if she has a meltdown, better she has it now when her retakes are months away.

He gives me a big hug, leans down and kisses me. 'Two weeks.'

Before that, I have to get through this stupid party Joshie is planning. Bless him, he wants to celebrate my birthday in style, and so he's invited everyone to come over, and hired a catering company so I won't have to do any work towards it. I feel awful that he's going to all this expense and effort just before . . . you know . . . but what can I do? I can hardly turn around and tell him he's wasting his time and money. So I'll just have to smile and look grateful. Try not to think about how humiliated he's going to feel when he has to explain to all our guests that I've left, a few days later.

Although, I'm thinking he'll want to hand his resignation in pretty swiftly after I break it to him, so at least he'll know he'll hardly have to see some of them again.

Poor love.

39

Paula

Of course, Alice and her new beau are late. Far be it from her to ever miss the chance to make an entrance. Robert and I are offered a seat at the bar, or the option of going straight to the table, which is the one we take. It's not as if we're on a date and want to prolong the evening any more than we have to.

'This is lovely,' I say, looking around. That's my best effort at making conversation.

'Mmm. It is.'

The waiter appears and we order wine and sparkling water.

'God, I hope he's not an arsehole. I hope he doesn't spend all evening telling us how rich he is.'

Robert laughs. 'He definitely will.'

'Do you think she asks for their bank statements before she agrees to go on a date with them?'

'No, because most of them are conmen, so far as I can tell. She's just too trusting.'

'Poor Alice. Why is she so hung up on going out with rich men, though? I don't get it.' That's not true, I do. It's because she has no income of her own and no intention of ever getting a job, even if anyone would have her. But I'm not going to say that to Robert. I'm trying to be nice.

'I think that's just the kind of men she meets,' he says, always keen to let his sister off the hook.

'How old is this one?'

He shudders, no doubt remembering the (very wealthy) near-octogenarian she introduced him to once. He'd had the gall to keel over without ever getting around to changing his will in her favour.

'God knows.'

We both pick up a menu and browse. I will the evening to be over.

A couple of (silent) minutes later and we're greeted – well, Robert is – by a shriek of 'Robbie!', and there's Alice in a baggy vintage dress that shows off her skinny frame. Everything else is the same – tousled hair, kohl-rimmed eyes, floaty scarf. Trailing behind her is a presentable-looking man in – I would say – his late forties. Maybe early fifties, if he has good genes and an even better surgeon. I was expecting either an Adonis or a wrinkled old prune with cash falling out of his pockets. Ivan is neither. He's pleasant-looking. Unremarkable.

Alice thrusts him forward like he's won a prize. 'This is Ivan.'

Ivan, I have to say, seems like a perfectly nice man. I warm to him, because Alice keeps trying to big him up and he keeps undercutting her boasting.

'Ivan is a film producer,' she says proudly.

'I work in property, really,' Ivan says, smiling at her indulgently. 'Doing up houses and selling them, that kind of thing. A couple of times I've put a small amount into a film purely as an investment. But do I know anything about the film business? No.'

'Ivan lives in a huge house on Wildwood Road,' she says, mentioning a road not that far from us where all the houses are huge.

'Wow,' I say. 'Lovely.'

Ivan does a little eye roll. 'It's my latest project. I'm staying on site while I renovate it.'

'Oh, do you do the work yourself then?' Robert says, articulating what I was thinking. I'd imagined Ivan sitting in a penthouse office and telling people what to do.

'Most of it. Not everything, obviously, I have to get the trades in. But the basics, yes. That's the only way to make money, really. You have to be hands-on.'

'So, how do you do that if you've got a load of properties on the go at once?' I'm worried he'll think I'm interrogating him, but I'm genuinely interested.

'That's why I don't. I do one at a time. Big projects. And I project-manage each one myself.'

Alice is looking a bit put out. Somehow, rather than presenting himself as Harvey Weinstein, her boyfriend is allowing us to think he's Bob the Builder. I, on the other hand, am quite impressed, and I can sense Robert is too.

Robert has always loved the idea of house-flipping. He used to talk about it as his alternative career choice if it all went tits up with the acting. Of course, he knows nothing about it in reality, can barely change a plug. I think he imagined himself swanning around choosing paint colours and granite worktops all day.

He happily quizzes Ivan on his trade secrets and Ivan seems happy enough to engage. I turn to Alice and mouth, 'He's nice,' and, even though I can see she's irritated he hasn't kept up the front that he's a Hollywood player, I can also tell that she's pleased we like him.

'I'm nipping to the loo,' she announces when there's a gap in the conversation. 'Paula, come with me.'

Alice has never done this. Never tried to engage me in girls' talk or act as if we're BFFs, not just thrown together by our relationships to 'Robbie'. I'm intrigued. I follow her to the ladies'. Thankfully, she's not expecting me to go into a cubicle with her, because that would be a step too far. Once the door is shut, she grabs my arm.

'You like him? He's lovely, isn't he? I told you.' She's looking a bit hyper.

'He seems really nice. Not what I expected.'

'He's downplaying the film stuff, obviously . . .'

'I think he has a really impressive job,' I say, interrupting.

'Well, it would be better if he had a permanent place to live rather than on a building site, but he's just done it like this since his divorce because he says it makes sense.'

'Does he have any kids?' I'm looking for the downside because, knowing Alice's taste in men, there must be one.

'No. Not . . . Paula, you can't breathe a word of this, not even to Robbie yet . . .' She takes hold of both my hands. I just know what's coming.

'I'm pregnant.'

I do what everyone does in these circumstances. I can't resist a glance down at her belly. Nothing. It's practically concave.

'Wow. Alice . . . that's . . . are you pleased?'

'Of course I am! It was an accident, obviously, but, imagine, I'm going to have a baby! Ivan's going to need to find somewhere to live sooner than he thought, of course . . .'

'What does he think about it?'

'I haven't told him yet. I'm not even two months . . .'

'You are going to tell him, though?'

'Of course! I'm just waiting till I'm past the dodgy bit.'

'And how do you think he'll take it?' I can't help it. I've known Alice for too long. I'm looking for the angle, the trap. Although her excitement feels real. And, if she were going to use a baby to try and solidify a relationship, wouldn't she have done it with one of the ones she thought would keep her in luxury?

'It'll be a shock because we've only been together such a short time but, honestly, I think he'll be thrilled. He's always wanted kids. His ex-wife couldn't . . . they went through loads of IVF, everything.'

'And where is she now?' What's the catch? He's still married to her? She has a contract out on him?

'Devon. She's remarried. I've met her. She came up for his niece's wedding with her husband. She seems nice, bit dull. She's an office manager.'

'Right.'

'Aren't you going to congratulate me?' she says suddenly, looking a bit teary.

'Of course! Congratulations! Sorry, it was just a shock . . .'

'I'm so happy, Paula, truly.'

I give her a hug. Feel her skin and bone. 'I'm not nagging, but you have to start eating. No more dieting and picking away at your food, like you think we won't notice you're just moving it around your plate.'

'I don't!'

I raise an eyebrow at her. 'I'm not even joking. If you want this baby, then you have to be healthy.'

'OK. I will. I promise.'

'Don't think I won't be checking up on you. And stop with the vaping. I mean it. God knows what's in those things.'

She nods like a compliant child and I think that, maybe, this new dynamic between us might work. I boss her around and she lets me. I like it.

'Do you want me to come to your next appointment with you?'

Her face lights up, making her look ten years younger. 'Would you? Oh God, Paula, I'd be really grateful. None of my friends live nearby.'

I refrain from saying, 'What friends?' I know she's driven most of them away over the years with her sense of entitlement and the way she uses people. It suddenly strikes me as very sad. Alice. Her whole life. Maybe this really will be the making of her.

'I like him,' Robert says in the cab on the way home. 'He seems like a good bloke.'

'I really like him. Good for Alice. Maybe this is the one that's going to work out for her.'

'Stranger things have happened,' he says, but I can't think of many.

40

We're watching the episode where Melody breaks the news to Hargreaves that she's finally pregnant. Robert is inordinately pleased with himself. I can tell he thinks his performance – shock, disbelief and then joy – is award-worthy. Saskia plonks her way through the lines with all the subtlety of a carthorse at the ballet, pulling faces that – and I can only hazard a guess here – imply relief and happiness.

This morning I sweated up a storm next to her again. I'm thinking that, after it all kicks off, I should just keep going to the class. Doggedly stick it out so she feels she has to be the one to leave. Maybe mutter, 'This town ain't big enough for the both of us' at her when she's attempting to be zen. I know she could just switch to the earlier or later one, or go somewhere else entirely, but it would be a small victory. I know how much she loves her weekend routine.

I knew I was in for a treat because she texted me yesterday, saying, '*Told R about S and J!!! He's fuming! That'll put the cat among the pigeons haha!!!*' I resisted about five different caustic stroke sarcastic replies and sent back '*Haha!!! Amazing!!! Can't wait to see what kind of mood he's in this evening haha!!!*' I thought about adding some more exclamation marks or even another 'haha!' but I restrained myself in case she realized I was taking the piss.

I didn't get a chance to ask her about it before class but, as soon as she joined me at the café (post-shower), I was all questions. What exactly did she say to him? Was he devastated? Did he agree not to go straight to Samantha and tell her what he now knew?

Of course, she'd had time to work out her answers.

'I went to his dressing room,' she said, all big eyes and fake excitement. 'Which, as you can imagine, was a bit of a shock for him! It's not often you'd find me in there!'

No, Saskia. Of course it's not.

'Samantha wasn't in so I knew there was no chance of surprising them . . . you know . . .'

She waited for me to acknowledge that, yes, I did know.

'I told him that, the day before, I'd walked past the window of her dressing room – hers is on the ground floor – and I'd seen her and Jez in a clinch. You should have seen his face! I said I thought he deserved to know, given he was risking his marriage for her.'

I arranged my face into a look of delight. 'So what did he say?'

Saskia dabs at her mouth with her napkin then places it back on her lap. 'Well, he swore, I can tell you that much. Quite a lot. Kept going on about what a bastard Jez was, so I said, "But he doesn't even know about you and Samantha, I assume. I mean, she's hardly likely to have told him."'

'Genius.'

She smiles. The cat that got the cream. 'I thought so. Anyway, he was fuming. Picked up his phone as if he was going to call her pretty quick, so I had to start begging.'

She adopts a grovelling pose, hands together in a prayer position, puts on a voice.

'"Please, Robert, don't say anything. They'll know it was me who told you" – oh, I forgot to say that I'd told him that they saw me. Samantha looked out of the window and our eyes met just for a moment. I said that I'd smiled and waved at her as if nothing was happening but that if anyone reported back to Robbie . . . Robert . . . she would know it was me —'

'And he went for it?'

'Not at first. I had to really lay it on thick about how I already felt half the cast hated me and I couldn't bear it if I actually gave one of them a concrete reason to do so . . .'

You'd think I'd laugh at this point, wouldn't you? I'm proud of myself that I managed not to. I just took a big sip of my juice. Held it in.

'. . . Anyway, to cut a long story short, I said the thing about maybe I should find out if it was true for sure before he started throwing accusations around. Oh, and then just to make sure I said, "You don't want to get into a fight with Jez, do you? So you need to have all your facts in place before you say anything." Well, he went pale at that point, you can imagine.'

I laugh in what I think sounds like a delighted but cruel manner. 'I bet he did.'

'And then, of course, he agreed that he shouldn't do anything hasty. I promised to keep my eyes and ears open and report back. I even told him I would try and start up a conversation with Samantha about Jez, without her suspecting anything, just to see what she says about him.'

Her story is starting to unravel a bit. There are holes in it wide enough to drive a truck through. I wonder if this is because she hasn't practised as much as I thought or just because she thinks I'm such an easy touch that she can get away with telling me any old crap and I'll believe her.

'But she knows that you know, doesn't she? Or, at least, Robert thinks she does. Wouldn't he worry that, if you start talking to her about Jez, she'll know what you're getting at?'

She looks flustered for a split second but then she covers well. 'Yes, of course, but I was banking on him not thinking rationally. That he'd just see my offer as a life raft and grab for it.'

I reward her with a big smile. I want her to think she's won. 'And he did, by the sounds of it. God, well done, you.'

'It was a stellar performance,' she says. 'I really am quite proud of myself.'

'So, what now?'

'I'm trying to think. I need your help – you're so much cleverer than me. Obviously, we want to keep this going, but we don't want to push it so far that he confronts her.'

I pretend to think. 'Although we do want him to break it off with her.'

'Yes, but without her thinking it was anything to do with me seeing them. I mean, I don't really care what she thinks of me, but I do not want to encounter the wrath of Jez, any more than Robert does.'

'So . . .' I pick up my latte, have a long drink just to keep her waiting. I always order both a coffee and an orange juice with our brunch. No wonder I always need the loo on the way home. '. . . We have two options. Either you tell him you've talked to Samantha and the Jez thing was a blip. It's over before it's even started. But that might mean he just forgives her and they carry on where they left off. Or . . . if we want to seed some proper doubts in his mind, we have to find a way to keep it going but not push things so far that he confronts Samantha. Not until we want him to, anyway.'

'Exactly,' she says. 'I'm still clueless as to how.'

'I think, for now, just tell him you haven't had a chance to talk to her on her own, string him along for a bit, and then maybe throw him something like you overheard her asking someone where Jez was, or saying she was going to his dressing room to go over lines or something. Just enough to keep his paranoia going. He'll start getting needy and suspicious and, hopefully, that'll drive her mad. Especially as we know she isn't really up to anything. Well, except the obvious.'

'OK. I'll do my best. This is quite exciting, haha!'

'I'm really grateful, you know that.'

'Oh, it's nothing,' she says magnanimously. 'Anything to help you out. He shouldn't get away with it. How are you coping?'

I lower my eyes. 'Oh, you know. Hurt, disappointed. Furious. Mostly furious.'

'Furious is good.'

'I can't wait for this to be over. To be honest, I just want him out of my life – well, as far out as he can be when we have a daughter together. I have absolutely no feelings left for him at all. None.'

'I'm not surprised. And how was he on Friday night? Did he seem like a man who had just found out his mistress had something else going on on the side?'

'He did seem in a funny mood, actually. I wondered if it was because you'd said something.'

Oh, please. Having to make myself seem like a gullible idiot is galling, to say the least. I watch as a smug smile takes over her face.

'Haha! See, he's rattled! I've got to him!'

I smile back at her. Yes, Saskia. Yes, of course I believe that's the case.

41

Saskia

Hook, line and sinker. Really, I should get some kind of award for my performance. Paula is totally eating out of my hand, lapping up every word like a hungry dog. I'm really quite proud of myself. I just wish I could share my success with someone. It doesn't quite feel real when it's only me that knows about it.

I think I've done enough. I don't really need to add any more fuel to the fire. She's on the verge of kicking him out. He has a bolt-hole, a place to run to, when she does. It's all about to come together.

I've been trying to persuade him he shouldn't come to the party. I think it's rubbing salt into the wound for Joshie – not that he'll realize it, not till later, anyway. But it feels needlessly cruel. Robbie tells me Paula is insisting they come. Of course, I know it's because she's hoping to see him and Samantha in action. He's just confused about why she suddenly wants to crash his social life. I've tried to say to her that it'll be dull as dishwater and that Samantha probably won't even come, but how can she resist the possibility?

Thank God Paula's not the type who would confront Samantha herself. Can you imagine! The whole thing blowing up right in front of my face! Robbie finding out what I'd been saying! I'd just have to deny everything. I'm a good enough actress. He'd believe me.

I wasn't even going to invite Samantha. Or Robbie, for that matter. I've tried saying to Joshie that maybe we should keep it to close friends only, make it an intimate do rather than a full-on party, but he isn't having it. He's invited practically everyone I've ever met. It's going to be like an episode of *This Is Your Life*.

Still, we just have to get through it. And once it's over, then the countdown can really begin.

42

Paula

I haven't seen Josh since the other night. There hasn't been an opportunity and, besides, it's too dangerous. My head is full of images of us together and what I want to do to him. And him to me. And I do want to wait. I do want to be able to look Robert and Saskia in the eye and say, 'I would never have done what you've done.' And I want it to be true.

We've talked every day. Planning our big move. Getting our story straight. Now that we know they have the nest, there's no panic about Josh having to move out of the house right away. He's still insisting he'll sell it and give Saskia half the proceeds, but I keep telling him to wait it out. Not to make any grand gestures in a hurry.

Oh . . . and the best news of all: it looks like Josh might be lining himself up another job. The production company who make *Farmer Giles* have another show that's about to go into production and they need a safe pair of hands. He had an informal chat with the head of production – someone he knows well – about it and he thinks he might have persuaded her that *Farmer Giles* could be run by any old hack at this point (I'm sure he didn't put it quite that way, but that was the underlying message, I believe) but that *One Night* – the six-part thriller that has just been given the green light by Channel 4 – needs careful handling. She seemed keen, he tells me. It would just be a question of finding someone else to step in and run *Farmer Giles* at short notice.

We haven't discussed what – if anything – is going to happen between us once it's all over.

The party is on a Friday night, post-filming. Lucky for me, Robert has the day off and so, I tell him happily, we can travel all the way together, I won't have to hang around the studio gates like a groupie. Robert is confused as to why I want to go at all. He keeps trying to claim that he'd much rather spend the evening relaxing on the sofa.

'You always want to go to the parties,' I say when he brings it up for the third time, thinking but not saying, 'Or at least you did before I started inviting myself along.'

He sighs. 'I just don't feel like it. I see enough of these people at work.'

We're walking – my suggestion, but he took me up on it happily. The stroll to the pergola via the café is no longer far enough for me, so we've gone south, up across Primrose Hill and down through Regent's Park. It's a nice day. Sunny, but just the tiniest hint of autumn in the air. It feels like new beginnings.

'But I don't. Please can we? I feel as if we hardly ever go out . . .'

'Let's go out to dinner then, just us?'

'We can do that any night. It's not as if this happens every week. I really enjoyed the last one.'

To give him credit, he doesn't say, 'We were only there five minutes and all you did was throw a drink down Saskia's top.' God, that feels like a long time ago. A lifetime.

'OK,' he says. 'But we'll take the car again. Stay an hour, tops, and then escape.'

'Sure,' I say. 'Whatever you want. Let's go and buy lunch from Villandry and bring it back and eat it in the park.'

He looks at me as if I'm insane. 'It might rain.'

'It won't. Go on, live dangerously.'

Robert laughs, and I'm glad. We might as well have one last nice day together.

Myra helps me plan what to wear. Her first suggestion: 'Nothing. Show them how good you look.'

'Be serious.'

'I don't know,' she says, stacking a pile of plates. Now the schools have gone back, we get a rush every morning, just after drop-off time. We have a local reputation as being very tolerant of babies and pre-school toddlers, so the exhausted young mums often pop in after saying goodbye to their older children at the gates. 'What have you got?'

'Well, I can't describe my whole wardrobe to you. Just what kind of thing?'

'Something fitted but not tarty. You don't want to look like a hooker he's just picked up.'

'Really? Because that was exactly the look I was going to go for.'

She rolls her eyes at me. 'You know what I mean. You need to look as if you know you look good but you're not showing off about it.'

'You read too many crappy magazines,' I say, wiping the surface underneath the stack when she lifts it to put it away. 'Is it going to be warm at the weekend?'

'What am I? The internet?'

'I think there's supposed to be a little heatwave. That'll affect what I wear.'

We're saved from ourselves by the arrival of three customers, who all head to different tables. 'I'll keep you posted,' I say as I head towards the one nearest the door.

'Oh do!' she says. 'I'll be thinking about nothing else.'

'Haha!' I say, before I can stop myself. And then I think, that's how easy it is. One day you're laughing at someone for an irritating habit and the next you're doing it yourself.

In the end, Friday is a beautiful, warm, cloud-free day. I try to control the nerves that are threatening to overwhelm me. I call Josh on my walk to work, and he answers, so I know Saskia is nowhere near.

'Everything OK?' he says. We're both worried the other might bottle out at the last moment.

'Yes. Well, no, I feel sick, and I'm terrified, and I'm thinking about running away and never coming back, but I'll get over it. You?'

'Same. With added exhilaration.'

He runs through the plan one last time – you can tell he's a producer – and we try to pre-empt any possible curve balls and work out what we would do in each case – random interruptions, either Saskia or Robert refusing to be corralled into the room in the first place, our chosen room (Josh's study, on the ground floor, two sofas, but far enough from the living room/ kitchen party fulcrum to mean we're not overheard) being occupied by some random party guest. My head is swimming with the possibilities.

Obviously, there are certain scenarios we can't legislate for – like one of them falling ill and demanding either to go home or go to bed – which would mean we had to abort. That feels like the worst eventuality of all. Now we've decided to do it, I just want it over with. I want to move on with my life.

Before I left this morning I had breakfast with George, who is off today for her last hurrah before Eliza leaves for uni next weekend (she went through clearing, has ended up doing Speech Sciences at Cardiff) and she starts her new college the week after. Hence the reason she was up so early, because they are travelling up to Leeds by coach. No working for them this weekend, just pure hedonism. I have to stop myself thinking hysterical thoughts like, 'This might be the last weekend of her innocence.' She's not due back till Monday night and, whatever happens tonight, I'm sure, by then, Robert and I will have worked out how best to break it to her when she returns. He'll know that the me-and-Josh thing was a lie and that we've known about him and Saskia for months now. He won't have any reason to cause a scene.

I over-compensated by cooking her a huge breakfast of eggs and beans and toast.

'Oh my God, Mum, that's lovely but, no way,' she said, as she shuffled in and flopped down at the table.

'It'll keep you going in case there's no food on the coach.'

'There's not going to be any food on our coach. It's a ten-pound return – they're hardly likely to provide food. We'll be lucky if there's even a loo that works. We're making sandwiches to take, remember?'

'Even better then. Eat this and then you won't be tempted to eat all your sandwiches in the first half-hour.'

'I'll eat the eggs,' she said, and then proceeded to wolf the whole lot down. I watched as proudly as if I were watching her walk on stage to collect an award.

'See,' I said as she clattered her fork down on her empty plate.

Georgia groaned. 'It'll be your fault if I'm sick on the coach now.'

I leant over her and gave her a big hug, and she was too full of food to fight me off.

'Have a good time. Don't do anything . . . well, you know.'

'I will. Or I won't. Whatever the right answer is. When's Dad getting up?'

'No idea. But wake him before you go. He'd hate it if he didn't get to say goodbye.'

'I'm back on Monday,' she said in a tone that screamed, 'Stop fussing!'

'I know. Ring us at some point. Just so we know you got there OK.'

Myra gives me a pep talk before I leave work, which is basically her saying everyone else is a lying, manipulative bastard and I need to remember that and protect myself. Apart from Josh, of course, who seems OK, and who she would happily take off my hands if I decide I don't want him.

'Thanks,' I say. 'I'll remember that.'

When I get home from work I change clothes, put my trainers back on and head out for a run. The walk from the café – the walk I couldn't do all in one go for several weeks when I first started, months ago – now feels like a warm-up to the main event. I run down towards the park, trying to clear my head, trying to concentrate on the sound of my feet hitting the pavement, on the rhythm of my breathing in and out. It's hopeless. My brain feels scrambled, a mixture of fear and excitement.

At one point, I get into a major panic and decide I'm going to phone Josh and call the whole thing off. I even get as far as stopping at a bench and pulling my mobile from my pocket. What stops me is a text from Saskia, which sits there looking at me as the phone springs to life.

'Can't wait to see you tonight!! Lots to tell about R and S!! We need to find a sneaky five minutes and I'll fill you in!!! xx'

I shove the mobile back in my zip pocket, start running again.

Robert is making coffee when I get in, back from a wander to the shops.

'Want one?' he says, as I appear red-faced and sweating in the kitchen doorway.

'In a minute. Shower first.'

'How far did you go?' he asks when I re-emerge, hair wrapped up in a towel. He fires up the machine again and it growls as it churns out a coffee. Robert has never been able to get his head around the fact that I prefer instant. I think he thinks it's an affectation.

'Just down to the bottom of Regent's Park and back.'

'"Just"?' He laughs. I know what he's getting at. I have always had a habit of undercutting any personal achievement by qualifying it.

'OK, not "just". Down to the bottom of Regent's Park and back.'

'Better.' He raises an eyebrow to show he's teasing me, not being patronizing, just so you know. It's an old routine we have, and it started because he thought I always undervalued whatever I did. And he was right.

It's good that we're getting on, that we're going to go to the party as happy a couple as we can seem to be these days.

I take my time getting ready. I want to feel at my best. In the end, I wear my summery knee-length dress with its fitted top and flared skirt. I know I need to take a cardigan because it might get chilly later but, for as long as I can, I intend to show off my toned bare arms to anyone who cares. I blow-dry my hair, brush it till it shines. Add a second coat of mascara. Slip into the nude open-toed heels I've bought specially for the occasion.

When I'm done, I look at myself in the full-length mirror. The same mirror I stripped off and looked in the night Alice was here. I actually well up at the transformation but, luckily, I realize that if I allow myself to cry I'll have to redo all my make-up, and I don't have time for that, so I pull myself together just in time. I'm going to allow myself to feel proud, though. I deserve to.

'You look great,' Robert says when I emerge. He's only just out of the shower, but I know he'll be ready in ten minutes. He just needs time to dry his hair and fluff the dark brown powder in to thicken it up. I wonder if it ever comes out on Saskia's hands in the throes of passion. I have to suppress a laugh.

'Thanks.'

I'm dying for a glass of wine. I need whatever courage I can muster. I stop myself, though. It's imperative that, tonight of all nights, I keep a clear head.

Josh has put fairy lights up in the tree outside the house. Or, at least, I assume it was Josh. I can't imagine Saskia up a ladder. The place looks magical as we pull up. I can tell there are a few people there already from the cars outside. We find a space along the road and walk back. I can still smell the honeysuckle, even though it's nearly autumn. My heart is beating like a hammer on a very stubborn nail. I feel as if, if I looked down, I would be able to see it pounding out of my chest, trying to escape. I breathe in and out slowly, try to calm myself down.

Josh and Saskia are at the front door, like a pair of club hostesses. Of course, I have to remember that Robert has no idea Saskia and I are friends and that she believes Josh is clueless about this too. She and I discussed it last time we met. We're friendly, we went for coffee once, but we're not friends. We haven't seen each other since.

Josh, I am only meant to have met the one time, at the previous party. I go for polite but friendly all round. Not big, effusive gestures or OTT hugs. Just 'Thank you for inviting me, I'm very happy to be here.' We all seem to get away with whatever particular version we are supposed to be getting away with. It occurs to me that only Robert is completely in the dark. In his own naïve way, he just believes he is having an affair with the woman in the red strappy dress and that he is getting away with it faultlessly. I almost feel sorry for him.

Saskia winks at me as I move further into the hall. A

waiter – actually, he's at pains to tell me, one of the runners on the show topping up his pitiful wage with a bit of work on the side – hands me a glass of something fizzy and I accept before it even occurs to me that I should say no. I remember that Josh said he was going to get caterers in and people to serve, ostensibly so that he could persuade Saskia that a party would be no trouble, but really so he could give his full attention to what we are about to do and his guests would still be well catered for.

The plan, such as it is, is this. We allow the party to get going, and Saskia and Robert to have a couple of drinks. We decided it would help if their judgement was a little off. Once everyone is having a good time and Josh has done a round of saying hello to all the guests, we – separately – somehow get our partners to accompany us to Josh's study. He has described in detail to me where it is – I have a terror of not being able to locate the right room and blowing the whole thing that way – but he's also promised to try and show me if we get a moment away from the others beforehand.

Josh thinks that it will be easy to lure Saskia with the promise of a birthday surprise. I am not so confident about Robert. If he's midway through a story to a captivated audience when I get Josh's signal (a very sophisticated poke in the back) that the time is now, then I have no idea how I'm going to persuade him to leave the limelight and come with me. I think I'll have to feign an emergency. Make it seem to him as if I'm going to cause some kind of a scene if he doesn't. Embarrass him somehow.

Once we have them in the room (the potential for so many things to have gone wrong already by this stage is almost infinite), Josh and I will sit next to each other on one of the little sofas, take each other's hands and he (thankfully, I'm not sure I could carry it off personally) is going to say, 'Sit down, Paula and I have something to tell you . . .'

We have no idea, of course, how they will react. Whether one of them will say, 'Actually, the two of us are a couple too, how do you like that?' or – and, in Robert's case, I think much more likely – 'How could you? I'm devastated.' We've tossed around the possibility that one of them might storm straight out and announce it to the gathered guests but, on balance, we both feel that they are way too proud and would never want to be seen as the cheatee rather than the cheater. They'd both want people to think they're the desired one, not the one who's been discarded for a hotter model.

If they admit their own affair, then our plan is to say, 'Gotcha! We knew all along and we just pretended to be an item to force you to tell us.' If they deny it, it gets a bit more complicated. We'll still have burst their bubble, but we won't have outed them. What we have decided to do in that case it to give them a night to stew on it (and to possibly feel a little the way they have made us feel; not that we think they will care about losing us, it's way too late for that, but they might feel foolish, laughed at, belittled) and then, next day, if neither of them has come clean, tell them it was a performance. That we know. That we've known for ages. Job done.

Either way, by the time they go back to work on Monday and Georgia is home, we will have killed any idea that we – Josh and I – are the ones who have strayed, and

Robert and Saskia will have been forced to come clean. How they handle it after that is up to them.

We've only been there five minutes – I'm chatting to a woman called Clare, who works in the costume department, Saskia and Robert are in a big group nearby, mostly made up of cast members, from what I can tell – when Samantha walks in. I look at Saskia, and she looks right back at me, raising her eyebrows. Samantha greets everyone – including Robert, because why wouldn't she? – with an enthusiastic kiss on the cheek. And they're all – Robert included – clearly happy to see her. She's obviously well liked. I remember that Saskia claimed to have more gossip and I determine to try and get it out of her before our big revelation. I want to see how far she's prepared to go. I want her to dig herself a bigger hole.

She's looking over again so I make a tiny head gesture that means 'Let's go over here.' I tell Clare I'm off to the loo and I go, hoping Saskia will follow immediately. When I get to the bathroom door she's right behind me.

'Let's go into the garden,' she says. 'It'll look weird if people see us coming out of here together.'

She's right. I follow her through the kitchen to the back door. It's still warm enough that a few people are milling about the beautiful courtyard. There are fairy lights here too, and small speakers pumping out tasteful music at a low volume.

'Oh my God!' she squeals, when we're far enough away not to be overheard. 'Did you see the way she kissed him?'

'To be fair, she kissed everyone.'

'I know,' Saskia says, waving over a boy with a tray of

drinks who has just ventured outside. It's not the same one I spoke to earlier, but I assume he's another runner. We both take a glass, replacing our empties on the tray.

'Thanks,' I say. Saskia doesn't even look at him.

'But it's slightly different doing it to Robert, don't you think?'

'I suppose she could hardly have kissed everyone else and missed him out. That would really have looked odd.'

I can see Saskia is getting frustrated with me. She wants me to buy into her gossip. 'Well, anyway . . .' she says, slightly huffily.

I try to match her mood. 'So, go on, what did you have to tell me?'

'Oh, that,' she says, not playing now. 'It was probably nothing.'

'Oh, come on, you can't leave me hanging like that. Tell me!'

She relents. 'She's asked to move dressing rooms. To the first floor. Which is where Robert is, as you know.'

I know from years of production tittle-tattle that the first-floor dressing rooms are considered far superior to those on the ground. They're bigger, and more private, because they don't have windows that everyone can gawp through as they walk past. Sooner or later, according to Robert, every new cast member throws a fit and asks to be moved upstairs. I don't need to let on to Saskia how clued up I am, though.

'Wow.'

'I know! And so, of course, I planted the seed in Robert's ear that it was because she knew I'd seen her with Jez and she wanted more privacy. You can imagine his reaction.'

I pull my best 'amazed' face. 'Brilliant. Now he'll be really unsettled.'

'I think he's getting tired of her anyway. Between you and me. Well, obviously between you and me, haha! Because no one else knows, do they?'

'Really, why?'

'I get the impression she's quite demanding. Bit of a diva.'

I think of the open, friendly-looking woman greeting everyone like she was happy to see them.

'I can imagine.'

'And because she's so young, you know . . . I think he's starting to find her annoying.'

'Has he told you this?'

'Not in so many words. But you can see it in his face when he talks about her.'

'So maybe this Jez thing will push him over the edge.'

'Exactly. I reckon he'll dump her within a week. And then you can make your grand gesture, and out into the street he goes. You *are* still going to go through with it, aren't you? Even though Georgia's still at home?'

I'm not sure I've ever told her about Georgia's results, but I let it pass. 'Definitely. She's eighteen. She's got months till her retakes. She'll be able to deal with it. Especially if he's not running straight into the arms of someone else.'

'Good for you. Girl power, haha!'

'Haha!' I say. Haha, indeed. Hahaha, in fact. Hahahaha!

43

Saskia

What a minefield this party is. Joshie has no idea! Well, obviously!

I'm trying to remember what I've said to who (to whom??) about what. Who I'm friends with. (Whom I'm friends with? No, Saskia, that's not right). Best thing I can do is keep smiling and talk about the weather.

Joshie has done a fabulous job, I have to give him that. The house looks beautiful. I'm going to miss it – I can't even tell you. I've put so much love into this place. He hired a firm of caterers, and they have made nibbles to die for. In our kitchen! Apparently, they just show up with their ingredients, make all this fabulous food, clear up after themselves. I'm sure it cost a fortune.

He has the three latest *Farmer Giles* runners – I forget their names, two boys and a girl. All way too drippy to make an impact in the industry IMO – acting as waiters, hovering with trays of champagne and glasses of fizzy water. Not that anyone is drinking the water, haha! Our parties are notoriously boozy. The day after is always one long parade of people coming to collect their cars because they got too drunk to drive home. Usually, I just hide upstairs and pretend I don't see them because I'm never at my sparkly best with a hangover.

And hangovers become far worse when you're forty blah blah, let me tell you that. God, what am I really now? Forty-three? Forty-four in a few days. It doesn't bear thinking about. And I try not to think about it, in case I accidentally give myself away. Joshie knows, of course. Robbie has never asked, so I'm keeping quiet. You're as old as you feel. Or, at least, as old as other people think you are. Although I have started to wish lately that I'd only knocked off two years instead of five all those decades ago. I'd much rather people thought I looked good for my age than that I was a bit ropey for thirty-eight. Still, nothing I can do about it now. Imagine the field day if I came clean!

I'm avoiding Robbie as much as I can, without it looking impolite. I always do at these things – and he does the same – hence our reputation for disliking each other. It gives me a buzz, though, to know he's in my house. It always perks our sex up for a bit after we've been at one of these dos together. Not that it needs perking up, you understand, but a bit of added spice never hurt anyone, did it? Robbie likes to tell me how he couldn't take his eyes off me, how much he wanted to have me there and then and sod the consequences.

I feed Paula a bit more Robbie and Samantha 'gossip'. She laps up the stuff about him getting bored of her, and I wonder for a moment whether she's thinking of pretending it never happened. Letting him off the hook, when he doesn't even know he's been caught. She's made of stronger stuff, though, I think. She's on a mission to reclaim her life.

Jez wasn't invited, by the way. It's pretty much considered

the worst faux pas on any show – but especially a long-running one with a regular cast – to invite all the players along to something but leave out one person. It's as if the rest of us have signed a secret pledge, though. No one has mentioned the party to him, and no one will talk about it in front of him on Monday. It'll be as if it never happened. He's too much of a loose cannon. He could start a fight in a nunnery (although, to be fair, some of those nuns can be quite feisty, haha!) and I didn't want anyone to ruin my night.

It's fabulous, it really is. All my friends gathered under one roof to celebrate my birthday. So much love. And it'll be the last time, I know that. I'm sure Robbie and I will have spectacular parties in the flat, don't get me wrong. I fully intend to make it the place everyone wants to be. But we won't have the space or the garden. Not for a while, anyway. It won't be the same.

So I just need to enjoy this last hurrah. Before we blow everyone's worlds apart.

I'm still out in the garden, now chatting to Grace, wife of David (Farmer Giles himself), about baking – a subject I know nothing about and have no opinion on, but she seems to find it fascinating – when I hear a shout coming from inside, followed by a mix of laughter and gasps. There's a tangible change in the atmosphere and I know, I just know, something has happened.

'Let me just go and see what's going on,' I say to Grace, glad of the excuse to get away, truthfully.

I don't know what it is I expect to find. Everyone turns towards me as I walk in. It's as if everything is in slow motion. Like in a Western when the piano player lowers the lid and everybody swivels around to stare at the stranger who's just strolled in.

I instinctively look for Robbie in the crowd. He's standing at the door to Joshie's study, his face a mix of disbelief and anger.

I step further into the room, push my way through the gathered crowd, in an effort to see what's going on.

44

Paula

Fuck, shit.

This is not what was supposed to happen.

After my little chat with Saskia in the garden I headed back inside and decided to try and locate Josh's study. I wanted to be as prepared as I could be. Across the room, I could see Robert deep in conversation with a man I didn't know. If he'd noticed me sneaking off to talk to her, he wasn't giving anything away.

I wove through the groups of people in the living room, opened the first door I came to, but that turned out to be a cupboard. The next led to a flight of stairs. I was heading for the third door, thinking that must be where it was, when I became aware of Josh by my side.

'It's just through here,' he muttered. He walked through a square archway and I followed, after a quick look around to check no one was watching. There was a door to the right that I remembered was the bathroom where I first struck up a conversation with Saskia. Josh opened the door straight ahead and went in. Confident that no one could see me in the little recess, I went after him. Shut the door behind us.

Inside was a small but beautiful room with dark wood bookcases lining the walls. There was a desk against the window, looking out on the tiny front garden and the road, with a computer and a pile of scripts on top of it. On either side of the (real) fireplace were two small leather sofas, each just barely big enough for two people.

'This is it,' he said. 'So, if we sit ourselves here,' – he indicated one of the sofas – 'next to each other.'

'OK,' I said. My heart had started pounding again at the thought that we were actually going to go through with it.

'Are you feeling ready?'

I nodded. 'As ready as I'll ever be. We are doing the right thing, aren't we?'

'Well, I don't know about that, but we're doing something to make ourselves feel better, so that has to be a good idea.'

'I suppose.'

He put his hands on my shoulders. 'Listen, Paula, we can back out any time we want. If either of us doesn't want to go through with it, then we just forget it and wait for them to tell us the truth in their own good time.'

'Oh God. It seemed like such a good plan, but now I feel as if we're just being vindictive.'

'Let's remember we didn't start this, though . . .'

'I know. But do we want to sink to their level?'

He dropped his hands. 'I don't know. Shit, maybe this was a stupid idea. Shall we just forget about it? Your call.'

'I don't know. I don't know what to do.'

'Neither do I.'

'Fucking hell. We could toss for it.'

For a moment Josh actually looked as if he was thinking that might be a good idea. 'We need to be a hundred per cent certain if we go ahead. Any doubt, we should bail out.'

I had no hesitation. 'Let's bail out then. Fuck.'

He laughed. 'What a pair of idiots.'

'Well, at least Saskia got a nice birthday party out of it.'

'What if she decides that she's so grateful she doesn't want to leave me any more?'

I couldn't help it. I started laughing too and couldn't stop. I think we both had a case of mild, relief-induced hysteria.

'We've made her fall back in love with you! All it took were a few canapés and half a glass of champagne.'

'Shit! What have I done?'

I leaned against the desk, feeling slightly light-headed. 'We should become marriage counsellors.'

'Wife having an affair? Dress a runner up as a waiter – that'll have her wanting to renew her marriage vows in no time.'

'Don't,' I said, clutching my side. 'I'm going to have a heart attack.'

'Worried that your husband's cheating? Offer him a bit of goat's cheese and tomato on a stick.'

Eventually, we laughed ourselves out. I felt a lot better for it. Like I'd opened up a valve and let the pressure go down.

'OK,' Josh said finally. 'We need to go back out there. Otherwise, they'll be wondering where we are.'

'You're sure?'

'Sure.'

And that was nearly that. We were almost home free. But then Josh took hold of my hand as I passed him on my way to the door – we had decided I should leave first and then he'd follow a few minutes later, just in case.

'Seriously, though, I can't wait for this to be over,' he said.

I felt my stomach flip. 'Me neither.'

'It's driving me crazy.'

I could have taken my hand away. Could have moved towards the door. Instead, I looked right at him and he held my gaze with his intense, beautiful brown eyes. I could hear the low music from next door, the murmur of voices.

He put his hand under my chin. I don't know who made the first move, who kissed who but, next thing I knew, we were in a clinch like we'd been on a desert island and neither of us had seen anyone of the opposite sex in living memory.

Remember when you were a teenager and a kiss could last an ecstatic twenty minutes? When self-imposed boundaries meant you emerged the other end a sweaty ball of anticipation and arousal but still with your clothes more or less intact?

That.

I don't know *how* long it lasted, actually. I know it felt incredible. I know it lived up to every fantasy I'd been allowing myself to indulge in since Josh reappeared in the café and told me it was over with Saskia. At the back of my brain, a niggling voice kept telling me that this wasn't the time or the place, that we shouldn't be taking a risk like this. But I ignored it.

And then there was a squeal. A noise that said someone had seen something they shouldn't. And a ripple of laughter. Someone said, 'Whoa!' in a really loud voice.

'Oh my God, sorry!' a woman's voice said.

It all happened so quickly. Josh and I stepped away from each other, both straightening our clothes, but it was too late. Gathered in the doorway was a group of three people, two men and a woman, none of whom I knew, which, I suppose, was some kind of a relief. Behind them, alerted by the squeal and the shout of 'Whoa!', about eight or nine more, including David and Grace. And, at the back of that little group, his face a mixture of shock and disgust, Robert.

'This isn't what it looks like,' I said, although what else it could possibly be I couldn't say.

I saw Robert turn and walk away, and my first instinct was that I should go and explain myself to him. I stayed rooted to the spot, though, because I couldn't face fighting my way through the sniggering crowd.

'Introduce us to your lady friend, Josh,' said some tosser I recognized as the actor playing a brash young toff from the village 'big house'. Several people laughed.

I heard David trying to shoo people away and was grateful that they mostly did as they were asked. I finally managed a look at Josh.

'OK, fun's over,' he said to the stragglers, as if he'd just realized what was going on. 'Let's all go and get another drink.' I could see him scanning the crowd for Saskia, as was I. Then I saw a huddle and, in the middle, a blonde head. She looked over just at that moment and caught my eye. She didn't acknowledge me, just turned back and allowed herself to continue being 'comforted' by the crowd around her.

'You OK?' Josh said to me, under his breath.

'Not really. You?'

He took hold of my hand, out of sight of the remaining few, and quickly squeezed it. That, more than anything, gave me courage. At least I never had to see any of these people again. Josh had to work with them every day – had to somehow garner their respect as the boss – for as long as he remained at *Farmer Giles*. I couldn't even imagine how difficult that was going to be.

'I need to go and . . .' he said, indicating where Saskia was still standing at the centre of a small group, a sea of hands petting her.

'Me too.'

I put my head down and braved the other room. I heard someone say, 'Who is she, anyway?' and I was glad for Robert's sake that everyone hadn't yet put two and two together.

There was no sign of him. I made my way towards the kitchen, giving Saskia and her friends a wide berth.

'How could you?' I heard her shriek, and I assumed that Josh had reached her. Everyone went quiet again, a captive audience. Saskia, of course, wasn't going to miss this opportunity to play the wronged woman. Even though I felt bad for her – it can never be great having all your colleagues witness your husband copping off with another woman, whatever the state of your marriage – I also knew that we'd played right into her hands. Josh could be the bad guy, she could be the heartbroken, devoted wife. Everyone would understand why she had to kick him out and, if she took up with Robert a few weeks later, then who wouldn't sympathize? Who wouldn't turn to an old friend at a time of crisis?

I knew that, of course, Josh was way too much of a gentleman to turn around in front of all these people and tell her what he knew. He'd save that for later. He'd allow her to have her moment at the centre of a tragedy.

There was no sign of Robert anywhere and, when I wandered out of the front door, unsure where to look next, I saw that the car had gone. Great.

I couldn't really face going home, and the recriminations that would follow, but I didn't know what else to do. So I sat down on the steps and called an Uber. Of course, there was nothing in the area so I ended up waiting nearly half an hour, shivering in my summer dress, as the night had turned chilly, but way too self-conscious to go back inside to find my cardigan. And besides, for all I knew, the heartbroken character Saskia had created might have murderous tendencies.

Several people left as I was sitting there. A couple said goodnight, but mostly they just ignored me or I caught a snigger as they passed. Ironically, the only person who showed any concern was Samantha.

'What are you doing sitting here, babe? You'll freeze,' she said, as she tottered towards her waiting (obviously pre-booked) taxi.

'Waiting for my Uber. I'm fine. Thanks.'

'Do you want me to wait with you? I don't think you should be sat here on your own.'

'No. That's really nice of you to offer, but I'll be OK.'

'Or I could give you a lift – I'm going to Clapham, if that's any good?'

'Opposite way. Really, I'm fine.'

She went off eventually. It crossed my mind to try to

explain to her what the situation really was. Specifically, how Saskia had used her name in her manipulations but, even to me, it sounded insane. Another time.

Just as my car arrived, my phone beeped and a message from Gail aka Josh appeared. '*Where are you? Are you OK?*'

'*On my way home,*' I replied.

'*Jesus, what a fucking mess. I'll call you in the morning. All kicking off here xx*'

I didn't know what to say, so I just sent back '*XX*'. I didn't imagine either of us was going to have a good night.

45

Saskia

Whatever Robbie and I have done, we've done it in private. Gone to great lengths to make sure we're not humiliating anyone. And this is the thanks we get?

Paula! Paula, of all people. Josh must have been drunk. Or she initiated it. Some kind of desperate attempt to prove she's attractive. And he just got swept up in the moment. But to be caught! And in my own house! At my party! It's like the script for a farce.

I was seething, I'll tell you that much. All those people watching my husband with his hand inside some woman's dress. At least, that's what they tell me. I made Geri and Fedrico from the make-up department give me all the gory details. They were the first ones in there. Them and Sharon, the third assistant. They said they were looking for the way out to the garden, but they've all been here many times before, so that's not true. Probably off to snort a few lines in private. I'm glad they don't tell me. Our parties might be boozy, but they're never druggie. I abhor that stuff.

Anyway, so the story goes, they were in the middle of a passionate kiss – Joshie and Paula, that is, not Geri, Federico and Sharon, haha! He had his hand on her boob. She had one of hers – well, you can imagine. On the outside of his jeans, not the inside, thank God.

Federico says they didn't know what to do, they were so shocked. So they just stood there for a minute, by which time half of the rest of the room had seen. From what other people tell me, they drew attention to it by squawking and squeaking all over the place. And, even if they hadn't, they're the world's biggest gossips, so it would have been all round in no time.

Of course, everyone's first concern was for me. There was no shortage of people fussing around 'making sure you're OK'. I could feel the excitement, though, if that's the right word. Like they wanted to be involved in the drama, but, in fact, they couldn't wait to leave so they could talk about what had happened. Laugh behind my back. I'm not so naïve that I think all those people really had my best interests at heart. They just wanted to be able to say they had a front-row seat.

And, all the time, all I was thinking was 'Where's Robbie?' Had he seen? Did he care?' I was struck with an absolute fear that he might be heartbroken and realize he had really loved her all along. I kept scanning the room for a glimpse of him, but he was nowhere to be seen. Was he with her?

Eventually, I heard someone say, 'Where's Robert?' and someone else answer, 'Left, I think.' And next thing I knew, Joshie was by my side.

'How could you?' I said, in the loudest voice I could. Might as well milk it.

The crowd around me shushed, obviously hoping the second act was about to start. Josh tried to usher me away, but I was having none of it.

'Where's she gone?"

'I don't know,' he said. 'After Robert, probably.'

I gathered myself. Put the steeliest look I could muster on my face and said, 'I have nothing to say to you.'

That put him in his place.

Now we're about to be on our own. The last two people are saying their hurried goodbyes. Josh has pretty much thrown them all out, telling them he'll see them on Monday. Being all matey, as if nothing has happened. So it's about to be just me and him.

As he corrals them to the door I find my mobile and try Robbie's number. Sod protocol. He answers almost immediately.

'What the fuck?'

'Are you OK?' I say, meaning, 'This hasn't made you change your mind, has it?' but knowing he'll take it at face value.

'Did you have any idea?' he splutters.

'God, no! None.'

'In front of all our friends!'

'Where are you now?' I say. I can hear Joshie saying his final goodbyes.

'Driving home.'

'Where's Paula?'

'No idea,' he says. 'Fuck her, humiliating me like that.'

'Call me tomorrow. Or I'll call you, OK? And drive carefully.'

'I will,' he says, sounding a bit calmer. 'You know I love you, don't you?'

A weight lifts off my shoulders. 'You, too. And, listen,' I say, whispering now. 'Don't tell her anything. We can come out of this smelling of roses.'

He actually laughs. 'You might be right. They'll be the homewreckers. We'll be the ones everyone feels sorry for. Brilliant.'

'I hate people feeling sorry for me,' I say. It's true, I do. I can't stand to be a pity object. 'But in this case, I'll make an exception.'

I hang up just as the front door closes and Josh walks into the kitchen, a sheepish look on his face.

I stand up, look right at him.

'I can't wait to hear what you've got to say.'

46

Paula

By the time I get home Robert is sitting at the kitchen table, nursing a huge glass of red wine.

'So,' he says, without looking at me. 'Want to explain yourself?'

'Not really,' I say. 'It wasn't meant to happen, we're not having an affair.'

'That's all you've got to say? It wasn't meant to happen? What? You got taken over by aliens for a few minutes and you had no idea what you were doing?'

'Obviously not.'

'So don't give me that bullshit. How long has it been going on?'

'Nothing is going on. I've kissed him twice before. Well, three times, technically speaking. That's it. We haven't had sex.'

Robert gives me a look that tells me he doesn't believe a word of it. Well, good for him. Now he'll know how I feel.

'And that makes it OK? Because you haven't had sex, you've just groped each other like a pair of teenagers?'

'This was the first time with the groping.'

I can see he's struggling to understand why I'm being so belligerent. Why I'm not begging for forgiveness.

'Great. Be facetious about it.'

'I'm not actually,' I say, sitting opposite him. I reach down to take my shoes off because my feet are killing me. 'I'm just trying to be truthful. I think everyone deserves that.'

'You're not even sorry. You've humiliated me in front of all my friends and colleagues . . .'

'That, I am sorry for. Genuinely. I would never have wanted that to happen.'

'How the fuck am I going to show my face at work on Monday?'

How was Josh meant to show his face once all those friends and colleagues found out about you and Saskia, I want to say, but I don't. Not yet.

'That's rough. I'm sorry.'

He's not even listening, though. 'And what do you mean, you've kissed him before? Where? When?'

I don't want to give too much away yet but I don't want to lie to him either so I just avoid the issue.

'It's not something I'm proud of. But it's true when I say we're not having an affair. We just met up a couple of times and it happened.'

He's fiddling with the salt cellar on the table – a china pig who we've had since George was little and who has long since lost his peppery friend – and I worry he'll accidentally snap off its little tail. 'Met up how? You didn't even know him.'

'It was a mistake. I'm not trying to justify what I've done, but haven't you ever made a mistake?'

He puffs his chest up like a toad. Assumes the moral high ground. 'I've bought hundred-watt light bulbs instead of forty, if that's what you mean. I once got off the tube at Mornington Crescent instead of Camden. Have I ever snuck around meeting up with your boss for some kind of adolescent necking session? No, funnily enough, I haven't.'

He's incandescent with self-righteousness. I try to stay calm, rational. I wonder how Josh is getting on with Saskia. An image of him declaring his love for her and begging for forgiveness gatecrashes my brain. I push it away.

'Not with my boss, obviously . . .' I must remember to tell Myra this detail, I think. Once it's all over. She'll be horrified that the idea of Robert and her even entered the universe.

'. . . but with anyone? Ever?'

He doesn't even flinch. 'No, because I thought we were a family. I thought that was part of the deal. For God's sake, how could you do this to George?'

Really? 'Georgia doesn't have to hear about this.'

'Let's hope none of those arseholes thinks it's funny to tip off the gossip pages.'

Shit, I hadn't even thought of that. There are always leaks to the press which can only be attributed to cast or crew. It's entirely possible that one of the party guests will think they can earn a few quid or a few favours by tipping off the papers that Robert Westmore's wife is having a thing with Saskia Sherbourne's husband. I blush at the thought of it. For a second, I lose my nerve.

'God, I hope not. You don't think they will? They couldn't print anything anyway, could they? Not without corroboration.'

He shrugs. He's not letting me off the hook that easily.

'OK, well, let's assume that doesn't happen. There would be no reason for George to ever find out.'

He looks me right in the eye. I want to look away, but I can't quite make myself.

'Let's hope not. It would devastate her. Finding out her mother's been running around with some other bloke . . . how could you?'

OK. That's it. I've had enough.

I load my big gun.

'What would be worse?' I say. 'In your opinion. Kissing someone a total of four times and never going any further than that, or having a full-on affair for years – I'm not sure exactly how many – but a full-on, all-out, sneaking-around relationship?' I give him a forced and, I imagine, quite creepy smile. 'Asking for a friend.'

'What the hell are you talking about? You want me to congratulate you because you and Josh haven't had sex yet?'

'I know,' I say, and now I'm the one who's forcing eye contact. 'About you and Saskia.'

47

Saskia

So, Joshie knows all about me and Robbie. He waited, thankfully, until we were alone to tell me this, the last guest having been forced to leave their front-row seat. He let me accuse and reproach in front of them, and he said nothing.

Once the last one had left, and just as I was preparing myself for the big showdown, he said, 'You can quit the act now, Sas.'

I tried to protest, of course I did. He was having none of it. And, in all honesty, I didn't have it in me to fight. We were going to tell them in a week or so anyway – why put him through the agony of having to fight to hear the truth? I did resist for a little while – I wanted to punish him for the public humiliation he had just put me through – but then he mentioned the flat and I knew I should just give it up, for his sake. I owed him that.

I sat down on the ottoman before my legs gave way beneath me. All this time, I'd been thinking we had the upper hand, and they knew. I suddenly felt very cruel.

'I'm sorry,' I said finally. He had sat down opposite me on the sofa. 'I'll tell you everything.'

'I think I pretty much know it all,' he said. He didn't even shout at me. He didn't give me a hard time at all.

And that almost made it worse. 'I just wanted you to admit to it. I wanted you to stop treating me like an idiot.'

'I don't understand what's going on with you and Paula,' I said, as if I had any right to know the truth, after the way I'd been behaving. I was struck with jealousy, I'm not going to lie. The idea of Joshie, his hands all over another woman, his lips locked on hers, it was killing me. Hypocrite? *Moi?*

He told me from start to finish about their – pretty chaste, I was glad to hear – relationship. And despite what all my party guests would say, I believed him. They were not having an affair. I couldn't understand why I felt so relieved.

'I'm sorry if you were embarrassed. That was never our intention.'

I didn't like the way he said the word 'our'.

'I'll live,' I said. He was looking wretched. I could see that he was racked with guilt. I reached out and took hold of his hand. And he let me.

I looked at him. At his kind, handsome face. 'Can you ever forgive me?'

48

Paula

'What on earth are you talking about? Me and *Saskia*?'

There's an almost comedy moment where he blinks about four times.

I nod slowly. I want to savour this moment. 'I've known for months. Josh too.'

He actually goes pale.

'I have no idea what you're talking about, but there is no me and Saskia. I mean, really, is this how you're going to try to get out of what you've just done? What I saw with my own eyes?'

I expected him to deny it. Coming clean has never been Robert's strong point. And, besides, why would he tell the truth now, when Josh and I have just handed him a get-out-of-jail-free card?

'I know about the heart she gave you, and her knickers in your dressing room and the fact that she calls you Robbie.'

I know I'm rambling. I try to bring it back, stick to the important stuff. 'I know you're planning on leaving. I know about the flat.'

That gets him. I can see his hand is shaking. He bumps the wine glass down on the table.

I'm not finished. 'So don't give me that about Georgia.

You're planning on leaving and setting up home with Saskia in Chiltern bloody Mansions, without a second thought for Georgia. Two bedrooms, balcony, views to the park. I know everything about it. So just stop lying to me, Robert.'

He can't hide it. I can see it on his face. Busted.

He puts his hands on the table, pushes himself up to a standing position.

'I have no idea what you're talking about. It's late. I'm going to bed.'

I stay there, stunned. That's it. I'm out of ammo. Without a confession, we have nothing, guv. I'm floored by the fact that he's just going to brazen it out. He's going to attribute the breakdown of our marriage to me having an affair with Josh. He has witnesses. I have the flat, but that doesn't prove anything, because it's all in Saskia's name. Other than that, I just have a carved heart and a bit of hearsay about a stray pair of pants.

I sit there, defeated.

My phone beeps to tell me I have a message. Josh.

'Jesus Christ, what a night. Hope you're OK. Sas has told me everything. Talk tomorrow. Xxx'

Hallelujah.

49

Saskia

It's odd how good it feels, offloading it all. The more I tell him, the more I feel as if a weight has been lifted off my shoulders. Of course, it helps that he seems to know it all anyway. No horrible surprises, although I imagine they were when he first discovered them.

As soon as I've admitted my affair, I obviously have to stop giving him a hard time about him and Paula. It's eating away at me, though. What was going on there? He told me they have just kissed a few times and, obviously, that's only a one on the scale of bad things, whereas me and Robbie are a twelve. Out of ten, haha! And I believe him. I absolutely do. That's the thing about Joshie, he's all principles.

But, even so, I want to know the details. How it started. Why. Was it just a spur of the moment reaction to finding out about me and Robbie? He wanted revenge and she just happened to be there? And probably gagging for it. Did she think she was getting one over on me, seducing my husband? Well, if she wants a competition, I'm in. We'll see who he thinks is the biggest prize.

The thought of everyone laughing at me is horrendous, I'm not going to lie. I'll be a laughing stock at work for weeks. My husband got caught with his hand on some fat woman's boob. Josh said I just have to front it out. He's going to tell people that it was all a big mistake. Too many glasses of champagne. It'll all die down, he said. It will go away.

I felt hypocritical even worrying about that after what Robbie and I have been doing, but, like I said before, we were always discreet. Well, apparently not so discreet that Josh and Paula didn't work out what was going on, but you know what I mean. We never got caught in the act.

Even though I'm feeling embarrassed and hard done by, I beg Joshie for forgiveness. And I mean it. I want him to forgive me. I couldn't bear him to think badly of me. Ridiculous, isn't it? But he's such a good man. His default position is to think the best of everyone. I don't want to be the exception to that.

He tells me he does. That he wishes me the best. Me and Robbie. I'm confused. I thought he would be the one begging.

'I don't know . . .' I hear myself say. 'Everything's different now, isn't it?' I suddenly feel in a blind panic at the thought of losing him.

'Different how?' he says, in a way too unemotional voice.

'Now that it's all out in the open. We can work out what went wrong. Why on earth I did what I did . . .'

'That's just the thing, Sas,' he says. 'I didn't think anything had gone wrong. I thought we were happy till I found out.'

'We were!' He looks at me sceptically. 'I just got a bit carried away, that's all.'

'You were going to leave in a couple of weeks, right?

You were going to set up home with him, make it impossible for me to carry on doing my job. That's hardly getting "a bit carried away".'

He's cross with me. I expected that. I deserve it. But what upsets me more is that he doesn't sound it. He sounds resigned. Too rational, too calm. Too much like he doesn't really care.

'All of that . . . I don't know what I was thinking. I wasn't thinking. Please, Joshie . . .'

'It's OK,' he says and, just for a second, I allow myself to hope. Because I know exactly what I want now. Now the explosion has happened, now everything is real, I just want my husband. I realize I haven't even given a thought to how it's going with Robbie and Paula.

'Please, Josh. We're strong. We can get over this. I love you. I've never stopped loving you, and that's the truth, whether you believe it or not.'

He leans over and puts his hand on mine, giving it a squeeze.

'We should go to bed,' he says. 'Sleep on it.'

It's only when I'm getting undressed that I think to check my phone. Five missed calls from Robbie. One text.

Stay strong xxx

I don't reply.

50

Paula

'You and Saskia need to get your stories straight,' I say. I hold my mobile up to show him Josh's message. For the first time, he looks rattled.

'He's got a cheek, sending you a text when he knows you're with me.'

'What do you think that means? *"Saskia's told me everything?"'*

He blanches. Scritches his beard. 'God knows. You know what a diva she is. She's probably made up some story to get back at him. Tit for tat.'

'Robert. I know. Just tell me the truth. Let's sort this out before George gets back.'

'I'm going to bed,' he says again, and he huffs off down the corridor, a cloud of smug piety billowing behind him.

'And by the way,' I call after him, 'it's true that me and Josh aren't sleeping together. But we're going to now. I can't wait.'

I hear him stomp back towards me. He pokes his head around the door, face like fury.

'You've really sunk to new depths this time. Is this really how you want people to think of you? George?'

I don't even respond. Wait until he storms off again. Pick up my phone to call Josh. Listen as it rings out. I don't leave a message.

51

Saskia

This morning I got up super-early and made break-fast. This is an event, let me tell you! I'm not the domesticated type. Usually, it's a bowl of sugar-free granola, and even that is prepared by Josh.

Today, though, I find ripe avocados in the fridge and I mash them up with a little olive oil and cumin, like I saw someone do on TV the other day, spread the mixture on crispy toast and pop a poached egg on top. My poached eggs are a disaster, I'm not going to lie. They look like brains, and there's water leaking from them, so the toast goes soggy in no time. But it's the thought that counts.

I put the two plates on a tray with a pot of coffee, two mugs and some milk, salt and black pepper. I can hardly lift the bloody thing but I manage to lug it up the stairs with minimal spillage. Josh is still asleep, so I gently nudge him awake and present my offering.

I don't think either of us got much sleep last night. I could sense that he was awake as much as I was, and at one point I risked it and snuggled into his back, draping my arm across his warm body. He didn't react. But he didn't push me off either, so that was something. He felt so safe, so solid. I whispered that I was sorry into his hair, but he didn't reply so maybe he was sleeping after all.

'I'm not really hungry,' he says now. He looks wretched. Dark shadows under his beautiful eyes. I probably look no better myself.

'It does look pretty inedible, doesn't it?' I slide back under the covers next to him. 'I know you didn't marry me for my culinary skills, haha!'

He rewards me with a half-smile and my stomach does somersaults. In my head, I try to calculate how much money I would lose if I cancelled the rental agreement on the flat. Three months, I think, the notice period is. Maybe we could sublet.

'It's kind of you,' he says. 'But I'll just have the coffee.'

I pour him out a cup, hands shaking. 'It'll all be OK. I'll make it up to you. And I'll get over you and Paula. We'll tell everyone you'd mixed antibiotics and alcohol or something. That you had no idea what you were doing. We'll put on a united front and laugh about it.'

He looks at me. Deep brown eyes holding my gaze. I want to put my hand out and feel the rough stubble on his chin, but I know I have to leave it up to him to make the first move.

I wait.

52

Paula

I wake up in George's room, not knowing where I am. I lie there for a moment, taking in all her familiar things. Shelves full of books, a jumble of make-up, Stuffy, the bear that we gave her for her second birthday, the cute Cath Kidston suitcase we bought her before she found out she wasn't leaving home yet after all. I give myself a minute to take it in and then I get up, making sure the bed bears no sign of me having slept there.

There's no sign of Robert. The door to our bedroom is closed, so I assume he's sleeping off his hangover. I leave him to it.

There are no more texts from Josh. No missed calls. I pull on my trainers, put a hoody over my pyjamas and head down to the street. I deliberately don't take my mobile with me. I need to clear my head, and running is the best way I know how. Of course, I've forgotten I have no bra on, so I have to run with one arm strapped across my chest, but I manage about five kilometres anyway. By the time I get home my head is still buzzing, though. Georgia is home tomorrow and, whatever else happens, I have to make sure Robert doesn't greet her by saying, 'So, your mum got groped at the party in front of everyone . . .'

I need to talk to Josh and find out what's going on. If Saskia's told him everything, then Robert's going to have to tell the truth eventually. I just need that to happen sooner rather than later.

He's sitting at the kitchen table like a big angry bear when I walk in. If I was hoping sobriety and a good night's sleep might make him see sense, I realize I was wrong when he says:

'So. What have you got to say for yourself this morning?'

I pick up my mobile. I don't even care that I'm going to call Josh in front of him. 'Give it up, Robert.'

I hit on Josh's number. It rings and rings again, and eventually clicks on to voicemail.

'Not answering?' Robert says with a smug look. 'He's probably begging Saskia to take him back right now.'

'As if,' I say. But I'm not feeling as confident as I was. 'You're ridiculous'.

'You said some very hurtful things last night.' Robert pours himself more coffee. He doesn't offer me one.

'Jesus Christ, Robert. Give it a rest.'

'We can't come back from this, you know. You and him.'

'Forget me and Josh. There is no me and Josh. But yes, it's over. It's what I want, it's what you want. It's done. You and Saskia can run off into the sunset now. I'm past caring. I've been past caring for months, to tell you the truth. We just need to handle this like adults, for George's sake.'

He looks at me levelly. 'You should have thought of that last night.'

'I have no intention of telling her about you and Saskia, if that's what you're worried about. We can just say we've decided to live apart for a while and then take it from there. I would never want her to think badly of you, what-ever's happened. You must know that.'

He still won't budge. He's assumed the superior posi-tion and he's staying there.

'That would be because there's nothing to tell. What she'd think about her mother and some random man giv-ing a room full of people a floor show, I have no idea, though.'

It's all I can do not to punch him. He's so pleased with himself, so self-righteous.

I hit Josh's number again. Nothing. Where the hell is he? I think about all those times Robert moaned that he was weak, ineffectual. I know how persuasive Saskia can be. I know how much Josh values his marriage vows, even though his feelings for her have changed. It would be typical of the person I've come to realize she is if she con-vinced him to stay with her just to spite me.

I have no idea what to do.

And then the doorbell rings.

53

Paula

I open the door, and there they are, Josh and Saskia, standing on my doorstep.

Robert and I have spent most of the morning in different rooms. I am a furious ball of frustration; he is doing his best turn as the disappointed husband let down by his cheating wife. I have no idea how long he can keep this up. All I want is for him to tell me the truth, and then we can move on.

My eyes go straight to Josh first. I want reassurance. He smiles, but I feel as if it doesn't reach his eyes. I put a hand on to the door frame to steady myself. Saskia is looking anywhere but at me.

'You'd better come in.'

I take them straight through to the living room, where Robert is now sitting up. Any thoughts I had that Saskia might have communicated their upcoming visit to him dissipate when I see the look on his face. He stands up to meet them head on.

Of course, he has to stay in character – by which I mean he has to remember that his main motivation is supposed to be anger at Josh, not guilt, or even love, on seeing Saskia.

'What's this all about?' Robert barks at Josh.

'I thought we all needed to talk.'

'I don't think I've got anything to say to you,' Robert says. I wonder whether I'm supposed to offer to make our visitors tea. I'm not sure whether there's a rule for good etiquette in these circumstances. I decide that leaving the room would be a bad idea.

'Well, we've got plenty to say to you, haven't we, Sas?' She looks at him, like a shelter dog looks at the person who's finally taking them home. And he looks back at her with a reassuring smile. That's it, I think. That's the look that tells me they've decided to save their marriage.

I try to focus on what's important. When I started this, Josh was never part of the plan. I just need to flush the truth out of Robert. I just have to stop him announcing to our daughter that I'm the one responsible for the break-up of our marriage.

'Sit down,' I finally manage to say. They perch next to one another on the sofa. Saskia reaches out and takes Josh's hand. For the first time, she looks at me. I had thought that maybe she was feeling guilty, but it's a look of pure defiance. Robert, back in his armchair, can't hide the fact that he's noticed either. His mask slips for just a second and shows the shock and hurt underneath. Well, that's something, I suppose.

Josh gives Saskia a little nod of encouragement. She smiles weakly.

'We . . . that's Joshie and I . . . thought we should all handle this like adults . . .'

I snort. I can't help myself. Saskia ignores me.

'. . . and clear the air. After all, some of us have to work together.'

Robert pipes up, as if he's still working from an old script, unaware that the rest of us got the rewrites. 'That's going to be hard after what we witnessed between these two last night, frankly.'

Saskia practically does a double-take. She obviously assumed he would have admitted the truth to me by now.

'And after what we've been doing, Robbie. You and me.'

He blusters. 'What are you talking about?'

'I've told him. About us. The flat. Everything.' She turns to me, puts on her best penitent face. 'This is going to hurt me as much as it's going to hurt you.' Obviously, Josh hasn't completely filled her in. 'I'm really sorry to have to tell you this, Paula, but Robbie and I have been having an affair.'

She waits for my big reaction. Instead, I just laugh. 'I know. I've known for as long as I've known you. Did "Joshie" not tell you that?'

'Don't be so ridiculous.' Robert is glaring at her, willing her to shut up. 'I don't know what your game is, Saskia, but we're here to talk about Josh and Paula.'

'Actually, Robert, we're not,' Josh says. 'We're here to talk about you and Saskia.'

'There is no me and Saskia! How many times?'

'Robbie, I've told him everything. There's no point trying to deny it any more.'

'She showed me these, look.' Josh produces a bunch of scraps of paper from his pocket. He holds one up. '*Tomorrow afternoon? Told P I have golf. Hotel? Or your place if J is at work? R xx*'.

'You old romantic, you,' I say. His face has gone purple. Josh starts on another one. '*Darling S . . .*'

'Oooh,' I say. 'Better'.

'. . . *a thousand apologies for yesterday. I just get so jealous when I see you . . .*'

'OK. Enough,' Robert barks.

'There's more.' Josh holds the rest of the scraps of paper aloft. I notice for the first time that there are cards in there too. 'A lot more, as you can see.'

I catch Robert looking at Saskia. She doesn't meet his eye.

There's silence for a moment, and then Robert says, 'At least we tried to protect you from the truth.'

That's too much for me. 'Since when was that a good thing?'

'And besides,' Josh says, 'I assume that, when you moved into together, we might have noticed.'

Robert ignores him. 'I'm sorry, Paula. I never meant to hurt you. It just happened.'

'Did you swallow a dictionary of clichés? What next? "It's me, not you?" "I love you but I'm not in love with you"?'

Josh lets out a small laugh. 'So, how long?'

'I thought Saskia had told you all the details,' Robert snaps.

'I'd like to hear them from you,' I say.

So then he tells me, finally, all the details I already know, and a few more I don't like: where they used to go if they couldn't go to Saskia and Josh's house (a small but discreet hotel in Bayswater), and when it first happened (after a particularly gruelling location shoot, when they decided to reward themselves with a few drinks in the bar of the hotel). I listen to it all in silence. I don't really care, except with the forensic interest of a coroner. What's really bugging me is what's happening between Saskia and Josh.

Eventually, Robert runs out of steam. 'So, yes,' he says, 'I love Saskia.' He looks at her, and she still doesn't look at him. 'And, yes, we have found a flat, and we're moving in together.'

'See,' I say. 'It wasn't that hard, was it?'

He grunts like a sulky child.

'So,' I carry on, and now I'm addressing him and him only. 'We need to decide what to do about George. Whatever that is, we need to present a united front. No mud-slinging. No telling her about my non-existent affair with Josh to make me look like the bad guy . . .'

'I won't,' he says, and he finally has the good grace to look a bit sheepish.

'It's going to come as a massive shock to her that you have a girlfriend in the first place, let alone that you're moving in together, so we have to do as much damage limitation as we can. Agreed?'

'Agreed.'

'Let's just all behave like grown-ups and get through this without hurting anyone else, OK? It might, for example, be a good idea if you went somewhere else temporarily, instead of straight into the flat. Let her get used to the whole idea of you and Saskia slowly. Even if it was just for show – not that I'm encouraging any more lies.'

'We could do that,' Robert says. He looks to Saskia for confirmation. She looks at her fingernails. I have no idea whether Robert has picked up that there's something not right, but I definitely have.

'Good,' I say. 'That's a start.'

Robert actually smiles, as if we're all friends now. Finally, he can have his cake and eat it. I'm not going to say that doesn't irk me, but I remind myself it's the end result that matters.

He puffs his chest up. 'I must say, Paula, you're being very reasonable about this, and I want to tell you I appreciate that. And Josh. Hopefully, we can all stay friends.'

He actually said that. I look at Josh, hoping to share a smirk, but he seems to be looking at Saskia's fingernails too.

Suddenly, she speaks.

'Actually, Robbie, things have changed. I'm not . . . I don't think I'm going to be moving into the flat after all.' She turns to Josh and gives him a big, beaming smile. I fight the urge to throw up.

'Joshie and I have decided to make it work. He's forgiven me . . . well, he's going to try . . . and I've forgiven him for, you know . . .' She casts half a glance at me at this point. I imagine she can't resist the urge to see the shock on my face. I try to remain impassive. I felt it. I knew something like this was coming.

Of course, the real drama is playing out in Robert's expression. His mouth hangs open. Eyes wide. It's almost comical. Or it would be if I didn't feel so wretched myself.

'I'm so sorry,' Saskia says. 'It just took me a while to realize what I really wanted.'

I, I, I. As usual, Saskia is able to justify any bit of bad behaviour, because it's what she wants. And what Saskia wants, Saskia gets.

'Good for you,' I say, mustering as much genuine

warmth as I'm capable of. I look at Josh as I say this. I'm not giving Saskia the time of day. 'I hope it works out.'

'Oh, it will,' she says, with a patronizing smirk.

Robert has coloured a nice shade of puce. 'But . . .' he splutters. 'What are you talking about? Your marriage is dead, you've told me that a million times.'

'I wasn't thinking straight.'

'For two years?' He's raising his voice. 'I risked everything for you.'

'And I did for you,' Saskia says. She's holding on to Josh's hand now. His fingers look as if they're turning white. 'But things have changed. It happens. I'm not trying to hurt you.'

'Well, you're doing a bloody good job of that.'

'Robbie, please . . .'

'So that's it? After everything we've been through, all the sacrifices I've made for you . . .'

I almost laugh here – the idea of Robert making any kind of sacrifice for anyone. It's all I can do to get him to put the bins out.

'. . . you're just going to tell me that you're staying with . . . him?' He spits the last word out as if it's poison.

'I am. I'm sorry.'

'Stop saying you're sorry. You're not sorry, or you wouldn't be doing it.'

I watch back and forth. Josh does the same. It's like being at Wimbledon.

Saskia, for once in her life, keeps quiet. But Robert isn't finished yet.

'So, for the record, what you're saying is that you no longer love me?'

The words hang out there in the room. You could hear a pin drop. All our eyes are on Saskia. I feel like saying that if either of them could channel half this emotion on screen, *Farmer Giles* would be an entirely different show, but, of course, I don't. I don't want to break the moment. After all, isn't this what we've been working towards all these months? The implosion of Roskia? Even if I had started to hope it would be under different circumstances. Saskia gives a little sigh.

'No. I mean, yes, I don't think I do. The bottom line is that, when it came to it, I realized I still loved Josh.'

Robert looks like a dog toy after fifteen rounds with a Rottweiler. As if all the stuffing has been knocked out of him. He crumples.

'Unbelievable.'

'I'm so sorry, Robbie, it's over,' Saskia adds, just in case he hadn't got the message.

'So . . . nothing I could say . . .' Robert says, and it's so pathetic I almost feel sorry for him.

Saskia looks over at Josh again, gives his hand a little squeeze. He rewards her with an encouraging smile.

'Nothing.'

I can't bring myself to look at them, love's old dream. I can't believe for a minute it won't still end in tears further down the line. Saskia is way too much of a narcissist to spend the rest of her life with one man. Or maybe he'll just let her go off and do her thing and still be sitting there patiently when she decides to come home.

I assume this is where we all part ways. Where Saskia and Josh go off into the sunset and I'm left with the husk formerly known as Robert. Saskia must read my mind, because she turns to Josh, gives him another sickly smile, and says, 'Shall we go home?'

I'm half standing up, eager to see the back of them – although not so eager to have to spend time alone with Robert – when something stops me in my tracks.

Josh looks right at me and, I don't know if I'm imagining it, but I think he gives me the tiniest of winks.

Then he places Saskia's hand very deliberately back on her own lap.

'Well,' he says. 'Thank fuck that's over.'

PART THREE

54

Three months later

Paula

I hardly recognize her when I see her. The hair's the same. Tousled and blonde, looking as if it could do with a good brushing. And the eyeliner. But precious little else.

Pregnancy suits her. At least, the fact that being pregnant has made her look after herself for a change suits her. She's lost that tortured-artist look. For the first time since I've known her, Alice looks happy.

She gives me a big hug when she spots me, laughing that her considerable bump gets in the way. She still basically just says, 'Mwah! Mwah!' into my ear rather than kissing me, but I feel as if she does it with affection.

I hold her at arm's length.

'You look fantastic.'

I look pregnant,' she says, rolling her eyes.

'You definitely do.'

We're here for her scan. I missed the last one because, in the aftermath of my and Robert's break-up, I felt as if I should stay away. I assumed that she would take Robert's side – Christ knows what version of the truth he would have presented her with – and that she wouldn't want anything to do with me out of loyalty to him. Truth is, I felt rather relieved not to have to deal with her any more.

Then, a couple of weeks ago, she got in touch with me. She missed me, she said. (Really?) She still wanted me to be an auntie to her baby. (Why?) In the end, I agreed to meet up with her just because I didn't quite know how to say no.

'OK, awkward stuff over with first,' she says as we wait for the lift. 'I'm very cross with Robbie, and I've told him that. The way he's behaved towards you . . .'

This from Alice. Alice who has practically made a career out of dating married men.

'Thanks, but you don't need to apologize for him.'

'I'm just saying I told him he'd been a dickhead. He should have appreciated what he had when he had it.'

'How's Ivan?' I ask, to change the subject.

She breaks into a huge smile. 'He's well. Lovely, actually.'

'He's happy about the baby then, I take it?'

'Delirious.'

Good old Ivan. I can only assume he's behind her change of heart towards me too. Either directly or, more likely, indirectly. She's finally met a decent bloke and it's occurred to her that it would be nice if they were all like that.

'We're buying a flat together. Mine's not big enough for the three of us so I'm selling it, and, of course, he's been living on site . . .'

'That's brilliant,' I say. 'Where?'

'Southgate. It's so much cheaper than Islington, and it'll be nicer for the baby . . .'

Alice, voluntarily living in the suburbs. Well, practically. Worrying about the cost and whether it's a good place to bring up a child rather than if it fits her image.

'It will be,' I say encouragingly. 'And it's still on the tube, at least.'

'Come round. When we move in.'

'I will,' I say, and I mean it. 'Try keeping me away from the baby.'

'You'll always be its auntie,' she says. 'Because Georgia will always be its cousin. I hate calling it "it", don't you? I can't wait to find out.'

The lift deposits us on the sixth floor.

'I'm trying to remember everything,' Alice says as we walk towards the reception desk. 'How I feel, how I stand, how I walk. Just in case, you know, I get cast as a pregnant woman in the future.'

'Every experience is method in the bank,' I say, parroting one of Robert's and my former teachers. I'm actually bizarrely pleased that the old Alice is still in there somewhere. Just – hopefully – without the nastier bits.

'Exactly! Oh . . . did I tell you I went for an audition . . . ?'

I don't get home till nearly six. Even so, I change and go out for a run, having checked – as subtly as I can – that George is home for the evening. By 'subtly', I mean I say, 'Are you in this evening?'

At the moment, she seems to be sticking to her promise only to go out at weekends. She volunteered that, by the way. I didn't insist. With Eliza gone, she has made a new group of friends, who seem nice enough, and I've made the effort to get to know their mums, just in case we need to compare stories in the future.

'How was Auntie Alice?' she says as I'm lacing up my trainers.

'Good. Like Alice, but nicer. She's happy, I think.'

'Did you tell her I'm going to audition for the dramsoc play?'

This is news to me. 'Are you? Since when?'

She shrugs. 'I just thought I'd give it a go.'

'Gosh,' I say. 'Well.'

'It won't interfere with my work if I get it,' she says defensively.

'No, it was just . . . I didn't know you were interested in acting.'

'I don't know if I am, do I? Not till I try.'

'Whatever makes you happy,' I say.

I say a silent prayer that she'll decide it's not for her. I'm not sure I could take another actor in the family.

'Dad said he'll help me prepare.' Georgia sees her dad all the time. He's living in a rented flat in Maida Vale while he looks for somewhere to buy. Close enough that she can visit easily. Not so close that I keep tripping over him every time I go out. I let him stay in our flat for a couple of weeks while he looked for somewhere and while we negotiated our way around telling our daughter that we were separating. She took it surprisingly well, once we convinced her that we were still going to be friends (we're not, by the way, but we are going to be civil enough to each other so that she will think we are), and that neither of us was running off with someone else. There's no need for her ever to know about Saskia.

'Thank fuck that's over.'

Saskia looked down at her hand, now back in her own lap and no longer being held. Josh scooted away to create a space between them.

'Joshie?'

I could feel the shift in the air. Saskia was looking at Josh like a lost puppy. Robert kept turning to me as if I might hold the answer, but I had no idea what was going on.

'Of course we're not going to make a go of it,' Josh suddenly said, and only then did he flash me a big smile. My stomach flipped. 'Of course Saskia and I aren't going to stay together. It's over. I just wanted the truth to come out. I wanted Robert to see exactly what you were like, Sas. How you'd drop someone like a hot brick if it suited you.'

Saskia's face crumpled. Except for the bits that had had Botox, which stayed defiantly where they were. She turned to Robert.

'He begged me to stay with him. I felt sorry for him, that's all. It doesn't change anything between us.'

'Ha!' Robert let out a big guffaw. And I knew then that we'd done it. We'd broken them up for good.

'For the record,' Josh said, looking at me, 'I didn't. I think, Sas, that everything for you is a competition. You didn't want to stay with me because you wanted me, you wanted to stay with me so you could make a point that I chose you over Paula. Well, I didn't, OK?'

I couldn't look at her then. I could feel she was glaring daggers at me. I tried to suppress the smile that was trying to take over my face.

'So you're really going to be with her now?' She made the word 'her' sound like something she'd found at the bottom of a very smelly pond.

Josh smiled at me. 'I don't know. If she'll have me, then yes, I'd like to give it a try.'

The smile won, took over my face whether I liked it or not. 'Let's take things day by day,' I forced myself to say, even though I didn't really mean it.

'Exactly,' Josh said. 'Let's do it right this time.'

Robert stood up. 'I think you should both leave now.'

'Of course. I'll drive you back to the house,' Josh said, standing and looking down at Saskia, who was sniffling on the sofa. She looked older suddenly. 'You can stay there and I'll get a few things and move into the flat. Just for now. Till I can find somewhere else.'

'Do you want me to move out?' Robert said quietly.

'Yes. But not today. We need to put on a show for George. Break it to her gently. Make her think it's not going to be too bad.'

'Thank you,' he said gratefully.

Saskia walked out without looking at either me or Robert. Good riddance. There was no reason our paths would ever have to cross again.

As he went to follow her out, Josh gave me a hug. I allowed myself to lean into it, not caring that Robert was there. 'Sorry I had to put you through that,' he said into my hair. 'I couldn't even look at you in case I couldn't pull it off.'

'Nice work,' I said. 'Good plot twist.'

The short version of what happened next goes like this. Robert, to give him credit for once, agreed that we should speak to Georgia calmly and rationally on her return. We would cite our having grown apart. No big drama. He would start looking for a flat to rent right away. She and I would stay where we were, in the home that I love. Like

I said, she took it remarkably well. Maybe she'd been picking up on the signs for years but hadn't felt she could say anything. Who knows, maybe in some ways this was a relief for her? Either way, she has no idea there was anyone else involved for either of us, and we're both going to make sure it stays that way.

I imagine things *chez Farmer Giles* were a bit awkward on the Monday. Josh told me that he made a point of going around the people who had seen him and me together at the party and trying to make light of it. We had had a glass of champagne too many. It was a stupid spur-of-the-moment thing and we both felt like the worst kind of idiots. He asked them not to spread the gossip, for Robert and Saskia's sakes, and, though I'm sure they must have all laughed about it behind closed doors, it's never leaked out any further, in so far as I know. Not even when the papers picked up on the fact that both Robert Westmore and Saskia Sherbourne had split from their spouses within weeks of each other.

No one even linked the two of them in the press. Mostly, I think, because they were never seen together, but also because their reputation for loathing each other was suddenly stronger than ever.

And then, of course, there were those pictures in the tabloids of her and Jez sitting outside a restaurant, even though it was nearly November, leaning in towards each other, his hand holding hers. I can only imagine what Robert thought when he saw those.

I've gone full-time in Myra's. I like it. It keeps me occupied and it pays the bills. One of these days, I'll think about what I want to do with the rest of my life. Chas has been hinting that, with my dedication, I could eventually get some qualifications to become a trainer myself. I could inspire my clients with my own story of reinvention. I'm not sure I'm ready to be a role model, though. Not while I'm still a work in progress myself.

Josh and I agreed on a three-month cooling-off period where we could sort out our home lives and make sure we really did think there was a spark between us. My suggestion. I didn't want to be sneaking around, hoping George or a random journalist didn't spot us. And I didn't want to enter another relationship and then realize further down the line that one of us had done it just because we were scared of being on our own, or as a two-fingered gesture to our faithless spouse.

We talked all the time on the phone, don't get me wrong. I was the first person he called when he found out he'd got the *One Night* job. He was the one I phoned when Myra told me she and Chas had had a one-night stand and I didn't know if I was going to be able to look either of them in the eye ever again. (Just for the record, he got a bit clingy, wanted a rematch; she saw it totally as a bit of fun with a (much) younger, good-looking bloke and had zero interest in anything more. I felt horrible for having introduced them in the first place, and I had to endure several training sessions where he banged on about how he thought he was in love with her before he finally, thankfully, came to his senses.)

That three-month period is up today. We are going on our first official date. That is to say, I'm going down to the flat in Marylebone (he completes on a new place in a couple of weeks. Still in the same area. He likes it) and, even though we've talked about going out for dinner, we both know that's not going to happen. We haven't set eyes on each other for nearly twelve weeks. I think eating is the last thing on either of our minds.

I've told George I have a date and I've been honest about who Josh is. I've just left out our history.

'Don't do anything you wouldn't want me to find out about,' she says with a big smile as I wait for my Uber.

Josh is standing at the door to the flat as I get out of the lift. He's smiling at me. I inwardly breathe a sigh of relief that he still looks like the Josh in my head.

'What if we take one look at each other and think, Yuk??' I'd said in an email the other day. 'Maybe we were just attracted to each other as a reaction to what was going on.'

'I don't think that's going to happen,' he said in his reply. 'And, to be honest, at this point I'd probably still go for it anyway. It's been a long time, just saying.'

'Haha!' I wrote, and then I deleted that and put, 'Very funny.'

It's my first time in the nest, and the irony isn't lost on me. We're surrounded by the things Saskia chose so painstakingly but never got to enjoy herself. The elegant white sofa, the rich dark wood coffee table. The bed.

'Drink?' he says.

'Definitely.'

'No, I mean, what?'

'Oh. Red wine. Sorry. Nervous.'

'Me too.'

'I'm out of practice at this . . . kind of thing . . .'

He laughs. 'What? And you think I'm not?'

He hands me a glass and I take a big gulp. 'Shall we just get it over with?'

'That,' Josh says, 'might be the most romantic thing anyone's ever said to me.'

'I'm just being honest,' I say, and I take his hand and lead him into the other room.

Acknowledgements

Huge thanks to Myra Jones, who bid so generously to have a character named after her in this book and helped raise money for Clic Sargent, the charity for children with cancer.

www.clicsargent.org.uk

Also by
Jane Fallon . . .

'A deliciously edgy read full of
double-dealings and divided loyalties'
Good Housekeeping

He just wanted a decent book to read ...

Not too much to ask, is it? It was in 1935 when Allen Lane, Managing Director of Bodley Head Publishers, stood on a platform at Exeter railway station looking for something good to read on his journey back to London. His choice was limited to popular magazines and poor-quality paperbacks – the same choice faced every day by the vast majority of readers, few of whom could afford hardbacks. Lane's disappointment and subsequent anger at the range of books generally available led him to found a company – and change the world.

'We believed in the existence in this country of a vast reading public for intelligent books at a low price, and staked everything on it'
Sir Allen Lane, 1902–1970, founder of Penguin Books

The quality paperback had arrived – and not just in bookshops. Lane was adamant that his Penguins should appear in chain stores and tobacconists, and should cost no more than a packet of cigarettes.

Reading habits (and cigarette prices) have changed since 1935, but Penguin still believes in publishing the best books for everybody to enjoy. We still believe that good design costs no more than bad design, and we still believe that quality books published passionately and responsibly make the world a better place.

So wherever you see the little bird – whether it's on a piece of prize-winning literary fiction or a celebrity autobiography, political tour de force or historical masterpiece, a serial-killer thriller, reference book, world classic or a piece of pure escapism – you can bet that it represents the very best that the genre has to offer.

Whatever you like to read – trust Penguin.